THREE MINUTES TO ZERO!

Between the counts the silence was heavy and oppressive, the glow from the test site ominous.

"Ten . . . nine . . . eight . . ."

"Now!" yelled the voice.

A brilliant yellow flash lit up the New Mexico desert. Instinctively Snyder and Nakamura dropped their heads. A thunderous roar crashed over them and a boiling cloud of kaleidoscopic colors spread outward, forming the cap of a mushroom. For what seemed like minutes, matter continued to soar upward, feeding the boiling cauldron some ten thousand feet up.

"I'll be goddamned!" Snyder gasped, staring at the awesome panorama.

"Or the damned of God," Nakamura said grimly.

"WELL-PLOTTED, WELL-PACED . . . CONVEY(S) THE URGENCY SURROUNDING THE BOMB IN THOSE FINAL DAYS OF THE WAR."

—*Houston Chronicle*

*Books by George E. Simpson
and Neal R. Burger*

GHOSTBOAT
THIN AIR

FAIR WARNING

George E. Simpson
and
Neal R. Burger

A DELL BOOK

Published by
Dell Publishing Co., Inc.
1 Dag Hammarskjold Plaza
New York, New York 10017

Dell ® TM 681510, Dell Publishing Co., Inc.

ISBN: 0-440-12478-6

Reprinted by arrangement with Delacorte Press

Printed in the United States of America

First Dell printing—September 1981

With love to our wives,
Jean and Maureen

Acknowledgments

Gratefully:
Jeanne F. Bernkopf, *editor*
Stuart M. Miller, *authors' agent*

Fair Warning is fiction. While certain events remain faithful to history, those of Operation Big Stick are entirely our creation.

Rather than fabricate an imaginary President, Army Chief of Staff, Secretary of War and other key personages, we have elected to use public figures in a speculative manner, basing their words and actions largely upon historically known attitudes, while taking certain necessary liberties.

With all due respect to the memories of Truman, Stimson, Marshall, Groves and others, the decision to use nuclear weapons in 1945 was an act that changed the world for all time, and therefore deserves interpretation.

S-1, Manhattan Project and the atomic bombs dropped on Hiroshima and Nagasaki are historical fact. But the line separating what was from what might have been prevented is embodied in this book.

The Authors

FAIR
WARNING

PART 1

June 6, 1945: Washington

By 1945 Washington was bursting at the seams. So many people had flocked to the nation's capital during the war years that the city could hardly hold them. On a spring day thousands of young office girls filled the streets at noon, their bright dresses splashing color among the drab military uniforms.

Germany's surrender in May had brought an emotional turnaround from the devastating shock of Roosevelt's sudden death in April.

The first wild reaction was over. Excitement had peaked and now everyone was geared up for the final surge against Japan. The entire nation was moving with a purpose. Washington was the fulcrum, the center of that effort.

Secretary of War Henry L. Stimson grimaced in the sudden explosions of light. He held up the plaque and again shook hands with Stefan Thyssen. Both men smiled and more flashbulbs popped.

Reporters crowded in past the photographers. Stimson glanced at Thyssen, a tall, Nordic bear of a man with a ruddy face, a deep voice and an unashamedly protruding stomach.

"On this first anniversary of D-day, our European invasion," Stimson began, "it is most appropriate that we honor a man who has pursued peace with the same courage and diligence as those fine warriors who landed at Normandy.

"Stefan Thyssen and his small contingent of Swedish diplomats personally negotiated with Himmler in the last days of the war, endeavoring to save countless political prisoners and concentration camp inmates from Germany's final solution."

Thyssen looked down, embarrassed by the praise. Stimson continued to outline his accomplishments while Thyssen tried to form the words he had come to say to the Secretary of War in private.

At last the agony was over. Stimson handed him the plaque. Thyssen clutched it and smiled once more for the photographers. Then he was ushered out of the lobby and into Stimson's office. Coffee was served and the two men relaxed alone.

The war against Germany had ended on May 8th and Stimson was curious to hear about the aftermath in Europe. Since Thyssen had just returned from touring some of the hardest-hit areas, he was able to describe the devastation vividly.

"I am glad to find you interested in this, Mr. Secretary," he said, "because it leads me to my own reasons for coming here today."

Stimson looked up, puzzled.

Thyssen hesitated before going on. "I was in England," he continued, "just before D-day and by chance ran into an old acquaintance, a very prominent physicist."

Stimson's lips pursed but he said nothing. He hooked a finger into his coffee cup and slowly brought it to his lips.

"He was quite candid but swore me to secrecy. He had a great deal to say about an atomic bomb under development in the United States."

"Mr. Thyssen," said Stimson, "I don't think you should go on with this."

"Please hear me out, Mr. Secretary. I have come a long way at your invitation, but I must tell you, it is my own conscience that has brought me here."

Stimson's brow furrowed.

"I will not accept any denials of the bomb's existence. I wish only to voice the very human concern that such a weapon not be used in haste. If there is any way to avoid it entirely, I believe the United States must try."

Stimson sat back slowly and frowned at the window.

Thyssen picked up the plaque and smiled. "This is hardly in order, you know. My efforts were rigorous, but we were completely deceived."

"What do you mean?"

"While I was negotiating with Himmler, trying to save lives, he was very busy accelerating the slaughter. He bought time from me to finish the job in the concentration camps." He put down the plaque and his smile turned rueful. "The Nazis will be branded murderers for generations to come. The United States cannot afford that label. And if you use that bomb against the Japanese—"

"It's not the same," Stimson said sharply.

"It is mass murder. Only the method is different."

"Mr. Thyssen, I can't discuss this any further."

Thyssen waved a hand. "I quite understand. Have you considered a demonstration?" Thyssen's eyes bored into him.

Stimson did not flinch. He was seventy-seven years old, a thirty-five-year veteran of Washington politics who had been Secretary of War since 1940. He was also Senior Advisor to the President on S-1, the Manhattan Project. He studied Thyssen with forced disinterest while deciding how to deal with him. With security so stringent, how had a foreign national become so conversant with his problems?

"Mr. Secretary," said Thyssen, "let us take a hypothetical approach, shall we? Let us suppose that you have considered demonstrating your bomb to the Japanese in order to convince them to surrender. And you have decided not to. Why? Because you are not certain it is going to work. Can I conclude that it has not been tested yet?"

Stimson flinched. Thyssen was very close.

"Bad enough if you drop it on Japan and nothing happens, but if you invite a group of Japanese observers over for a show and it fails, you are going to look extremely foolish."

"Very astute," said Stimson, recalling the same reasoning from the Interim Committee meetings only last week.

"Thank you. So you cannot show them anything, but you still want to warn them somehow, let them know that if they do not capitulate, the consequences will be dire."

"Wouldn't that be an empty threat, Mr. Thyssen? Certainly it would have to be something dramatic or they wouldn't believe us. Hypothetically speaking, of course."

Thyssen allowed himself a little smile. "I agree. Drama is very important in dealing with the Japanese. The buildup is everything. Now, your President is shortly going to be meeting with Churchill and Stalin in Potsdam. It would seem to me that he would want to develop a unified front against Japan. Of course, it is common knowledge that the Russians and the Japanese have a nonaggression pact. Not so common is the knowledge that the Russians are prepared to break it. August eighth, I believe."

Stimson met Thyssen's gaze. "Some of your information is very accurate, Mr. Thyssen."

"Some of my thinking is, too. For instance, I do not think it would be in America's best interest to have the Soviets interfering in the Far East."

"That's politics. No comment," said Stimson.

"None needed. It is just logic. Now, in order to keep the Russians out, the war must be concluded before August eighth. Do you have any indications that the Japanese will surrender before that date?"

Stimson shook his head.

"So the United States is being pushed by circumstance into a drastic and probably regrettable course of action: using the atomic bomb. I cannot believe that you want to do this, Mr. Secretary."

Stimson cleared his throat. "Considering you've come to me, Mr. Thyssen, you must think that I'm the man most responsible for the bomb's development. Therefore, what makes you believe I would be against using it?"

"Good point. I hope I am a better judge of character now. I do not see you as another Himmler."

Stimson bristled but couldn't find his voice for a moment; then he said, "Suppose it's out of my hands?"

Thyssen studied the ceiling for a moment, deep in thought. "Are you telling me that there is already an official policy to use the bomb as soon as possible and not to give the Japanese any warning?"

"That's your conclusion."

"An obvious one, I think. Otherwise you would be going out of your way to warn them."

"Not necessarily. Japan is run by a group of military fanatics determined to fight to the last man. How are we supposed to reason with people like that? Perhaps the only demonstration that will work is tactical use."

Thyssen paced a moment, then faced Stimson again. "Would you consider an unofficial warning?" he asked.

Stimson looked up slowly.

"After the test, and if it is successful," Thyssen added. "If so, I would be willing to undertake such an effort."

Without committing himself Stimson said, "How?"

"Through Swedish trade channels I believe I can reach into the highest echelons of the Imperial government. Of course, the substance of any warning would be up to you."

"I see." Stimson's mind raced. "How soon could you do this?"

"When is the test?"

"I can't tell you that."

Thyssen shrugged. "Let me just say, then, that I will work as fast as I can and assume that there is great urgency."

Stimson frowned uncertainly. The test was scheduled for mid-July. How much time Thyssen might have beyond that depended on its success.

Thyssen leaned over the desk and looked at him with deep sincerity. "Mr. Secretary, if you use this horrendous weapon against anyone, it will destroy America's image as defender of the oppressed. It is no fitting way to end this war. But if you warn them first, you may bring about what you want most—unconditional surrender."

Stimson was quiet a long time. Finally he stood up. "Are you staying in Washington?"

"Yes."

"I'd like to talk again tomorrow, Mr. Thyssen."

"I am at your disposal."

Stimson saw him to the door, then called in his secretary. "What's my schedule for tonight?"

"Nothing booked, sir."

Stimson thanked her, waited till she left, then reached for the phone.

* * *

Stimson stopped talking as a servant came in to pour brandy. General of the Army George C. Marshall waited patiently for the ritual to be completed, his brow furrowed in thought as he digested what Stimson had just told him. Marshall was sixty-five, Chairman of the Joint Chiefs of Staff, a VMI graduate who had fought in World War One, had been Pershing's aide-de-camp in the early '20s and was presently head of the most powerful military machine the world had ever seen.

The servant quietly left the den and closed the door. Stimson swirled his brandy and looked to Marshall for comment.

"In the first place, Henry, even listening to Thyssen was a mistake."

"I had no idea what he was going to say."

"You should have cut him off and kicked him out."

"George, he made some good points. The same things we've been discussing for weeks."

"But it all comes back to the same problem. Truman doesn't want to warn the Japanese. Up until two weeks after he became President, he didn't know anything about S-1. You tossed it in his lap and he responded like a kid with a new toy. He hasn't lived with it as we have."

Stimson heaved himself out of his chair and reached for his cane. "George, even under Roosevelt there was never any question about our using the bomb. And I always supported that position. But now, with the responsibility almost on us, I have qualms."

"We both do. But we have to deal with reality. This man is suggesting treason."

Stimson sighed. "Perhaps, but he may have hit on the right way to do it."

"There's no right way to commit treason."

Stimson shook his head. "We *will* tell the President, but not just yet. First, we'll put the whole thing together. Then, at the appropriate time, offer it to him as a viable alternative. If we lay the proper groundwork and keep it simple, we can be ready to go at a moment's notice. Then if Truman rejects it, no harm done. But George, it's worth a try."

Marshall shook his head. "I don't believe there will be an

appropriate time. We're getting close to Potsdam. The President is talking about using the bomb as a way of pushing Stalin into line. He would resent any interference, and I don't think we have anything to gain by trying to subvert him."

Stimson nodded thoughtfully. "I agree, but the President needs guidance. We can't just sit back and let an inexperienced viewpoint dominate. That would be a *real* disservice."

Marshall was not convinced. He rubbed his brow and stared at his brandy.

"George, Stefan Thyssen is no fool. For a man who has spent the war in Europe, he had a surprising grasp of what's going on here in Washington. It comes down to this: we better start thinking about the future as more than just winning wars and cutting up the political pie. Weigh the consequences of *not* warning the Japanese."

Stimson dropped into his chair. Marshall studied him carefully. "You feel that strongly about it, Henry?"

"Yes."

"You trust Thyssen?"

"So far."

Marshall steepled his hands. "Then I better meet him."

June 13: Trinity

The sun blazed hotly over weathered rocks and sand in the Jornada del Muerto, the southern New Mexico desert known as "Journey of the Dead."

In the midst of the vast, parched wasteland, a herd of technicians labored like an ant army, digging and building at a furious pace, fighting the heat and an ever-encroaching deadline.

Snyder sat quietly in the Jeep with the motor off, sipping a warm Coke and watching the activity in the distance.

He squinted at the Trinity test site a mile downrange, feeling a twinge of pity for the Army engineers who were fitting together the mysterious steel cylinder, a massive funnel of metal surrounded by a seventy-foot tower that rested on a concrete foundation. It was supposed to represent the structural strength of a twenty-story office building. If the first test was successful, scientists hoped to study the effects of the blast on that tower.

Snyder finished his Coke and chucked the bottle away. He pulled a rag from his pocket and wiped sweat off his brow, then looked at himself in the mirror. The sun had baked him almost brown. His chiseled features, dark hair and brown eyes seemed to belong on another face. He stretched the flexed aching muscles.

Captain Patrick Timothy Snyder was thirty years old, Regular Army, a mustang who had come up through the ranks. Whenever he thought about where his career was going, Snyder always wondered what had become of the proud, rigid young soldier featured on all the enlistment posters. Was he lucky enough to be an Intelligence officer, scooting around the desert in a Jeep? Or was he lying dead in some foxhole in Europe? It always came down to that—the life-or-death comparison.

He watched a Jeep come up from the south and race toward him. He grunted to himself. Fifteen minutes it had taken those two moron MP lieutenants to find one map and a stack of notes. Snyder sighed.

He had just finished a two-day survey of the perimeter checkpoints around the desert site, a journey covering hundreds of miles and turning up far too many weak spots. He would never tell Colonel Tully, but he fully believed that the only security element that really worked out here was the desert itself.

The Jeep fishtailed to a stop and a soldier got out—not the two lieutenants he was expecting.

Staff Sergeant Steve Taylor walked over, smiling and holding out a manila envelope. "The stuff you wanted, sir." Taylor squinted in the sharp sunlight.

"Thanks." Snyder took the envelope and pulled out its contents. "Those two cream puffs decide to take a break?"

"Colonel Tully appropriated them, sir."

"Good. Then you can do their work." Snyder unfolded the map and glanced over Colonel Tully's proposed security checkpoints and the suggested trails for roving patrols. Taylor moved in to look with him.

"We've got patrols where we don't need them, and where we need them—nothing." Snyder reached under his seat and fished out his own map and notes scribbled on a clipboard pad. "I want you to take my findings and coordinate them with Tully's plan," he said. "Just do an overlay on a new map and make up a presentation on paper. Okay?"

"Yes, sir."

Snyder reacted to another Jeep roaring up from the south. "What's this—a convention?"

"Might be the Colonel, sir."

"Orders?"

"I think it's a transfer, sir."

Snyder blinked. He couldn't believe it. He had been in the desert eleven months, assigned to Tully, Officer in Charge of Security and Intelligence, Western Division,

Manhattan Project. They were the top security team at
Alamogordo, handling a scientific community rapidly suc-
cumbing to cabin fever. Snyder had never loved the routine, the daily inspections of the test site and the constant
conflicts with the civilian work force, who had dubbed him
"Iron Balls." But at least he fully understood the need for
what he was doing. He was part of the S-1 fold, the "family," with full knowledge of the ultimate end of the project.
And he subscribed to it wholeheartedly. It made absolute
sense to him to develop a weapon that would destroy more
enemies in one blow than any other single act of war. Still,
he was sick of the desert. He would be happy to say good-
bye to the jackrabbits, the rattlers, the scientists and Tully.

Snyder got out of the Jeep as the approaching vehicle
pulled to a stop. He walked over and saluted Colonel Tully,
a lean, thinly moustached man with piercing blue eyes and
a nasty disposition.

Tully remained in his Jeep. He handed Snyder a set of
orders and said with controlled anger, "What's this all
about?"

Snyder took the papers and peered at the black print. He
was being transferred to the War Department in Washington.

He thought quickly, trying to imagine what it meant. A
top-level briefing, then reassignment to an Intelligence unit
overseas?

"I don't know, sir," he said finally.

"You've got friends in Washington?" Tully asked.

"Colonel, I don't know anything about it."

"That makes two of us. I tried to get it scotched and was
told in no uncertain terms not to interfere."

Snyder sensed the Colonel's boiling point rapidly approaching. "I'm sorry, sir. But this is the first I've heard of
it."

Tully eyed him mistrustfully. "Goddamnit, Snyder, I
don't like anything done behind my back. We have an important job here. When I get a responsible officer trained
to do it well, I want to keep him. I just spoke with two
lieutenants who couldn't tell me in plain language what
they'd been doing with you for two whole days!"

"Sir, I've given all that information to Sergeant Taylor. He'll prepare it for you tonight."

Tully eyed Taylor, who was standing stiffly at his Jeep. "Does he know what he's doing?" Tully said.

"Yes, sir. I trust him completely. But I really think he's been a sergeant too long."

"What does that mean?"

"If you need to replace me, you might give him a chance."

Tully glared at him, then called out, "Taylor!"

Taylor jogged over and saluted. "Yes, sir?"

"You're out of uniform."

"Pardon, sir?"

"Get those sergeant's stripes off. You're now a second lieutenant. . . . Congratulations."

Taylor stared from Tully to Snyder, incredulous.

"Colonel," interrupted Snyder. "It might be better if he outranked those other two—"

"First lieutenant!" Tully barked.

Taylor's eyes widened and he grinned with excitement. "Thank you, sir!"

"Don't mention it. Snyder, get moving. They want you in Washington on Friday. And Snyder—" Tully lowered his voice to a threatening monotone. "I hope I don't have to caution you about watching what you say."

Snyder's mouth opened and for a fleeting moment he wondered if this transfer might be just another security check to see if he could be trusted. That sort of thing was done all the time, and anyone who failed the test got himself a one-way ticket to the back side of the moon.

"Colonel," he said, hoping his next words were furthest from the truth. "I'll probably be back in a week."

June 15: Washington

Snyder hadn't quite settled into his chair when he was asked to step into the Secretary's office.

Henry Stimson looked up from his desk, waved a hand to the sideboard and said in a friendly voice, "There's coffee if you want some, Captain."

Snyder thanked him and helped himself.

"I hope you had a pleasant flight," said Stimson, buried in paper work. "I'll be with you in just a moment."

"Take your time, sir," Snyder said, his eyes taking in the banked flags and the seal of office behind Stimson. His hand froze on the cup handle when an inner door opened and General Marshall walked in.

"Good morning, Mr. Secretary," Marshall said. He flashed a smile and added, "You too, Captain Snyder." He pointed to a chair in front of the desk.

"Good morning, sir," said Snyder, sitting down, his eyes glued to the file jacket under Marshall's arm. What the hell was going on? Nobody pulled a captain out of the desert just to have coffee with the Secretary of War and the Army Chief of Staff.

Marshall sat next to Stimson and scanned the 201 file. "You have quite an interesting service record, Captain," he said. "Enlisted in 'thirty-six. What made you choose Military Police?"

Snyder drained the cup, scalding his throat. "It wasn't my choice, sir. They needed men to fill out a roster."

Marshall nodded and examined the top sheet more closely. Stimson finished whatever he was doing, stacked his papers, and gave the proceedings his full attention.

"You took correspondence courses," Marshall said.

"Yes, sir."

"Did that interfere with your regular duties?"

"No, sir. That was on my own time." Snyder recalled long hours at night, missed weekend passes, trying to cram knowledge into a head woozy from lack of sleep.

"I see you're credited with three years toward a degree."

"Yes, sir. I would have completed, but the war . . ." He shrugged.

"Of course," said Marshall.

"Tell us about New York," Stimson interrupted.

Snyder felt dampness spreading under his arms. What had he done wrong? What were they after him for? "I headed a security team weeding out Nazi sympathizers in Yorkville," he said. "Right after Pearl Harbor. We infiltrated a spy ring on the New York waterfront. They were radioing ship movements to U-boats offshore."

"Were you commissioned by then?" asked Marshall.

"Yes, sir. Just."

"And why were you picked for that job?" Stimson asked.

"I don't exactly know, sir. Nobody ever gave reasons."

"Could it be because you had studied German, Captain?" Marshall asked.

Snyder sat very still. He felt they were trying to mousetrap him. "I was sure we were going to be at war with them sooner or later, sir," he said. "But it wasn't my German. It was because I had the Gaelic."

They both looked at him, puzzled.

"I'm Irish," he explained. "Grandma Gilhool lived with us until she died. She insisted my brother and I learn the old tongue. I posed as an Irishman from Dublin with strong anti-British feelings."

"And it worked?" said Marshall, impressed.

"Wouldn't have worked in Dublin, sir. But in New York the Bundists were not the brightest people in the world."

"But their leader was a member of German Intelligence. What about him?"

"You tell me, General," Snyder said quietly, tired of the game. "You both seem to know everything else."

Marshall regarded him quizzically, a tiny smile at the corner of his mouth.

"Sir, if I'm here for a reason, I would appreciate knowing it before we go any further."

Marshall smoothed his silver hair and almost absently asked, "What's your opinion of the Japanese?"

Snyder was wary. "I suppose, like everyone else, I'd like to see them beaten and the war ended."

"You suppose?"

Now that he knew it was the right answer, Snyder had no trouble putting conviction into his voice. "I'm very sure."

"I understand you lost a brother at Guadalcanal," Marshall said.

"Yes, sir." Snyder's lip tightened.

"Has that affected your feelings toward the Japanese?"

Snyder stared in disbelief. He stumbled over his words. "It hasn't endeared them to me, sir . . ."

After a silence Marshall said, "Of course. I'm sorry about your brother, Captain Snyder."

Snyder nodded.

Then Marshall leaned forward and patiently explained, "We want to know if this is a hatred for all things Japanese, or just their military."

Snyder frowned. "Forgive me, sir, but I don't know what you're getting at."

Marshall was silent a moment, glancing at Stimson. "We'll come back to that," he said finally.

Stimson took a deep breath. "Captain Snyder, we have an opportunity to end the war quickly." He paused.

"That would be very welcome, Mr. Secretary."

"It's only a matter of time, anyway. Our best assessment tells us the Japanese can't hold out through the end of the year, even though their leadership may want to."

Snyder's inner alarm went off. What was he doing here discussing politics and grand strategy with these men?

"The Japanese mentality is a far cry from that of the Germans," Stimson continued. "Let me explain something about them. They have what they call the code of Bushido, which means unquestioning loyalty, valuing honor above life. The Emperor is their god, and if he says die for me, all his followers ask is when and where."

Snyder nodded. "I'm familiar with their customs, sir."

"Oh. Novels?"

"No, sir. Briefings."

Stimson chuckled. "Well and good, but there are certain political details invariably left out of briefings. It isn't so much the Emperor who must be dealt with, but the military factions who are in power in his name. They are fanatics intent on continuing this war till the last loyal samurai has gone to his Maker. The political climate in Japan is viciously tense, to say the least. However——" He paused and leaned forward. "In all probability they would surrender if they were shown that their imminent fate was complete and total devastation."

Snyder listened intently, his mind racing ahead, trying to figure his part in all this.

"Captain Snyder, we're talking about the bomb."

Snyder snapped alert. Almost by rote he announced, "Sir, I am under orders not to discuss anything regarding S-1."

"Commendable reaction, Captain," said Marshall. "But I relieve you of that responsibility in the confines of this room. After all, the Secretary here is the head of S-1."

"Yes, sir." Snyder felt foolish.

"The bomb," Stimson repeated. "The atomic bomb. How do you feel about using it on the Japanese?"

Snyder had never really considered the question before. "I've always assumed we were going to use it," he said. "Either on the Germans or the Japanese."

"But do you think we should?" Stimson said carefully, and Snyder realized the answer was important to them.

"If there is no other way of bringing about their surrender, then yes."

Stimson nodded. "The only alternative would seem to be a massive invasion, which would cost millions of lives on both sides."

"Then I don't see much of a choice, sir."

Marshall frowned and rose, clasped his hands behind his back and faced Snyder directly. "Don't you think, Captain, that if the Japanese had any notion of the power of this weapon, they might alter their thinking and perhaps surrender that much faster?"

"Possibly, sir, but——"

"I wasn't exaggerating when I said millions of lives," said Stimson quietly. "Conservative estimates put our first-day losses at five hundred thousand."

Snyder stared in disbelief: the figure was staggering.

"So anything we can do to avoid that should be explored as fully as possible, don't you agree?"

"Yes, sir. But it seems to me that it's the Japanese you have to convince."

"Precisely," said Marshall. "That's why you're here."

Snyder sat motionless for a moment. "I don't quite follow," he said.

Stimson folded his hands on the desk and leaned forward again. "The idea of the invasion is repugnant to me," he said. "But the alternative, using the bomb, puts this country in a difficult moral position relative to the rest of the world. We would be setting a terrible precedent. Do you understand?"

Snyder looked down at his knee and tried to think. Too much politics coming too fast. His moral responsibility in this war had been cut and dried for three and a half years.

At last he looked up into their waiting faces. "Mr. Secretary," he said, "I'm an Army officer. If I'm given an order, I obey it. I don't know a thing about policy."

"That's why you don't have gray hair," said Marshall with a smile. "But we're not throwing the burden of decision on your shoulders." He left the thought hanging and Sndyer felt only uncertain relief.

"Then what do you have in mind, sir?"

There was a silence, then Stimson said point-blank, "We want you to lead a special mission to warn Japan of the consequences of an atomic attack."

Snyder stared at him, aghast. They had the wrong man. They should have had some diplomat sitting here, someone who knew exactly what they were talking about, all the options and enough people in high places at the other end. Certainly not someone whose own brother had been killed by the Japanese.

"We need a good man," said Marshall, "to run a top-secret military operation. You won't be required to negotiate with anyone, just deliver the people who will."

Snyder swallowed hard. "Are you asking me to volunteer, General?"

"Asking you?" Marshall echoed. "No."

Snyder looked back at Stimson. "Sir, we don't even know yet if the device works."

"We will—after the test in July," said Stimson. "And that's when you would leave. But we want to start laying groundwork now."

Snyder was overwhelmed. It still didn't make sense to him. "Sir, suppose we send this mission and they still refuse to surrender?"

"At least we will have made the attempt," Stimson replied.

Snyder nodded at the logic, then said, "Why me? I can't believe you just pulled my name out of a hat."

Marshall chuckled. "Not quite. The Secretary and I conducted a discreet and exhaustive research to find someone totally familiar with S-1 who knew his way around the project, and who had dealt with the scientists."

"And we did not want a field-grade officer," Stimson added. "We felt that for this kind of operation, to start shuffling generals would attract too much attention."

Snyder pointed to his file. "I'm sure there's one thing the records don't show about my status with the scientists. They call me Captain Iron Balls."

Marshall smiled. "As of now you're Major Iron Balls."

Snyder squirmed and mumbled his thanks. "I'm sure that will make a difference," he said, and saw Stimson fighting to suppress a grin.

"We won't be running a popularity contest, Major," said Marshall. "Just a quiet operation. If you think of it that way, I'm sure it's well within your capabilities." He noticed Snyder's frown deepening. "Anything wrong, Major?"

"Colonel Tully didn't seem to know anything about this."

"Make sure he doesn't find out," said Marshall. "The need to know extends only this far—you and I and the Secretary, and the people who will work directly with you. No one outside. That's part of your responsibility, and it's at least as important as accomplishing the mission. We cannot tell Colonel Tully, or anyone else in S-1 security, particularly General Groves."

"May I ask why not, sir?"

"Because he wouldn't approve of the mission. He would take a dim view of his two-billion-dollar effort going down the drain."

"Excuse me, sir, but why are *you* so willing to shunt it aside?"

"We are not tossing it away at all. All we are doing is giving the Japanese a limited amount of information to impress them with a situation they already know to be hopeless. The decision is up to them."

Snyder had no reply. They had worked it all out to their own satisfaction, so how could he question it?

"Well, Major?" Marshall looked down at him.

"I guess I'm your man, sir."

"Fine," said Marshall. He sat down again and leaned forward, his eyes boring in on Snyder. "You'll be working out of the Berkeley Radiation Lab. Contact Dr. Allen Lasch. You will have all the proper authorization, but our names will be left out of it. Understand?"

"Yes, sir. What about Dr. Lawrence?"

"He won't be involved. We'll keep him away and see that he knows nothing about this."

"He'll be at Los Alamos most of the time anyway. The work at Berkeley is, for the most part, done. I don't anticipate any trouble from that quarter."

"So introduce yourself to Lasch," said Marshall. "We'll supply you with convincing orders to clear you through Rad Lab Security, but the less you have to show to Lasch, the better. Once you're in his good graces, you and he will select a team of scientists to make the journey to Japan. You will assemble a packet of highly secret information, which will include photos of the Trinity test."

Snyder nodded, then asked, "Since S-1 security is not going to be in on this, will I have full jurisdiction?"

"Yes," said Marshall.

"And will you back me up in case of trouble?"

"Set up a scrambler phone and keep in touch."

He didn't really answer the question, but Snyder was reluctant to pursue it. Another matter occurred to him: "There's still something missing, sir. Is it just me and a group of scientists?"

Stimson stood up and walked to his inner door again. "You will be under the diplomatic wing of the Swedish government, acting as neutral negotiators," he said. He opened the door and nodded to someone in the next room.

Snyder stood up as the tall, paunchy Swede walked in, beamed at him and bowed from the shoulders.

"Major Snyder, this is Mr. Stefan Thyssen."

PART 2

PART 2

June 16: San Francisco

Snyder peered through the rain-splashed windshield and cursed the ineffectual wiper blades of the staff car he had requisitioned from the motor pool at Hamilton Field. The tires stopped thrumming as he came off the Golden Gate Bridge and crossed to the toll plaza.

He handed the attendant a trip chit, then eased the Plymouth out into sparse late-night traffic. It was nearly 3 A.M. Washington time, and he half-wished he had checked into the BOQ instead of heading home. But he'd had a little too much Army in the last forty-eight hours: he needed time to think. How could the Secretary of War and the Army Chief of Staff worry about using the bomb? Who would question us? We're in the right. The Japanese made war on *us*. Maybe Stimson and Marshall could forget that, but he couldn't. Not with Dennis' bones rotting in the Marine cemetery on Guadalcanal.

And why verbal orders? The Army never functioned without the written word, yet here he was—a dumb mick without a scrap of paper to back him up. Why were they leaving him so vulnerable?

He couldn't figure it out. His mind was too groggy. He hoped his parents were asleep: he couldn't face them now. Time enough for a reunion tomorrow morning.

He turned off Van Ness to Twenty-second Street. The brownout and the rain forced him to slow down. He passed Dolores Street and began searching for a parking space. He was amazed to find a slot near the house.

Snyder pulled his B4 bag from the trunk, shut the lid and sprinted through the rain toward the covered porch.

The house was dark. Water dribbled off his plastic cap cover and ran down the upturned collar of his raincoat as he stretched, his fingers scrabbling for the key hidden above the front window frame. As he drew back, the weak street light in front of the house illuminated two stars on the service flag in the window. The gold star, signifying a death in action, glinted dully.

He closed the door quietly and stood in the hallway, dripping water on his mother's polished wooden floor. No sound from upstairs. He took off his raincoat, shook it, then hung it up on a peg inside the hall closet door. He waited for his eyes to adjust to the gloom, then headed for the stairs with his bag in one hand, automatically skipping the steps that creaked. He paused on the landing. Still no sound from the second floor.

He passed his parents' bedroom, turned the corner and saw a faint flicker playing on the wall across from his bedroom. Fire, he thought, and moved quickly to the open doorway.

Two dancing candles flanked a small statue of the Virgin Mary. They sat on a shelf beneath a silver crucifix mounted on the wall. The crucifix was centered among pictures that Snyder couldn't quite see, but he didn't have to. He knew right away what the arrangement was. Directly under the crucifix he could make out the yellow Western Union telegram, the one from the Navy Department that began: "We regret to inform you . . ."

He closed his eyes and muttered a sigh.

"Dennis?"

Snyder froze and felt the back of his neck go cold.

A small figure sunk in the old chair by the window craned its head and stared at him anxiously.

"No, Pop. It's me, Patrick."

Patrick Senior let out a startled grunt, then rose with difficulty. He lurched across the room and threw strong, wiry arms around Snyder. They stood in an embrace almost a full minute before the old man spoke: "Why didn't you call and tell us you were coming?"

"Spur of the moment, Pop. Didn't have time." Snyder held his father at arm's length and caught a sour whiff of whisky.

"Let me get your mother up. She'll be so glad—"

"No, don't do that. I'll see her in the morning. Hey, Pop, looks like I might be here for a while." He smiled.

Patrick Senior brightened. "Well . . . well, that's fine, it is. We're always glad to have you," he said thickly.

"Okay if I turn on a light?"

"Sure—wait, I want you to see something." Patrick Senior held his son in place and reached for the wall switch. He snapped the light on and indicated the wall proudly.

Snyder had to react anew to the pictorial record of his dead brother's brief life spread out over one whole wall. He drank it in with his eyes and managed a smile of approval, but he felt sick inside.

His father, still clutching his rosary, looked on anxiously. "Like it?" he asked.

Snyder tore his eyes away and studied his father. He had aged. In the harsh light of the overhead lamp, his face appeared deeply lined, his body thinner. He was stooped and his head looked more hawklike than Snyder remembered.

"It's a shrine," explained Patrick Senior.

"It's terrific, Pop." He paused. "When did you do this?"

"Oh—just after your last leave, I think. I wanted some way to—I mean, so your mother and I could still have our boy with us." There was a stiff silence.

Snyder wanted to reassure him, but the words wouldn't come. He felt his stomach churning with the strain.

"It's your room now, I know," Patrick Senior went on. "We promised it would always be yours, but—"

"Pop, that's okay—"

His father moved to the shrine and gazed at the pictures wistfully. "I hope you don't mind," he said softly.

"Of course not." Snyder pulled him around, let him see a smile.

His father stared into his eyes, then seemed to change his mood abruptly. He stood back and said, "Well now, let's have a good look at you. Sweet Jesus!" He stared at the gold oak leaves. "You're a major!"

"Shh, Pop. You'll wake up Ma—"

Patrick Senior laughed and tears ran from his eyes. Snyder was suddenly quite sure they weren't all tears of joy. But his father put on a good act. "She *should* be up to see this," he said. "Oh, you look so *grand*. If only your brother was here to see you now. He'd be proud . . ."

The two men stood awkwardly, Snyder trying not to see his father's tears. How vulnerable and pathetic the old man seemed now, so different from the strong-willed disciplinarian he had been throughout Snyder's youth.

"Pop, are you okay?"

"Sure I am."

"Have you been holding up all right? The job—"

Watery blue eyes snapped. "You sound like your mother. And Father Carr."

"Father Carr?" Snyder was surprised. "Are you back in the Church?"

"Seven o'clock Mass at St. Charles' every morning." He didn't say it with pride; it was stated fact.

"You're back on speaking terms with Father Carr?"

"After a fashion: he talks, I listen."

"About Dennis?"

Patrick Senior nodded.

"What does he say?"

"That it was the Lord's will."

Snyder winced. "Do you accept that?"

"No. We're at a standoff."

"But you still go to Mass. Why?"

He put a hand on his son's shoulder and said, "I pray to the same God, and in the same House as the good Father. But I don't pray much for souls. I pray for something different."

"What?"

"If it was the Lord's will to take Dennis away from me, then I pray He does the same to that accursed race across the Pacific."

"The Japanese."

"Aye, them."

"Take it from me, Pop—they're losing. We're kicking the crap out of them."

"That's not enough. Send every last one of them to hell! That's what I pray. Then maybe your brother's soul will rest!"

And yours? Snyder wondered to himself. He watched the hatred slowly drain from his father's face.

Patrick Senior fingered the gold oak leaves on his son's uniform. "Major," he said with a smile. "You'd better get some sleep. Your mother will be wakin' you early." He went to the door and paused to look back. "Good night, son. It's grand havin' you back."

" 'Night, Pop."

Snyder waited till he was gone, then blew out the candles. He undressed, crept to the bathroom and washed, then came back and buried himself under the bedclothes. As he drifted off to sleep, he wondered what his father would say if he learned about the mission. It would probably put him round the bend.

"All right, lazybones—up!"

Snyder's eyes sprang open and for a long moment he couldn't remember where he was; then he saw his mother's stern face looking down at him, a kitchen towel slung over one forearm. She wore a faded print dress that he remembered vividly—her household uniform. She had gained weight and her face had gone wrinkly. Red-brown hair was pulled back into a bun and her arms, always her most prominent feature, looked strong and dangerous. Snyder remembered that towel well—she could swat with it faster than the eye could see.

"Wait a minute," he said, the fog of sleep clearing. "I'm not a kid anymore. Why does everybody treat me like a kid when I come home?"

"Every mother has an answer for that one," she said, then her face softened into a smile and she sat down on the edge of the bed. Snyder pulled himself up and they looked at each other.

"How about a bone-crushing hug?" he said.

It was more than he bargained for. While his father had lost much of his overbearing power—it had all shrunk up into a tiny frame—his mother still resembled a bear. She held him tightly a long time, then said, "All right, breakfast—ten minutes."

"What time is it?"

"Seven thirty. Come on, your father's already at Mass. He'll want to take you out when he gets back."

Lillian Snyder stood up and smoothed her dress, watching her son roll out of bed in his shorts. "Good Lord," she said, "from the neck up you're as brown as a meat loaf. Where've you been?"

"Can't answer, Ma. You might be a spy."

He ate breakfast with his mother and listened to a torrent of gossip. His mother was wired into every family in the neighborhood and particularly wanted to apprise him of the fate of several old girlfriends. "You should have snapped up Katie Milbride when you had the chance," she said, scooping more eggs onto his plate. "She had the eye for you and there's no doubt about that. She married some farm boy from Nebraska. Imagine!"

"Good for her," mumbled Snyder. "I talked with Pop last night," he said, maneuvering her away from that subject. "He's changed a lot."

"Aye, and not for the better."

"That's some museum upstairs."

"Aye," she said without comment.

"I notice you're not going to Mass with him."

"I did once." She sat down and looked at her plate. "I couldn't take it. Sitting there, listening to him spout all that hate at the Japanese. It calls too much pain to mind, you know?" Her eyes filled. "I do miss Dennis," she added. "Sometimes terribly. But I know we've still got you."

Snyder reached for her hand. "And each other, Ma."

"Oh—little enough company that is these days." She reflected to herself for a moment, then her eyes twinkled happily. "You've had a promotion."

"Shows you how wrong the Army can be."

She smiled, rose and cleared the table. Snyder followed her into the kitchen and grabbed a dish towel.

"Do majors help with the cleaning up?" his mother asked.

"Depends on your CO."

"Then mind you don't break any dishes. I seem to remember you were incurably butterfingered."

"I'm better now—only one plate in twenty."

"When your father gets back from Mass, he wants to call the O'Haras and the Sheans. They haven't seen you in ages."

"Mom, I'm going to be busy." He held out a dish to quiet her protest. She snatched it out of his hand.

"Look," he said, "I didn't come home to socialize. I wanted to see you and Pop, but I've got a lot of work, and I'll drop in when I can, but please don't make plans for me, okay?"

His mother finished rinsing the sink in silence. Snyder could tell she was disappointed. She took the towel from him and wouldn't let him help anymore. It was her way of sulking. But she always got over it quickly.

"Patrick," she said after a few moments, "does your father worry you?"

"I wasn't prepared for last night."

'Well, you have to understand—he wasn't prepared for what happened to Dennis."

"I know that."

"And though he talks of nothing else most of the time, I think his real concern is you."

Snyder met her questioning gaze. He wasn't so sure she was right. But he said, "He's got nothing to worry about. I'm not going anywhere dangerous." The lie almost stuck in his throat. But she seemed relieved, and he hoped it wouldn't come up again.

Afterward Snyder went upstairs and spent the day checking maps, Army directives and the stack of bogus orders the War Department had issued to him. He worked on the bed, facing the window, so he wouldn't have to look at the memorial wall.

June 18: Berkeley

On Monday morning Snyder drove out to the University of California, a sprawling campus in the Berkeley foothills. As he turned off Bancroft to Telegraph, he kept his eye on the Campanile, a peaked bell tower that could be seen for miles, Berkeley's most prominent landmark. He went through Sather Gate and turned up South Drive. It was the week after finals and the only students around were a few women and GIs. He passed an ivy-covered building on his left, then the Campanile. He relaxed as he saw the security gate ahead. A fence surrounded most of the buildings at the east end of campus.

The MP came out of the guard box to examine Snyder's credentials, asked him to park along the drive, then called for another MP to escort him over to Security.

Snyder passed between two huge buildings and was taken to a Quonset hut backed up against another, forming a T shape. He was ushered into the first office.

Captain Browne stood up. He was pale, young and dark-haired, with sharp features and suspicious eyes. Browne motioned him to a chair.

"What can I do for you, Major?" he asked.

Snyder opened his briefcase and produced the set of orders that Stimson's office had cut for him. Browne scanned them: Snyder's transfer from Colonel Tully's command to the direct authority of General Groves, his posting to the Radiation Lab at Berkeley on "special assignment" and orders that Captain Browne and his staff were to follow all of his instructions to the letter.

Browne gave Snyder a curious look.

"Read paragraph five," Snyder suggested quietly.

Browne pulled out the last sheet and read aloud: " 'On pain of strict disciplinary action, you are not to reveal the source of Major Snyder's authority to anyone. Further, Major Snyder's requirements take priority over all Berkeley security activities. Signed, Leslie R. Groves, General, commanding.' "

Snyder added nothing. The orders were, of course, a complete forgery, prepared to perfection by a team in the War Department.

Browne grunted to himself.

Snyder cracked a smile. "Does it sound ominous?"

"I'm used to these little games, sir."

"It's no game, Captain. I don't want to disrupt anything here, nor do I want to be consulted on routine security procedures, but if I ask for something, I'll expect it fast. Is that clear?"

"Perfectly, sir."

"I'll need a security badge, a sticker for my car and quarters."

"Yes, sir. Have all that for you today."

"Very well." Snyder rose with a warm smile. "Now, if you could take me over to see Dr. Lasch?"

Browne led him back to one of the two big buildings he had passed on the way in: Le Conte Hall, a three-story white stucco structure housing the physics department and Rad Lab offices. On the way Browne enthusiastically explained his security procedures.

"We've got a company of MPs here," he said. "Sentries rotated on a two-hour schedule. Once an hour, two-man teams patrol the buildings and check every room. Shifts are four hours on, eight off."

"Internal security force?" Snyder asked.

"Yes, sir. Any goof-off gets a swift transfer to oblivion. The attrition rate is about ten percent, and that's low. I hear it's higher in Alamogordo."

Snyder gave him a light-switch smile. "Your people have it easy, Browne. No hot sun, no rattlesnakes, just coeds, girls, paradise. I'm not surprised that ten percent of your people are slobs."

Browne's face sank. He looked like a wounded puppy.

"Where do we find Dr. Lasch?" Snyder asked.

"This way," Browne mumbled. He led Snyder into Le Conte and up the stairs.

They stepped out on the landing and walked down a long hall between two rows of offices, their heels clicking sharply on the worn linoleum. Everywhere Snyder looked there was glass and institutional green paint. People worked in small cubicles with a minimum of furniture and a maximum of paper. His eyes traveled over photographs lining the walls: eight-by-ten black-and-whites of men and women in lab coats, standing in small groups near huge pieces of equipment, most of it unfamiliar to Snyder.

At the end of the hall he spotted a woman leaning over a desk. Browne was headed that way, so Snyder took the trouble to look her over.

She was slim, in her midtwenties, he guessed, wearing a soft yellow dress girded with a black patent leather belt. Brown hair looped gently to her shoulders; a curl fell straight down, concealing her face.

When they were almost upon her, she looked up. Her eyes swept past Browne and scanned Snyder quickly. His interest took a leap as she straightened and he saw her face: lovely, with high cheekbones and intense green eyes.

"Miss Martin, this is Major Snyder. He'd like to see Dr. Lasch," Browne announced.

She scrutinized Snyder carefully, mumbled his name to herself, then checked her appointment book. "Is he expecting you?"

"No, ma'am," Snyder admitted. He looked past her at the closed door and the black letters: DR. ALLEN C. LASCH, DIRECTOR OF SPECIAL PROJECTS.

"I see," she said. "I'm afraid you'll have to wait. He's away from his office right now. He'll be back shortly." She turned to Browne. "Can you leave him here, Captain?"

"Yes, ma'am. He's cleared." Browne seemed reluctant to go.

"I'll see you after I'm through," said Snyder, hinting he was no longer needed. "To pick up those passes."

"Uh, yes, sir." Browne glanced uncertainly at Miss Martin, then turned and walked back up the hall.

She indicated a chair. "Please have a seat, Major."

He sat down and watched her settle back to work. She perused papers as if he didn't exist.

He was quiet for a moment, then said, "P.T."

"Pardon?"

"P.T., my name. P.T. Snyder."

She blinked at him quizzically, then jotted it down. "That's not a name," she said. "It's initials."

"Patrick Timothy."

"Irish?"

"Sure and begorrah."

She smiled tolerantly and he said, "What do I call you?"

"Miss."

"Miss what?"

"Elizabeth Martin."

"Very nice."

"Thank you. My parents will be pleased to know."

"And they live where?" She didn't answer. "Well, you're not from California."

"Major, that's none of your business."

"Okay, then if we can't talk about you, we'll discuss Lasch. How long has he worked here?"

"Three years," she said, sticking a sheet of paper into her typewriter. Rolling it through, she straightened it and began rapping the keys at a machine-gun pace.

"I understand he's Associate Chairman of OSRD."

"Yes," she said.

"That's a pretty big job. He must be in awfully tight on S-1."

She stopped typing. "Major, please."

"Oh. None of my business, right?"

She rapped the keys again, really ignoring him now. He smiled to himself, amused.

"What's your title, Elizabeth?"

She glanced up, rolling her eyes to herself. "Administrative assistant. And call me Beth."

"Happily."

"Major, if you'll excuse me, I do have work."

"Oh, sure. Sorry," Snyder said innocently.

He sank back in the chair and tried to imagine her on a date. Plied with good wine, soft music and candlelight, would she relax and open up or just sit there planning the next day's work?

He looked up sharply. A tall, thin, almost handsome man with a hawkish face came down the hall, head bent and brow furrowed. His long legs snapped out in front of him; his hands were buried in his waist pockets. Snyder stood up.

"Dr. Lasch?" he said.

The tall man stopped and squinted at Snyder, trying to place him. Beth stopped typing. "Dr. Lasch," she said, "this is Major Snyder. P.T. Snyder," she added.

Lasch withdrew a bony hand from his right pocket and clasped Snyder's. "Very pleased to meet you, sir," said Snyder. "Can we talk privately?"

Lasch nodded and mumbled, "My office." He opened the door and let Snyder enter.

The room was small and stark. There was a rickety chair behind a heavy schoolteacher's desk, and two others, mismatched, in front of it; a lumpy leather sofa along one bare wall, and a small bookcase oddly dropped into a corner. On the wall behind the desk was an MIT diploma, a framed photograph of Lasch in cap and gown among a small group of dons; beneath the picture was the legend: Cambridge, 1938. Snyder craned to see it better, then was distracted by Lasch's voice outside.

"Is she back from Chicago yet?"

"Due in this afternoon," said Beth.

"I'll want to see her. Have somebody put a message on her door to get right over here. No excuses."

Lasch strode in and closed the door. He slid behind his desk and sat down, motioning Snyder to a chair with a forced smile. "What does the Army want with us now, Major? Haven't we been good boys and girls?"

"Dr. Lasch, what I'm going to tell you is top secret—"

"And otherwise hazardous to my health," Lasch finished. "Yes, Major, I'm used to this. Just get on with it."

Snyder paused, feeling a twinge of indignation at his condescending tone. "I want to put together a group of people to explain the Manhattan Project."

Lasch frowned. "Why?"

"We'll get to that. Can you come up with a handpicked

group of scientists, each with specialized knowledge about the bomb? And quickly?"

"What for?" asked Lasch. "Are we going public?"

Snyder fixed him with a reproachful stare. "Can you do it?" he repeated.

"Well, if Oppenheimer, Teller and Lawrence are available, certainly."

Snyder shook his head. "We have to set our sights a bit lower."

"Maybe you'd better explain."

"You and I are going to coordinate a mission to warn the Japanese about the atomic bomb."

Lasch stared in astonishment at Snyder, who outlined the mission rapidly. When he was finished, Lasch said, "Do you expect me to accept what you're saying on faith?"

"No," Snyder answered. "If you did, then I wouldn't want you involved."

"Then hadn't you better show me some authorization?"

"If you call Captain Browne, you'll find that I've satisfied his security requirements."

Lasch reached for the phone and called Security. He asked Browne if there were any orders pertaining to Snyder's authority.

"Yes, sir. He's cleared all the way up to the top."

Lasch grunted, then asked, "By whom?"

"Sorry, sir. I can't tell you that. It's part of my orders."

Lasch frowned. "Weren't there any orders for me?"

"No, sir."

"Look, Captain, Major Snyder wants certain cooperation from me that I can't give without something in writing."

"That's between you and the Major, sir. I'm satisfied."

Lasch growled a thank-you and hung up. He looked at Snyder uncomfortably and said, "Major, the government has spent enormous amounts of money and manpower developing this weapon, and now you show up telling me that they're looking for a way to avoid using it. That's quite a reversal in policy."

"Does that bother you?"

"Well, it's . . . mysterious."

"Do you have any personal objection to being part of such a mission?"

"I . . . I don't know. I would be in a better position to answer you sometime in mid-July."

"I need an answer today."

Lasch seemed to freeze.

"Dr. Lasch," Snyder said, "you've been selected because of your high ranking in the Office of Scientific Research and Development and your overall knowledge of the project. You're the keystone. I'm sure we could find someone else, but right now you have the best qualifications."

"How do I know this isn't your idea and yours alone?"

"Call the Swedish consulate in San Francisco and ask to speak with Stefan Thyssen. He's going to be our diplomatic liaison." Lasch frowned in suspicion. "I think you'll find out," Snyder continued, "that once we get things in motion, my authority extends far beyond what you might believe. I'll have no trouble getting clearances or moving people around. I don't think any ordinary Army major, acting on his own initiative, could accomplish that. That's the only verification I can give you at this time. But I need to know right away if you'll cooperate."

Lasch buzzed for Beth and asked her for the San Francisco phone directory. He had no trouble reaching Thyssen, who promised to send over a paper outlining the proposal, which Lasch would be free to examine, although it had to come right back.

When Lasch hung up, he faced Snyder thoughtfully. "Just how much do you intend to tell the Japanese?"

"Enough to scare hell out of them, sir, but not enough for them to use."

Lasch grunted. "I have some work to do," he said. "So while we're waiting for Thyssen's papers, how would you like to see the lab?"

Snyder relaxed, anticipating a pleasant hour with Beth Martin.

"Keith, would you step into my office, please?"

The Chief Administrator for Special Projects snapped his intercom switch down and said sharply, "Right away."

Keith Fulbright leaned back in his chair and sighed in annoyance as he surveyed the mess on his desk. If everybody would just leave him alone, he could get things done, but work at the Rad Lab was nothing but a series of interruptions. He rubbed tired eyes. He had been here since 7 A.M., his usual starting hour, well before anyone else.

He pushed the chair back and got up, stretching his short frame, and reached for his coat. He walked briskly up to Lasch's office, avoiding eye contact with Beth Martin. She had been there long enough for him to get used to her, but envy died hard. He hadn't liked it when Lasch had brought her in "to ease his work load," and he had liked it less when she became a fixture and Lasch's confidante. Fulbright felt that more and more he was being pushed into the background, left to handle the details while Beth dealt with personnel.

Often, as he sat in his office having lunch alone, he plotted revenge. But now, at least, Lasch had called for him, not her.

It turned out to be not much of an assignment. Give the Major a guided tour. Fulbright led Snyder downstairs and quickly sank into monotonous patter as they went through the Crocker Lab.

The building façade gave no indication of what went on behind the walls. To Snyder it looked like a factory, a tool-and-die works. There were experiment cubicles packed with strange instruments and men in white lab coats. There was chemistry equipment mixed with electronics, long worktables piled with half-built devices. In a corner he saw a large object that looked as if it had been torn apart by metal-eating mice. Fulbright explained that it was the remains of a cyclotron that had been cannibalized for parts.

The presence of students mingling with professors made it all the more ordinary, unlike the rigid professionalism of Alamogordo and Oak Ridge.

"We've got six cyclotrons," Fulbright explained "Electromagnetic mass accelerators used in separating U-235 from uranium isotopes."

"I see," said Snyder, playing dumb. "Could you explain how they work?"

"That's classified, Major."

"Isn't that funny? I couldn't either."

Fulbright reddened. Sndyer had thought his remark

would break the ice, but it had the opposite effect. Fulbright cut his patter to the bare minimum. "Want to see more?" he said.

"Rather have some coffee."

Fulbright walked Snyder down South Drive, across a bridge over a creek, then up to the faculty lounge. They entered a large room with tables and a cafeteria line. Snyder paid for coffee and rolls and they went to find a table.

Fulbright selected one that was away from everybody else and sat glumly nursing his coffee. Snyder studied him curiously. "How long have you worked here?" he asked.

"I started with Dr. Lasch in 1942. We came out from Washington together."

"Is he a good man to work for?"

"Work with, Major—with."

"My mistake." Touchy little fellow, he thought. "Where were you before that?"

"With Grumman Aircraft, Navy liaison."

Snyder nodded. "Must have been a good job."

"This one is better."

"I can see how much you like it."

Fulbright looked up sharply. "Major, if you had to deal with a lot of undisciplined slide-rule jockeys who haven't the slightest concept of organization, you'd have troubles, too."

Snyder grinned. "Hey, I've been around plenty of them. I know exactly what you mean."

Fulbright eyed him narrowly. "You do? How?"

"My family," Snyder lied.

"Scientists?"

"Loads of them. Got 'em under the bed." He laughed.

Even Fulbright managed a smile. "Christ," he said. "I'd give anything to get rid of all of them."

"Tell me about Miss Martin."

Fulbright's eyes glazed over and he became sullen again. "How does she fit in?"

"She picks up my excess," said Fulbright. "She deals with personnel directly and does a lot of Lasch's work with Washington."

"OSRD?" Fulbright nodded. "She must know a lot about S-1."

"No more than I do," Fulbright said defensively. "Anyway, Major, we shouldn't be discussing this. I don't know you."

"Of course. She seems . . . dedicated."

"When she wants to be."

"What does that mean?"

"Major, I don't carry stories."

I'll bet you don't, Snyder thought.

The overhead loudspeaker blared: "Keith Fulbright, please report to Administration."

"That's us," snapped Fulbright. "Lasch wants you back."

He didn't wait for Snyder to finish his coffee. He jumped up and started toward the door. Snyder followed, aware of the cold looks they were getting as they passed men in lab coats. Fulbright must have a hell of a reputation, he thought. But that wasn't always a liability. Sometimes, the least liked were best qualified . . . like Colonel Tully.

Lasch regarded Snyder grimly, his fingers tapping on his desk. "I've examined the Swedish papers," he said. "They seem to be in order. So as long as Captain Browne is satisfied and what I've seen is legitimate, we'll have no problem. I'm ready to put myself and my staff in your hands. But I would like to speak to Dr. Lawrence first."

Snyder shook his head. "He's not in on it, Dr. Lasch. He's not to know anything about it."

Lasch frowned. "But he's head of the Rad Lab. I can't do this under his nose."

"You can and you will."

Lasch shifted uncomfortably. "I suppose if that's the way they want it . . ."

"It is."

"Then we should get right to work."

They were alone in the office. Fulbright had left them and returned to work. Beth was outside. Lasch circled the desk and listened to Snyder.

"First step is to make up a list of candidates for our team by determining which areas of the project would be most likely to provide convincing information for the Japanese."

"That's easily done. I can put one of my assistants on it," said Lasch.

Snyder smiled. "Sorry."

"Why not?" Lasch seemed shocked. "Miss Martin and Mr. Fulbright have the highest clearances or they wouldn't be working here."

"They haven't been cleared by me."

Lasch hesitated. "Major, if you want to give the impression that nothing's out of the ordinary, then I'll have to throw a lot of work to my assistants. I think they ought to know why."

"Dr. Lasch, everybody on S-1 is used to secrecy. Your assistants will get along just fine if you give them the right orders."

Lasch smiled tolerantly. "That's the military way, Major. Don't tell anybody anything, and hope they do the job right. Look at it this way: they can help coordinate details. You won't have to bring in outsiders. We can keep it in the family."

Snyder shook his head. "I'm sorry, Dr. Lasch, I don't know these people well enough."

Lasch reflected for a moment. "Before you walked into my office, you didn't know me either."

"I've seen a complete dossier."

Lasch showed a flicker of surprise, then he sighed. "Maybe I can give you the opportunity to get better acquainted with them."

"How?"

"On a social basis. We've all been invited to a party on Wednesday night. You can go and make your own observations."

Snyder said sharply, "I don't want to waste any time."

"In the long run," said Lasch, "this will save time. Besides, I need to think." His determined gaze met Snyder's. He buzzed the intercom and Beth Martin came in.

"The Major will be your escort Wednesday night to Louise Daniels' party. Better give him directions to the Nunnery."

Beth's mouth opened in dismay. Snyder was also taken by surprise. Lasch turned to him. "You *will* be available, won't you, Major?"

"How could I refuse?" Snyder said.

June 19: San Francisco

Thyssen led Snyder into a small, ornate sitting room at the rear of the Swedish consulate and closed the door. It was hot and stuffy. Thyssen opened his coat before he sat down with a tired sigh.

"I have been attending the final sessions of the United Nations Conference here," he said. "Have you been following that?"

"Not really."

"It could be a marvelous thing—international cooperation on an unprecedented scale. Or it could be another League of Nations—a fizzle." He mumbled something to himself, then slapped his knees. "To cases," he said. "I have already extended feelers to Japan through our embassy in Tokyo. And I am working on my trade connections." He made a fist to show determination. "By God, Major, we will bring this off." Snyder made no reply other than a curt nod, so Thyssen said, "What have you come up with?"

Snyder leaned forward and looked Thyssen in the eye. "The safest place to hold the meeting is American-held territory close to Japan. I recommend Okinawa. We can make the flight in one C-54, in three stages: San Francisco to Hawaii, then to Wake Island, then Okinawa."

Thyssen held up a hand. "Is it feasible," he asked, "to go all the way to mainland Japan?"

Snyder stared at him. "No."

"Why not? Security?"

"Obviously," said Snyder. "On American soil we can guarantee it. The other way presents problems."

"Of course, but perhaps the Japanese will have the same reluctance."

"That's not my concern," Snyder said coldly. "I'm responsible for a group of high-level scientists and a package of sensitive information."

Thyssen waved at him again. "Consider the possibility, Major. You would be under the protection of my neutral government."

"I'm sorry. That's not good enough."

Thyssen sighed again. "Well, the first step is to see if they are receptive to a meeting at all—without telling them what it is about, of course, beyond a hint that it is a peace feeler."

"Who are you planning to meet with?" Snyder asked.

"Oh, a few key Cabinet members, military advisers, someone representing the royal family . . ."

"You could drop a very subtle hint."

"How?"

"Request a physicist."

Thyssen brightened. "Wonderful!" he said. He reached into his coat pocket for a small leather notebook and jotted that down. "Now then," he said, "what about the aircraft crew?"

"We'll assemble them as late as possible to hold down the risk of exposure."

"Fine, Major. That is your domain." He closed the notebook and tapped it on his knee. "Now, what is your feeling about Lasch?"

"He has to get used to the idea. I'll give him till Thursday. He's sending me to some party tomorrow night, hoping I'll find his associates trustworthy."

"Why?"

"He wants them in on it."

Thyssen frowned. "Is that wise?"

"I have to work with him, sir. As soon as we've settled this, we can start assembling the team."

"Any thoughts on how you will go about it?"

"Yes." Snyder hesitated, formulating his thoughts. "I would like it to be the smallest possible group representing specific but key fields. Rather than having everybody say the same thing, let's divide it into important areas."

Thyssen smiled happily. "Excellent. Major, I had no idea you were so thorough."

Snyder nodded patiently. "Mr. Thyssen," he said, "we will get along much better if you drop the diplomatic flattery. I don't need encouragement."

Thyssen burst out laughing. "And direct!" he added.

"Yes, sir. One other thing."

"Yes?"

"I consider the entire cargo of that plane—the people and the information—to be sensitive material, and if I can't guarantee its integrity, I'll do everything in my power to get that meeting called off."

Thyssen stopped smiling. He scrutinized Snyder carefully as he spoke. "Major Snyder, are you in favor of this mission?"

Snyder looked right back. "The more I think about it, the less I like it."

"Will I be up against you as well as the Japanese?"

"No, sir. But at least I won't get carried away with enthusiasm."

"Are you implying that I might?"

Snyder flashed a killer smile. "I'll keep my eyes open."

June 20: Berkeley

"The Nunnery" was a three-story brick building, U-shaped with three wings surrounding a central courtyard facing the street. Snyder got out of his car and checked his uniform in the side mirror, then walked up to the entrance. He pressed the buzzer next to Beth Martin's name. There was a loud answering buzz and the front door clicked open. He took the stairs to the second floor, then searched for her apartment.

He knocked at the door. It was opened by a woman he had never seen before. "I'm looking for Miss Martin," he said, confused. The number was right.

The woman stuck out a hand and said with a distinct European accent, "Marion Cypulski, Major Snyder. Please come in." Snyder stared at her before entering. She was about thirty-five, with a stocky frame on a small body. Her blond hair was pulled back into a severe bun. She was wearing an outfit that even Snyder could see was far from stylish.

She stepped back and he saw two men in the living room stand up. Beth Martin came out of the kitchen with a plate of crackers and cheese. She was dressed in a pale blue gown with a string of pearls around her neck. She looked wonderful. But that didn't take the edge off Snyder's surprise.

"Good evening, Major," she said. "You're very prompt."

"And confused," he said.

She glanced at the others, then said, "I thought that since there were so few of us we should all go together. I hope you don't mind." Without waiting for his answer, she made introductions. "You've met Dr. Cypulski? This is Dr. Harris Emmett, and Dr. Karl Gottlieb."

Snyder acknowledged them. Emmett was a tall, toothy man with a bird's nest of wiry red hair. He waved an empty wineglass at Snyder and said hello. Gottlieb flashed yellow, uneven pipe smoker's teeth from a sallow, lined face. His hair was cropped into a Prussian crew cut.

"Sorry to impose on you this way, Herr Major," said Gottlieb with a cough.

"No problem," Snyder said, aware that Beth was avoiding his gaze. "Where's Fulbright?"

There was an abrupt silence as if he had uttered an embarrassing obscenity. Then Emmett said, "Still working. He'll slide in under the door later."

"Harris," Beth said sharply.

" 'Scuse me for speaking ill of the living." Emmett raised his empty wineglass. "To dear old Keith," he said. No one joined him in the toast.

Snyder checked his watch. "Is Dr. Lasch close by?"

Marion reacted sharply. She put down her wine, said, "I'll get my coat," and went toward the closet.

Snyder frowned. Beth smiled to make light of it. "He's not coming," she said. "He never goes to parties."

Snyder couldn't believe it. He had been sandbagged twice in five minutes. Lasch had set this up knowing full well he wouldn't be around, and Beth had seen fit to surround herself with a ring of protection. She held the plate out to him and said brightly, "Have some cheese, Major."

"No, thanks, Miss Martin," Snyder replied. "Maybe later."

"Suit yourself."

He went to the door. "Ladies, gentlemen—shall we?"

Getting into the car was a choreographed charade. Snyder opened the front passenger door and said, "Miss Martin?" But Gottlieb zipped by with a quick *"Danke,"* and plunked himself down. Beth opened the rear door herself and slid in ahead of the others.

Snyder sighed. The evening was off to a rousing start. He drove through Berkeley and headed across the Bay Bridge. In guttural English, Gottlieb chattered about some weekend he had recently spent in Sausalito while in the backseat Beth and Marion argued in hushed tones. He strained to hear them but caught only snatches of words, like "Chicago . . . Lasch . . . petition . . ."

He interrupted, asking if someone would mind telling him where they were going. Beth gave him an address in Pacific Heights.

"You're kidding," he said.

"Anything wrong, Major?"

"That's pretty ritzy."

"Scientists go to ritzy parties, just like everybody else."

"Like who?"

Beth smiled. "I promise you the guest list will include a large quantity of officers. Louise makes a point of having them sent over from the Presidio, and they love it. Most of them are on their way to the Pacific anyhow."

"And are you attached to one of them? Or have you got someone overseas?"

Beth sighed. "I'm not attached to anybody. And I'm not planning to be in the near future, either."

"Got something against officers?"

"Not yet. Do you need directions?"

"No, thanks. San Francisco is my hometown."

"Is that so, Major?" said Gottlieb, coming in as if on cue. "Where do you live?" He monopolized Snyder again, giving him the impression that this, too, had been arranged beforehand. Snyder was getting impatient with being out-maneuvered.

Emmett was completely silent, huddled in the far corner, looking out at the scenery. After a while Snyder was able to tune out Gottlieb and pay closer attention to the talk in the backseat. Marion was complaining:

". . . didn't even give me a chance. Just locked up all my papers. Everything I got in Chicago."

"Marion, he doesn't want that material circulated around the lab," said Beth.

"But he treats me like a child! I haven't done anything wrong. I believe in something, that's all. I wanted to convince him, but he started yelling right away—"

"He'll get over it and so will you. He's under a strain—"

"But I have a right—!"

"Marion, not now."

Beth had caught Snyder looking at them in the rearview mirror. Suddenly Emmett piped up. "Damn foolishness," he said, and aimed a disapproving pout at Marion.

"What's that?" she said sharply.

"It's idiotic," he said, clarifying. "All that crap in Chicago. I know what goes on there—"

"You don't know a thing!" Marion retorted.

"Okay," said Beth, "that's enough from both of you."

They fell silent, Marion glaring at Emmett. Beth met Snyder's gaze in the mirror again. He said nothing.

They pulled up in front of an imposing three-story stucco house on Vallejo Street. As they got out of the car, they were immediately enveloped in tendrils of mist. The Presidio, very close by, was completely blanketed in fog. Snyder stood still a moment, regarding the house.

"Still too snazzy for you, Major?" asked Beth.

Snyder looked humble. "We don't get up here too often, ma'am. My father's a motorman on the Powell Street cable car line. But what the heck, isn't this what we're all fighting for?"

He moved past her and up the stairs to hold the door for the group. Beth came in last. "I'll try not to embarrass you," he said.

"I didn't realize you were so sensitive."

"I'm not—just considerate." He flashed a smile and said, "After you."

She waited for him in the vestibule. The others went down a long hall to an archway in the rear. Off to the left Snyder could see a huge living room crowded with people. The noise was deafening. He went up to Beth and motioned her ahead of him, but she stood there a moment, looking at the floor.

"Listen," she said finally, "I'll call a truce if you will."

"Agreed."

She stuck out her hand and they shook on it. Then she said, "Just don't end the evening by asking me for a date."

"I wouldn't dream of it. You have too many chaperons."

She smiled. He was beginning to like that smile. He wished she would use it more often. She hooked her arm through his and they walked together down the hall and into a wall of noise.

The living room was enormous, filled with expensive antique furniture. The men were either in uniforms or dark suits. The women were dressed as if there were no such thing as wartime shortages. Snyder was instantly grateful he wasn't the only military man here. It helped put him at ease.

They stood near the archway with Gottlieb, Marion and Emmett. Beth spotted their hostess at the hors d'oeuvres table and waved to catch her eye.

Louise Daniels waved back eagerly and pushed through the throng to reach them. She was a ravishing blonde, younger than Snyder would have expected, the same age as Beth. She wore a Veronica Lake coiffure and a low-cut gown exposing ample bosom.

"Beth, darling!" Louise cooed, throwing out her arms to embrace her old friend. "It's been so long!" Her eyes swept over the little group as she said hello all around. She locked on Snyder. "You're new here, aren't you, Major?"

Before he realized what was happening, Louise had eased him away and taken him on a whirlwind of greetings to a blur of people. He had the strange feeling it was for only one purpose: not to help him make new friends, but so Louise Daniels could size him up for some sacrificial rite to follow. Once he looked around to see what had happened to the others. Marion, Gottlieb and Emmett had drifted over to the fireplace, where they looked out of place and insular. Beth apparently knew more people and was reacquainting herself with no trouble at all. He watched her approach the bar. A dapper, fiftyish fellow behind the counter put a paternal arm around her shoulder and earnestly dispensed advice. She listened and nodded but didn't seem convinced. She kissed the man once on the cheek then slipped away with the drink he had made for her.

Snyder tried to catch her eye for rescue, but found Louise looking up at him curiously.

"I want you to meet someone special," she purred. She took his hand and led him toward the bar, a carved wooden counter built into the wall by the front window. Snyder looked at the bartender more closely. He was an elegant gentleman wearing a white-on-white shirt with French cuffs and a silk tie. His blue suit coat was draped over the stool behind him. He dispensed drinks with measured precision, chatting amiably with each customer.

"Bernard, darling," said Louise, getting the bartender's attention. "I want you to meet one of Beth's friends."

Bernard looked up with an expectant, eager smile, then put down the drink he was preparing and wiped his hands as they were introduced.

"Major Snyder, this is Bernard Bowen—my dearest friend and savior. The domestic agency failed us tonight so he agreed to tend bar. Isn't that sweet?"

Snyder saw a way to escape Louise's clutches. "You look like you could use an extra pair of hands, Mr. Bowen."

"Ah," Bowen sighed in relief. "Major, you're a godsend. Please make yourself at home. You probably know much more about this than I do. Louise, forgive me—I am appropriating your guest."

"That's all right," she said, stepping up to the bar. "He can start by making me a Cuba libre."

"One rum and Coke coming up," Snyder said.

Bowen smiled happily, then said, "Major, I must warn you: you're going to get awfully tired of this."

They worked steadily until there was a lull in the demand. Louise went off to greet more people and see to the food. Most of the guests had arrived, so business at the bar fell off.

"Thank you, Major, you've been a great help," said Bowen, glancing at Snyder's tan. "Shall I mix you something to wash away the desert dust?"

Snyder gave a start, then recovered. "Never heard anybody call Honolulu a desert," he said.

"My mistake." Bowen smiled. "What will you have?"

"Scotch—rocks."

Bowen poured generously, then asked Snyder, "Shall we talk about the Pacific?"

Snyder pointed west. "It's that way."

"Aha—very good." Bowen handed him the drink. It was a double, and then some. "So you're a friend of Beth's. Very sweet girl. We were just talking before you were dragooned here. I'm quite fond of her. Did you know that she and Louise were classmates at Smith College together?"

"Back east?"

"That's right. They're very close. Sometimes, to hear them tell stories, you would think they were still teenagers."

"You see a lot of them?"

"I haven't seen Beth for quite a while. Those friends she brought tonight must keep her terribly busy. They're scientists, you know," he said in a confidential tone.

"Really?"

Bowen nodded sagely. "Very hush-hush. They think their work, whatever it is, is vitally important. A dreary group on the whole, and so helpless. Look at them sitting over there." He clucked at the shame of it. "What's your interest in Beth?"

Snyder grinned. "What do you think?"

"Ah, Major. She's not easy."

"Don't tell me you—?"

"Oh, no. What do you take me for? I . . . Oh, my God, here we go again."

A second wave of thirsty guests began to build up. Bowen touched Snyder's arm. "Thank you for helping, but I'm sure you would rather track down Miss Martin, eh?" He winked and propelled Snyder away from the bar.

Snyder moved off, avoiding jostling elbows. He held his drink up high and looked around for Beth. He couldn't spot her anywhere.

"Szilard says we can only have an effect if we speak with one voice," Marion said quietly.

Gottlieb laughed. "When have we ever done that?"

"At Chicago," she replied.

"Ach, Marion. You keep on about Chicago as if it were the promised land. Please, those people may all be our colleagues, but they are ready to hop on the bandwagon for anything."

Snyder was at the other end of the sofa, only half paying attention to a tiresome banker reminiscing about the trenches of World War One. He was more interested in the intense discussion between Marion and her cohorts. For the last ten minutes they had been arguing in low tones over some recent gathering of scientists at the University of Chicago. Snyder had recognized several names mentioned, particularly Dr. Leo Szilard, one of the founding fathers of the atomic energy project. According to Marion, Szilard may have recently turned against the project.

"We are acting from conscience," Marion explained to Gottlieb, "not self-interest. We're not against peaceful use, only military."

"That's a load of crap." Emmett waved his drink and slurred, "If we felt that way at the beginning, we wouldn't have taken part."

"My friend, you are wrong," said Gottlieb. "We were never sure it would work. We thought we were in a race with the Nazis, who it now turns out were not even in the running."

"Then that bunch in Chicago are hypocrites!" said Emmett, his voice rising a shade too loud. "They'd use it against the Germans, but—"

There was a sudden silence. Snyder looked around to see what had happened and saw Marion with a finger to her lips, aimed at Emmett, who angrily sank back into the sofa.

Marion caught Snyder looking and stiffened.

Snyder cut the banker off just before the Meuse-Argonne offensive, rose and excused himself, then joined Marion and the others.

"Can I get you a drink, Dr. Cypulski?" he asked.

She shook her head, plucking a glass from the end table to show him she was already well supplied. Snyder pulled up a chair and huddled with them. "Cypulski," he said, mulling over the name. "Does it end in 'y' or 'i'?"

"Polish," she replied. "From Warsaw."

Snyder nodded. "I've always wanted to see Europe," he said.

Marion's hand fluttered. "You wouldn't like it as we left it."

"That's going to change. Things will get back to normal. Cities will be rebuilt, families reunited and eventually there won't be any sign there ever was a war."

"I disagree," said Gottlieb. "The scars will remain for

many years." Snyder listened to him but watched Marion—she seemed distracted.

"You can rebuild brick and mortar," Gottlieb continued. "But flesh and blood? Once they are spilled, how do you repair them?"

"Make sure it doesn't happen again," Snyder said.

Marion looked at him. "That's very interesting, coming from a soldier."

Snyder grinned. "You'd be surprised how many of us don't like war."

"I think the military thrives on it. They may not like fighting," she conceded, "but they love exercising authority."

"You're talking about Nazis," Snyder said.

"No—all military."

Snyder shrugged. "I don't want to argue that point, Doctor." He sat back and sipped his Scotch. It was the familiar anti-Army line of most scientists on the Manhattan Project. They hated the security system and the people who ran it. Marion suddenly got up. Snyder rose with her.

"Stay where you are," she said. "I'm just going for a refill." She slipped away before Snyder could volunteer.

"How did you get roped into this thing tonight, Major?" asked Emmett.

"Beats the hell out of me, chum." Snyder slapped Emmett on the knee and went off to find Beth. He spotted Marion at the bar, leaning on the counter, waiting for Bowen to return her glass.

"Major, what would you think if I told you I'm going to have a headache in a half-hour?" Beth whispered in his ear. She had come up out of nowhere.

"I thought these were your sort of people," he said.

"I can only take so much. You should hear what they talk about. Except for the uniforms you wouldn't know there was a war going on."

"Maybe they come to these things to forget."

"Don't be naive."

He was about to inquire what that meant when he spotted a familiar figure standing in the archway, furtively looking around. It was Fulbright.

"Look who just walked in," Snyder said.

Beth followed his gaze. "Oh, great," she muttered. "That makes the evening complete."

"What's between you two?"

"Absolutely nothing," she snapped.

Fulbright spotted them and maneuvered over. "Hi," he said with a quick nod. "How's it going?"

"Fine," said Snyder, turning to Beth and discovering she had left his side. "The bar's over there." He pointed.

"I don't feel the need to indulge right now, Major."

Snyder shrugged. "Plenty of women here."

Fulbright sniffed. "Not my type."

"Your associates are over there by the fireplace." Snyder indicated Gottlieb and Emmett. Fulbright nodded, said nothing, just stood with Snyder watching people. Snyder grunted to himself. It would be tough getting back to Beth with Fulbright in tow.

"You know, Major, I learned early on in life that people like this don't give a damn whether you live or die," said Fulbright. "They've got theirs, they're going to keep it, and all they're interested in is seeing that you don't get any of it."

"That's a pretty grim point of view," said Snyder.

"If I had one percent of the wealth of any one of these people, I could be satsified for the rest of my life."

"Really? Don't you think you'd get like them and want more?"

Fulbright pulled out his handkerchief and shook it open. "Probably, but I've never had the chance to find out. I had a fiancée once. 1937. I was headed for big things, fresh out of business school. I got a job at Grumman, a clerk in purchasing. A good start. But Lorraine thought it was common. The middle of the Depression, I got a job, and she thought it was *common*. She figured I wouldn't be able to support her. So off she went." He shrugged. "No loss. But it taught me a lesson."

Surprised by Fulbright's sudden willingness to confide, Snyder had to play along. "What lesson?" he asked, expecting a great revelation.

"Do your job but look out for yourself."

"Interesting philosophy," said Snyder.

Fulbright puffed himself up. "It got me from purchasing clerk to where I am today," he said. "And I did it on my own. Is that common, Major?"

"No, it's extraordinary." Snyder wanted desperately to get away. His gaze settled on the hors d'oeuvres. "Why don't you at least get yourself something to eat?"

Fulbright squinted at the food, then nodded and without another word headed for the table. Snyder drained his drink. He was ready to murder Lasch for setting him up. Of course, he had already decided that in the interest of expediency he would give in to Lasch and explain the mission to Beth and Fulbright, unless something went terribly awry tonight. Fulbright was a depressing character but not necessarily a bad security risk. He seemed so worried about maintaining his position that he probably wouldn't dream of doing anything to jeopardize it. Beth, on the other hand, was a level-headed, perceptive lady with very few illusions.

He saw Bowen waving at him from across the room. Snyder threaded through the crowd, his eyes stinging from smoke and his nose rebelling against an overdose of perfume.

"Could use your help again," Bowen said plaintively.

Snyder slipped behind the bar and reached for the ice bucket.

"Who was that dreary little fellow you were talking to?" Bowen asked.

"He works with Beth."

"Ah—I should have known. That crowd—they're all the same. Now, shall we discuss the Pacific?"

"If you want."

"You think the war will end soon?"

"Just a matter of time."

"That's good news." Bowen smiled. "But I hope we've learned our lesson."

"What do you mean?"

"Look at the mess in Europe."

"What mess?" Snyder asked, wary of getting caught in another philosophical discussion.

"The Russians." Bowen spat distastefully.

"What about them?"

"They can't be trusted. Their word means nothing. And they will steal everything that isn't nailed down. Whole countries at a gulp."

"We're allies, Mr. Bowen."

"I'm surprised at you, Major. Are you defending them?"

"I've never even seen a Russian."

"I have. I have an antique business and I once dealt with a Russian furniture expert. Mind you, that does not make me an authority on their national character, but he was an *experience!*" He laughed grimly. "If you read the newspapers, you'll see the difficulties we're headed for. Look at Central Europe. Those poor countries endured the Nazis for so long; now they've exchanged one set of conquerors for another. It's deplorable. I'm sure there's a certain amount of barracks talk, eh?"

Snyder finished making a bourbon and water for Harris Emmett, who had been leaning on the bar listening, then said, "A lot of Army people would agree with you about the Russians. But then, that's politics, and the experts don't listen to latrine rumors."

"Experts!" Bowen exploded. "And when will we learn not to leave things in their hands?"

"Right!" barked Emmett, raising his glass in a salute. "Blow 'em all to hell!"

"You know, I must tell you," Bowen said, gripping Snyder's arm, "I don't mix in politics, but the day the White House comes to me for a desk in French provincial, I shall not hesitate to offer my opinions on the state of the world."

"We can do it," said Emmett, trying to attract Bowen's attention.

"But I give you this thought," Bowen said to Sndyer. "If we let the Russians walk over everybody, then that will be the end of these lovely parties, and we will all end up as tractor mechanics."

"Not me," said Emmett.

"Nor I," Bowen said. "As an antique dealer, I shall be confined to repairing only *old* tractors." He fixed Emmett with a benevolent smile. "And what about you, my friend."

"Blow 'em all to hell," Emmett repeated proudly. Snyder was beginning to regret having made him that last drink.

"Who?" Bowen asked.

"The Japs! We can do it, you know."

"Pardon?"

Emmett shook his head. "One plane, that's all—"

Snyder took away his drink. "Dr. Emmett," he said quietly, "why don't you go sit down?"

"Gimme back my glass."

"You've had enough." Snyder looked around for Beth. If she knew he drank, why didn't she watch him?

"Gimme it," Emmett insisted. "You don't pull any weight here—" He was beginning to draw attention. He turned to Bowen for support. "Tell him to gimme back my drink!"

"I think you've had quite sufficient, my friend," said Bowen. "The Major's right. You should sit down."

"Fuck the Major!" Emmett slurred. "I'm not sittin' down until I get my drink!"

Snyder poured it into the sink.

Emmett's eyes glazed over in surprise. "Why'd you do that?" He looked around at all the men in uniform, then shook an angry finger at Snyder. "I'm on *your* side! I'm for all of you!" he shouted. Conversation died around him and people stared at the bar.

"We're gonna end the war," he said, eyes open in wonder as if he'd just discovered the elixir of life. "You and me, Major, we're gonna end it. No invasion! No more kamikazes—one plane!" His voice dropped and he rasped, "One bomb!"

Snyder eased around the bar, smiling at Emmett and saying, "It'll take a lot more than one bomb, and if you'll step outside, we'll have a drink and discuss it." He took Emmett by the arm and without appearing to use force, propelled him toward the archway. Emmett lost his balance and stumbled along.

Snyder wouldn't let him stop. People glanced over in surprise, then looked away in embarrassment as they swept by. Beth Martin loomed in their path.

"What happened?" she said.

"Stay out of it," Snyder mumbled, helping Emmett up the two steps to the archway, then getting him into the hall. He found a room and shoved Emmett through the door.

They were in a study. Snyder snapped on a light and

dumped Emmett into a chair. Emmett straightened his rumpled coat and said, "What the hell do you think you're doing?"

"Deciding whether you're going home or to a Federal prison for the next five years," Snyder replied.

"Bullshit. You're bluffing—"

"Am I?" Snyder grinned thinly. "I could prefer charges tonight. Dr. Lasch would have my report on his desk before 0800 tomorrow, with copies to Washington, Oak Ridge and Alamogordo. If that's what you want."

The names jarred Emmett. He began to perceive a genuine threat. "What did I do?" he groaned.

"You opened your big mouth about S-1. You did everything but take an ad out in the *Chronicle*."

"I did not." He tried to get up; Snyder shoved him back.

"Don't move. I'm going to get the others and we're leaving, right now."

Snyder backed away and turned, then froze. Beth was standing in the doorway, regarding them both with amazement. Snyder quickly snapped, "Some den mother you are."

"What are you doing with him?"

"We're leaving. Go tell your friends the party's over. Fulbright, too."

"He just left."

"Smart boy."

She studied him curiously. "Are you really going to prefer charges?"

"The longer we stand here talking, the more I'm inclined to."

She looked past Snyder at Emmett slumped in the chair, scared and pale. "Let's compromise," she said. "Let Marion and Gottlieb stay. They can take a cab home. I'll help you with Dr. Emmett."

"Miss Martin, I'm not making deals."

Her eyes flashed. "*He's* the only drunk!" she snapped.

Snyder looked at her and grunted. "Okay. You make excuses."

"Thanks," she said, and disappeared.

Snyder helped Emmett to his feet. "I don't feel so good," he said.

"That's all right, Doc. When we get you outside, I'll make you better in a second."

He had Emmett propped up in the hallway and was helping him on with his coat when Beth returned with Louise, who was greatly concerned.

"The poor man," she said. "I'm so sorry this happened. I hope he feels better."

And gets out of my house, Snyder was tempted to finish for her. "Mrs. Daniels, it's been a nice party," he said.

Louise brightened. "Don't be a stranger. Come again."

Snyder grabbed Emmett. "Say good night, Doc."

Emmett mumbled, "I don't feel good . . ."

Louise pecked Beth on the cheek, glanced at Snyder and whispered, "Don't let that one get away. And call me soon, darling." She squeezed Beth's hand and walked them to the front door.

Bernard Bowen stood at the window and watched the three shadowy figures make their way through the fog toward the cars.

"May I have a refill, please?" asked a voice behind him.

He frowned and turned back to the bar. Marion Cypulski held up her glass. "That was bourbon and soda?" he asked. She nodded. He mixed the drink and watched her. She stood with head bent, unwilling to offer conversation.

"Here you are," he said. He handed the glass back and their eyes met.

Snyder coaxed Emmett to the car, assuring him he would be fine. Propping him against the fender, he opened the front door for Beth. She slid in, wondering how he was going to get Emmett in the back. She watched him lift Emmett up bodily and haul him toward the bushes. Snyder grabbed his coat collar and bent him over. Emmett shook his head and hollered, "I'm okay, I'm okay!"

Snyder's right hand doubled into a fist and plowed into Emmett's stomach. He jackknifed over and heaved several times.

"Oh, for God's sake," Beth cried, opening the door. "Was that necessary?"

"Better here than in the car," he replied. He pulled Emmett upright and looked into his green face, then he reached inside the scientist's coat, found his handkerchief and handed it to him. "Wipe your mouth, Doc. We're going home."

Emmett staggered back to the car and waited for Snyder to open the back door, then he tumbled inside and lay on the seat groaning. Snyder slammed and locked the door, then slid in behind the wheel. Beth stared at him, fuming.

"You like to beat up on drunks?" she said.

"I don't know why you're mad at me, lady. He's your friend."

They rode in silence, except for an occasional moan from Emmett, until they reached the middle of the Oakland Bay Bridge. Beth sat huddled in her coat, right up against the door, as far away from Snyder as she could get.

"I don't see what you're upset about," Snyder said, trying to cut the chill. "I did us all a favor. Maybe you haven't spent any time driving home with a puking drunk in the backseat, but I have."

"I'll bet," she said.

"I didn't hurt him." She gave him a withering look. He glanced back and called, "Hey, Doc, how are you doing?"

Emmett's hand curled up over the top of the seat and he peered at Snyder. "Fine," he groaned.

"See?" said Snyder. "He appreciates it."

"Well, I don't. I don't see where you get off acting like a barbarian with my friends. And just what was all that stuff about sending him to prison and putting reports on Lasch's desk?"

"I'm with S-1 security."

She folded her arms in disgust. "Well, that's just marvelous. Of all the dirty tricks—"

"What are you talking about?"

"I don't like being spied on," she snapped. "Who put you up to this? I can't believe Dr. Lasch would—"

"Wait a minute. Nobody's doing any spying."

"Then what do you call it?"

"Dumb luck."

"What?" she said incredulously.

"Look, would you rather I had let him tell everybody

about the Manhattan Project? Not only would he be going to jail, but your fanny would be in a sling, too!"

"I see. You saved my ass, is that it?"

"To put it crudely, yes."

They both fell silent, stewing angrily. Snyder shot off the bridge at fifty miles per hour, right into another thick fogbank. He slowed to creep through the streets of Berkeley.

"How many other people did you know at that party?" he asked.

"You want names?"

"Just a rough estimate."

"Maybe ten," she said.

"And how many of them know where you work?"

"Major," she said in tired exasperation, "we are all very security-conscious. This is the first lapse we've ever had."

"Uh-huh, but when you have them, they're beauts."

"Are you going to file charges?"

Snyder looked in the mirror at Emmett, passed out on the backseat. "I'm going to let him sleep it off."

"Are you going to tell Lasch? Or anyone else?"

"Look, I wasn't planted here to check up on anybody. It was Lasch's idea that I get acquainted with some of his people."

"Why?"

"Because I'll be working with you for a while."

"Doing what?"

"Asking questions. For instance who is Louise Daniels?"

"I don't think I want to inform on my friends."

"Where is her husband?" Snyder persisted.

"In the Navy. Look, Major, I really don't want to talk about Louise. She's my oldest friend, but sometimes she tries my patience."

"Why is that?"

"I don't see how it could be important to you. Besides, it's her life, not mine."

"Then let's see what I can figure out," he said. "Husband at war, young and beautiful wife left at home, more money than she knows what to do with, lots of free time, likes to keep people around so they'll remember she exists. And she's—"

"Sleeping with Bernard Bowen," Beth finished.

"The bartender?" Snyder asked. Beth nodded. "Now that I wouldn't have guessed."

"Yes, I'm afraid the field isn't clear, Major. She's not available."

Snyder looked at her. "That's a relief. She's not my type."

"Then why were you asking?"

"It seems odd to me that your crowd would be invited to a party like that. Except for you, the whole bunch sat in a corner like a pack of wallflowers."

Beth's eyes narrowed. "Major, it's going to be a joy having you around."

They pulled up to the Nunnery. Beth helped Snyder take Emmett to his apartment. She sat in the living room while Snyder undressed him and put him to bed.

"Thanks for waiting," he said when he came out. "I'll take you upstairs."

At her door she turned and stuck out her hand. "Delightful evening, Major. I'd ask you in, but I'm tired of answering questions."

"I don't always ask them. Maybe we could get on a better footing at dinner tomorrow night."

She smiled. "I warned you not to ask me out."

"Does that mean no?"

"In any language." She shut the door.

Snyder expelled his breath and walked heavily down the hall. From the courtyard he looked back up at the building, wondering why they called it the Nunnery.

Louise Daniels said good night to her last guest, closed the front door and leaned wearily against the heavy wood, her eyes half-closed. She stayed there a minute, then puckered her face in annoyance, bothered by sounds from the living room. "Leave everything for the maid, darling," she called, pushing away from the door.

Bernard Bowen continued stacking dishes as she entered. "This food must go back in the refrigerator, Louise. It will spoil."

"Don't lecture me about waste, Bernard. I used a caterer, so you needn't worry about ration stamps." Louise raised Bowen's hands and framed her cheeks with his long, manicured fingers. Her lips brushed his palm; she nibbled the skin webbing between his thumb and index finger. "Interested?" she asked.

"Of course," Bowen said quietly. "After we straighten up a bit."

Louise threw her arms around his neck and nuzzled his throat. "Damn the food," she murmured, pressing her body against his. "Take me upstairs before I die."

Bowen paused, a peculiar look of astonishment dancing around in his eyes, then he smiled, bent slightly, put one arm behind her knees and picked her up.

Louise lay on the bed, cradled against Bowen's chest, letting his hands roam her naked body. Her long nails stroked the tight white skin of his back in response to his probing fingers.

Bowen shifted and lowered his head. His lips brushed her neck, then sought a breast. Louise moaned. Her body arched and fell to the rhythm of his flicking tongue. His hand moved downward, his middle finger sliding through pubic hair until it found warm, moist flesh. Her legs parted. She shuddered and reached for his penis. He stiffened and pulled away from her hardened nipple. His hand circled her wrist and he muttered, "Don't."

Her eyes opened. She looked up at him looming over her. She put a hand behind his neck and pulled him down to her breast again. "Now, darling," she demanded. "Now!"

Bowen rolled between her legs and braced himself. Eagerly and firmly, she grabbed him again, then gasped with pleasure as he entered her. She raised her legs and locked them behind his back, falling into his rhythm and accompanying each stroke with her low-throated moans. Her pace built while his remained steady and constant. When he sensed she was nearing climax, he cupped her writhing buttocks and pushed upward. Her legs tightened. He heard the familiar catch in her throat. Then she slammed into him, her body rocking, shuddering. Her breath exploded in his ear. She wailed and jerked spasmodically. He pushed in and held himself deep. She groaned once more, and then her taut muscles relaxed. Her hands eased off his neck and fell to the sheets. Her legs unlocked and slid down. She was splayed out, bracketing his body with hers—flushed and spent.

After a long moment of repose she looked up at him with glazed eyes. She wiped a thin sheen of moisture from her upper lip. "Oh, darling," she murmured, "that was lovely."

Bowen smiled.

Louise shifted a bit then stopped. "You're still hard," she gasped.

His chin moved up and down and his gaze bore into her, answering an unspoken question. She opened her mouth to speak, but his words came first: "That was for you. The next one is mine."

Louise chuckled thickly then felt him throbbing inside her, contracting his penis, making it move without hip thrusts. A wave of emotion spread through her and she felt tears well up. "My Bowen," she said. "My guardian, my friend, my angel." She caressed his face and he kissed her hand.

"Shh," he said.

She closed her eyes and sucked her lower lip with a sharp hiss as he shoved into her again. She locked her legs around his waist once more. In a moment she was pumping in wild abandon.

At 1 A.M. Bowen slipped quietly from Louise's bed, checked to be sure she was asleep, then scooped up his clothes and went downstairs to dress. He grabbed his coat and hat and left the house.

Gottlieb paid the cab fare and refused Marion's offer of half. He wished her good night as they went into the Nunnery. As Marion opened the door, a folded note slipped out of the jamb. She bent to pick it up, then closed and locked the door.

She stared at the note, then crumpled it and threw it away angrily. The nerve of Lasch, calling her on the carpet one minute and trying to seduce her the next. She loved him, but there were times when she found him exasperating. No, she would not stop in for a nightcap. Let him stew for a while, she decided.

Marion reached into her overcoat and pulled out a pale green envelope. She slit it open and spread the letter out on her desk. She bent over it and savored her mother's prim handwriting. She devoured the latest news, grateful to read Polish again. Her mother was, as usual, long on praise for Russia as she went into detail about conditions at the refugee camp. There were hardships, but both of Marion's brothers were now back from the war and they had promised to make things easier. They sent their love to Marion and hoped for the day when the family would be reunited. And since the war in Europe was now over, perhaps that would be sooner than they had imagined.

Marion read the letter several times through and cried softly to herself each time she came to her mother's blessing at the end of it. She switched the light off and sat in darkness a long time, trying to imagine how her mother and brothers would look today. She had only very old pictures—those and the letters. . . . Her thoughts shifted to Allen Lasch and the deception she had used on him for the last two years, but tonight she couldn't feel guilty. She was still angry with him. Maybe it would be better if she made a clean break, stopped stringing him along with false hopes. But she didn't want to lose him, either. He was the only man in her life at a time when she desperately needed someone to cling to. . . .

She slipped the letter back into its envelope, opened a carved wooden box on the edge of her desk and placed it reverently on top of the others.

"Come on, baby," he crooned. "I promise you'll like it."

"I don't know," Marylou mumbled, her hand playing with him. "How about a nice half-and-half?" she said hopefully.

Fulbright waved a ten-dollar bill. "Once up the ass," he said, and stuffed it between the fingers clutching his erection.

The prostitute frowned, letting go of him, turning around and bending over the bed. "Be care—Ow!"

He was in her before she could protest. He grabbed her thick hips and burrowed in like a rabbit.

Marylou cursed to herself and swore never again—no more spindly little creeps with leers and furtive looks. They always wanted something out of the ordinary. But this? She would expect this from a merchant seaman, not a square john out for a quick lay. And all the subterfuge, the sneaking around, having to crawl in a side window so she wouldn't be seen. Who the fuck did he think he was— Respectable Roscoe?

"Not so hard, baby," she said. "Don't want to hurt me, do you?"

Fulbright didn't answer, but an extra shove brought the message home: she better not interfere. She rested on her elbows and felt herself pushed and pulled, back and forth. His hands snaked up to squeeze her breasts and she groaned. She pushed one hand away: he had managed to find one of last night's bruises and it hurt like hell.

She could feel him stiffening but he wasn't panting yet. He was still working at it, she realized, not feeling it. God, what did it take to get this jerk off? "Hey, honey," she offered, "stand still and let me do the work, what do you say?"

He stopped for a moment to see what she could do. She rotated her hips seductively and rocked back and forth. "Oh, you're so big, honey," she moaned, going into the hooker's chant. "You're the biggest!"

"Shit," she heard him mutter. Then he took over again. He shot his hips forward, burying himself to the hilt. Her gasp of pain and surprise goaded him on. He slammed into her again and again. Their body heat mingled. Her stale perfume filled the room and he loved it. He loved the feel of her fleshy warmth, the smeared lipstick, the raunchy odors, the power he had over her, the absolute command of this body.

He was a long way from home but the first stirrings were there, starting deep. Just a bit more and—

The phone rang. Once, then again. It went off over and over, an insistent high-pitched clatter, practically in his ear. He slowed and felt himself wilting. He clenched his teeth and swore angrily, then pulled out. Marylou gasped and

crashed to the mattress. He staggered back and groped for
the nightstand. He snatched up the phone and snarled,
"Hello!"

"Good morning, Keith," said the silky voice.

Fulbright's anger faded, replaced by a heavy feeling in
his gut. He glanced at the clock: it was after two. He took
the phone into the bathroom, turning so he could watch
Marylou and make sure she knew it. She rolled over on the
bed and looked at him.

"What do you want?" he said into the phone. "I can't
talk now."

"Just a little business, dear boy. Chicago."

Fulbright frowned. "That's a lot of horseshit. Doesn't
mean a thing."

"Still—I would like to see something. Can you prepare a
report?"

"Tomorrow."

"Names, Keith. All of them."

"I can't give you *all* of them," Fulbright growled.

"Whatever you can manage, then. I didn't take you
away from anything, did I?"

"Not at all," Fulbright squeaked. How did he know?

"Oh—and one other thing," said the voice. "Who is this
Major Snyder?"

Fulbright silently cursed and said, "I'll find out."

"Do that." The line clicked.

He hung up, furious. Marylou followed him into the
bathroom and looked her customer over. He'd gone limp.
She ran her tongue over her lips and made a sucking
sound.

"Why don't you wash off, honey? Then I'll take care of
you. Same price, too. Instead of that other stuff."

Fulbright glared at her. He turned to the faucet, ignoring her look of relief. He washed and stared at the phone.
Damn Bernard Bowen, he thought—the man is everywhere. Can't even knock off a piece of ass without interruptions.

June 20: Berkeley

Fulbright walked into the administrative wing of the Rad Lab at 7 A.M. As he had expected, it was deserted. He opened up his office, then walked to Beth Martin's work area and snapped on the light. He dialed the combination on one of her file cabinets and slid the bottom drawer open. He rifled through the dividers and plucked out a manila folder, flipped up the one behind it, then closed the drawer.

He went to his own office, settled into his chair and opened the folder. He spread the papers across his desk and stared at them. A wave of anger surged through him— he was still furious over Bowen's phone call. The bastard had no right to interfere with his private life. He was getting more and more demanding: information about this, policy on that, sketches, diagrams—and all of it putting Fulbright to enormous amounts of early morning work, taxing his photo-retentive memory. He was getting damned tired of memorizing all this crap, carrying it around in his head until he could meet with Bowen, then spilling it all out. Fulbright never left the lab with a single shred of incriminating evidence. Until Security found a way to look inside his head, he was safe.

And if that son of a bitch Bowen ever tried to double-cross him, he had plenty to fall back on—exactly 9225 dollars squirreled away in a safe deposit box in Oakland. He also had a letter in there, detailing his seven-year involvement with Russian agents, starting when he had become expediter in the blueprint department at Grumman.

Fulbright sat back and tried to recall the oily manner of

the big man who had met him one day after work at Grumman and had introduced himself as a representative of Vought-Sikorsky. The man had offered cash for certain plans and Fulbright needed extra money, so he agreed to supply them. But he refused the use of a small camera, impressing his new "friend" with an ability to draw blueprints from memory. That started him on his long career.

At first he had thought it was cut-and-dried industrial espionage. He was surprised when the Vought-Sikorsky man turned out to be a Russian trade attaché. From then on he was in for keeps. At first he was scared, but he quickly realized that his contacts were as careful about discovery as he was. The relationship was mutually beneficial and comfortable.

Advancements at Grumman had led him into the Navy liaison group in Washington at the beginning of the war. There he met Allen Lasch, who responded to a Grumman recommendation and had Fulbright brought into his OSRD staff. Once at Berkeley, Fulbright's Russian contacts narrowed down to one man, Bernard Bowen, with whom he entered into an uneasy relationship. He knew Bowen was contemptuous of him, and he was frustrated by the man's condescending attitude.

Someday he would kiss the bastard off, take his money and start a legitimate business. Bowen couldn't touch him without risking his own exposure.

Fulbright picked up the first page, a petition, originating from the University of Chicago and signed by some of the biggest names in the Manhattan Project. It called for a reappraisal of American nuclear policy and some consideration of the moral aspects of using the bomb.

Fulbright clucked to himself. What a useless exercise. All this stuff Marion had brought back, and Lasch was so upset about, was nothing more than a load of crap. He scanned the sheet through once, then read it line by line, carefully memorizing everything on it. After five minutes of study he closed his eyes and recited the entire contents of the page to himself, then he checked it through to be sure he was right. He did the same with the rest of the papers, which included mimeographed flyers calling for other project facilities to join the cause, statements by prominent physicists in favor of a protest and a letter from Marion Cypulski addressed to Lasch, supporting all of it and requesting permission to promote it at the Rad Lab.

Fulbright steamed over that one. Like hell she was going to conduct a political dialogue under his nose. Damn fool woman. How did Lasch tolerate her? Always leaping on the latest white horse—and Lasch was forever knocking her out of the saddle.

He finished as much as he could handle, then put the papers back in order and closed the file. He tucked it under his arm, checked his watch—it was nearing 8 A.M., he had to hurry. He went to his door, opened it and looked out. No one else in yet. He started across the hall then stopped abruptly, hearing something.

Footsteps echoing from the stairwell.

He froze, uncertain whether to hide the file or try to return it. He waited too long. Beth Martin stepped into the hall, and he quickly moved back into his office, standing still for a moment, fighting panic, listening to her heels clicking as she came up the hall. He looked down at the file in his hand and cursed to himself. Moving to his desk, his back to the open door, he pretended to be searching through other files.

He heard her pass by without so much as a good morning. But that was typical. She never wasted words on him. He watched her take off her coat and hang it up. She sat down behind her desk and unlocked it, pulling out papers and pencils and all her paraphernalia.

Coffee, he thought. She'll make coffee, then I can go back. He glanced at his watch. Eight o'clock straight up. Lasch would be coming in shortly. He heard more footsteps. Everybody else was arriving. He turned and looked out the door, straight at Beth. She wasn't getting up to make coffee: one of the other girls went past his door carrying the pot. Beth stayed at her desk, checking through her calendar, then picking up the phone.

Fulbright's heart leaped—the phone might be enough of a distraction. He waited till she started speaking, then snatched up the file and bolted through the door. He strode across the hall, letting her see a dark scowl.

"Damn!" he said as he went right for the file cabinet.

She kept talking, but turned to watch him. He dropped to one knee, opened the bottom drawer. His hand shot to the flipped-up file and he jammed the other one in front of it. Then he relaxed and began systematically going through the other folders, looking for something.

"Thanks, Janet," Beth said into the phone, then hung up. She swiveled around and said, "What are you doing, Mr. Fulbright?"

"Looking for last week's cost sheets," he said. "Pulled the wrong file."

Her eyes went to the combination lock at the top of the cabinet. "You opened up my files?"

"Sure. How else am I gonna get it?"

"I wasn't aware you had the combination."

He looked at her. "What's that supposed to mean? I've got the combination to every file on this floor. Don't just sit there—help me find this damned thing."

She glared at him, then got up and walked over. He stood up while she kneeled down and reached into the drawer. Fulbright glanced at her exposed knee and suppressed a sudden desire to grab it.

Beth yanked out a thick file and held it up. "Right here under 'C,'" she said.

"Thanks." He took the file and shuffled through it, pretending to study figures. Beth stood up and waited for him. "Ah—just what I wanted," he said and handed the file back. "Thanks very much."

"Next time just ask, Mr. Fulbright."

"You weren't here." He watched her close the drawer and spin the combination lock. She stood back, giving him room to pass, making sure there would be no physical contact. He slipped around then turned.

"By the way," he said, "how did it end last night?" He paused. "With Emmett, I mean."

Beth settled in at her desk. "We took him home," she said.

Fulbright scratched his chin. "Who is this Major Snyder anyway? What's he doing here?"

"If you're supposed to know, you'll be told," she said coldly.

Fulbright scowled and walked away. "Not normal procedure . . ." he mumbled.

He stepped back into his office and rubbed a finger along his forehead. It came away oily. He pulled out his handkerchief and wiped his face. "High and mighty bitch," he muttered, and looked across at her, sitting primly behind her desk. "I can find out all about that fucking Major without you," he whispered, closing the door.

Lasch came to work in a foul frame of mind. Not only had Marion failed to respond to his note last night, but she had turned him down for breakfast this morning as well. She was carrying resentment too far, he thought, and all because of this damned Chicago business. Why couldn't she just *support* a cause? Why did she have to *embrace* it?

He nodded to Beth and stepped into his office. Snyder was waiting for him. He closed the door and opened his briefcase on the desk. "Morning, Major," he said.

"That was some stunt you pulled last night," said Snyder. "Not showing up for the party."

"I find them dull and useless," Lasch explained.

"Not this one."

"Yes, so I heard. I bumped into Gottlieb this morning. He said Emmett got a bit out of hand."

Snyder leaned over the desk. "Do you want my impressions of your scientific colleagues?"

"I'm sure it's the standard military view," Lasch said with a quick smile. "No, I'm more interested in knowing if we can bring in Miss Martin and Mr. Fulbright."

"Only if you're committed."

Lasch sat down and rubbed his eyes. "I still have some doubts but yes, I'm committed."

Snyder was not happy with that answer, and he tried to let Lasch see it in his expression. But Lasch just said, "Shall we get them in here?"

Beth took a chair and Fulbright went to the sofa. They looked at Snyder expectantly. "Dr. Lasch has asked me to involve you in a project of vital importance," he began. "There's a certain amount of risk, and before I go into detail, I want to give you the opportunity to back out. In other words, if you don't want to be involved, then leave the room now."

Nobody moved. They sat staring at him, waiting for more. "I take that as yes," Snyder said. "Very well."

Carefully and slowly he explained the mission to them. Fulbright listened with a stone face, now and then glancing at Lasch, and seemed to be calculating the work that lay ahead. Beth gazed at Snyder with growing wonder.

Snyder finished with another warning. "I'm sure you can understand my concern about security. If you think Captain Browne's regulations are hard to live with, I guarantee you mine are worse. If I suspect even a hint of breach, I'll deal with it quickly and it won't be pleasant."

Beth regarded him distastefully. "If this means I could be punched in the stomach, like Harris Emmett . . ."

Lasch looked up in surprise.

"Maybe if you were as drunk as he was," Snyder said quickly, "you'd be grateful for my delicate touch. I won't put up with that behavior."

His gaze fell on Fulbright, who spread his hands and said, "Don't look at me. Remember, I'm not a boozer."

"I'm concerned about talk."

Lasch leaned back in his chair. "I think we understand, Major. Please get on with it."

"Any questions?" said Snyder.

They were silent a moment, then Lasch said, "I have one. Have your superiors considered the repercussions? A lot of people aren't going to like this—when they find out."

"You mean scientists?" Lasch nodded. "That's not my problem."

"Most of us have worked extremely hard and believe in what we're doing," continued Lasch. "Some may not see this mission as the panacea your superiors evidently think it is. They may say that we're betraying everything they have worked for."

Snyder listened patiently but simmered inside. "The object is to end the war," he said.

He had caught Lasch off guard. "Of course. That's what we all want, Major."

"Then don't worry about public opinion." Snyder turned to Beth. "Do you have anything to offer, Miss Martin?"

"I think we should have a woman along on the mission."

She sat with her legs crossed and regarded the men thoughtfully. Then she said, "Some people won't like it, as Dr. Lasch says, but a growing number of scientists have come to feel disenchanted." She paused and looked at Lasch. "You can't disregard Chicago."

Lasch took a deep breath and frowned.

"What about Chicago?" Snyder asked, recalling the bits of conversation he had overheard last night.

"There's something of a protest going on," Lasch explained. "It started at the university." He shot Beth a warning glance and went on: "I understand there's a petition . . ."

"What petition?"

"To the War Department. To put it simply, they don't want the bomb to be used."

"Can I see it?"

"It hasn't arrived here yet," Lasch lied.

Snyder glanced at Beth and Fulbright—they shifted uncomfortably. He sensed they were holding something from him. "I can tell you right now, it won't have an effect," he said. "Policy has already been set and our mission is part of it. If we don't succeed, the bomb will be used."

"If it works," added Fulbright.

Snyder nodded. "But we don't have the luxury to debate this," he said. "You're involved now, and we're going to follow through with no more arguments. Understood?"

No one answered. Beth rose, smoothed her dress and went to the door. She looked back at Snyder. "I suppose you'll want an office," she said.

"Please."

She went out. Snyder waited for Lasch to say something. The tall scientist finally swallowed his pride and grumbled, "You're right. Perhaps if we just throw ourselves into it, we'll come to ignore everything else. Is that what you want?"

"Precisely," said Snyder.

Fulbright stood up and limply shook hands with Snyder. "Count on me for anything you need, Major." He left. Lasch got up and followed Snyder to the door, then closed it for a moment and turned to face him.

"I think we should have a woman along on the mission."

Snyder had a sinking sensation. "Beth Martin?" he asked.

"No, no. A physicist. Someone you met last night. Marion Cypulski."

In a jumble of recall Snyder tried to reconstruct everything about her. Stalling, he asked, "Why?"

"She's eminently qualified. An expert in her field, which is one of the crucial areas we will need to lay out for the Japanese."

Snyder was wary. "What's her background?"

Lasch got defensive. "Are you worried because she's Polish? She happens to be a naturalized American citizen."

"How long?"

"Oh, for God's sake," said Lasch. "Two years. Don't you understand? She's beyond reproach! She's as trustworthy as all the Germans working here who fled Hitler—more so! She lost her entire family in Poland." Snyder appraised him keenly but made no comment. Lasch felt compelled to go on. "Her father was a newspaper publisher. He was one of the first to be executed when the Nazis took Warsaw."

"I'm sorry to hear that," Snyder said carefully. "But what does it have to do with her usefulness to us?"

Lasch bristled at this pragmatism. He held up a finger. "She's a woman," he said.

"Is that an advantage?"

Lasch beamed. "The Japanese are a male-oriented society. The idea that a woman participated in developing this weapon could have a tremendous psychological effect on them. Don't you think?"

Snyder's mind raced. He recognized a trade-off. Lasch would climb down from the fence if Snyder threw him this bone. And now he recalled one important fact that stood out about last night: Marion Cypulski had been angry with Lasch in more than a professional way. He decided to ask about it.

"Is there anything personal between you and Dr. Cypulski?"

Lasch looked him in the eye. "Yes . . . but that does not influence my conviction that she would be an asset."

"I appreciate your being honest with me, Dr. Lasch, but don't tell her anything yet."

"Of course not. Thank you, Major."

Snyder went out and stopped by Beth's desk. "If I'm not in the office and I have to be reached, Browne is giving me quarters down in the Security huts."

"How cozy," she said.

"Isn't it?" He winked and walked away.

June 21: Washington

"What's to stop Stalin from backing out of his commitment?" Truman asked, pulling down his glasses and pinching the bridge of his nose.

"Why should he do that, Mr. President," Stimson replied, "when he's so anxious to gain a foothold in the Far East?"

Truman was absorbed in a late night strategy session in the Oval Office with Stimson, Marshall and the still unconfirmed Secretary of State James Byrnes. They were discussing the commitment made at Yalta by Stalin: that Russia would attack Japan three months after the German surrender.

Byrnes was being hopeful. "Stalin could have changed his mind. The Russians are stretched thin. Most of their forces are tied up in Europe."

"Not quite right," Marshall pointed out. "Intelligence reports Soviet troops moving into the eastern border areas. It's now fairly certain they will be able to attack on or about eight August."

"And we can't mount an invasion until November at the earliest," said Truman, unbuttoning his double-breasted suit coat. "That means the Russians will get into it whether we want them to or not, and they'll give us a hell of a jurisdiction problem in that whole area." He turned to Stimson. "When will that damned bomb be tested?"

"Mid-July, Mr. President," Stimson replied, then added, "Suppose the Japanese surrender before it's used? Wouldn't that solve all our problems?"

Marshall tensed, following Stimson's line of thought. If Truman would agree to the Thyssen-Snyder mission . . .

Truman shook his head. "It won't happen," he said. "We won't settle for anything less than unconditional surrender, and they insist on keeping their Emperor, so there we are. . . . Can't have that, can we?" He jumped up and paced energetically. "If they surrender, fine. If not, those sons of bitches are going down in flames."

Stimson sat back, tired, his worst fears confirmed. The President was determined to play the heaviest hand possible. How could he and Marshall hope to turn the man around, particularly with Byrnes giving him total support?

He considered telling the President about the Thyssen-Snyder mission now, but it was clear he would get a flat no. He would have to tell Truman sometime; the question was, when? For now, there was nothing to do but wait and see how things developed. He gazed at the President. The man seemed anxious to destroy the Japanese: was that sound political thinking or a much more basic desire for revenge?

June 22: San Francisco

Bernard Bowen Antiques occupied the ground floor of a four-story commercial building on O'Farrell Street near Market. Keith Fulbright walked into the shop late Friday afternoon and signaled Bowen that he wanted to talk. For the benefit of Bowen's aging assistant, Mrs. Beach, a sweet little mouse of a woman just past seventy, they conducted a familiar charade concerning a certain chair. Fulbright asked to see some others and Bowen invited him into the back room.

It was a small warehouse piled high with furniture in various states of repair and restoration. Bowen shut the connecting door and led Fulbright to his desk, cluttered with papers and account books. Fulbright sat down in an ante bellum rocker while Bowen pulled out his steno pad and fountain pen.

"Your colleague Dr. Emmett was rather careless the other night," commented Bowen.

"That's blown over," said Fulbright.

"Really? I should think an indiscretion like that would warrant a severe reprimand."

"He got that, all right."

"He's a reckless fool. So, Keith, what have you got for me?"

Fulbright began dictating information while Bowen took it down in coded shorthand. Fulbright enjoyed this: it was the only aspect of their relationship in which Bowen was subservient, something like a faithful secretary. He rocked gently back and forth, spoke in a steady monotone as he recited from memory and punctuated his remarks with an occasional, "Got that?"

He reeled off the names of the scientists who had signed the Chicago petition. Amused, Bowen shook his head and muttered, "Like little children . . ."

Bowen filled up six pages in his book, then relaxed and said, "Now, as to this Major Snyder—anything there?"

"Oh yes," said Fulbright, gleefully anticipating Bowen's reaction. "But it's going to cost you extra."

Bowen smiled thoughtfully. "Keith, if your information is valuable, you know I never quibble."

Like hell you don't, thought Fulbright, returning Bowen's smile. He stopped rocking and leaned into the lamplight. "Major Snyder has a very unique assignment, and I have been taken into his confidence."

Bowen nodded, acting impressed.

Fulbright carefully described the mission exactly as Snyder had outlined it, reminding Bowen that he was in a position to keep tabs on it.

Bowen listened intently, then made some notes. "This is quite interesting, Keith," he said. Fulbright nodded, knowing full well it was more than that. "And I agree with you," Bowen added. "It is worth more money."

Fulbright waved a magnanimous hand. "I leave that to your usual generosity."

"Have they determined who's going yet?"

"No. But Lasch for sure, and Snyder. I'm getting together a list of scientists to be considered for it."

"Anybody else from the Rad Lab?" asked Bowen.

"Lasch wants his girlfriend."

"Cypulski?"

Fulbright nodded again.

"Well, Keith, I'll expect you to keep me apprised of further developments."

"Naturally."

Bowen unlocked a drawer in the desk and drew out a wad of cash. He counted out 250 dollars, better than two weeks' salary for Fulbright, then placed another 50 on top of it. "Satisfactory?" he asked.

Fulbright shook his head. "This is really important news," he said in a wheedling tone.

Bowen shrugged then peeled off two more twenties and a ten. "Three fifty," he said, putting away the rest. "Let's see where this leads."

Fulbright scooped up the money and stuffed it into his wallet. They stood up and Bowen led him to the back door. He unlocked it and Fulbright stepped into the alley. "Good work, Keith," said Bowen.

Fulbright let him have a tiny smile that tried to suggest who had gotten the best of whom, then he walked quickly down the alley and disappeared around the corner. Bowen closed and locked the door, then returned to his desk to examine the notes.

Alexei would have to hear about this right away. Of course, it would take Bowen some study to turn it to his advantage, but he already felt it had the makings of a major breakthrough. This went beyond the pure scientific information he had been funneling to Moscow over the last three years. This would be of major interest to the policy-makers in the Kremlin. And to think it came from that toad, Fulbright!

Bowen's nose wrinkled in distaste. The network was riddled with men like that, even in Moscow. He sighed. He had grown to expect that the true gems of information would invariably come from dirt: it was a natural law of espionage.

He glanced into his cash box. 350 dollars this had cost him. In 1929, when he was stranded in Berlin, he had killed a man for that much money: it was his passage back to New York.

He had been born Peter Bernardovich Bolwenkov in Petrograd, Russia, in 1893, the only child of a Czarist export minister. With the revolution of 1917, his family had escaped to the United States and settled in New York City in the midst of the emigré colony. Spurning the aristocratic remnants of old Russia, Peter Americanized his name to Bernard Bowen and tried to assimilate himself into the new culture, against his father's vehement objections. His mother's death removed the only buffer. Anxious to break away, Bernard moved to Greenwich Village and went to work for an antique dealer.

His great opportunity came in the '20s, when he was

sent alone on a buying tour to Europe. But this job ended
when his employer died while Bernard was in Berlin. Try
as he might, he could not earn enough for passage home.
Broke and unhappy, he fell in with the Berlin Communists, who sustained him with food and ideology for several
years.

The Depression struck, and even the Communists
couldn't hang on. Desperate, Bernard tried to swindle a
man and was found out. To protect himself, he murdered
then robbed his mark. He returned to New York, putting
the incident behind him, intent on reuniting with his father
and impressing him with his newfound beliefs.

Upon learning that Bernard had embraced the principles
of Lenin's Marxism, his father threw him out of the house.

Forced to take menial jobs in New York, Bernard grew
bitter and disillusioned. He wrote to his Berlin friends and
after six months of silence suddenly received a train ticket
to Canada, a forged passport, money and instructions for a
quiet departure from the United States.

He ended up in Moscow, where most of his friends had
fled. He was emotionally welcomed back. For the first
time in his adult life Bernard felt wanted. He was easily
recruited for espionage work.

In 1936 he was smuggled back into the United States
through Canada. Playing on his enthusiasm for antiques,
the NKVD gave him a complete backgrounud and set him
up in business in San Francisco. He spent the prewar years
building up his trade and clientele. By 1941 he had managed to lose nearly all trace of his European accent.

He became the top Russian agent on the West Coast. In
1942 his area of concentration narrowed to the Manhattan
Project. . . .

He was disturbed by a knock on the connecting door.
Mrs. Beach timidly stuck her head in and mentioned something about an impatient customer. "I'll be right out,"
Bowen said, smiling to himself. She was so fiercely loyal
and so totally unaware of his outside activities. Not a suspicious bone in her frail body.

He reached for the phone and dialed the number of the
San Francisco Chronicle.

"Classified Department," he said. He waited for the order clerk to come on the line. "Hello, this is Bernard Bowen Antiques. I would like to place an ad to run in tomorrow's edition, as follows: 'From new shipment—portable writing desk. Inquire first.' "

He hung up and got to his feet, anticipating a meeting with Alexei as soon as the paper hit the stands.

June 24: Sausalito

Marion Cypulski and Allen Lasch patched up their differences on Sunday when, after apologizing to her, he managed to coax her to Sausalito for a cruise in a rented sailboat.

They bought food and set out in a twenty-foot day-sailer. Huddled in the cockpit against a brisk wind, they drank wine and relaxed. They had been out like this before. The sun, wind and water always conspired to create a romantic atmosphere.

Marion fixed sandwiches while Lasch waited for the right moment to tell her his news. They ate in silence until he said, "Marion, I have something very important to tell you, along the lines of Chicago—but it's *official*."

She put down her sandwich. "What are you talking about?"

"You have to promise not to say a word about it."

"Allen—"

He cut off her protest. "Not a word, Marion."

She stared at him. "I promise," she said meekly.

Lasch took a deep breath. "There's a plan to warn the Japanese about the bomb."

Marion's mouth opened, but she was speechless.

Lasch went on. "The Swedish government is making the arrangements. We'll just be a small group of scientists. We'll meet with the Japanese. If we're successful, the war's over."

"And no bomb," she finished. He nodded. She began to tremble with excitement. "Oh, Allen, this is incredible, just incredible. How long have you known?"

"Only a few days."

Her excitement subsided and she asked pointedly, "Does Major Snyder have anything to do with this?"

"Everything. And if you want to come along, you'll have to satisfy him that you're—"

"Come along?" she repeated. "Oh, God, Allen, do you really mean—?" He nodded again, please with her reaction. She stared at the water passing around them, then up at the clouds, her mind racing to absorb the news. She faced him again with a trembling smile. "Thank you," she said and put her arms around him. "I do want to be part of it. It'll be the most important thing we have ever done."

He held her tightly and they rocked gently with the motion of the boat.

"When it's over," he said quietly, "can we discuss marriage again?"

He pulled back and searched her eyes, hoping to find some indication that he had at last cracked her resistance.

"We'll discuss it," she said simply.

"How about now?"

She shook her head. Her fingers traced a path along his cheek and she looked at him sorrowfully. "I've put you off so many times," she said. "But you must be patient."

"Why?" he said urgently. "Marion, for God's sake, tell me why."

She kept shaking her head, then suddenly her mouth was on his, silencing his questions; diverting him with passion.

Lasch came about and sailed behind Belvedere Island. He dropped anchor, then they crawled into the cuddy to make love.

Marion slipped away from her sleeping lover and went back to the tiller, buttoning up her blouse and lighting a cigarette. She felt pressured by her terrible burden. Though convinced she was doing the right thing, Allen would never see it that way. To him, it would be treason. But the Russians were the only ones who had helped her find the family she had left behind in Poland. The International Red Cross hadn't been much help, telling her only that her father had been executed by the Nazis and the rest of the family had disappeared.

She knew no one would ever understand the frustration, the fear and the guilt she suffered at that time. Her father was a wonderful man who had defied convention to send Marion to the United States in the 1930s to study physics. Her grandparents had been horrified: in their eyes that was not fit work for a woman. Ignoring family protests, she had gone off to America and made the most of her opportunity, grateful for it. But after the blitzkrieg and her family's disappearance, she'd felt trapped.

She had responded eagerly when the Soviet embassy contacted her, producing letters as proof that her mother and two brothers were living in a relocation camp in Russia. They had offered a way for her to correspond but had insisted she keep it quiet. Accepting their rules, she had begun exchanging letters. She was promised that her family would be brought out, but when the Germans invaded Russia in June of 1941, all Polish refugees had to be moved to camps farther east, and getting them out became impossible. Still, Mama had written that they were safe and well, that her two brothers had volunteered for an all-Polish unit fighting with the Red Army against the Germans.

When Marion came to Berkeley in 1943 to start her work on the Manhattan Project, she still followed their rules: lying on her security clearance, hiding the facts about her family. Why not? Her family was the most important thing in her life.

And when the Soviet agents came to her, wanting information about her work, it didn't take much to convince her she should cooperate. If the Russians wanted something in return for working to get her family out, maybe they deserved it. Besides, weren't Russia and the United States allies in this war? Shouldn't the S-1 secrets be shared?

It was easy to find justification, much easier every couple of months when she got the fresh packet of letters.

So in February of 1944 she had begun passing atomic secrets to Bernard Bowen.

The afternoon wind chilled her. She called to Lasch and stirred him from his nap. Clinging to each other, they brought the boat back to Sausalito. She felt so close to him that more than once she was tempted to tell him the truth about her family. That would answer his questions about marriage: she couldn't make any other commitments until she had her mother and brothers with her again. But he seemed happy and she didn't want to break that mood—she needed a little happiness as much as he did.

June 25: Berkeley

Snyder's office at the Rad Lab was up the hall from Lasch's, a cramped room with two desks, two file cabinets, two telephones and a couple of chairs. One of the phones was a security line with a scrambler, so he could talk to Washington safely.

Beth walked in with a list. She stood in front of the desk and handed him his copy. "Dr. Lasch and I spent Saturday morning putting this together," she said. Snyder scanned two columns of scientists' names opposite their job descriptions. He picked up a pencil and crossed off six of them.

"Some of these people are too important," he said. "I'd like you to go through it again with that in mind. And if there's anybody in here who could be considered politically unstable, remove him. I'd like the final candidates brought to the Rad Lab for interview no later than Wednesday."

"That's two days," Beth protested.

"Less," he said, handing back the list. "And getting them here is your job. Lasch wanted you in, so you are."

She glared at him and said crisply, "I'll do my best, *Major*."

"Get Fulbright to help you."

"I won't need him. You'll have everything when you want it." She walked out. He smiled to himself. She wasn't so hard to handle after all.

He closed the door and locked it, then sat down and picked up the security line. A military operator came on immediately. Snyder gave her the Pentagon extension number Marshall had instructed him to use. While he waited for the call to go through, he checked his watch. He was a few minutes early for their prearranged conversation.

"Marshall," said the voice on the other end.

"Snyder," he answered.

"Go ahead."

Snyder quickly brought the Chief of Staff up to date. Marshall was pleased and urged Snyder to keep things moving. Then he added, "The Secretary has come up with a new element. It means including another man if we can find the right one."

"To take over, sir?"

"No, Major. A Japanese POW who's bright, bilingual and cooperative."

Shocked, Snyder mumbled, "What for, sir?"

"You'll need an interpreter. We don't want to use anybody from State or the military."

"If you say so, General," Snyder said unhappily. "But where will you find someone who can interpret the sort of technical information we have to get across?"

"That's a problem, but we'll solve it."

"Sir, you know the sort of people we're working with. It'll be difficult enough just shepherding them. I don't know how they'll react to the idea of traveling with a POW. And I'll have to watch *him* like a hawk."

"Major, have you ever met a Japanese POW?"

"No, sir."

"Once captured, they see themselves as disgraced and dishonored, considered dead in their own country. I think whoever we select will welcome the opportunity to become the savior of his nation."

"I see," said Snyder, not liking it despite the explanation.

"Good. I'll want you back in Washington on the twenty-eighth to discuss progress."

"Yes, sir."

Snyder hung up and thought about the POW. This mission was hard enough without him. All he could hope was that Stimson and Marshall wouldn't find a suitable candidate.

Just before noon Beth returned with a new list. She and Lasch had cut the names down to fifteen, and she was worn out from making arrangements on the phone. "I've got hold of twelve of them," she began, but Snyder held up a hand.

"Let's go to lunch," he said. "We'll discuss it there."

She started to protest, but he cut her off.

"This is business, Miss Martin. We have to get it done and I'm starving, so we'll do it at lunch."

She frowned. "Only if we go Dutch."

"Naturally."

They went to the faculty lounge and ordered sandwiches. Snyder steered Beth away from the inside tables and took her out to the glade. They sat under a tree and ate. She handed him the list and said between bites, "Of the twelve I talked to, four said that their work was at a crucial point and they just couldn't get free. The rest are coming Wednesday and I've scheduled them two an hour beginning at 1 P.M."

"That's fine," said Snyder.

"What are you going to ask them?" she said.

"Just a few questions. . . . How would you handle it?"

Beth gave it some thought. "You're not going to tell them why they're being interviewed, are you?"

"I can't."

"So I guess you just have to fish for attitudes—see which ones would be inclined not to use the bomb."

"Something like that," he agreed, "but I wouldn't want anybody who couldn't follow instructions."

"You mean take orders."

"This isn't going to be a scholastic exercise. It's a military operation involving scientists. But they're not running it."

Beth leaned against the tree and studied him. "Authority is everything to you, isn't it?"

He shook his head. "Only when it applies. Look, if we don't present a unified approach, the Japanese will sense it, and then we'll fail. I'm not going to have this go down the drain because one scientist decides it's a crusade. I don't want any hotheads. And in order to keep that from happening, I've got to select carefully."

She nodded, understanding, then asked him, "How do you feel about the mission?"

Snyder was surprised. "You're the second one to ask me

that," he said. "I'll give you the same answer: I was assigned."

She stared at him. "That's no explanation—that's an excuse."

He looked back at her tightly. "I can't help it. My feelings have no place in this."

"How convenient. You ask Dr. Lasch and some others to do an about-face on what they believe in, but what about you? Is this just another job, or are you committed to it?"

"I'm committed to the Army. The mission was dumped in my lap. I wasn't given a choice."

Beth was skeptical. "Come on—you must have an opinion. Either you want to give the Japanese a chance to avoid catastrophe or you don't. Which is it?"

Snyder's look hardened. "My brother was killed at Guadalcanal. I can't work up much love for those people."

Beth's eyes widened and her confident jawline sagged. Devastated, she tried to search past his flat stare. She recovered her directness and said, "Then you'd rather we did use the bomb."

He lowered his gaze and reached for his Coke. "I don't know. It's not simple, is it?"

"No, it's very difficult. In fact, I've been thinking about it all weekend. But you must give the rest of us some credit. Everyone on that list is dedicated to his work but also terribly concerned about what the bomb is to be used for."

"Really?" Snyder said doubtfully. "And not public opinion? Lasch brought it up himself. If we use the bomb, then after the war somebody will point the finger and say, 'You built the damned thing!' " He held up the list. "You know what I expect? I expect these people to *jump* at the chance to whitewash themselves!"

"You're basically a cynic."

"And how long have you known what you were working on?"

"That doesn't matter. I've always been uncomfortable about it."

"Then why didn't you quit?"

"How could I?" she said sharply, her eyes flashing. "If it's used, we're *all* responsible! Most of us working here have struggled with that. You may not trust civilians, Major, but at least we make our own decisions!"

Snyder was taken aback. He looked at his Coke bottle, then drained it.

"I'm sorry about your brother," Beth said softly.

Snyder shrugged and pulled his knees up to his chest. He looked across the glade, trying to calm himself. One thought emerged clearer than any other: she was right. He couldn't be just a man doing a job; in the end he would be forced to make up his own mind.

June 26: San Francisco

Bowen sat on a bench at one end of the aquatic pool in Fleishhacker Park. He was joined by a large, beefy-looking man carrying a flat briefcase: the Russian vice-consul, Alexei Portiakov, who sat down, pulled up one leg and massaged his ankle. His heavy-lidded eyes scanned the children and few adults cavorting around the pool. When he was satisfied that they were not attracting attention, he spoke softly to Bowen.

"Moscow was quite taken with your information," he said.

"Thank you."

"Very good for the son of a Czarist," Portiakov added with a sly smile.

Bowen stiffened. Portiakov took a particular delight in holding Bowen's father over his head.

"It is not in our best interest for that mission to succeed," Portiakov said. "It would end the war prematurely. If it accomplishes a surrender, we would have a hard time enforcing our territorial claims."

"Then what are my instructions?" asked Bowen.

"Do nothing. It would be silly to move before we find out if their weapon works. And I can assure you they won't bother sending such a mission without that knowledge."

"I'll keep watching then."

"Yes," said Portiakov. "By the way, we were delighted to hear about events in Chicago." He laughed, deep and bubbly. "Americans can't even control their own scientists. Do you know what Molotov asked? How many of them were on *our payroll*? We couldn't ask for better representation!" He guffawed.

"Alex," Bowen interrupted, "you must get Marion Cypulski's mother to write more letters."

Portiakov put down his leg and stamped his foot. He grimaced, then said, "I don't think that's possible."

"Why not? Is she no longer cooperative?"

"She is no longer—period.".

Bowen blanched. "What do you mean?" he whispered.

"She has been eliminated," Portiakov whispered back.

"But that's insane!"

"Please don't give it labels. She stopped being useful some time ago."

"But the letters—?"

"The last three came out of Department Five."

Bowen was aghast. "Forgeries?"

Portiakov sighed. "Have they been discovered?"

"No, but—"

"Then why concern yourself?" Portiakov gave him a pious look. "You may, if you wish, light a candle."

Bowen stared at him.

June 27: Berkeley

"This will do," said Snyder, walking into the small, bare office at the north end of Le Conte Hall that Beth had suggested he use for the interviews. He opened the back door and looked out on a flight of stairs.

"I'll need a squad of MPs stationed out here from twelve forty-five," he said to Captain Browne. "I don't want the scientists to have any contact with each other before or after the interviews. When each one is finished, he goes out here and you take him to the airport or the train terminal."

"That'll tie up a lot of men, sir," said Browne.

"Can't be helped. Just do it."

"Yes, sir."

At one o'clock Beth called to say she was ready to bring in the first one, Franklin Kirby.

"Okay," said Snyder. "Come ahead."

He flipped open a security file and did a quick refresher. Kirby was an expert on the physics of bomb development and a middle-level associate director on all projects at the Chicago Metallurgical Laboratory. He was fifty-three, a family man with three grown daughters and four grandchildren. His security record was spotless and the file listed several pages of awards and degrees.

Beth knocked and brought Kirby in. Snyder stood up and shook hands with a tall, lean, slightly stooped older man with deep pouches under his eyes. He wore a baggy brown suit with a gold fraternity pin over one lapel.

"Please have a seat," Snyder said, waiting for Beth to go

out and shut the door. Kirby sat down, looked around at the bare walls, then settled a curious gaze on Snyder.

"Dr. Kirby, we're conducting a preliminary survey on the anticipated effects of an atomic attack. We're interested in any opinions you might have, based on your particular field of research."

Kirby nodded. "Happy to help if I can, and if you can tell me who this is for."

"State Department," Snyder lied.

"And what are they going to do with it?"

"They're preparing a policy for the United Nations."

Kirby's interest rose. "Really? And the Army is helping?"

"Yes."

"How ironic. Well, what do you want to know, Major?"

"How effective do you figure the bomb will be?"

"Anywhere from five to twenty thousand tons of TNT, but at this stage we can only guess."

"Can you estimate the extent of damage?"

"What's the point? You'll have that answer when it's tested."

"We have to prepare a position paper now," Snyder said patiently. "We'll supplement it later. Besides, it may never get beyond the one test."

"What do you mean?" asked Kirby.

"The war might end, or it could be a dud."

Kirby shook his head sadly. "It won't be a dud. I can guarantee that."

"Would you be prepared to go before a committee to explain in theoretical terms why it should work?"

Kirby shrugged. He couldn't see where the questions were leading. "A committee of what?"

"Some laymen, fellow scientists, members of the military. How complete is your knowledge of bomb development?"

"I'm a consultant to Oppenheimer and his unit at Los Alamos. My job transcends compartmentalization."

Snyder nodded and made a note.

"Major, I get the feeling you're going to ask me to make a speech someplace."

Snyder smiled. "How do you feel about using the bomb on an enemy?"

Kirby fixed him with an iron gaze. "Not good. But I see the necessity."

"Which is?"

"Strange question from an Army man."

"This is an objective survey, Doctor. I gather that you feel it's going to be used anyway, so what can you do to stop it?"

"Close enough."

"You must be aware of what's been happening in Chicago." Kirby looked momentarily lost. "I'm speaking about the protest, Doctor. Did you participate?"

Kirby stiffened. "Is this what you're really after, Major?"

"I'm not trying to trap you."

"No? I've been in little rooms with little men and their wire recorders before."

"I'm sure you have. But this is just you and me. I give you my word."

Kirby sighed. "I was curious. I attended a few meetings. I sympathize with their intentions, of course, but not their methods. They're too antagonistic and emotional."

"So you don't support the protest?"

"Look, whether the bomb is used or not, I'm against giving information about it to other countries. That's part of what the protest is about and I think it would be inviting disaster."

Snyder concealed his surprise. Lasch hadn't explained that there was a serious move afoot to share atomic secrets.

"What fraternity?" he asked. Kirby looked surprised. Snyder indicated the pin on his lapel.

"Oh. Sigma Alpha Epsilon."

"Uh-huh. The drinking man's frat."

Kirby looked up sharply. Then he shook his head and smiled. "Not at MIT, Major."

Snyder grinned then spent a few minutes verifying Kirby's background and filling in details missing from the security report. Then he asked a hypothetical question: "If this were a year ago and we were still fighting in Europe,

where do you think the bomb would be most effective—
against the Germans or the Japanese?"

Kirby shook his head with a sad smile. "Regardless of
who it's used on, Major, God help us all."

Snyder closed his notebook. "Thank you very much, Dr.
Kirby."

He took Kirby to the back door and put him in the
hands of the MPs. He liked Kirby. He was almost exactly
what Snyder was looking for—unemotional, direct, knowl-
edgeable, able to communicate, and not overbearing. Snyder wondered if he would be as lucky with the rest.

Two men in succession turned out to be losers. Horace
Mills had a huge red face gone slack and puffy from
drinking. Snyder just went through the motions with him.
E. W. Schweiber only wanted to talk about his domestic
problem, an imminent divorce. Snyder could get nothing
out of him about his work.

Julian Bliss sat down and eyed Snyder warily. He was
short, overweight and balding, with wisps of black hair
combed across the top of his head. He lit a cigarette and
jammed it into the corner of his mouth. During the interview he kept the pack in one hand and played with a
lighter in the other.

Snyder picked up a dossier but was immediately interrupted.

"I didn't know this was going to be an Army interview,"
Bliss blurted out.

"Does that make a difference?"

Bliss indicated the papers. "Is that my file?" he asked.

"Yes."

Bliss shifted. "What have I done?"

Snyder smiled, trying to put him at ease. "Nothing, Dr.
Bliss. I'm here purely for information." He repeated the
same story he had given the others but refined it a bit.
"We're going to inform the members of the United Nations
about what we have and how dangerous it is."

"*Instead* of using it?"

"That hasn't been decided yet."

"Well, I think you should do it quick," Bliss snapped.
"Cut all the red tape, just get right to it."

"Why the urgency?"

Bliss snorted. "Just like the Army. You can't wait to drop that thing on the Japanese."

"I didn't say we wanted to. But what if we didn't get to the United Nations in time?"

"Then you wouldn't have to bother at all. The whole world will see the results. That's one way of ending war forever."

"Do you consider that the ultimate purpose of S-1?"

Bliss laughed and his whole torso shook. "No, Major, it's a by-product. It's what we'll end up with, and I personally couldn't be happier." He put out the stub of one cigarette and lit another.

"If I had to send you before a mixed bag of people to convince them of how awful this weapon is, do you think you could do it?"

Bliss sat up and looked at Snyder with strained patience. "Major, do you have any idea what effect radiation has on living bodies?"

"I think so," said Snyder, leading him.

Bliss snorted. "I doubt it. I'm on a steering committee of biologists studying the extrapolation of blast and radiation effects. I've just been down to Los Alamos explaining all this to Oppenheimer and Teller. Even they found it hard to accept."

"Explaining what?" Snyder asked.

Bliss puffed hard on his cigarette, then became professorial. "Takes a good fifteen minutes to charbroil a steak, doesn't it? Reduce that to milliseconds, from raw meat to well done in the blink of an eye, and you have a fair idea of an atomic blast effect. However, if you're unlucky enough not to get fried in the initial explosion, something far worse will happen to you. You'll be hit with a tremendous dose of radiation. You'll literally cook from the inside out—slowly. It could take days, and it's gruesome. We believe more people will die from radiation exposure than from the blast itself."

Snyder had no trouble reading the agony of responsibility in Bliss' face. His disapproval was manifest in his nervous habits. He drew hard on the cigarette and calmed down.

"Could you explain that to this group we're talking about, but in less emotional terms?" Snyder asked.

Bliss stared at him. "Why should I bother being less emotional about it?"

"Because it will be more convincing."

Bliss shrugged. "You're probably right. You know . . . I've got a wife and two kids, and I always wanted them to respect me and appreciate my work. But someday when they find out about this—the way I think they're going to find out—things will get pretty grim at home. They're intelligent people, see? And they have deep regard for human life," he said pointedly.

"And so do you, I'm sure, Dr. Bliss. Would you have been willing to use it on the Germans?"

Bliss hesitated. "I don't know. Hard to separate the needs of war from conscience." He stubbed out his cigarette and fingered the pack. "So when do you want me to see this group?"

"I'll let you know."

"Don't wait too long. Now that you've brought it up, I'm going to worry about it."

"Keep your worries to yourself, Dr. Bliss."

Bliss stared at his pack of cigarettes. Snyder thanked him and led him to the back door, wondering how much of Bliss' idealism was deepseated belief and how much came from a sense of guilt. He was more emotional than Snyder would have wanted, but perhaps that could become an advantage. He buzzed Beth to send in the next one.

DeWitt Hillerman knocked his pipe ashes out into the wastebasket and thought over Snyder's last question: "How can we measure the effects of radiation?"

"Simple," Hillerman replied. "After we've flattened some city in Japan, we go in and do a complete study. I mean, hell—it's the best testing ground in the world. And frankly, we won't know what that bomb does until we *really* use it."

Snyder winced. "But you're in biological studies. Haven't you estimated the extent of human vulnerability?"

"Yes, but that's still theory. Let's find out!"

"Would you have used it on the Germans?"

"Major, who are you kidding? With all the Kraut refugees we've got running around on this project, there isn't a chance it would have been used on der Fatherland. But the Japanese—?" He snorted in contempt.

Snyder smiled thinly and cut the interview short. With all his faults, Bliss was infinitely preferable to Hillerman.

"You helped set up the Hanford plant in Washington," said Snyder.

"That's right."

"But since early last year you've been on K-25 at Oak Ridge."

"Right again."

"Doing what?"

Paul Willard eyed Snyder suspiciously. He was rosy-cheeked, blond, handsome and young, but there was a cold-blooded maturity in his manner. "Gaseous diffusion," he said. "You wouldn't understand."

"I would if you'd explain it to me plainly."

"I can't do that, Major. It's what you boys call top secret, isn't it?" He smiled, then leveled a penetrating gaze at Snyder. "Look, I don't swallow this crap about the United Nations. What's your game?"

"No game," Snyder said simply. "As a matter of fact, I know plenty about the gaseous diffusion process. It's the method that has proved most productive in separating fissionable materials. Now, I want to know if you can express it to a layman."

"Oh, sure," Willard said lightly: "I could even make it clear to the Japanese."

"Very funny," Snyder said. "If it were possible to end the war without using this weapon you've spent so much energy developing, how would you feel?"

Willard thought a moment, then said, "Fine."

"But if we don't use it, how will anybody understand its potential?"

"Ah . . . Bring foreign observers to Alamogordo to witness the test. If that doesn't convince anyone, I don't know what will. Actually, Major, I don't accept the idea that we have to wipe out a whole city just to show what we can do. When we thought the Germans were developing the same thing, it was a race to get there first. Turns out the race was one-sided. Okay, now we've got this thing, but let's use it as a threat and nothing more."

Snyder relaxed. Willard was a man after Stimson's heart. Cold, logical, clear-thinking and well qualified, he would make the perfect counterpoint to Bliss.

Marion Cypulski took the chair and gazed at Snyder with eager anticipation. Snyder wondered what she expected. He glanced at her file once more. She would be the ideal expert on U-235 extraction and the electromagnetic method.

Snyder asked several innocuous questions. She was eager to give answers and rattled on amiably about cyclotrons and calutrons for ten minutes. She made herself so clear that even Snyder had no trouble following her. When he stopped her and launched into his United Nations story, her face clouded over.

"What's the matter?" he asked.

"I had a different impression," she said, rubbing her knuckles along the tops of her legs.

"Of what?"

Marion thought carefully before she spoke. "Going before the United Nations is fine, Major, but the Japanese should be told first."

Snyder hesitated. "Of course," he said.

"I understand why you had to concoct this little story for the others, but I think *we* can speak plainly."

"Please do, Doctor."

"I want to be part of it. I've worked hard, you see—for a long time. But I couldn't live with myself if I didn't take some steps to help end the war humanely. And the hope that you're holding out is more important than anything I've done so far."

Snyder stared at the desk, struggling to control his anger. Somebody had told Marion Cypulski about the mission. He asked one more question to be sure. "Do you think the Japanese will believe us?"

"Of course. Dr. Lasch and I have already discussed points that must be brought out. You don't have to worry," she said confidently. "We can do it."

"I'm sure you can. You won't mention it to anyone else though, will you?"

"Of course not."

For a moment, Snyder was at a loss for words, then he said, "Thank you, Dr. Cypulski, I'm glad we see eye to eye."

Lasch looked up in surprise as Snyder stormed in and slammed the door.

"Did you tell Marion Cypulski about the mission?"

Lasch stared at him then said quietly, "Yes."

"That's just fine. Anybody else?"

"No."

"How do I know that?"

"Now, just a minute, Major—Marion is as trustworthy as I am."

"Right now that's not a high recommendation."

"All right, Snyder, I get the point. I'm sorry. Slap my hand."

Snyder bristled. "You and your colleagues may be wizards in the lab, but you're not running this operation. I don't care if it falls through. In fact I might be damned grateful, for a variety of reasons. But I won't have it blown because of carelessness!"

Snyder stalked out and caught Beth staring at him. "I want to see you right now," he said. Startled by his behavior, she followed him back to the interview room. He went behind the desk and ran a pencil down the original list of names, circling three of them.

"Kirby, Bliss and Willard," he said, handing her the list. "Make Ozalid copies of their files so I can take them back to Washington. Put all the others in a safe."

"What about Dr. Cypulski?"

Snyder was prepared to reject Marion, but he picked up her file and studied the qualifications page once more. Scientifically she would be an asset. He handed it to Beth.

"Hers, too," he said. She took it and their hands touched. "You ran this pretty well," he added.

"Thank you, Major. I wish you were this diplomatic all the time."

He sighed. "Takes too much willpower. But I'll keep it in mind. In fact, my first act of diplomacy will be to take you to dinner . . ." She shook her head, but he cut in before she could turn him down, ". . . when I come back from Washington. That'll give you time to get used to the idea."

She laughed.

June 28: Washington

Snyder had flown back to Washington on the night of the twenty-seventh. He met with Stimson and Marshall in the morning, tired and bleary-eyed from lack of sleep. He handed over the copies of the files on Kirby, Bliss and Willard and said, "We're covering three different fields with these people: physics of bomb development, radiation biology and the gaseous diffusion process of extracting fissionable materials. They are all qualified and I'm satisfied they're up to our specific needs."

"Just three?" asked Marshall.

"No, sir." Snyder handed him Marion Cypulski's file. "Dr. Cypulski would be the expert on the electromagnetic process. She was personally recommended by Lasch."

"A woman?" questioned Marshall, flipping open the file.

"Yes, sir," said Snyder.

"You held her back, Major," said Stimson. "Any particular reason?"

"I thought we should discuss her a bit, sir. She's the only foreign-born candidate in the group."

"She's a naturalized citizen," said Marshall. "But I do question the wisdom of taking a woman."

"Dr. Lasch feels that it would have a great impact on the Japanese mentality."

Marshall sighed. "The right impact?"

"I think we should run a final security check on all of them anyway," said Stimson. "I'll send these files down to Intelligence. It won't take long."

"While you're at it, sir, I'd like to see Dr. Lasch's file

again, and whatever you've got on his two assistants, Elizabeth Martin and Keith Fulbright."

Stimson wrote down the names. "I'll send them to your quarters tonight." He put all the files aside and said, "Now to the matter of our Japanese candidate. We've located someone who should be perfect. He speaks English and he's a physicist educated in this country. His name is Shinichiro Nakamura and he's a major in the Japanese Army. He's being held at Sand Island in Oregon."

Snyder squirmed. "I still feel that watching a POW will present an added burden."

"He was captured late in December 1942," Marshall explained. "I don't think he'll be much of a problem. He's had quite a bit of time to accept his fate."

Snyder's brow furrowed. "What's a physicist doing in the Japanese Army? How was he captured?"

Stimson handed him yet another file. "This should give you a clear picture of the man. He was taken on Guadalcanal . . ."

Snyder felt a cold chill work up his spine. Guadalcanal . . . December 1942 . . . just around the time Dennis was killed. There couldn't be a connection: it was pure coincidence. . . . Marshall was looking at him strangely.

"I'll study this carefully," Snyder said. "And let you know my opinion."

"He'll have to do, Major," said Marshall. "I guarantee you we're not going to find anyone better."

"Yes, sir. Has he agreed to cooperate?"

"He will if you can convince him. And you'd better try hard."

"Yes, sir."

"Next on the agenda," said Stimson, "Colonel Tully has been making inquiries about your transfer. He's upset that you were removed without explanation."

"We've managed to short-stop him," said Marshall, "but we couldn't avoid offending him in the process. You'd better watch your step."

Snyder smiled ruefully and shook his head. "Anything else, sir?"

Stimson nodded. "I've arranged for you to get with a

member of my staff, Bud Veneck. He'll be your liaison from now on. Set up a communications link with him. He's going to be the funnel for Trinity data. Films, tech reports, all that will automatically go to him. He'll make available whatever you need."

"Okay, sir," said Snyder. "Just set up a time for us to meet."

"We'll need a code name," said Marshall. "How does Big Stick suit you?"

Snyder grinned. "Fine, I guess."

"Teddy Roosevelt would be proud," said Stimson.

"While we're on the subject of presidents," said Snyder, "I have a question."

"What's that?"

"Why can't President Truman simply contact the Japanese through regular diplomatic channels and avoid all this pussyfooting around?"

Stimson leaned back in his chair and smiled grimly. "Because at this point the President doesn't know what we're doing."

Snyder stared from one to the other.

"And wouldn't approve if he did," Marshall added.

Snyder's eyes widened in shock. "Do you realize what you're saying, sir?"

"Perfectly, Major." Marshall stood up and looked down at him. "But *we're* taking the risk."

"With all due respect, General, if anything goes wrong at Berkeley, it's *my* ass that's on the line! You haven't played straight with me. *Nobody told me this was unauthorized.*"

Stimson looked at him calmly. "Our reasons are quite sound. At the appropriate time we will inform the President—when we judge him to be receptive. At the moment he's not."

Snyder had trouble controlling himself. "But I told Lasch that this was cleared at the highest level!" he protested.

"As far as you're concerned, it is."

"What if my authority is challenged? What do I fall back on?"

"I don't see why you're concerned," said Marshall. "Everything has gone smoothly so far. There's no reason to expect the worst. If you have problems, you know where to reach us."

"That's a comfort, sir," Snyder mumbled.

"Our effort goes beyond the end of the war, Major Snyder," Marshall continued. "Future policy. It's the core of what we're trying to do. You're acting as our instrument, not as an independent force."

Snyder nodded dumbly. "You know best, General. Maybe someday you'll explain it to me."

June 29: Washington

Bud Veneck was a bright young kid who would have been in uniform if it weren't for the case of polio that had left him with heavy leg braces. He greeted Snyder warmly in his Pentagon cubbyhole. He handed over a top-secret War Department code book and said, "Use this for all future written communication and send everything direct to me. We're gonna have a ball, Major."

"I'll bet," said Snyder, not so sure about the fun at his end.

"Was everything okay on those first orders we cut for you?"

"My compliments to the forger."

"Oh, thank you, sir." Veneck beamed.

"You?" said Snyder.

"I specialize in General Groves' signature."

Snyder laughed. Veneck added, "Would you believe we had courses in forgery at Georgetown?"

"No."

"Well, I must have learned it somewhere." He dug out several files and slapped them on the desk. "The Secretary said you would be asking for these. Allen Lasch, Elizabeth Martin and Keith Fulbright. He also said to tell you to proceed on the basis that those other four scientists are cleared for Big Stick."

Snyder shoved the folders into his briefcase and listened to Veneck explain how communications would work. They would use the scrambler phone or coded teletype, and a mail pouch system for Thyssen. Satisfied with everything, especially Veneck and his infectious enthusiasm, Snyder returned to his quarters at Fort Myer.

He spent the weekend combing through the files, familiarizing himself with everyone's background. There were no surprises in either Lasch's or Fulbright's dossier, but Beth Martin had a rather tantalizing background—one marriage annulled after two weeks, and a short period of alleged one-night stands. It made fascinating reading, but Snyder resolved to put it out of his mind, for it would only color their relationship, whatever that was going to be. Besides, Security had passed her with no reservations. He was interested to learn that she was the only daughter of D. Wesley Martin, President of the Martin Steamship Company, a huge firm run by the same old-line New England family for nearly one hundred years. So she came from wealth. She certainly didn't act rich, but what did he know about how rich people behaved? He'd met so few of them.

He stalled as long as he could, but the Nakamura file lay conspicuously waiting for him on the corner of his tiny desk. Sunday morning he opened it.

Shinichiro Nakamura . . . born Tokyo, 1905 . . . father's occupation, toy manufacturer . . . educated Dartmouth . . . graduate study, physics, Caltech, late 1920s . . . returned to Japan 1931 . . .

There was a huge gap between that date and the next, 1939, when Nakamura returned to the U.S. and took a research job back at Caltech.

. . . October 1941, returned to Japan, personal reasons . . . captured by Marine patrol, Guadalcanal, December 1942 . . . at time of capture was major, Japanese Army, highest ranking officer in American custody . . . sent to Australia for interrogation . . . presently interned POW camp, Sand Island, Portland, Oregon . . .

Snyder stopped reading and wondered why they had selected someone with such huge gaps in his history. He flipped pages and found material described by an Intelligence Section cover letter as "friendly contributions by Conrad Einfeld, a physicist at Caltech." It consisted of interrogation summaries and statements signed by Einfeld. Also included was a microfilm blowup of a letter to Einfeld written on International Red Cross stationery, signed by Nakamura. It was dated June 1943, and was filled with comments on "the ironies of war," along with reminiscences of their past association together at Caltech. In it Nakamura openly wished for the day when the war would be behind them and they could work together again.

Snyder was unmoved: it sounded wheedling. He turned to the Einfeld material, all of which was dated recently. In fact, one of the statements was a complaint by Einfeld deploring the security practices that had "prevented him from receiving the Nakamura letter at the time it was written."

The interrogation reports on Einfeld contained what he knew of Nakamura's background. In particular, the big gap was covered quite thoroughly. Upon returning to Tokyo in 1931, in the aftermath of the Manchuria Incident, Nakamura had participated in protests against Japanese territorial expansion. According to Einfeld, Nakamura believed his government's policies would lead to disaster. His family disagreed with his views and sent him to Kyoto to cool off. He spent a year doing manual labor, then decided he'd had enough and went to the Riken Laboratory, where he was befriended by Dr. Yoshio Nishina, Japan's leading physicist. He was hired as a research assistant and within a few years was elevated to full status. But according to Einfeld, Nakamura never learned to keep his mouth shut and became very vocal against Japanese war aims. During this period he had a run-in with the *kempeitai*, the secret police. They pressured Nishina to shut Nakamura up. Nishina refused but warned Nakamura what could happen to him: prison, exile or worse.

Nakamura fled back to the United States, armed with recommendations from Nishina. In 1939 he was back at Caltech and worked there with Einfeld until October 1941.

According to Einfeld, Nakamura's last trip to Japan came about because he learned that his father was dying. Reading this, Snyder was not entirely convinced. How did Nakamura go from a known opponent of the government to a major in its army? How did he end up on Guadalcanal? It made no sense.

A report from the Provost-Marshal at Allied HQ, Australia, stated that Nakamura had been only minimally cooperative during his interrogations after capture. He had limited his statements to name, rank and Army identification number. Only because they knew he spoke English were they able to trace his background in the States. He was considered a prize catch at the time but Intelligence had never figured out a way to capitalize on him.

But now apparently Stimson and Marshall had, thought Snyder. He was still upset about the Guadalcanal relationship. Nakamura couldn't personally have had anything to do with his brother's death, but *he had been there.*

July 2: Sand Island

Snyder arrived in Portland, Oregon, and took a navy launch to Sand Island on the Columbia River. The POW camp was a fenced compound of Quonset huts guarded by MPs. The commandant examined Snyder's papers, another Bud Veneck masterpiece, and had an MP escort him to a sparsely furnished interrogation room.

After a twenty-minute wait Major Nakamura was brought in. He was a short, slight man, clean-shaven and dressed in a rumpled set of American Army fatigues a full size too large. He looked comical and helpless, hardly a dangerous enemy.

Nakamura bowed from the neck and kept his eyes on the floor.

"Sit down, Major," said Snyder, taking a chair for himself behind a long table.

"Thank you," said Nakamura. He sat across from Snyder with his hands below the table.

"My name is Snyder. I'm here from the War Department to ask you a few questions."

He offered a cigarette, which Nakamura declined, saying, "I answered questions a long time ago."

"You didn't say very much."

"I don't have to."

Snyder opened his briefcase and drew out Nakamura's file. "Even without your cooperation we've managed to learn a great deal about you." He produced a copy of the letter Nakamura had written to Einfeld. "Remember this?"

Nakamura leaned over to study it without picking it up.

He was silent a moment, then said. "This was a personal letter. It never reached Dr. Einfeld?"

"Did you get a reply?"

Nakamura shook his head.

"To be honest, Major, he was not permitted to answer you," explained Snyder. "And he was very upset about that." Snyder pushed over another paper, Einfeld's letter of protest about security.

Nakamura scanned it and grunted. "Why are you showing me this?"

"I thought you'd want to know he's still your friend." Nakamura didn't reply. "You're a physicist," Snyder continued. "What were you doing in the Japanese Army?"

Nakamura smiled. "My name is Shinichiro Nakamura—"

Snyder waved a hand. "Don't bother. This is a pretty thick file, Major. Let's go back to my question. Is it the practice of the Japanese government to reward its dissidents with a commission in the Army?"

Nakamura's gaze hardened. "Major Snyder, there is no way you can use my past to get me to help you."

"I haven't asked for any help."

"You will." He leaned forward. "And if it has anything to do with broadcasting, the answer is still no."

Snyder was puzzled. "What are you talking about?"

"Your psychological warfare department has been after me for two years to broadcast propaganda into Japan. If this is another attempt, may I suggest we save ourselves some time?"

"I'm not here for that, Major."

"No? What then?"

"How would you like to go back to Japan?"

Nakamura regarded him without emotion. "As what?" he asked.

"Part of a team that will try to convince your government to surrender."

Nakamura smiled, then said calmly, "Please explain how this is different from broadcasting propaganda."

"Okinawa is lost, Major. The next step is the invasion of the home islands. That means death and destruction on both sides. There is a way to prevent that, but it requires the cooperation of a Japanese national who speaks English."

Nakamura shot him a bitter look. "Then you don't want a prisoner of war."

"Why not?"

"In my country I am nothing. I'm dead. I would be useless to you. They would never listen to me."

Snyder thought for a moment, then said, "Doctor Nishina would."

Nakamura's eyes came alert and swept over Snyder, who pretended to ignore his sudden interest. He took back his papers and stuffed the file into his briefcase, saying casually, "That's all for now, Major. One thing you should know, however—I didn't come to see you just because you're Japanese. It's your background as a physicist I'm depending on."

Nakamura's eyes followed Snyder to the door. Snyder called the guard, then turned back to him. "I'll be in touch with you again. I hope you decide to cooperate. It would affect the lives of thousands of your countrymen."

As Snyder walked across the hard-packed earth, he felt curious eyes on him. Glancing around, he saw Japanese prisoners sitting or squatting around the huts. Most seemed exactly as Marshall had described them: quiet and docile. The few who watched him pass did so with mild interest, no great concern and without any trace of hostility. For all the fight that was left in them, perhaps they were, in a sense, dead.

He took the launch back to the city. Nakamura was far from the stereotyped enemy, Snyder thought as he gazed off the stern at the rippling wake. There was something he hadn't expected in Nakamura's personality, a dignity. But more than that—an air of detachment, as if he were an observer of his own fate, a performer marking time, waiting for his cue.

July 4: San Francisco

Golden Gate Park was awash with flags, bunting and people. Across the top of a speakers' platform was a huge replica of a war bond and a banner above that that read CONGRATULATIONS SAN FRANCISCO. There were picnic tables, rows of chairs, food stands, a beer bar and an enormous covered object in a roped-off area. The Presidio Army Band played patriotic marches and children ran squealing through the park.

"I think it's a statue," said Beth. "They're dedicating a statue."

Snyder stood with her at the edge of a rope barrier and tried to imagine what was beneath that huge tarpaulin.

"Are you a betting lady?"

"Depends."

"Fifty cents that's no statue."

"Agreed."

He walked her back to the table where his mother was laying out food from her bottomless picnic basket. His father sat quietly in a chair, nursing a battered hip flask.

"See—it's not so bad," Snyder said, indicating the crowd.

"No," Beth agreed, holding on to her big picture hat. "I just thought you were rushing things a bit."

"You wouldn't go to dinner: I had to improvise." He grinned.

"But you've got it backwards," she said, indicating his parents. "I'm the one who's supposed to be chaperoned."

Snyder laughed. "My dad's been called many things in his life, but never a chaperon. Right, Pop?"

Patrick Senior hefted his flask and said, "Right. When are we going to eat?"

"As soon as you all sit down," said Lillian, crooking a finger at Snyder. "Help with the sandwiches."

"Let me," Beth offered, moving to the table.

Snyder watched her fill the paper plates. Bright sunlight streamed through the straw weave in her hat, casting a pattern of shadows across her face. Her skin sparkled with golden warmth, and her mouth curled in a secret smile. This was hardly the same woman he dealt with daily at the Rad Lab.

"What are you standing there for?" demanded Lillian. "Sit down and eat."

Snyder obediently dropped into a chair and took the plate Beth handed him. His fingers touched hers and their eyes met furtively.

"Waste of time," said Patrick Senior. "I shouldn't be here."

Lillian put a plate down in front of him. "Don't start that," she said. "You deserve the award."

As the top bond seller in the transit union, Snyder's father had been invited here to be recognized for his efforts.

"I just did my part," mumbled Patrick Senior. "Don't need any damned award . . ."

"You'll take it and be gracious about it," Lillian insisted. She sat down and smiled at Beth. "Sit here next to me, Elizabeth."

Beth ate sparingly while Lillian made conversation. "So you're from Massachusetts. Do you have relatives in Boston?"

"One uncle."

Lillian was pleased. "Patrick's Grandmother Gilhool lived there sixty years before we talked her into coming here to be with us. We have cousins all over the east."

"That's nice," said Beth. "I've always missed not having a large family."

"You haven't any brothers or sisters?" Beth shook her head. "No family out here?"

"No."

Snyder caught Beth's eye. "Watch what you say. She'll take out adoption papers."

"If I waited for you to make a move," Lillian snapped, "I'd never have a daughter."

Beth turned red. Snyder laughed and held his head in his hands. "Oh, brother," he said. "Thanks, Mom."

Lillian took Beth's hand. "I meant nothing by that, Elizabeth," she said sweetly. "You're a lovely girl."

"I'm having a wonderful time, Mrs. Snyder," Beth said, breaking into a laugh.

"Oh, Lord," groaned Patrick Senior. "The mayor's going to make a speech. We'll be here all day." He raised his flask and closed his eyes, blotting out everything.

"I think you'll be putting that away now, Mr. Snyder," said Lillian, her eyes narrowing in distaste.

"When I'm through with it," he growled back.

Patrick Senior was right. The mayor droned on for thirty minutes. Finally the entertainment began and Snyder took Beth for a walk.

"You'll have to make allowances for my dad," he said.

"Why?"

"He drinks when he's nervous. Doesn't like crowds. And for all his bluster it's going to kill him to walk up on that stage."

She nodded. "My father is so different."

"In what way?"

"He only shows emotion over a balance statement. And he has a nasty habit of buying and selling people." She smiled tightly.

"What about your mother?"

"She'd never do anything to get him angry. She hates *scenes*. And we've had a few, Daddy and I. She's never dared to take my side."

"Where does that leave you?"

"At the age of eighteen I became a social commodity. If my father could have thought of a way to sell shares in me, he wouldn't have hesitated. You belong to a family—I was just property."

"That sounds a little harsh."

"No, realistic." She stopped, looked at his uniform, then into his face. "You don't want my life story, do you, Major?"

"I've been listening. And do me a favor, will you? Drop the rank."

She smiled. "Okay. What do I call you? P.T.?"

"Fine."

Their eyes met and she studied him warmly. He thought of leaning over for a kiss but was interrupted by a drum roll from the bandstand, signaling that the ceremony was about to begin. Their mood broken, Beth frowned to herself. She let Snyder take her arm and lead her back to the picnic table.

Patrick Senior was still working on his flask and muttering comments about the keynote speaker, a local theatrical impresario who had taken upon his shoulders the responsibility of San Francisco's bond drive. He filled the summer air with superlatives about how the city had exceeded its quota. Then he moved to the edge of the platform and gestured dramatically toward the mysterious covered object below. "And to demonstrate that your money is being put to good use," he said, "here's just a sample of what you've bought!"

A troop of Boy Scouts pulled down the tarpaulin, revealing a bullet-riddled Japanese Zero, intact except for half a wing. The crowd roared its approval, their cheers merging into the thumping of drums and the blare of brass as the band burst into "Stars and Stripes Forever."

Snyder's father lowered his flask and stared at the plane.

Beth felt Snyder's lips close to her ear, whispering, "It's okay—you can keep the fifty cents." She glanced at his cocky smile.

As the final strains of music died away, the speaker began to call the roll of honorees. One by one they went up onstage to get their awards. Patrick Senior was up fourth. Snyder helped him rise and pointed him toward the platform. He stumbled a few steps then walked forward, glancing nervously at the Zero.

Snyder stood with Beth and his mother, who beamed with pride. Patrick Senior shakily accepted a scroll and a medal with red, white and blue ribbon.

"Representing the San Francisco Transit Union, Patrick Timothy Snyder!" bellowed the speaker. There was a short round of applause, most of it from Lillian.

"This man really has a stake in our war effort, ladies and gentlemen," said the speaker. "He lost his youngest son at Guadalcanal."

The crowd rose to its feet, acknowledging the sacrifice. Snyder froze; his mother stopped clapping.

Patrick Senior stood before thundering hands and his eyes shifted slowly to the Zero. The applause rose in his mind like the sound of warfare—engines and machine guns merging with Dennis' dying scream, the same scream he had tried so hard to banish from his dreams . . .

He burst into tears. Snyder rushed up to the platform. Misunderstanding, the crowd cheered the emotion. Snyder brought his father back to the table, shouldering through unwitting well-wishers and back-slappers.

They sat down and Patrick Senior came apart in a passionate outpouring of grief for his lost son. Lillian took his hand and pulled him close. "Find your strength," she murmured.

Beth watched helplessly. Her gaze shifted to Snyder, who stood with his back to the table, staring angrily at the Zero. She went to his side.

"Maybe we should leave," she said.

Snyder helped Lillian get his father up to bed. Beth waited below. The old man wanted whisky, so Snyder said he would go for it.

Lillian grabbed his arm and whispered, "She's a fine girl. I hope she doesn't think badly of us."

"I'm sure she understands, Mom."

Snyder went down to the living room for the whisky. Beth stood up. "How is he?" she asked.

"He'll survive."

"I'd like to see him."

Snyder hesitated, then waved her to the stairs. They went up together and entered the bedroom. Patrick Senior was huddled under a blanket. Embarrassed, he looked away as Beth approached. She went right to his side, unhesitating and direct.

"Mr. Snyder," she said, "I think you're a very brave man."

He still wouldn't look at her. She bent over and lightly pressed her lips to his cheek. He looked around in surprise.

"I suppose I am," he said.

"Sure you are," said Lillian, taking the whisky bottle from her son and handing it to the old man. He clutched it to his breast and closed his eyes.

Snyder took Beth's arm and led her away. Lillian followed them downstairs a moment later. She dropped into a soft chair and sighed. "Now don't let this ruin the rest of your day. Run along and have a good time."

She took Beth's hand and smiled warmly. "I hope we'll see more of you, Elizabeth."

"I'd like that, Mrs. Snyder."

Beth went to the hallway and Snyder kissed his mother's forehead. He felt her iron grip on his arm and found himself looking into her blazing eyes, which sneaked a look at the woman waiting in the hall and seemed to say, "If you let this one get away, you no-good Irish peacock, you'll have to deal with me."

"Okay, Ma," Snyder whispered. "I get the hint."

Her jaw stuck out to make sure there was no mistake. He fled the room quickly.

"You went over big," Snyder said, touching Beth's glass with his in a silent toast. They were sitting in the Drake, having cocktails and looking out at the skyline, watching dusk fall. "Hasn't been much of a day for you," he said.

"Are you worried about your father?"

"That and other things."

"Tell me."

"What for? You can't feel it the way I do. He's an old man now, busted up about my brother—it's an obsession. He hates the Japanese, blames them for all his problems. If he ever found out what I'm doing . . ."

"You're not going to tell him, are you?"

He looked at her dismally. "How can I? It would kill him."

"Then don't. Even after the war's over, you don't have to tell him."

Snyder nodded agreement. "You know, I'm not so wild about this thing myself. I stood looking at that shot-up Zero this afternoon and suddenly felt that I've let myself get mixed up in something I don't believe in."

"Couldn't you request reassignment?"

He shook his head, then took a drink and slapped the table. "The hell with this," he said. "Irish families are too close. We take each other's problems too much to heart."

"That's not a handicap," said Beth. "In my family we had just the opposite: a lot of interference but no real caring. While I was growing up, it was nice to have anything I wanted, but when I turned off the flow and left, I didn't miss any of it—because the one thing they'd forgotten to give me was love."

"Is that why you left home?"

She took more of her drink and looked at him, weighing a decision. Finally she said, "I married someone my father didn't approve of."

Snyder recalled that from her file, but feigned ignorance and surprise. "You have a husband?" he said.

She laughed, *"Had.* In a funny way my father was right. The boy was no good. He was a second lieutenant in the Air Corps. I met him at a ball in Washington. We drove to Maryland to get married."

"The same night?"

"No, a week later. Sounds stupid, doesn't it?" Snyder didn't comment. He watched her stretch with both hands behind her neck. Her breasts rose beneath the light cotton summer dress. Then she laughed again. "I brought him home to meet my parents, and he suddenly developed a weak backbone."

"How so?"

"My father was able to buy him off." She said it offhandedly, and he realized she wasn't trying to shock him, just stating fact.

"For how much?" he asked.

"Five thousand dollars." Her lip curled in amusement. "We got an annulment and he walked out of my life."

"Were you in love with him?"

She thought it over, then said, "I was wildly infatuated. And I was furious with my father for meddling. I suppose it was understandable. He was trying to be protective, looking after my interests . . . I thought. But then he did something unforgivable. He tried to smooth things over with a paternal chat. Up till then he had hardly acknowledged me as a thinking human being, so it just made me see how shallow he really was."

"But that wasn't the end of it?"

"No," she said, smiling again. "I got even . . . then I left home for good."

She wouldn't elaborate, and Snyder was left wondering what she meant by getting even. "I did a lot of things I'm not proud of," was all she added. He nodded and looked around for a way to change the subject. His attention was drawn to the small combo and the people dancing.

"Nice music," he said. "I haven't danced in a long time. How about it?"

She listened to the music a moment, then tapped her glass. "I'd like another drink. These are very good. And I'm hungry."

Snyder grinned as the food was served. "Another victory for the United States Army," he said. "I finally got you to dinner."

She smiled and dug into her food. They went through the meal, dessert and coffee with Snyder telling Beth about his boyhood in San Francisco. She listened attentively for a while, then was drawn to the music. She interrupted him. "Do you still want to dance?"

He was careful not to hold her too closely and this amused her. Obediently she kept her distance and floated along in a mellow haze, closing her eyes and letting him guide her around the floor.

He drove her back to the Nunnery and they walked up to her apartment in silence. He opened the door for her and stood aside. She took back her key and flashed him a beguiling smile. "I had a lovely time, Major."

He held up a finger. "P.T."

She stood up on tiptoes and gave him a kiss, her lips just brushing his. "Good night, Patrick Timothy."

She closed the door and Snyder stood outside, rooted for a moment. Then he walked toward the stairs, recalling the last time he had brought her home.

"Patience," he said to himself, "does indeed have its rewards."

July 4: Washington

Music from the Marine Band concert at the Washington Monument drifted through the open windows of the Oval Office at twilight. Truman and Stimson sat with Byrnes, who was in a buoyant mood, having that day finally been confirmed as Secretary of State. They were discussing the upcoming conference at Potsdam with the Military Advisor to the President, Admiral William D. Leahy; Truman's old political crony, Brigadier General Harry Vaughan; and the White House Advisor on Russian Affairs, Charles "Chip" Bohlen.

Despite the heat, Truman kept his jacket on and alertly watched the men around him. Nothing passed his notice.

Stimson's aides had drafted the text of a proclamation to be sent jointly from Potsdam by the United States and England. It was, in effect, a final demand for Japan's surrender, and it threatened destruction of the home islands if she didn't comply.

Stimson had included a provision allowing the Japanese to retain the Emperor if they would give in to all other terms unconditionally.

Truman was amused. "It's hardly unconditional when you give them a condition, Henry," he said.

"I think it would help to show them we're flexible, Mr. President," Stimson replied.

Truman pursed his lips. "That might be fine for the Japanese," he said, "but it's not the impression I want to convey at Potsdam."

"I don't understand."

"There's a twofold purpose in using the bomb, Henry,"

explained the President. "One, it will end the war. And two, it should convince those Russian sons of bitches that we're not to be taken lightly." He turned to Bohlen. "Chip, don't you think that using the bomb on Japan will make a hell of an impression on Stalin?"

Bohlen sat up and glanced at Stimson. "Well, yes, sir," he said. "Since he's so dependent on the display of force himself. However, is it necessary to use the bomb in order to defeat Japan? It's my understanding that the empire is close to collapse as it is."

"Japan will fall," said Truman, "but if it's after August eighth, it's a question who she falls *to*."

General Vaughan stood up and clasped his hands behind his back. "Gentlemen," he said, "nothing is quite so awesome and convincing as the first sight of an invasion fleet coming up on your doorstep. That will do the job."

Truman closed his eyes a moment. He tolerated Vaughn's excessive military views only because he was an old friend. "You better pray that bomb works," he said; "unless you want to be the first man ashore."

Vaughan sat down. Leahy sided with Stimson, pointing out that to demand an unconditional surrender might only serve to antagonize the Japanese and prolong the war, costing more lives.

Truman was silent a moment, then said he would take the matter under advisement and make a decision while en route to Potsdam.

Stimson was amazed. Perhaps the arguments were beginning to have their effect and he wouldn't have to send Big Stick after all. And he might never have to tell the President that it had been planned behind his back.

On July 6th, Stimson stepped aboard the transport USS *Brazil* for the Atlantic crossing to Marseilles, seeing a glimmer of hope in the days ahead.

July 9: Berkeley

"We're calling it Operation Big Stick."

Lasch smiled. "You people come up with more damn funny names . . ."

Thyssen chuckled. "Appropriate, though."

They sat behind closed doors in Lasch's office with Fulbright taking notes. Thyssen was detailing his progress in setting up the meeting.

"Through our trade channels," he began, "we have contacted a close friend of Prince Konoye. He wanted more information but indicated that Konoye might be willing to meet with anyone who displayed serious intent. However, unless I am able to tell them ahead of time what is going to be discussed and whom they will be meeting, it will be hard getting them to commit."

"We can't give them that information yet," said Snyder. "You'll have to work around it."

Lasch frowned. "Why can't we tell them?"

"The whole idea is to shock them into reality," said Snyder. "If we tip our mitt before we have a face-to-face meeting, we lose the impact. To say nothing of the obvious security problems." He turned to Thyssen. "You'll have to be more persuasive: rope them in on faith."

Fulbright took everything down in a rapid pencil scrawl and eyed Snyder furtively.

Thyssen sighed. "I did manage to extract a small concession. If we are able to convince them to meet with us, then Okinawa is acceptable, as long as my government guarantees safety."

"Did you request a Japanese physicist?" Snyder asked.

"Not yet. That is one reason I wanted to meet with you, Dr. Lasch. I am hoping you could suggest someone specific."

Lasch lowered his arms and frowned thoughtfully. "As I recall, their three top men were Fuchida, Miyaki and Nishina. They were all at the Riken before the war."

"Make it Nishina," Snyder interrupted. Lasch looked at him, surprised. "I'd better explain something. We're taking along a physicist named Nakamura who, it happens, used to work with Dr. Nishina."

"Where did you find him?" Lasch asked.

"Prisoner of war."

Fulbright took this down eagerly. "Will he be brought to the Rad Lab?" he asked.

"When it's time, yes," said Snyder.

"Has he been told what the mission is?" Lasch asked.

"Not yet."

"Just how far are you going to carry this secrecy business, Major? You haven't told any of the scientists what they're going to be involved in. Suppose they refuse to go?"

Snyder smiled. "You're forgetting they were selected very carefully . . . with your help."

"But how long do you intend to keep them in the dark?"

"Once we get everything set up and we have the results of the Trinity test, we'll bring them here under tight security, and then we'll tell them. Frankly, Dr. Lasch, that's my worry. Don't concern yourself."

Lasch nodded, expecting that answer. "I *will* meet with this Nakamura, won't I?"

"Soon. When is the test?"

Lasch leaned back. "I'm going to Los Alamos on the eleventh to supervise placing the plutonium core into the test device. I believe we can expect detonation within a week after that."

"Get us the exact date," Snyder said.

"As soon as I know it."

"Have you got anything else?" Snyder asked Thyssen, who shook his head, stood up and extended a hand to Lasch.

"A pleasure meeting you, sir," he said. He and Snyder left together.

Fulbright folded his notebook and looked at Lasch. "Hell of a way to run things," he said.

"Yes," Lasch agreed slowly.

July 10: Sand Island

Nakamura didn't seem surprised to see Snyder again. He went to the table and sat in the same place as before.

"Are you ready to cooperate?" Snyder asked.

"Under certain conditions."

"Okay, what?"

"No propaganda broadcasting or anything else that would compromise me against my country."

"Agreed. And if you'll take my word on it, we should get moving. I can't tell you any more until I have you under my own security. If you change your mind then, you'll have to be isolated for the duration, which I can promise you won't be long."

Nakamura studied him with interest, then nodded once, deeply. It was almost a bow.

Snyder stood at the door with the two MPs he had brought from Berkeley and watched Nakamura pack his few belongings into a GI canvas satchel. Nakamura paused at a bookshelf and ran his hands over a meager collection of worn and soiled detective novels. He glanced at Snyder. "They belong to the commandant," he said wistfully. "It's like leaving old friends."

"You'll make new ones," said Snyder. "We've got plenty of books where you're going."

Nakamura grunted, picked up his satchel and said, "I'm ready."

A line of prisoners stood quietly at the fence, paying silent homage to their ranking officer as he walked out of the camp, led by Snyder and flanked by the two MPs.

Nakamura's eyes swept across their faces as he moved by, and he felt mixed emotions—a surge of hope dampened by a feeling of betrayal. Once past the line, though, he never looked back.

They flew out of Portland by military transport and landed at Hamilton Field a few hours later.

Nakamura sat in the back of a car between Snyder and one of the MPs and gazed impassively out the window. He came alert as they wound through Berkeley, went up Bancroft Way and entered the U.C. campus. His eyes locked on the small sign at the gate: University of California Radiation Laboratory. He turned to Snyder, who anticipated him and said, "No questions just yet."

The car pulled up to Security and Nakamura was taken into Captain Browne's office, where he was photographed and fingerprinted. Then Snyder escorted him to quarters deep in the back of the rear Quonset hut.

They walked down a narrow hall to an open door with one MP posted outside as guard. It was a single room with a bath and closet behind a partition. There were some casual clothes on hangers, bedding stacked on the cot, one battered easy chair and some toilet articles on the sink. There were bars on the windows, but it was twice the size of Nakamura's Sand Island quarters.

Snyder went to the sink and lifted a safety razor. "Can I trust you to use this as it was intended, Major?"

"Of course. What about meals?"

"They'll be served here. Schedule's been written out and posted on the back of the door, just like a hotel. We call it the El Solitaire."

Nakamura smiled wanly. "I'll miss having company."

"Not for long, I hope," said Snyder. "If it's any comfort, my quarters are in the front hut, and they're just as meager as yours." He closed the door so the MP wouldn't hear what he had to say next. "Sit down, Major."

Nakamura sat on the bed. Snyder perched on the edge of the desk. "For the past three and a half years the United States has been developing a new weapon, based on research into nuclear energy. As a physicist, I'm sure you have some knowledge of this."

"Yes."

"It's called an atomic bomb," said Snyder, "and we expect it will be ready for use very shortly. It's estimated that one bomb could wipe out a whole city."

Nakamura gave him a blank stare. Snyder wondered what sort of reaction he had expected. Certainly more than this. He went on: "We would like to avoid using it if possible, so we're planning to send a small group of American physicists to meet with members of your government to give them an idea of what they're up against if they refuse to surrender."

Nakamura frowned, then said, "Who's going? Fermi? Teller?"

"No one that important. Too risky. We've selected a few midlevel people who are best equipped to explain their research. But we need a Japanese national to interpret where necessary. And since we're requesting Dr. Nishina to take part in this, we need someone he'll listen to. You." Snyder fell silent.

Nakamura stood up and moved to the window. He stared at the bars, then said, "It seems like a very generous thing to do."

"I suppose it is."

Nakamura turned back and spoke guardedly. "But how do I know I'm not being used to pull off a monumental bluff?"

"I've been involved in this project a long time, Major. You have no idea how massive this effort has been, involving thousands of people and facilities all over the country. Your friend Einfeld has been part of it."

"Ah," Nakamura grunted. "But I must be sure."

"Well, what do you want? A tour of the lab? I don't think that would be convincing."

"Perhaps not, but I can't just parrot what your people will be telling mine. If Dr. Nishina is going to be there, he'll be more demanding than you might think. The questions he will ask must have convincing answers, and I can't provide conviction from hearsay."

"Major," Snyder said calmly, "you're not in a position to make demands."

Nakamura's eyes flashed. "Neither are you. But in order

to accomplish what you want, you'd better consider what I have to say."

Snyder stared at him. "All right. Go ahead."

"Have you had a successful detonation?"

"No."

"Will you test the bomb before it's used?"

"Yes."

"Then I have to see it when it goes off."

Snyder gaped at him, then said flatly, "No."

Nakamura smiled, then explained, "Don't you understand? Nishina won't accept this at face value. Somebody must be able to give him an eyewitness description in language he can understand. We have a special relationship—he was my teacher. If I try to deceive him or don't have enough conviction myself, he'll know it right away."

"Out of the question," said Snyder. "You can't be there, period. And it's not important anyway because we'll have films."

Nakamura snorted. "Made in Hollywood?"

"Don't be ridiculous."

Nakamura's voice lowered. "Major Snyder, you will not only have to convince Nishina, a very reasonable man, but I suspect the government officials at this meeting will be some of the same people who have carried on this war. If they choose not to believe you, they won't. You must go in with the strongest argument possible."

Snyder slid off the desk. "The strongest argument is to use the damned bomb!" he snapped.

"Then why do you need me?"

"Look, you can't dictate terms to us. We're trying to give your people a break!"

"Then do it properly. I won't be front man for a fraud."

"You're crazy!" said Snyder. "Do you think I can just walk you into the test site, put you in the bleachers and buy you a bag of peanuts?"

Nakamura shrugged. "Your problem."

Snyder was furious. If he tried to smuggle a Japanese observer into the Jornada del Muerto and got caught, Big Stick would go up in smoke and P. T. Snyder with it. But he could see the man's point. "I'll have to think about it," he said.

"I don't see the difficulty," said Nakamura. "I'm sure there will be other observers."

Snyder blew out his breath. "Major," he said, exasperated, "please remember that you're considered an enemy of this country. I can't just make some phone calls and clear it. There's probably no way we can do it legitimately."

Nakamura smiled grimly. "I leave it in your hands."

"Thanks," Snyder snapped. He left, slamming the door, furious at having been so easily outmaneuvered.

Nakamura sank onto the cot, drew his arms about his midsection and slowly rocked back and forth, staring at the floor in reflection. He had been bold with Snyder, but inside he was terrified. Fear had developed the first time Nishina's name had been mentioned. Now it had turned to dread.

July 11: San Francisco

Marion Cypulski parked on Market Street, walked down O'Farrell and entered Bernard Bowen's shop. She smiled at Mrs. Beach and browsed, waiting for Bowen to finish with a customer. Bowen saw her, waved and finally got free. He greeted her warmly, throwing a paternal arm over her shoulder and hugging her.

"How are you, Marion? Why don't you come into the back and share a glass of sherry?"

He closed the connecting door, went to his desk, opened the double drawer and pulled out a bottle of Sandman. He poured two glasses and offered a toast. "To us," he said. "May our friendship last forever."

He gave her the rocking chair and took his own seat at the desk. "I'm surprised to see you. I hope there's no trouble."

"About what?"

"Well, I didn't hear back from you regarding your mother's last letter. She's well, isn't she?"

"She sounded well. Is there any further news about getting her out?"

Bowen cupped his glass in both hands. "You must understand how difficult things are in Russia right now, my dear. We are doing all we can to repatriate refugees, but it's going to take some time. There's still the war in Asia. We can't tie up transportation until that's settled."

Marion nodded. It was the answer she had expected. "What if I told you that there's a chance the war might end sooner than everyone thinks?"

Bowen was impassive. "I would be delighted." He paused. "Is there such a chance?"

"Yes." Marion leaned forward and looked earnestly at Bowen. "Bernard, there's a plan to warn the Japanese about the bomb."

Bowen looked surprised. "There is?"

She nodded vigorously. "And I'm going to be part of it. I've been picked to go with a group to Japan to explain what the bomb can do. We're going to convince the Japanese that they haven't a chance of surviving a nuclear attack. And when we've done that, they'll have no choice but to surrender." She smiled excitedly.

"Marion, this is wonderful news! Absolutely marvelous!" He put a hand on hers. "I'm proud of you. Tell me more."

Eagerly she told him about Snyder, the interviews, Lasch's part in it, the fact that they would be taking along a wealth of information, including documents, films and test results—everything Lasch had confided in her before Snyder had stopped her. Bowen shook his head in amazement and kept exclaiming, "Marvelous . . . marvelous . . . exactly what should be done."

She finished and sat back while Bowen poured more sherry and proposed another toast. "To the Americans," he said, "for finally showing the good sense to share this with the rest of the world."

"Yes," said Marion, taking a sip of sherry.

Bowen tossed his back, cleared his throat, then said, "This means they will probably send the same information to Russia. Any idea when that will be?"

"No."

"Well, have you heard anything about it?"

Marion lowered her glass. "No."

Bowen was surprised. "Nothing at all?"

"It hasn't been discussed."

"But surely that's the ultimate intention. What good does it do simply to inform the Japanese? *They* are not America's ally."

"Bernard, I just don't know. I haven't heard."

Bowen seemed shocked. He sank back into his chair and stared at his glass, then set it down on the desk sharply. "Marion, this is very serious."

"But it's just the first step," she said meekly. "I'm sure America will share it with the rest of the world."

"Really?" he said. "Wouldn't it follow that if the United States can threaten Japan with it, she could also threaten Russia? Or anyone else?"

Marion frowned. "They would never do that."

"Why not—because we've been allies?" He laughed. "Don't let wartime illusions fool you. America has nothing to gain by sharing her atomic secrets, but she can force Russia into terribly unfavorable compromises by using the bomb as a sword against Stalin's throat!" His voice dropped. "And if the bomb threatens Stalin, it also threatens your family."

Marion stared at him, frightened. "But they promised—"

"Russia has protected and sheltered your mother, and your brothers have done great service fighting with the Red Armies. Do you think they would be permitted to travel to a country harboring such terrible intentions? And what makes you think the United States would let them in?"

Marion was reduced to sheer panic. "But we have to get them out!"

Bowen searched her eyes and tried to communicate his sorrow and compassion. He held her hand and said, "It means we still have work to do." She started to protest and he silenced her. "If anything, now we must intensify our efforts to get solid information across. They need much more on the gaseous diffusion process and the plutonium core housing."

"But I've given you everything I know—"

"Not quite," said Bowen. He waited till she calmed down and then said, "Haven't you just told me that a substantial amount of information on these sensitive areas will be assembled for this so-called warning mission? You must see how important it is for me to obtain all that."

Marion stared at him, then burst into tears. Bowen stood up and again put the fatherly arm around her. He stroked her head gently. "Now stop this, Marion. There's no need to cry."

"I want my family, Bernard. You can't keep pressing me this way. You hold them out and you take them away. You talk so much about politics and what's best for the world. Don't you see, I'm not concerned about that? I want my family!" she sobbed.

Bowen pulled his chair next to hers, sat down and took her face in his hands, forcing her to look at him. With his thumbs he wiped away her tears. "Marion, I'm not threatening your family. You must believe that. Do you?"

"I don't know . . ." She tried to turn away. Gently, he pulled her back and didn't speak again until their eyes locked.

"It's the Americans you have to fear. They're the aggressors. When Japan falls, they will establish air bases on Honshu and from there be able to use their new bombs against Russia. Look at a map, Marion. With a foothold in Japan and another in Europe, they would have Russia virtually surrounded. It's the future balance of power that's at stake." He gazed into her eyes and pleaded, "*No one country should have that bomb. It's too dangerous.*"

Marion sniffled and closed her eyes to avoid his look. She'd heard his argument so many times before that now it seemed like pure rote. She sighed in resignation, took his hands away from her face, managed a smile for him, then got up. She reached into her purse for a handkerchief, but Bowen handed her his own. She dried her eyes and gave it back.

"Thank you," she said. "I've always believed you were doing your best for me. I want to continue believing that. But I'm not stupid, Bernard. You must not try to pressure me, because you're just as vulnerable."

Bowen chuckled heartily, carefully refolding his handkerchief and replacing it in his breast pocket. "I'm sure everything will work out all right, Marion. I understand your fears, just as I know they are groundless. You *will* be reunited with your family, and soon."

He opened his arms and embraced her, then drew back and said, "But would you want them to come to a country that may turn into the next Germany? The seed is planted and growing, Marion—intensely apparent in their handling of this atomic bomb. It is the most corrupting weapon ever devised."

Marion nodded without looking at him. She was no

longer paying attention and he knew it. "Enough of that," he said. "Come, I'll see you to the door. You must get some rest and stop worrying."

He let her out the side door with a courtly kiss on the cheek. Then he watched her walk back up to O'Farrell Street, the gracious smile slowly fading from his face.

July 12: Moscow

Ambassador Naotake Sato arrived at the Kremlin for an evening meeting with Vyacheslav Molotov. The Russian Foreign Minister resembled a dyspeptic college professor as he sat down with Sato in a palatial conference room. They were alone and spoke Russian. Sato was nervous and kept his hands tightly around his briefcase.

Molotov got settled and said, "Please proceed."

Sato cleared his throat and bowed. "My government requests assistance in a matter of grave importance. I put it to you as a question. Would the Soviet government be inclined to intercede on Japan's behalf in certain peace negotiations with the United States?"

Molotov listened attentively, then said, "That's something I could not answer at this time, Mr. Ambassador."

"I quite understand." Again Sato bowed. "However, because of the urgency of the situation, the Emperor would like to send Prince Konoye as a special envoy to meet with you and discuss various possibilities. We hope your government will receive him and hear him out before deciding on the matter of intercession."

Molotov gave him a sympathetic smile. "Rest assured, Mr. Ambassador, that your request will be given proper attention."

"Thank you, Mr. Minister, and may we hope for a quick reply?"

Molotov nodded solemnly, then leaned over the table and clasped his hands, his eyes intent on the ashtray before him as he tried to impress Sato with the importance of what he had to say next. "Mr. Ambassador, certain activities of a

Swedish diplomat named Stefan Thyssen have come to my attention. We understand he is trying to set up a secret meeting between Japanese and American officials on the same subject you have just raised. According to my information," Molotov continued, "this effort is not bona fide. In fact, it is nothing more than a delaying tactic mounted by the Americans to wear down your government, so that you will be forced to end the war without any guarantee of the Emperor's continuance on his throne."

Sato's hands fluttered on his briefcase and Molotov distinctly saw him grow paler. "I am grateful to hear that your government is interested in the Emperor's plight," Sato said.

Molotov waved expansively. "The Soviet Union is always interested in maintaining order," he said. "I hope you will convey our concern to your government. We consider Thyssen's effort a shoddy piece of diplomacy."

"Thank you," said Sato.

The Japanese ambassador left the Kremlin quite shaken. The Thyssen matter had only recently come to his attention and had been touted as a genuine alternative. The Russian warning was most disturbing. Konoye would have to be informed immediately.

July 12-13: Trinity

On July 12 Louis Slotin and Philip Morrison, two scientists from the Weapons-Physics Division, used a field carrying case on the backseat of an Army sedan to deliver the plutonium core to the Alamogordo test site. At midnight Allen Lasch accompanied the nonnuclear components in a caravan from Los Alamos.

Next afternoon, Lasch stood with J. Robert Oppenheimer inside McDonald's ranch house, a four-room shack two miles downrange from point zero, and watched Slotin mount the two hemispheres encasing the active plutonium inside a capsule that held them slightly apart, to keep the neutron emissions from multiplying.

Once the capsule was fitted, Slotin rubbed his stubbly beard and invited Lasch over to inspect his work. "Put your hand on it," he said.

Lasch cautiously pressed his fingers against the capsule and was surprised to find it warm to the touch. He shrank back instinctively. Slotin grinned at his little joke.

"Don't worry," said Oppenheimer. "That's a uranium tamper coating. She's safe and snug."

"Looks like a black watermelon," observed Lasch.

An hour later he and Oppenheimer, along with Navy Commander Norris E. Bradbury, supervised as Robert Bacher's "G engineers" moved the core from the shack to the canvas tent at the base of the hundred-foot open-work steel tower. They labored under a searingly hot sun to pack the thirteen and one-half pounds of plutonium into the two-and-one-half-ton high-explosives assembly, between a thick rind of layered smokeless powder that would collapse the hemispheres together, then squeeze the solid metal until it reached critical mass and exploded.

There were twenty physicists and Army personnel at the tower base as Bacher attached the plutonium capsule to a chain hoist and slowly brought it down into the high-explosive assembly. When he saw that it wasn't going to fit, he called a halt. Immediately, the nervous Army men backed away, while the scientists tried to figure out what was wrong. It was Lasch who remembered the warmth of the capsule surface and suggested that perhaps the plutonium component, which had been under the desert sun almost a full day longer than the explosives, had absorbed additional heat and had expanded slightly.

Following his theory, Bacher lowered the capsule until it rested against the HE assembly and waited for the temperatures to equalize. The capsule slipped into place with a solid click.

Oppenheimer thanked Lasch for his help and the two men watched as the entire test platform was hoisted into a corrugated iron shed at the top of the tower. Oppenheimer was an incongruous figure in the desert, dressed in a tweed suit, showing no signs of perspiration despite the intense heat. Lasch stood next to him in shirtsleeves, sticky with sweat.

"You haven't been down here before, have you, Allen?" asked Oppenheimer, his face emaciated and tired-looking under his down-turned hat brim.

"No. It's impressive."

"Most of it is underground. Thousands of miles of electrical wiring for communications and monitoring."

Lasch smiled in appreciation. "Marvelous piece of work."

"The ingenuity is astounding. We've never seen its like before." He paused. "This is going to be some firecracker."

"Where are we going to be?"

"Take your choice. Three control stations: one each, ten thousand yards from point zero in the south, west and north. The base camp is nearly ten miles south. Most of the people from Los Alamos will be observing from Compania Hill, twenty miles northwest."

Lasch smiled wanly, unable to shake loose the burden of

guilt working inside him, worried what Oppenheimer and his colleagues would think when they learned about Big Stick.

"If the weather's okay, we'll fire at 4 A.M. on the sixteenth," said Oppenheimer. "You plan to stick around?"

"Wouldn't miss it for anything."

July 13: Berkeley

Fulbright ran back to his office to snatch up the phone on the third ring. It was a bad connection but he could make out Lasch's voice through the heavy static.

"Tell Major Snyder," Lasch enunciated, "we're set for 4 A.M. on the sixteenth. Got that?"

"Yes, sir. Anything else?" The static became too heavy, so Fulbright shouted a good-bye and hung up. He turned to see Snyder standing curiously at his door. "That was Lasch," he said. "They're going to fire the test at 4 A.M. on the sixteenth."

Snyder called Beth over and told her, then added, "Tell Kirby, Bliss and Willard to pack their bags and be ready to move at a moment's notice. Fulbright, you prepare an order for my signature, okay?" Fulbright nodded. "And make it brief."

When they left, Fulbright decided to risk a phone call to Bowen at his shop.

"Bernard Bowen Antiques," the familiar voice answered.

"That three-cornered table you've been waiting for?"

Bowen recognized Fulbright's voice but was slow to grasp that he was talking about Trinity. "You've got a delivery date?" he said finally.

"The sixteenth. Does that suit you?"

"Very well. Thank you."

Snyder walked over to Security. He had to figure a way to get Nakamura into the test area. First he would have to cook up some story for Captain Browne, and that wouldn't be easy. Browne had not liked the idea of guarding a Japanese POW, and when Snyder came in and said he would be taking the prisoner away for nearly forty-eight hours, he liked it even less.

"Why are we treating him like he's a guest here, Major? I don't get it at all."

"Don't worry about it, Captain. I'll see that he doesn't get away." As Snyder's attention wandered, he noticed a freshly pressed uniform hanging on the back of a door. Suddenly he knew how to handle Nakamura.

Back in Le Conte Hall a few minutes later, Snyder closed and locked the door to his office. He used the scrambler to call Bud Veneck and dictated a list of orders he wanted cut.

"Christ, I'll be working all night," Veneck complained.

"No you won't, because you'll have it all back to me in three hours by teletype." Then he explained about the items he wanted scrounged immediately and put on the next cross-country plane. Veneck took it all down faithfully, then sighed dramatically.

"I'm doing that now," he said, "because I'll be too pooped later."

"Someday you'll get a medal," Snyder said wryly. As soon as he hung up, he was buzzed by Beth. She said he had just missed a call from Thyssen. "He wants to see you. It's important and he won't be near a phone again today. He wants you to come to a party tonight at the home of the Swedish consul, and he said you should bring a lady." She hesitated, then added, "I'm busy—having dinner with Marion."

"No, you're not: you're both going with me."

Snyder picked up Marion and Beth at seven and drove them to the Swedish consul's house in Pacific Heights. "My social life has sure taken an upward turn," Snyder said as he led the ladies up the walkway.

A huge, baronial living room was thronged with local politicians, socialites and diplomats. Thyssen was standing in the reception line and excused himself to go off with Snyder's party. He escorted Marion and Beth toward a small group of people and introduced Marion to Josep

Wajda and Michal Sikorski, representatives of the Polish Government-in-Exile. Sikorski was a pleasant little man with an ingratiating smile; Wajda was dour and held his drink in a black-gloved hand. Marion was delighted to speak her native language again and began chattering happily.

Thyssen turned to Beth and said softly, "Well, I can see there is not much for you here, unless you speak Polish." He gazed at her hopefully.

"Don't worry," she said. "I'll be fine. You probably want to speak with the Major alone." She smiled at Snyder and went to get a drink. Thyssen looked after her appreciatively, then took Snyder's arm and led him upstairs to a sitting room. He closed the door and regarded Snyder uneasily. "I am sorry to have you come all the way over here, but there is some urgency."

"I thought so. Problems with the Japanese?"

"Yes. I suspect compromise. And I am not sure if it is at your end or at the consulate. Therefore, I find the telephone risky."

"I don't understand."

"The Japanese are using delaying tactics. I have been told they need more time to get their people together."

"What's unusual about that?"

Thyssen's brow furrowed. "When I first approached them, they felt as much urgency as I did. Now suddenly they are hesitating."

Snyder said coldly, "They don't have time to fool around. The test is set for Monday. Can you iron things out over the weekend?"

Thyssen sighed. "I will try. But we shall all have to be careful."

Beth sat on the couch, sipping her second drink, feeling left out and uneasy. She couldn't understand what was being said, but Marion was growing belligerent as she argued with the two Poles.

In their native tongue they had brought Marion up to date on what was happening in Poland. She had been shocked to learn that they were fanatically opposed to the Lublin government and to all Russian influence. She listened politely for a long time but at last couldn't help herself.

"The Russians saved my family," she blurted out in Polish. "I will not stand here and listen to you repeat such lies about them."

Wajda's face clouded over. "You have been out of the country a long time, Miss Cypulski," he said hotly. "Much has happened that you know nothing about. I assure you, Russian ferocity surpasses that of the Nazis. Poland has been victimized as much by one as the other."

"Not true," Marion insisted.

"No?" said Sikorski. "And what did the American newspapers have to say about Katyn?"

She glared at him impatiently. "The Nazis were responsible for that!"

Sikorski shook his head vigorously. "I beg your pardon. The *Russians* massacred thousand of Polish officers in the forest at Katyn and tried to make it *look* like the work of the Nazis!"

"I don't believe that," said Marion.

"Then what about Warsaw," Wajda interjected. "*There* was a masterpiece of deceit."

"What are you talking about?"

"I see you need a history lesson," Wajda said, putting down his drink and gesturing with his black-gloved hand. Bitterness crept into his voice. "In August of last year the Russians were camped on the banks of the Wista. The Germans pulled back from Warsaw to regroup and we thought it was a rout. In meetings with the Home Army staff, the Russians encouraged us to rise up and drive out the Germans, promising total support. We attacked. The Germans instantly brought up reinforcements and we were cut to pieces! And where was the great Red Army? Still sitting on their—" He paused, his face black with remembered rage. "We later learned that Stalin wanted to rid himself of all Poles he felt were unfriendly to the Lublin Communist government. So he ordered his Army to stay where they were and do nothing, to let the Germans annihilate everybody! Eventually those who were left had to surrender and were shot by the Nazis. The Russians waited until all the dirty work had been done for them, *then* they crossed the river and took the city, *liberating* it."

Marion was incredulous. She looked from one to the other, then said, "You're wrong. You're absolutely wrong!"

"We were there," Sikorski said quietly. "We were among the few who managed to escape."

Marion's eyes shot around wildly. "But I never heard any of this!"

"And what makes you think the Russians would admit to such a deed?" said Wajda. "Besides, they think nothing of the Polish people."

"Yes, they do," Marion said hoarsely. "My mother is in a resettlement camp near Moscow. The Russians have been wonderful to her. My brothers fought in the Red Army in an all-Polish unit!"

Sikorski scoffed. "Those groups. Sympathetic to Moscow. You know what happened to them? They became the nucleus of the Russian takeover."

Marion frowned. "That's not possible."

"What's the name of this refugee camp?"

"Sobinka," she replied. "It's a town about a hundred miles east of Moscow."

Sikorski nodded again. "I know Sobinka. There is no camp there," he said flatly.

Marion was suddenly panicked. "*You're wrong!*" she insisted. "I have letters from my mother. From Sobinka!"

Sikorski sipped his drink and regarded Marion sympathetically. "I would be happy to check out your story. Would you give me the names of your family?" She told him her father's name and Sikorski looked up with interest. "I remember him."

"He was executed by the Nazis," Marion said.

Sikorski took out a small leather case and handed her a card. "Why don't you take this and give me your phone number? I promise to get back to you."

Marion hesitated, then gave him her number.

Wajda tried to make up for his earlier antagonism. "Please understand," he said, "that we both hope you're right and that your family is safe, wherever they are. But you are wrong about the good intentions of the Russians. They always have reasons for what they do." He held up his black-gloved hand. "This was not a present from the Germans. Oh no—a *Russian* agent caught me in *London*. He stuck my hand in a fire as a lesson. And it was: I learned never to believe you are safe."

Marion stared at the glove. Her confidence completely shaken, she made her excuses to the two men and turned to find Beth.

"Are you all right, Marion?" Beth came to her side quickly. "What's been going on?"

"Nothing . . ." Marion mumbled. "I'm sorry. We talked so much . . . I'm a little dizzy . . ."

"Do you want to leave?"

Marion rubbed her forehead. "I'm getting a headache."

Beth got her a cup of coffee. By that time Snyder had returned and she suggested they take Marion home.

They drove back to the Nunnery in silence, Marion's gloom hanging like a pall in the car. Snyder kept glancing at Beth, hoping for elaboration, but she ignored him. She fidgeted and kept asking Marion how she was feeling. Snyder parked the car and escorted them into the building.

Marion thanked Snyder for the evening and hurried away.

He turned to Beth at the stairwell. "Can I buy you a drink someplace?"

"Not in Berkeley," she said. "Remember it's a college town, dry."

"Too bad."

"Why don't you come upstairs? I'll see what I have."

"What? No chaperons?"

She smiled and shrugged. "Coming or not?"

"Since you put it so nicely, sure."

Snyder sat on Beth's sofa and worked on a brandy. She took a chair a few feet away and sat demurely.

"What's Marion's problem?" he asked.

"I haven't the faintest idea. She was talking to those Poles and something upset her. I don't know what."

"Is she always this moody?"

"Sometimes. She probably misses Lasch."

Snyder frowned. Again he was forced to wonder about Marion Cypulski's stability.

"How's your father?" Beth asked.

"Fine. Keeps asking about you. I think he liked that kiss. Like father, like son," he said lightly.

"Not tonight, P.T. I think I'm getting a headache, too."

"Oh. Must be an epidemic." Snyder finished his drink, reached for his cap and followed her to the door. She gave him a peck on the cheek. He faced her, wanting more. She permitted him a single lingering kiss, then said good night.

He stared at the closed door and wondered how much of this arm's length relationship he could take.

July 14: Berkeley

Snyder followed the lunch tray into Nakamura's room, carrying a large box under his arm. He waited until the MP had cleared out and Nakamura had begun eating.

"Happy Bastille Day, Major," said Nakamura. "Care for some tea?"

"No, thanks. How are they treating you?"

"Very well." He eyed the box curiously. "Thanks for these," he said, pointing to a stack of newspapers. "It's going badly for Japan, isn't it?"

"Yes."

Nakamura lifted a sandwich and said, "Am I going to observe the test?"

"We're leaving tomorrow."

Nakamura nodded gratefully. "How did you arrange permission for a Japanese officer?" he asked with a smile.

"I didn't." Snyder opened the box and held up a khaki uniform. Nakamura stared at it. "Four forty-second Combat Team, Nisei Division, United States Army. I had the insignia flown in from Washington last night. My mother sewed it on this morning."

Nakamura was impressed. "Please thank your mother for me. What rank am I?"

"Captain. Sorry, best I could do. Let's see if it fits."

Nakamura stood up and Snyder held the uniform against his body. "Looks pretty close." He put the uniform on the cot, then took a large envelope from the box and spilled its contents on the desk. "ID papers, orders and some background in case we're questioned. You are now Captain Ben Ichikawa. Your father was a fisherman from San Pedro."

"Where is he now?"

"Manzanar. An internment camp—never mind where."
Snyder sat down across from him. "Now look," he said,
"I'm giving you a loaded gun, so to speak—uniform, papers, all this—I hope you won't decide to do anything
funny."

"Will you take my word?"

"I'll have to." Snyder got up and indicated the uniform.
"It's no disgrace to wear that, you know. The Nisei Division fought in Europe and won more purple hearts than
any other unit in the entire American Army."

"While their families were held in internment camps,"
Nakamura finished. "I find that very ironic."

"It's a tough life," Snyder said and walked out.

July 15: Europe

The *Augusta* docked at Antwerp and Truman was greeted with military honor guards. From there his party drove to Brussels, then flew on to Berlin. From the plane he watched a landscape carpeted with bombed-out, shattered buildings and brick rubble.

They were met at Gatow Airport by Stimson and Marshall. Accompanied by an MP escort, they drove another nine miles to Potsdam. Once they crossed into the Russian sector, the road was lined on both sides with Red Army soldiers, standing shoulder to shoulder and facing away from the motorcade.

Potsdam, once the seasonal retreat of Germany's movie colony, stood southwest of Berlin at the edge of Lake Griebnitz. The town was untouched by the war and only a short distance from massive devastation.

Truman's party stopped to admire the Cecilienhof Palace, where the conference sessions would be held. The enormous mock-Tudor country home, built in 1917 for the Crown Prince and named after his wife, Princess Cecilie, was a two-story, vine-encrusted architectural hodge-podge constructed around a central courtyard, which was dominated by a flower bed in the shape of the red star. The Russians had decorated all 176 rooms with magnificent furnishings freely liberated from neighboring homes.

The President was driven down to Babelsberg and given quarters in one of several villas assigned to the Americans. After a light supper he retired early, leaving word to be informed the moment any news came in on Trinity.

Stimson and Marshall went for a walk along the tree-lined shore of Lake Griebnitz. Stimson was upset because Truman had cut any mention of retaining the Emperor from the draft ultimatum.

"What did you expect?" asked Marshall.

"I don't know." Stimson brooded quietly, then blurted out, "All that destruction the President flew over today—do you think it might have the right effect on him?"

"I doubt it," said Marshall.

"But if he compares what's already happened here to what we'll be doing to Japan—it's ghastly."

"Again, Henry, I don't think he's making comparisons."

Stimson sagged perceptibly. "George, I feel we're being bounced in two directions at once. Maybe it's time we told him about Big Stick."

"Why now?"

"Because once he gets a taste of Joe Stalin, it could be too late for us. He might be intimidated into using the bomb—just to get even."

"If we have to tell him, let's at least pick the right time." Stimson began to protest, but Marshall silenced him. "We're ahead of ourselves. Let's see what happens at Trinity tomorrow."

Stimson shoved his hands into his pockets and stared wistfully at the serenity of Lake Griebnitz.

July 15: New Mexico

As a precaution he hadn't told Nakamura about, Snyder was carrying a holstered Colt .45 in his briefcase. But by the time they arrived at Biggs Field in the northwest corner of Texas, Snyder had lost his anxiety over Nakamura's disguise. "Captain Ichikawa" came through with no trouble at all.

Snyder checked out a Jeep. Since thunderheads were building up, he took the time to requisition ponchos as well. Once off the base, they set out on Route 54, up into New Mexico, through Alamogordo, then west on 380. Nakamura sat with his hands braced around his seat, watching the scenery.

"I'm still curious," said Snyder. "How did you end up in uniform?"

"Because I have a big mouth," said Nakamura.

"I wouldn't have guessed that from *our* conversations."

"I'm very eloquent when I feel strongly about something."

He fell silent and Snyder glanced at him again. "You're still not answering my question."

Nakamura sighed. "I went home two months before Pearl Harbor . . . to see about my father. I was too late. He died three days before I arrived. As the eldest son, I had to stay and handle some family affairs. So I was caught there when our planes attacked Pearl Harbor. I should have expected it. From the time I got home—even on the boat—there was so much talk of war, only a man deaf and dumb could have missed it. So I couldn't get out.

The only one I could turn to was Dr. Nishina. He offered me my old job back and I took it. But I was angry and kept shooting my mouth off. I disapproved of the war and didn't hesitate to say so."

"They commissioned you a major for that?"

"You don't understand Japanese thinking. My family had influence. I was given a choice—either submit to sentencing as a traitor or be put into a uniform and sent where I could be killed with honor."

"Guadalcanal?" asked Snyder.

"After China. I disappointed a lot of superiors. Somehow I managed to dodge all the bullets."

"That sounds crazy."

"Yes." Nakmura grinned. "But I lead a charmed life."

Snyder nodded. "Then this whole business about being dead in your country is just so much talk?"

Nakamura sobered. "No," he said. "It's all too true. No one in Japan will welcome me with open arms."

"What about your family?"

Nakamura frowned and stared straight ahead unhappily. "I've written home many times but never had an answer. Not once in two-and-a-half years. Six months ago a Red Cross representative advised me to stop trying. My family was no longer interested in hearing from me. I was officially declared dead. It's not just in the mind, Major. They made it *fact*."

Snyder was silent a moment then said, "Maybe when it's all over . . ."

Nakamura shrugged.

"Oh, come on, Major, you don't have it so rough," Snyder said. "You're still alive. No matter what anybody thinks, you've survived this war. And you got off Guadalcanal in one piece, which is more than I can say for my kid brother."

Nakamura glanced at him.

"He had everything to live for," Snyder continued in bitter reflection. "Nobody sent him there to die, but that's what happened. As for you—you're goddamned lucky."

Nakamura grimaced. "Major, there's all kinds of luck. I'm sorry about your brother. I hope you don't blame me."

"No," Snyder said hoarsely. "I don't blame anybody."

Halfway between Bingham and San Antonio, Snyder pulled the Jeep off the road and drove behind some rocks. He shut off the engine and gauged the sky. "Our chances of getting through are better if it's raining," he said.

"Getting through what?" Nakamura asked.

Snyder didn't reply. He hadn't yet told Nakamura *how* they were going to get within range of Trinity.

The rain began shortly after nightfall. Snyder raised the canvas top and screwed in the side curtains. He and Nakamura huddled in the Jeep in the midst of a fierce summer storm, replete with massive peals of thunder and sizzling forks of lightning that illuminated the barren landscape.

According to Lasch the test was scheduled for 4 A.M. That allowed them plenty of time to get into position. About 11 P.M. Snyder started the engine and headed the Jeep back onto the highway. He drove west, passing one of the dozens of military dirt roads and glimpsing a barrier, two trucks and the huddled forms of MPs standing out in the rain.

Snyder whizzed past, trying to recall from memory the security layout at this end of the desert. The highway was a two-lane blacktop raised about six feet off the desert floor, shouldered with gravel and graded down in a sharp slope to a two-foot gully, which came up again and flattened out into desert. The rain made visibility difficult for the perimeter patrols, but it could also turn the desert into a quagmire. If they went off the highway at any place other than a turnoff—which would be heavily guarded—they risked getting stuck in the gully. Snyder looked off to the right and in a flash of lightning saw water rushing down the base of the road.

He kept on, past another patrol. In an Army Jeep he wouldn't be challenged until he crossed the perimeter. He was beginning to remember the area: from the next patrol on the checkpoints were much closer together.

"Hang on," he told Nakamura. He slowed down, double-clutched into second, then turned the wheel to the left and went off the road onto the gravel shoulder. The Jeep plunged down the slope at a forty-five-degree angle. Nakamura held on tightly and fought the lean. Snyder turned sharply to cut across the gully and felt the rear wheels slew around, grabbing for traction on the gravel. The front wheels hit the water and it splashed up on the windshield.

Nakamura ducked. "What the hell are you doing?"

Snyder ignored him, working the gas pedal and the clutch, fighting to maintain traction and to nose up out of the water. The front wheels spun and slid back. He peered through the darkness ahead, looking for something he could hook the winch cable to. The Jeep rocked back and forth and the engine surged. The rear wheels caught and shoved forward. The Jeep shot out of the water and jack-rabbited up the other slope. They were on level ground again.

Snyder eased up on the clutch and the Jeep lurched off again. They bounded across the desert in butt-slapping rhythm. Snyder recklessly aimed for the nearest crest line and went over in a spray of mud. Once on the other side and out of view of the highway, he slowed to a crawl and handed Nakamura the map.

Nakamura opened it shakily and spread it under the flashlight. Snyder glanced at it, jabbed a finger into the center and said, "We're here . . . and there's Trinity . . . so we want to go here—Oscura Peak—the foothills on the west side." He moved his finger along and Nakamura pinched the map to mark the spot. "That'll put us about twelve miles from point zero."

"Are we inside the test area now?" asked Nakamura.

"More or less. We've got about fifteen miles to go."

"We seem to be avoiding the checkpoints."

"You noticed that?"

"Yes. Would you mind telling me why?"

"Simple. You're not posing as Captain Ichikawa to satisfy the curiosity of these guards, because it wouldn't satisfy them at all. This uniform was just to get you out of Berkeley and on a plane."

"You mean we're not authorized to be here?"

"Right."

"What if we get stopped?"

"You'll probably be shot as a spy."

Nakamura swore in Japanese.

"Especially if you talk like that," said Snyder.

"Major, you're crazy."

"Just remember—this was your idea."

Nakamura's jaw clamped shut and he stared straight ahead past the swishing windshield wipers. Two tiny points of light appeared ahead of them and grew larger.

"Company," Snyder muttered.

"What do we do?"

"We can't dodge them. Have to bluff. You get in the back and lie down. You'll find a tarp. Cover yourself. Keep your mouth shut and don't move."

Nakamura obeyed, slipping between the seats and tumbling into the back. He was down and covered in seconds.

Snyder watched the beams grow larger. Suddenly a bright spotlight stabbed through the rain, blinding him. He stopped and waited for the other vehicle to come alongside. They kept the spot glued on him and drew up within four feet. Though he couldn't see past the light, he knew they would have guns trained on him. That was a regulation he had personally initiated.

A voice growled at him. "Shut that thing off and get out slowly, Mac, and keep your hands where we can see them."

Snyder set the brake, opened the side curtain and stepped out.

"Advance and be recognized," the voice called.

Snyder took two steps to the side of the Jeep, his hands half-upraised. He was locked in the spotlight. Then he heard a familiar voice:

"Jesus Christ, Snyder—what the hell are you doing here?"

The spotlight flipped off, replaced by a much weaker flashlight. Snyder blinked and tried to make out who was in the Jeep. He saw three figures under the canvas top: the driver, holding a carbine leveled at him, a radio man in the back, also with a carbine, and an officer in the right front seat. He recognized the officer.

"Taylor?" asked Snyder.

"Yes, sir, Captain. It's okay, Corporal, I know this man. Come on around this side, sir."

Snyder walked around the front of the Jeep and stuck his head under the canvas top. Rain splashed off the back of his poncho. Taylor looked him over, suspicion flooding back. "I thought you were in Washington," he said.

"Can I speak to you alone for a minute, Steve?"

Taylor hesitated, then said, "Sure," and climbed out.

"And bring that flashlight," Snyder added.

They walked behind the Jeep, out of earshot and out of sight. Snyder's heart was pounding and he fought for perfect control as he turned to face Taylor, who repeated, "What *are* you doing out here, Captain?"

Snyder opened the top of his poncho, exposing his gold oak leaves. "Major," he said.

Taylor whistled. "Jesus. Congratulations." He watched Snyder dig further into the poncho and pull out a cellophane-wrapped packet of orders.

"Read the top sheet," said Snyder, "then forget it."

Taylor put his light on the packet. The top sheet under the cellophane was an order signed by General Groves, authorizing Major Snyder to attempt to penetrate the security of Trinity. It specifically prohibited any interference with the performance of his duties.

"Do you understand what this means?" said Snyder.

"You're checking up?"

"Correct. From the outside. I was transferred to Washington as a cover. They've assigned me to try to break through the whole apparatus we've set up here."

Taylor's mouth opened. "Jesus, sir, that's pretty slick." He shook his head over the lengths to which Security could go. "Well—we caught you." He grinned.

"You missed the point, Lieutenant."

"What's that?"

"I got through the lines."

Taylor blanched. "Yes, sir. You sure did. Should I radio Colonel Tully and inform him we've got a hole?"

"Negative," said Snyder. "Don't radio anybody. No one is supposed to know that I've been here until I make my report to General Groves. Is that clear?"

"Yes, sir."

"You've stopped me, so you did fine. But security in general is not what we thought it was. Let's get in the Jeep and have a look at the map."

For ten more minutes, Snyder crouched in the patrol

Jeep with Lieutenant Taylor and went over the map of the Jornada del Muerto valley, pointing out imaginary holes in the perimeter that would keep Taylor busy the rest of the night. Taylor swallowed the whole thing but wanted to know, "What am I supposed to tell Colonel Tully if I can't mention that you were here?"

"Very simple," said Snyder. "*You* found all this."

Taylor brightened and said he would take care of everything.

Snyder dashed back to his Jeep, started the engine, waved and took off. His nerves were high. He'd pulled the bluff but wasn't sure if he could do it again. Poor Taylor. It was a good thing he hadn't looked under the top sheet in that packet: the rest of the papers were duplicates of "Captain Ichikawa's" orders.

Then he remembered Nakamura. "How are you doing back there?" he said.

"Getting intimate with the floorboards," Nakamura replied. "I take it there's not going to be any firing squad."

"Not yet. You can have your seat back."

Nakamura climbed forward and looked straight ahead. His face was covered in sweat. "I won't ask how you did it."

"That's good, because I never reveal trade secrets."

Snyder drove south slowly for a full hour, without any lights, hoping the rain would conceal his presence and wondering how he was going to get out of here in the morning. Under a flash of lightning he saw that they were moving up into the rocky foothills along the western side of the mountain.

Oscura Peak rose to over 8600 feet on his left. He knew that Trinity was on a line due west from the peak. Snyder found it difficult to gauge distance in the darkness and rain, but a mile or so either way would make no difference. He could assume they would be safe here—at least as safe as the observers at base camp. If they could risk it, so could he.

Snyder kept the Jeep hugging the mountainside until he came to a little box canyon. He pulled to a stop. They got out in the pounding rain and carefully scaled the slippery side of a forty-foot rock. At the top they flattened out and

Snyder indicated the broad expanse of desert stretching into the west. "It's out there somewhere," he said. "They won't have any lights until just before the test, so that's how we'll know when she's going off."

It was nearly 1 A.M. and they still had a long wait ahead. "Will they hold off until the rain has stopped?" asked Nakamura.

Snyder nodded. "We'll come back up later." He tapped Nakamura's shoulder and motioned downward. They climbed down and returned to the Jeep. Huddling inside, Snyder opened C rations and a Thermos of coffee. They sat quietly eating and listening to the rain rap on the canvas top. Snyder was worn out from the drive. Despite the coffee, he dozed off, confident that Nakamura was too consumed with curiosity to make a bid for freedom.

At three thirty Nakamura shook Snyder awake and they went out again into the rain. Wearily they struggled back up the rock, this time with two pairs of smoked glasses that Snyder had brought along in his briefcase. The weather turned worse just as they reached the top, with thunder crashing around them and lightning stabbing the desert floor.

Snyder cursed to himself. "Let's hope it's the storm's last gasp!" he shouted. "Otherwise they'll postpone it and we'll be looking for a hotel. I don't want to be here again tomorrow night."

"Isn't there any way we can find out what they're going to do?"

Snyder shook his head. "Our Jeep doesn't have a radio. If it weren't for this weather, we could probably hear whatever's coming over their PA. This mountain we're backed up against should be a perfect sound reflector!"

Nakamura peered through the rain. "I can't make anything out," he said.

"It's there. Don't worry."

Nakamura clucked skeptically. "So far all I've seen is some men in a Jeep. You could still be putting on quite a show."

Snyder glared at him. "I'd love to take you in for the grand tour, but when that bomb goes off, frankly no one knows what's going to happen. I don't want to find out the hard way."

"What *is* out there, Major?"

"The bomb is on a platform at the top of a tower, then about a half-mile away there's a steel cylinder six stories high—supposed to represent the shell of a skyscraper. There's no siding, just the steel frame." Snyder described the concrete bunkers at the control stations and how the communications system worked. He talked at a low shout until nearly four o'clock, then his voice trailed off as both men noticed the storm's intensity rapidly diminishing.

They slipped on the smoked glasses and lay on the rock, peering across the desert, waiting, as the rain trickled to a stop.

S-10,000 was a reinforced concrete bunker, the control station 10,000 yards south of point zero. The single entrance was doorless and faced away from the blast site. The low room was filled with physicists, technicians and Army personnel, most of whom were psychiatrists brought in by Groves to keep the scientists calm.

Lasch waited nervously for the countdown. Oppenheimer was tense and irritable. Several times in the night he had exploded at his colleagues over some minor hitch in the proceedings. More than once Lasch had watched General Groves forcibly take him out for a walk in the rain to cool him off. The postponements had brought everyone in the bunker to a fever pitch of anticipation. At three thirty Groves and Oppenheimer had decided to postpone until five thirty. At 4 A.M., they stared out the observation slit and saw the rain end. Now their decision became firm. Groves passed the word via the PA and FM linkups to all control stations, vehicles and the base camp.

Samuel Allison took over the microphones to begin the countdown on Oppenheimer's signal. The mood in the bunker picked up.

The device was in place in its iron shed atop the tower, while Joseph McKibben lay on a bedroll in the sand below. He was head of the arming party, the last group still remaining at point zero. After fully arming the mechanism, save for a few last-minute electrical connections, McKibben had stayed behind while George Kistiakowsky, Ken Bainbridge and Jack Hubbard roamed the Trinity area with a couple of Army sergeants, sending weather balloons aloft. McKibben had been alone since midnight, snatching fitful intervals of sleep.

At four forty-five Bainbridge shook McKibben awake and said, "Better get out of here. We're going to shoot this thing."

"Jesus. Thanks for telling me," said McKibben. He rose, tossed his bedroll into the back of Bainbridge's Jeep, then went over to throw his final switches. He snapped on an immense floodlight, which could be seen at all the control stations; it signaled that the device was ready for firing. The tower was starkly illuminated against the clouded sky.

McKibben and the others jumped into three separate Jeeps and headed for S-10,000 at a cautious thirty-five miles per hour.

On their rock at Oscura Peak, Snyder and Nakamura shook the last raindrops off their ponchos and froze when they saw the floodlight snap on in the west. Seen from their vantage point, the detonation tower rose like a tiny needle in the center of a vast expanse of damp sand.

"That's it," whispered Snyder, checking his watch. "They'll fire anytime now. Stay down."

Nakamura obediently flattened against the rock.

When he saw the signal light go on, Groves turned to Oppenheimer and Lasch and shook hands with them. "Break a leg," he said, then hurried outside to a Jeep and drove south to the base camp at ten miles from point zero. Lasch stood at the open doorway and watched him go, wondering how he could remain so cool knowing about Big Stick. Lasch had decided for himself that Groves was the man behind Snyder, but he had refrained from discussing it with the General, still smarting from the last time he had crossed Snyder. Groves was the head of S-1, in command of Security, and if he wanted to talk about Big Stick, let *him* bring it up.

McKibben and his party drove up and hurried into the

blockhouse. By prior arrangement the last man to leave the bomb site had the privilege of firing it. McKibben took over the control panels. Allison began the countdown at twenty minutes to zero and made announcements thereafter at five-minute intervals. McKibben checked the photography setup and had the cameraman turn floodlamps on the dials and gauges so that measurements could be recorded on film. Around him men were posted to measure the blast and shock waves, spectrography, neutron emissions, gamma rays and nuclear efficiency. Navy photographers had cameras trained through the observation slits.

As the countdown progressed, Oppenheimer ordered everyone to lie on the ground inside the bunker, face down, bodies turned away from the blast, hands over closed eyes. Lasch got down next to Oppenheimer and placed a reassuring hand on his arm.

At base camp General Groves followed the same procedure, lying alongside Vannevar Bush and James Conant. Hans Bethe painted his face with suntan oil. Enrico Fermi tore up bits of paper and stuffed them into his hand. Only Klaus Fuchs remained upright, wearing smoked goggles and gazing toward point zero in the distance.

It was still dark, almost a half-hour before sunrise.

"Three minutes to zero." Allison's flat voice echoed across the desert, reverberating off the mountain behind Snyder and Nakamura. The Japanese physicist had finally cast aside any lingering doubts that this might be a show for his benefit. The distant PA made it real.

Between the counts the silence was heavy and oppressive, the glow from the test site ominous. Snyder dug his toes into a cut in the rock and lay frozen like a pointer, concentrating on the pool of light twelve miles away.

The countdown turned from minutes into seconds.

"There is a danger," Nakamura said quietly.

Snyder didn't hear him the first time. He had to repeat it. "What?" Snyder said hoarsely. "What danger?"

"Atmospheric ignition."

"What's that?"

"If something within this nuclear reaction interacts with the atmosphere, this whole desert could become an oven."

"Now you tell me—"

"Ten . . . nine . . . eight . . ." came the countdown, the numbers echoing, rolling over each other until Snyder could no longer keep track.

"NOW!" yelled the voice.

A brilliant yellow flash lit up the desert.

Instinctively Snyder and Nakamura dropped their heads and shielded their eyes. Even so, they were conscious of a blinding glare. They looked up in time to see a new sun rising from the desert floor, an expanding hemisphere of bright yellow, which swiftly became a ball of fire shooting into the sky, surrounded by a blue glow of intense radiation. It climbed upward, clawing for the heavens, sucking up tons of dust to form a thick brown pillar. The blue glow vanished, replaced by a dirty cotton-candy cloud of gray-white smoke.

Snyder looked down at a blanket of dust churning out in all directions and saw the shock wave rushing across the flatlands, blowing mud and brush before it. A gust of hot air slammed into them like a giant hand, lifting Nakamura from his perch. Snyder grabbed his arm and pulled him down. Around them pebbles skittered down the rock slope. A few feet away, a boulder was dislodged and rolled angrily toward them, hit a protrusion and flew over their shoulders.

A thunderous roar crashed over them and echoed across the box canyon. A boiling cloud of kaleidoscopic colors spread outward at the top of the pillar, forming the cap of a mushroom. The cloud fed on itself, exploding again from within as more material was ignited.

Snyder thought of Nakamura's warning about atmospheric ignition; he wanted to turn and run, to avoid a rain of fire from the sky. But it never appeared. For what seemed minutes, matter continued to soar upwards, feeding the boiling cauldron some ten thousand feet up.

Nakamura rose to his feet and stared at it.

Inside S-10,000 most of the observers were awed, some were wild with joy. General Farrell, Groves' representative, slapped Allison on the back and yelled, "What a wonderful thing that you could count backwards at a time like this!"

Oppenheimer had become tense at the moment of detonation, then seemed to relax into serene relief. Gradually, the observers got up and looked through the observation slits. Searchlights stabbed at the huge spectral cloud in the dawn sky. Oppenheimer led Lasch and a small daring group outside, where they climbed to the blockhouse roof to stare at the spectacle in the north.

Like most of the others, Lasch was speechless, and more than a little terrified.

In the trenches at base camp, Fermi dropped his fistful of torn paper and tried to gauge the distance they were carried by the blast wave.

Klaus Fuchs watched impassively, still standing, his coat torn open by the roaring wind.

Groves and Conant clasped each other in a relieved handshake.

The effects diminished and the cloud spread out to form a radioactive umbrella over the desert. Snyder and Nakamura looked for the remains of the test site. As the dust rained down and settled, they realized there was nothing left to see.

"I'll be goddamned," Snyder said, rising to a crouch on the rock and staring grimly at the awesome panorama.

"Or the damned of God," Nakamura said above the diminishing roar. "Not an easy distinction, Major."

PART 3

PART-3

July 16: Potsdam

Stimson and Marshall were eating lunch in the Secretary's quarters at Babelsberg when a cable arrived from Under-Secretary George Harrison in Washington. Stimson stared at it, then read it to Marshall:

> TOP SECRET
> URGENT
> WAR 32887
> FOR COLONEL KYLES EYES ONLY
> FROM HARRISON FOR MR. STIMSON
>
> OPERATED ON THIS MORNING. DIAGNOSIS NOT YET COMPLETE BUT RESULTS SEEM SATISFACTORY AND ALREADY EXCEED EXPECTATIONS. LOCAL PRESS RELEASE NECESSARY AS INTEREST EXTENDS GREAT DISTANCE. DR. GROVES PLEASED. HE RETURNS TOMORROW. I WILL KEEP YOU POSTED.

"The damned thing works," said Stimson.

When Truman returned from a tour of bombed-out Berlin, Stimson was waiting for him with the cable. The President was elated by the news.

"We need only one more thing," Truman said happily. "For Stalin to show up and tell us he can't get into the war on August eighth."

Stimson seized on that slim thread. "If that turns out to

be the case, Mr. President, we really *should* consider warning the Japanese."

"Possibly," said Truman, unwilling to discuss it further. "Why don't you take it up with Byrnes tomorrow morning?" He clapped Stimson on the shoulder. "Wonderful news, Henry. Goddamn, that's wonderful!"

July 16: Berkeley

"He's not here, Dr. Lasch," Beth said, glancing across the hall into Snyder's empty office. "I don't know where he is. Can I give him a message?"

Lasch hesitated on the phone. "Yes, tell him it was successful beyond our wildest dreams."

She felt a surge of excitement. "When?" she asked.

"This morning. Five thirty. Tell Snyder I'll see him as soon as I get back. And let Marion know."

"I will." She hung up. Fulbright was standing nearby, staring at her questioningly. She gave him the news and he sat down abruptly, surprised.

"My God," he said, "I never believed it would work."

"Neither did I," Beth said quietly. She got up. "I have to go find Marion."

"Uh—she called in sick."

"When?"

"This morning."

"Why didn't you tell me?" she said crossly.

Fulbright stiffened, watched her pick up the phone, then rose and walked back to his office.

"Marion?" said Beth. "I understand you're not feeling well."

"I'm okay . . . I just . . . I didn't want to infect anybody . . . I'm staying home . . ." She sounded clogged and stuffy.

"Can I bring you anything?"

"No!" she said firmly. "I just need some rest . . . have to think . . ." She trailed off.

"I just spoke with Dr. Lasch," Beth said. "The test was successful."

Marion was strangely silent for a moment. "That's wonderful. Did he say when he'd be back?"

"No." Beth sensed something wrong and wanted to pursue it, but Marion ended the conversation abruptly.

"Got to go. Thanks for calling, Beth."

She hung up and Beth leaned back in concern. She didn't have long to ponder it. The phone began ringing and she was plunged into work.

Fulbright sat in his office, contemplating this latest development. He had told himself all along that the bomb would never work, so what did it matter if he made a little money at the expense of the Russians? Who would have cared had he spied on an unsuccessful project? But now he was faced with harsh reality: he had been wrong. There was danger in continuing to supply what they asked for—the danger of discovery. He sat and weighed the consequences grimly, then the thought of the money ate away at his fears. Finally he regained his courage, reached for the phone and called Bowen.

July 16: Trinity

Snyder and Nakamura took advantage of the continued turmoil in the sky to scramble down off the rock, get back in their Jeep and drive out the way they had come in. In a race with the sunrise, Snyder tore recklessly through mud and scrub brush.

Nakamura sat stonily, looking ahead and clutching the handbar.

Snyder's mind worked feverishly, replaying what they had seen. He had never conceived of anything so awesome, so terrifyingly destructive. A bomb like this dropped on a city would mean instant obliteration for everything in a vast area. He was convinced that even Bliss, Kirby and Willard, with their specialized knowledge, had severely underestimated its power.

He glanced at Nakamura and tried to read his thoughts.

Nakamura turned his head slowly. "How soon will we leave for Japan?" he asked.

"Think you can face Nishina now?"

"Yes. But when can we go?"

"There's still a lot to put together—"

Nakamura leaned forward and caught Snyder's eye. "Major, we don't have time. I don't know whether we will be successful, but the sooner we try, the better."

"Jesus Christ, there's a point where reason has to take over. Japan may be run by fanatics, but they can't be blind as well."

"You still have a lot to learn," Nakamura said impatiently.

"For instance?"

"Using that bomb on Japan might prolong the war rather than end it."

"How? Japan is already beaten! You can't mean your Emperor will convince his entire nation to commit suicide!"

Nakamura swore in Japanese. "That's the difference!" he shouted over the engine roar. "Your people fight for a principle—mine fight for a god!"

Snyder jerked a thumb over his shoulder and said sharply, "That was just a *test*! We're in *production* on those things!"

"Will you destroy all of Japan?"

Snyder glared at him. "We can argue about this in our old age. Right now let's get back to Berkeley."

Nakamura fell silent and looked at the sun rising hotly in the east. The immense mushroom cloud had flattened out at the top but still had not dissipated. It hung in the sky like a malevolent shroud.

Snyder raced up the gravel incline to the highway then floored the gas pedal, heading back to Biggs Field.

It was late in the afternoon when they reached Nakamura's quarters and shut the door. On the drive in from Hamilton Field, Snyder had stopped to pick up a bottle of bourbon. He broke the seal and said to Nakamura, "We're going to get drunk."

Nakamura started to take off the Nisei uniform. "I suppose you'll want this back."

"Afraid so," said Snyder, pouring two glasses and adding a little water. "Sorry there's no ice."

"That's all right." Nakamura took the glass.

Snyder hesitated, about to make a toast. "Hell, what have we got to drink to?"

"A fast plane to Japan."

They drank to that. Nakamura made a face.

"Bad stuff?" said Snyder.

"No. My first drink in nearly three years."

"Is that so?" Snyder poured him some more, then leaned against the windowsill and stared at the bars. Nakamura slid back on the cot and with one hand removed his trousers.

Snyder raised his glass again. "Good-bye, Captain Ichikawa."

Nakamura put his glass down and folded the uniform carefully, placing it on the desk. Then he dropped back onto the cot in his shorts. "Interesting," he said. "You must have gotten a lot of propaganda mileage out of having Japanese fight for you."

"It wasn't done for that reason."

Nakamura smiled. "Well, I don't know of many Americans fighting for Japan."

Snyder drained his drink. "What about me?" he said and reached for the bottle again.

"They'll probably make you an honorary samurai."

"No kidding? I can't wait."

Nakamura smiled at the irony. "One of the things Japanese respect," he said, "is the grand gesture. You're giving us this chance. We mustn't waste it." He raised his glass again and said, "I salute an honorable man."

Snyder shook his head. "Don't drink to me."

Nakamura looked at him quizzically.

Snyder lurched away from the window, feeling the effects of the liquor. "I didn't want this job," he said. "I knew it would be a headache. Especially later. Your part in it is cut and dried. I'll be the one left facing the flak."

"What do you mean?"

"Some people are convinced the bomb should be used."

"Are you?"

Snyder swirled his drink, reluctant to carry this further. "Don't worry," he said. "We'll get you to Japan."

"Major Snyder, it's important that I know how you feel."

"No. It's what I do that counts."

Nakamura continued to look at him. Snyder went back to the desk and put down his glass. "Want me to leave the bottle?"

"No. You might need it. To take the edge off your conscience." He leaned forward on the cot. "Think of human beings, Snyder. Never mind the color of their skin or the shape of their eyes. People are going to be killed unless we do something to stop this madness. Your feelings matter to me if they're going to stand in the way of what we have to do."

"Who says they will?" Snyder smiled. He left the bottle, picked up the Nisei uniform and went to the door. "See you later," he said, and left.

When he returned to his office, it was five thirty and the floor had already cleared out. He sent a coded cable to Bud Veneck in Washington, instructing him to start the wheels turning.

Then he went down to his quarters in Security and collapsed on his cot.

July 16: San Francisco

Bowen opened the front door of his townhouse on Nob Hill. "Bernard!" Louise cooed. He brushed his lips gently across her hand. Then he turned to Beth and kissed her lightly on the cheek.

Louise scooted into Bowen's foyer and gasped with amazement. "Oh, Bernard, this is marvelous. Beth, you have to see what he's put in here!"

"Just a few odd pieces from the store," Bowen said modestly. "I'm so happy you both could come. It's not every day my house is graced with the presence of *two* charming ladies."

Beth returned his smile. She found his courtly manner decidedly off-putting, but she had promised Louise to be gracious.

Bernard Bowen ushered them into the living room. Beth was impressed with the selection of antiques about the room: a French armoire, a Victorian sofa, two Jacobean side tables, a carved mahogany-faced fireplace and a collection of delicate china figurines in a glass case. When Bowen opened the front drapes, all of San Francisco seemed spread out before them. Beth went to the window and admired the view. She turned back to Bowen.

"If this were my house, I'd never leave," she said.

"Naturally you're welcome to visit whenever you like." He smiled and took her arm. "Come. We'll have cocktails. Louise, what are you drinking?"

"The usual," Louise replied, floating to the Victorian sofa and settling into it.

Bowen opened a cabinet and displayed a well-stocked

bar. He mixed their drinks and served them from a tray. He led Beth to a chair and sat down between the two women. "I have a wonderful story to tell you," he said. "You know Dabne Hudson?"

"No," Beth said.

"I do and I don't like her," Louise said.

Bowen smiled. "Her father owns half the real estate in this neighborhood. She has always acted as though this entitles her to automatic ownership of anything she wants. She was picked up yesterday morning for shoplifting at Gump's."

Louise shrieked with delight. "That's marvelous!"

Beth looked confused. "It sounds unfortunate to me."

Bowen shrugged. "Not the first time. Up till now she's gotten away with it. Most of the better stores just send the bill to her father. But it seems she's victimized Gump's once too often. The rumor is they're going to press charges."

"Couldn't happen to a more deserving soul," clucked Louise, sipping her Scotch and water.

"Sounds more like a mental disorder than outright theft," Beth said. "I think they call it kleptomania."

"Who cares what they call it?" Louise said. "I call it just deserts."

"Whatever the outcome, I'm sure the family will stand by her," said Bowen, realizing that his little gem had met with a mixed reaction. "I must say I do agree with you, Elizabeth. It's an unfortunate human trait that urges us to take pleasure in other people's troubles. We should be ashamed of ourselves, shouldn't we, Louise?"

"Of course. I'm so ashamed I'll have another drink. Bernard, what happened to the Fowlers?"

"I don't think Elizabeth wants to hear about that, my dear."

"Oh, yes she does," said Louise, heading for the bar. "This one is a lulu, Beth. Go on, tell her."

Bowen sighed to let Beth see that it was unpleasant.

"You might as well," she said. "If you don't tell me, I know Louise will."

"Very well. It's such a sad thing, really. Tommy Fowler is one of the most respected lawyers in the city. Handles some of the best people. He's always been regarded as straitlaced, simon-pure and all that. Has a lovely wife and family, works for charities. . . . But Tommy has developed a slight problem in his advancing years, an inclination that no one ever suspected before . . ." He hesitated.

"He was caught wearing a dress!" Louise crowed. "In his office, of all places. His partner walked in on him." She dropped back on the sofa and grinned at Beth. "I understand it was a terrible outfit."

Beth couldn't help herself. She broke into laughter. "That's awful!" she said.

"Then let me tell you another one," said Bowen, leaning forward and launching into a wealth of juicy stories. For the next hour he had them gasping as he freely imparted gossip and destroyed reputations.

"God, Bernie," Louise howled, "you've got something on everybody!"

"Not at all," Bowen protested. "I know very little about Elizabeth, yet I'm sure there is much to be learned. She's more than just the charming creature we see before us. Isn't that so?"

"You won't get anything out of me," said Beth, giggling and working on her third bourbon and soda.

"Go on, Bernie," Louise implored. "Give it a try. I've seen him do it, Beth—he's wonderful! Should be wearing a turban and sitting behind a crystal ball."

"Please, my dear," Bowen said. "You make me sound like an absolute charlatan. I assure you, Elizabeth, I have no hidden powers, only a modest ability to estimate character. Sort of a hobby. But I would not even attempt it without your complete and total approval."

"Do it, Bernie," said Louise, egging him on.

Beth looked from one to the other, feeling giddy and reckless. She was perfectly willing to agree but just couldn't get the words out.

Louise slid off the sofa and plopped down next to her. "Beth, do you remember that funny little lady who came to our sorority? She was somebody's aunt and she took us one at a time into the study hall and looked into our eyes and told us everything about ourselves. Remember?"

Beth nodded.

"Bernard's better," she said in a stage whisper.

Bowen swirled his drink and gazed at the floor, waiting.

"Oh, hell," Beth said. "Go ahead."

Bowen looked up and smiled benignly. He stroked his chin and studied Beth from all angles. Then he said, "First, I must confess that Louise has told me a few things. But only a few. So, we shall see what I can divine. We know you are from the east, from wealth, from *old money*." He looked into her eyes and she gazed back unwaveringly. "You're self-sufficient, which is unusual for a lady of your background." He moved to the edge of his chair and reached for Beth's hand. "May I?" he said.

She nodded and watched him turn her palm over to scrutinize the lines in her skin. He traced them carefully with his finger. "You're an only child," he said. "You had everything. Clothes, friends, gifts—still you were lonely. Brief period of happiness in your adult life. Brief," he repeated.

Beth said nothing, uneasily trying to maintain a smile. Louise sat next to her, chin in hand, fascinated. Bowen studied Beth's face, then closed his eyes and thought aloud. "Not living at home now . . . family in the east . . . you here . . ." His eyes sprang open. "As far away from home as possible! You don't get along with them, do you? Some great resentment—"

Louise squealed with excitement. Beth looked at her sharply.

"If you had stayed at home," Bowen continued, "you wouldn't be working. Life would be uncomplicated. But for some reason you chose to escape the nest, to leave your parents and their values behind and get as far away as possible." He felt her hand stiffen, so he applied a soothing pressure and delicately stroked the inside of her palm. "I've struck a nerve," he said. "There's something you don't want me to know."

He stopped stroking and held her hand tightly. "Relax." She was still stiff and wanted to pull away, but gradually she gave in and relaxed her muscles. Bowen released the pressure and her hand lay limply in his.

"You're a secretive person," he whispered. She saw his eyes boring into her, dancing with the pleasure of discovery. "A mixed blessing," he went on. "It keeps you from sharing your problems with others. Trust is almost alien to you. It's even evidenced in your work. Why else would you select a job where a closed mouth is an asset? You enjoy the fact that the work is secret—"

Beth was almost lulled by his soothing voice, but the mention of her work set off an inner alarm and abruptly she pulled her hand away.

"What's wrong?" said Louise. "Oh, come on Beth—it's just getting good."

Beth glared at her. "How much have you told him?" She found her words slurring and was suddenly angry for allowing herself to drink too much. "How much have you told him?" she repeated, louder.

Bowen slid his gaze to Louise, offering no defense.

"Nothing!" Louise insisted. "I told you he was good."

"Not that good."

Bowen raised his arms in surrender. "Please, Elizabeth, it's just a game. I didn't mean to upset you. I was just guessing about your background. If I got too close, my apologies. As for your work, we all know you won't talk about it—ergo, secret."

Beth relaxed but still regarded Louise coldly.

"If you will excuse me," Bowen said, "we could use some hors d'oeuvres." He got up and left the room.

Beth moved unsteadily to the window and looked outside, trying to calm her anger. Surprised and hurt, Louise drained her glass and said, "You're awfully touchy."

"And you have a big mouth."

"I swear I haven't told him a thing about your . . . experiences." She giggled.

"Oh, Jesus," said Beth, whirling around. "Don't tell me he's clairvoyant!"

"I don't know *where* he gets it."

"You should—you're sleeping with him!"

Louise blanched. "I told you we weren't—"

"All right!" Beth waved a hand: she didn't want to hear any more. "But whatever your relationship, it doesn't give him the right to pry."

"Beth, stop it. You're being silly!"

"I am?" She laughed. "At least I'm honest with myself. I

don't have to hide behind a cloak of respectability. All those parties—the brave, cheerful hostess whose husband is off gallantly protecting his country, and the selfless philanthropist who spends two days a week working with underprivileged children—"

"Stop it!"

Beth advanced angrily to the sofa. "And in the evenings you sit here in this man's house and tell stories about your friends. You laugh at them behind their backs and you never understand that maybe they're laughing at you!"

There was an abrupt silence. Louise gaped at Beth in disbelief, then she took on a wounded look and said, "You don't mean any of that."

Beth stared back at her, realizing that Louise would never admit the truth. She lowered her eyes and managed a weak smile. "No, of course not."

Louise sank back, relieved. "Dear Beth," she said finally. "My oldest friend . . ." Tears filled her eyes and she looked up hopefully. "We do understand each other, don't we?"

Beth nodded. "I'm afraid so."

Bowen returned, the beaming host, carrying a tray of crackers and cheese and acting as if nothing had happened. He chattered about how difficult it was these days to get imported cheese, and he hoped they would both stay to dinner.

"I have to leave," Beth announced.

"Oh, really?" said Bowen, crestfallen. "I'm terribly sorry. You're not still upset, I hope."

"Yes, she is," said Louise, drying her eyes. "We've been terrible, Bernie, trying to extract all her deep, dark secrets. We must apologize. Say you're sorry."

Bowen looked genuinely concerned. "Elizabeth, what can I say? You make me feel ashamed. I can see now we had you at a disadvantage. I hope tomorrow you'll realize it was all in fun. May I drive you home?"

Beth shook her head. "My car's outside." She crossed to plant a kiss on Louise's cheek. "I'll call you later," she said. Louise touched her arm fondly.

She thanked Bowen for his hospitality and commented on his good taste in decor. He made her promise to forgive him and come back soon. At the door he kissed her hand and said, "I give you back your secrets."

She looked at him, surprised. "Thank you," she said, and left.

"Sometimes you go too far with your little games, Bernard." Louise pouted as he came back into the living room. "God, if I'd known that the things I told you in confidence would be used so carelessly—"

"My dear," he scoffed, "you encouraged it. But I assure you, I won't let it happen again. Now, let's forget this and enjoy a quiet evening together." He moved to kiss her and she held him off, petulant. Smoothly he whispered to her and nuzzled her neck. Her eyelids fluttered and she put down her drink. He was such perfect solace.

July 17: Potsdam

Stimson was still furious as he told Marshall about his early morning meeting with Byrnes. "He already knew about Trinity. The President must have told him last night. He was more than ready for me." He slammed his cane into the dirt of the wooded path bordering Lake Griebnitz.

"How did you broach it?"

"In two parts. Warn the Japanese—give them a chance to surrender. And guarantee something about the Emperor."

"What did he say?"

"That it would only encourage them to fight on, and it would make us seem weak and compromising. I think he got that from Cordell Hull. Also, he wants time to see how the Russians are going to behave at this conference. I told him that I don't see what that has to do with warning the Japanese. You know what his answer was? 'I know you don't, Henry.' Of all the snide remarks!"

"What about Churchill?" asked Marshall.

"No help there. If anything, he's worse. He sees the bomb as the perfect instrument of destruction. We drop it, Japan surrenders and Russia is paralyzed. He was emphatic that we tell Stalin nothing ahead of time. I said that would only damage relations, that we must deal with them frankly and openly." Stimson sighed. "That set him off. He said, 'Don't you understand? *They are the enemy!*' "

Stimson stopped at an embankment and stared into the water. "Frankly, I don't see how these three men are going to reach accord on anything."

Marshall smiled. "We still have time. Groves says the

bomb won't be operational sooner than August first. So if the Russians prove manageable here, then Truman should be satisfied. I still think we can talk him out of using it."

Stimson looked at him bleakly. "George, you're wonderfully optimistic."

Josef Stalin arrived by special train that afternoon, claiming that his doctors had forbidden him to fly. In truth, he had a deathly fear of air travel. Of course, there was an added benefit: crossing Europe by rail gave him a firsthand view of his conquered territories.

Having recently promoted himself to the rank of Generalissimo, he sported a new fawn-colored uniform, but it did nothing to hide his ungainly build. He was small, with a foreshortened trunk and unusually long limbs. His paunch was accentuated by the crippling effects of a childhood disease that had stiffened his upper left side and arm. Close-cropped hair, combed straight up in a Prussian brush, framed unnatural yellow eyes set in a sallow face. His distinctive moustache sat like a dark bush above a cruel mouth, which hid blackened, distorted teeth.

Churchill had said of Stalin and his Politburo, "They fear our friendship more than our enmity." And it was true. Stalin was paranoid about exposing his people to Western values. He perceived his wartime allies as an insidious threat to Russia's safety and well-being.

As he stepped off the train and acknowledged the Russian honor guard, he was steeled for his first meeting with the new American President.

"Well, he's damned determined to get into the war on August eighth. Never seen anybody so eager to let his own people get shot at," Truman cracked at dinner.

Surrounded by his top advisers, Truman was recounting his afternoon meeting with Stalin. "We discussed the agenda for the conference, then he jumped right in with both feet and tried to drive a wedge between Churchill and me. He said the British won't give us enough help in Japan because their own interests aren't served."

"Meaning his are," said Byrnes.

"Well, we all know that," said Truman. "On the other

hand, Uncle Joe says he's prepared to make an all-out effort. I told him thanks, but we had everything under control. But he's still going to come in around the eighth." Truman was quiet a moment, then he turned to Admiral Leahy. "You said that bomb would never work. You called it 'the biggest fool thing we have ever done.' "

Leahy looked up sheepishly. "I've heard about Trinity, Mr. President."

"Well, I just got another cable. We're ready with two functioning bombs."

Admiral King and General Arnold both shifted uncomfortably.

"Something wrong?" said Truman.

"With all due respect, Mr. President," said Arnold, Commanding General of the Army Air Corps, "I don't see the necessity. We're doing the same thing with conventional bombing."

Truman grunted and looked at King. "Is that how the Navy sees it?"

"Partly, sir. I think the blockade is doing the job just as well."

Truman turned to Marshall. "I know how you feel. And you, too, Henry. But you gentlemen are not dealing with that Russian horse trader."

"Agreed, Mr. President," said Stimson. "But I hope you're not miscalculating by planning to use the bomb as your ace with Stalin. The man does not respond to threats."

"We'll see about that."

"I suppose so. But don't forget that the difference between you and Stalin is that he doesn't have to answer to an electorate."

Truman bristled. "I can't speak for Uncle Joe, but I damn well know what Americans would feel if we had to take the high casualties some of you gentlemen have projected—then found out we had this bomb *and didn't use it*!"

The men at the table fell silent. Truman rose, glanced briefly at Stimson, then left the room.

July 17: Berkeley

Lasch paid the cabbie and wearily trudged up the walk to the Nunnery. He was tired, still shaken by what he had witnessed at Trinity and worried because he'd been unable to reach Marion all weekend. He went to his apartment, put down his luggage and called his office. Fulbright answered and asked to hear all about Trinity. "Not now, Keith," said Lasch. "Is Marion there?"

"No. Matter of fact, she hasn't been in since Friday. Have you tried her apartment?"

"I'll do that. Let Major Snyder know I'm back."

He took the steps two at a time and rapped on Marion's door. There was no answer. He called her name. Still nothing. Frowning, he knocked again. He was about to fish out the key she had given him when he heard the latch turn. The door opened and Marion stared listlessly at him, haggard and puffy-eyed. He was shocked by her appearance.

"What's wrong?" he asked.

Wordlessly Marion shuffled back into the living room. Lasch stepped in and closed the door. The apartment was in disarray. There were blankets bunched up on the sofa, overflowing ashtrays, dirty dishes and a pile of letters scattered on the coffee table.

Marion collapsed on the sofa and stared at the drapes. "Are you ill?" he asked. When she didn't reply, he sat down next to her. She kept her eyes turned from him, as if she were far away and lost. "Marion, look at me," he said.

Slowly she turned and focused on him. Gradually she seemed to recognize him. She raised her arms, sank to his chest and clung to him. "Oh, God, Allen . . ." she cried, and her words turned into great heaving sobs. He held her tightly.

"What's the matter? Please tell me," he begged. "Are you ill? Has something happened?"

"My family," she finally sobbed. *"They're dead."*

Lasch felt a crawling sensation.

"They're dead," she repeated. *"They're dead."*

He put his hand on her chin and lifted her face to look into it. "You've known that a long time," he said.

She shook her head. "You don't understand. They're really dead. I feel it."

Lasch was confused. "You're not making sense, Marion. What do you mean?"

She stared at him wildly. "I lied. I lied to all of you. They weren't dead. Just Poppa. My mother and brothers escaped to Russia."

"What do you mean?"

She indicated the letters. "Those are all from my mother. She was in a refugee camp. They took care of her—" Her eyes darted crazily back and forth, then locked on his. "Don't you see? It was inside Russia! I couldn't tell *anybody!*"

He stared at the letters, bewildered, then reached over and picked some of them up. He studied the pale green stationery and the thin pen scrawl. He couldn't understand the language, but he saw that every one of the letters was signed "Mama." He tried to sort it out. Why had she kept this secret? And if she had known they were alive before, now what made her think they were dead?

She must have anticipated his question. "I went to a party," she admitted, ". . . with Beth and Major Snyder . . . at the Swedish consulate . . . There were two Poles . . . They said terrible things . . . They insisted my mother couldn't be at Sobinka!"

"What does that prove? Aren't these your mother's letters?"

"I don't know anymore!" she wailed.

"You mean you've been sitting here all weekend, stewing about this, just on the say-so of two strangers? That's ridiculous!"

She looked up again, haunted. She wanted to tell him the

truth, everything about Bowen and her complicity with the Russians. But she couldn't bring herself to involve him, even now.

Lasch tried to reason with her. "Marion, at the least these letters indicate your mother is alive. Now just because two men you've never met before say she's not where you think she is doesn't mean they're right, and it certainly doesn't mean she's dead!" She stared back at him blankly. "I'd like to call them," he said.

"Don't!" Suddenly she was frightened.

Lasch strained to understand. "Marion, if I were you, I'd damned well want them to verify what they're talking about."

She shook her head vigorously.

"Marion, give me their number. Let me talk to them." He forced her to meet his gaze. Finally, she relented and pointed to a card on the coffee table. Lasch picked it up and looked at the raised lettering. Michal Sikorski's name was followed by a San Francisco business address and phone number.

He reached for the phone. Marion sat tensely staring at the table full of letters. Lasch was put through as soon as he told the receptionist he was calling on behalf of Marion Cypulski.

"This is Sikorski," said the voice at the other end. "What is your relationship with Miss Cypulski, Doctor?"

"Close friend," said Lasch, "which is more than I can say for you people. Do you make a habit of going around alarming your countrymen?"

There was a silence, then Sikorski said, "I have been trying to reach Miss Cypulski since Sunday. If you're in touch with her, would you ask her to call me?"

"Anything she needs to know you can say to me, right now."

"Dr. Lasch, I would prefer not to do this over the phone."

"Do what?" Lasch heard his voice rising. "Look, the lady has been upset ever since she met you and I'm trying to help her sort this out. So if you've got anything to say, let's have it."

Sikorski sighed heavily. "I hope you will repeat this with

utmost care, Dr. Lasch." He took a deep breath. "Miss Cypulski told us that her mother was in a refugee camp one hundred miles east of Moscow, in a village called Sobinka. We have reason to believe she was mistaken. In checking we have learned that there are *no Poles in Sobinka*. She also told us that her two brothers had volunteered for the Red Army. I am afraid this is also untrue."

Lasch clenched his teeth angrily. "How can you be sure?" he snapped.

"If you please, the rest is for Miss Cypulski only. It's very bad."

Lasch shot Marion a quick look. She was trying to read his expression.

"Is she there with you?" asked Sikorski, breaking the silence.

"Yes."

"I'm sorry. Dr. Lasch, I don't know where she has gotten her information about her family, but it is entirely wrong."

Lasch frowned at the letters. "Go on."

"We know that her father was executed by the Nazis. He was the key to our research. The family split up during the fall of Warsaw in 1939. Her mother was in a group that disappeared into the Russian zone and was not heard from again. But her brothers never left Poland. They were in the underground . . . which was wiped out by the Nazis during the 1944 uprising. They're dead, Dr. Lasch, and I'm quite sure of that."

Lasch held on to the phone, conscious of Marion staring at him. He didn't feel angry anymore, just sick. Sikorski went on.

"It's quite possible that Miss Cypulski's mother is somewhere in Russia, but she might not have wanted Marion to know the truth. She may have led her to believe this business about Sobinka and the boys in the Red Army . . . I don't know. I can't speculate. But we've run into this sort of thing before," Sikorski added. "I promise we will continue our efforts to locate the mother. However, the Russians have trouble enough feeding their own. Do you understand?"

"Yes . . ." Lasch thanked Sikorski and put the phone down. For a long moment he could not face Marion. Then he felt her hand take a grip on his. He turned and told her everything.

She stared at him and trembled as the shock took hold; then she seemed to explode with emotion. "It's all my fault! I deserve it! I should have seen the truth! Oh God!"

She lurched off the couch and stumbled toward the kitchen, still sobbing. Lasch was afraid she was going to harm herself. He grabbed her and she fought him.

"Let me go!" she yelled.

He held on tightly as she twisted to pull free. Then all resistance ended: she fainted in his arms. He put her on the sofa and hurried to the phone to call a doctor.

Beth had a hard time keeping up with Snyder on the way over to Cowell Hospital on the eastern edge of the campus. They followed a nurse down a corridor and entered a darkened private room. A small lamp next to the bed illuminated Marion's face framed on a pillow. Hovering by her side, Lasch glanced up and wordlessly held a finger to his lips.

"Is she all right?" Beth asked quietly.

Lasch nodded. "Sedated. She floats in and out."

"Why did you wait so long to call us?" said Snyder.

Lasch sighed. "It wasn't the first thing that occurred to me. She was hysterical; she needed attention right away."

Marion's eyes fluttered open and she looked around woozily. She focused on Lasch and grabbed his hand. "You're right," she said, her voice grating hoarsely. "It's not true . . . Why should I believe them . . . ?"

"Marion, take it easy—"

"Listen to me," she said. "The letters. They count for something . . ." She tried to sit up, then fell groggily back on the pillow. Snyder thought she was looking at him, then realized she was barely conscious and probably didn't know what she was seeing.

Beth whispered in his ear, "Maybe we should leave."

"Not yet," he muttered, his curiosity rising. "Stay with her a minute."

Beth obediently moved to the other side of the bed, sat down in a chair and took Marion's hand, rubbing it gently as she looked into half-glazed eyes.

Snyder put a hand on Lasch's shoulder. "Take a break, Dr. Lasch," he said softly. "Come on over by the window, just for a moment."

Reluctantly Lasch rose and moved away from the bed, following Snyder but avoiding his look.

"What brought this on?"

Lasch hesitated. "It's a personal matter. I don't feel I should discuss it."

"She's part of our group. We can't have any secrets."

Lasch frowned and thrust his hands into his pockets. With a glance over his shoulder at Marion, he said very quietly, "It's her family. Something about her mother and brothers. I'm sure you can understand," he said hopefully.

"Try me," Snyder said.

"Two brothers that she thought were alive may actually have been dead for more than a year."

"I see. . . . How did she find out?"

"From some men she spoke with at the party you took her to. I talked to one of them this afternoon and he was positive—"

"Hold it. According to Marion's file her family is missing. Now why would she have thought her brothers were alive?"

Lasch shook his head even before Snyder finished the question. "I don't want to go into it here. It's—"

"And what was she saying about letters?" Snyder pressed.

Lasch pulled a hand from his pocket and clutched Snyder's arm. He spoke in a beseeching tone. "Can't we let it rest a couple of days? Get her mind off it? Give her a chance to recover, then we can *all* ask questions."

Snyder was about to reply when Lasch turned away. Marion was struggling to rise again and calling for him. Beth held her down as she lapsed from English to Polish in a stream of barely audible sentences.

Lasch whirled to Snyder. "You've got to leave now. Please—both of you. I'll explain everything later."

Snyder took one more look at Marion's head lolling on the pillow, then let Beth lead him out. As the door closed behind them, Snyder turned back and stared at the room.

"She looked absolutely awful," Beth said anxiously. "What could have brought it on?"

"She just found out her brothers are dead," said Snyder. "But what made her think they were alive? It says in her file that her father was shot by the Nazis and the rest of her family disappeared in 1939. Now what the hell is going on? What happened at that party? Who was she talking to?"

"Two men," said Beth. "Mr. Thyssen introduced them: he must have known them."

"What did they say?"

"For God's sake how do you expect me to know? They were speaking Polish. Must you stand here playing Sherlock Holmes? Don't you ever stop?"

His eyes flashed angrily. "Marion is an important part of Big Stick; this breakdown is going to edge her right out of it!"

Beth stared at him, aghast, then grew angry. "You don't waste any time jumping right to conclusions, Major."

"I have to be realistic. The mission comes first. I wasn't assigned to play nursemaid."

She glared at him. "You really had me fooled. I thought you were human."

"Come on, Beth—"

"You know how much she wants to go. Can't you give her a chance? At least wait until you can talk with her, find out what this is all about?"

Snyder tightened. "I don't have time. We're going back to the Rad Lab. I want you to do two things. First, get on the phone and call Willard, Kirby and Bliss. I want them here on the morning of the nineteenth. Then get me the files on the people we rejected."

"If you replace her," Beth said quietly, "you'll probably lose Lasch as well."

"If he wants to be noble, let him. I can't put up with any more emotional prima donnas. That includes you."

Her mouth opened in astonishment. "You don't have to *put up* with anything," she said sharply. "And neither do I!"

She turned and stalked off.

* * *

Lasch sat on the bed and cradled Marion in his arms, trying to comfort her, but she remained drowsy and unresponsive. Until, in a half-awake moment, she urged him to go home.

"I'm all right," she said. "I'll rest. Come back tomorrow."

At last, reluctantly, he got up, kissed her on the forehead and left.

Marion sank back on the pillow and looked at the ceiling. She was not as groggy as she had led everyone to believe. She had to be alone to think. It all narrowed down to Bowen. She had to confront him with what Sikorski had told her. She had to see his reaction, then she would know. She clung to the slim hope that Bowen had told her the truth. But she was beginning to see the pattern of how she had been used.

Fulbright parked on Market Street and walked quickly down the alley to Bowen's side entrance. He rang the freight delivery bell twice and waited for the door to open. He couldn't make sense out of the latest development: Beth and Snyder returning separately to the Rad Lab, Beth angrily explaining that Marion was in the hospital, then flouncing back to her desk to make phone calls. He didn't know what it all meant, but he was sure Bowen would be interested.

The door opened a crack and Bowen peered out at him, then let him in with a smile. "Keith, this is an unexpected surprise."

"Yeah, and I don't like taking these chances."

"Something urgent?" Bowen asked when he had seated Fulbright at his desk.

"It's Big Stick. There's going to be a change. Beth Martin is rounding up the scientists, supposed to have them here Thursday morning."

"Are they leaving so soon?" Bowen asked, alarmed.

"Don't know that yet. Snyder just may want them around. But Cypulski's not going."

Bowen raised an eyebrow. "Really?"

Fulbright told him about Marion's breakdown and hospitalization.

"What do you think brought it on?"

Fulbright shook his head. "Got something to do with her family, about learning that her brothers were dead."

Bowen stared at him in a fleeting moment of panic at the thought of all his plans ruined, but he recovered almost instantly and was even able to show the proper concern. "Oh, that's a shame," he said calmly. "Under the circumstances, however, Major Snyder is making a wise move. Have you any idea who the replacement will be?"

"Uh . . . no," said Fulbright, disappointed that Bowen seemed unimpressed with the news.

"I'm curious, Keith. How did Cypulski come across such distressing news?"

"I don't know," said Fulbright, realizing he should have pumped Beth for more information. "I just thought you'd be interested," he finished lamely.

"I am," Bowen protested. He unlocked his cash drawer and drew out a wad of bills. He peeled off three fifties and Fulbright finally relaxed. "Is there anything else, Keith?" he said before handing the money over.

Fulbright shook his head. Then a thought occurred to him, a thought that had been nagging him since Lasch's phone call the day before. "A question," he said.

Bowen waved expansively. "Please."

Fulbright struggled a moment then blurted out, "Just tell me, did you ever believe that thing would actually work?"

Bowen smiled, finding him more dense than ever. He placed the money firmly in Fulbright's palm and said, "I learned a long time ago always to expect the unexpected. Why?"

"I don't know," he stammered. "Just thought I'd ask."

"Really, Keith," Bowen said smoothly, "haven't you felt all along that the bomb wouldn't work, that you were taking us for a great deal of money? And now you don't know what to make of it?" He stood up and Fulbright instinctively flinched. "Don't worry. You've done a wonderful job and we're proud of you. This has far-reaching implications and your role will be recognized."

Fulbright stared at him, completely dazzled. He got up heavily and thanked Bowen, who escorted him to the side door and checked to see that the alley was clear. Then he sent Fulbright off with a paternal pat on the shoulder, looking after him with contempt for his lack of imagination. That's what keeps him a money taker, Bowen thought, a man with no ideology to govern his daily needs and no conviction about the future.

He turned back and shut his door, beginning to worry about Marion.

Snyder sat fuming in his office, disappointed in Beth and angry that Lasch had been evasive when there was so much at stake. He was interrupted by a phone call from Security, asking him to come down to the gate to meet a Mr. Thyssen. Snyder hurried out, hoping this was good news.

"Get in," Thyssen said, opening the passenger door of his car. Surprised, Snyder slid in and shut the door. Thyssen turned the car around and drove down to the center of the campus. He parked and asked Snyder to take a walk with him.

"What's the problem, Mr. Thyssen?"

"I've discovered that no matter what security precautions are taken, it's never enough. Would it interest you to know why we were held up?"

"Yes."

"The Russians tried to interfere. The Japanese ambassador to Moscow was told personally by Molotov that I could not be trusted."

Snyder groped for understanding. "How much do you think they know?"

Thyssen laughed grimly. "I'm not sure. But I'm not surprised they stuck their noses in. They don't want the war to end just yet. There is one comforting possibility, however. Since it's probable they knew I was involved in peace negotiations with the Germans, they *may* have assumed that my actions with the Japanese were along the same lines. My mission, peace; to their advantage, no. So what they have done does not necessarily indicate any knowledge of Big Stick."

"Let's hope so," said Snyder.

"In any case, I think we have reestablished my integrity."

They stopped at a bridge over Strawberry Creek. Snyder said nothing about Marion Cypulski. He explained that the Trinity test had been extraordinarily successful and he was gathering the group and the information. "We can expect everything on the nineteenth," he said. "We'll keep them isolated at the Rad Lab until we're ready to go. So all we're waiting for now is approval from our friends at Potsdam."

"You will call me for any final briefings, won't you?"

"Yes, but as late as possible. Once you're in, you can't leave my supervision, Mr. Thyssen. Right now you're more effective on the outside."

"I wonder," said Thyssen. "If I've been compromised . . . and if the Russians suspect there's more to this than just a neutral peace feeler, I could become a distinct liability . . . at the least."

"Then watch your step," said Snyder.

Thyssen gazed over the side of the bridge at his mournful reflection in the water.

In the late afternoon Marion woke and rang for the nurse. She asked for a pot of coffee, and when it came she drank half of it. She got up, walked down the hall to a pay phone and called Bowen's shop. It rang but there was no answer. She struggled to recall his home number and after two misdialings got it right.

He was surprised to hear from her and said cautiously, "Is everything all right?"

"I have to see you."

He hesitated. "Sometime tomorrow?"

"*Now*, Bernard."

He sighed. "If we must, we must. I'll meet you at the shop."

"No, I'll come to your house."

"Marion," he laughed, "shouldn't we be a bit more discreet?"

"It's too late," she snapped. "I'm on my way." She hung up.

She went back to her room and dressed quickly. She slipped away from the hospital without anyone's noticing her. She walked down College Avenue all the way to the Nunnery, then around the alley to the garages in the rear.

She drove to San Francisco and parked in front of Bowen's townhouse on Nob Hill. Let him stew about his precious secrecy, she thought as she jabbed the doorbell.

Bowen swung open the door and stared at Marion with open concern. "Come in, come in," he said. "Tell me what's so urgent."

She walked past him. He closed the door and followed her into the living room. The lights were low and the front drapes were drawn.

"Would you like some coffee? Something stronger?"

"No, thank you, Bernard. This isn't a social visit."

He watched her pace back and forth restlessly. "You don't look well at all," he said.

"As always, Bernard, your concern is touching. Now, if it were only real."

"What are you talking about?"

Marion stopped pacing. Her voice trembling with emotion, she told him what she had heard about her family and from whom. Bowen listened impassively and when she finished, shook his head sadly and insisted they both sit down. He led her to the sofa and tried to sit close to her. She pulled away and said, "I came here for answers."

Bowen nodded slowly. "May I first ask a few questions?"

"No."

Bowen frowned. "I'm surprised to find you so quick to turn on me and so willing to believe two people you've never met before."

"Tell me why I shouldn't."

"I know about the London Poles. They are a discredit to your people. I don't presume to know their motives for telling you such lies, but they are *violently* anti-Russian. Don't you see what they were trying to do?"

As he spoke, his eyes probed Marion, seeking to learn if she could still be persuaded. But a mask had dropped over her face; she stared back at him blankly.

"Examine this with detachment," he said. "Put your emotions out of it for a moment and try to see the political side of it."

She nodded calmly. "Why would they feed me lies, Bernard? To further their own propaganda? You're not making sense."

Bowen shrugged. "I'm fishing for a motive," he admitted. "But in all honesty, what they have to gain is beyond me."

"They were in Warsaw a year ago. They gave me a different version of what really happened."

"Understandable. We know where their sympathies lie."

"I don't care about all that!" she snapped. "How could my brothers be in two places at once?"

"Well, your mother said they were in the army—"

"No! Your glorious Red Army sat back and watched! My brothers wouldn't do that! Warsaw was their home!"

"But the letters from your mother—"

"Not *one* from my brothers!"

"Your mother wouldn't lie to you—"

"Unless she was forced!"

She glared at Bowen, daring him to deny that.

"Marion," he said softly, "that's a very serious charge. Your imagination is running wild. From all my information none of this is possible. Your mother is at Sobinka and your brothers with the Army—"

"There is no camp at Sobinka," Marion declared flatly.

"Yes, there is—"

"Then bring her out. Bring them all out. The war in Europe has been over for ten weeks."

"What if I told you that's exactly what I'm trying to do?"

Marion was brought up short. She hadn't expected this. "When?" she said.

"I'm cutting through the remaining red tape. It won't be long. It's true, Marion. You've forced me to give you hope again and I can guarantee nothing. Only that I'm trying with all my power."

Marion shook her head. "How? They don't exist anymore!"

"You mustn't believe that."

She shouted, "They're all dead!" then broke into tears.

Bowen sat back with an incredulous look. "Marion, you're insinuating that they've fooled both of us! That's simply not true. I believe your mother is alive—and your brothers, too! *Think of the letters!* No one can be forced to write what they don't want to."

Marion wiped her eyes. "So easy," she mumbled. "Give me what I wanted so I would give you what they needed. Where is she, Bernard? *Where is she?*" She clutched his arm.

"Sobinka," he said flatly.

"You're lying."

"No! it's the truth—"

"*Lying! Where is she?* So help me, Bernard—"

"Marion, if any part of you still believes your family is alive, then don't do anything now that would jeopardize them. Trust me awhile longer so we can learn the truth together. Please believe me, if anything has happened to them, it was done without my knowledge. And if that's the case, I won't be a party to it. I'll help you expose the truth."

Marion stared at him, almost mesmerized, feeling a glimmer of hope. This was what she had come to hear, and with his face radiating sincerity, she was tempted to believe him. But her doubt and suspicion now overshadowed everything. She got up and paced again. "I can't go on the way I did before."

"Of course not," he said, rising and putting an arm around her. "Until this is settled, we don't give them a thing. Now, I want you to go home and get some rest. Try not to think about it. Let me follow through my sources. You've trusted me so long—just a little longer. Give me a chance to help."

Marion finally agreed and he led her to the door. She went out, walking quickly down the steps to her car.

Bowen stood immobile in the doorway until she started the engine and drove down the street. Then, with a momentary feeling of sadness, he looked at the black sedan parked at the corner. He flipped his porch light switch up and down twice. The sedan started up, made a U-turn and followed Marion.

Marion drove six blocks in a daze then stopped suddenly in the middle of the street. Overcome with emotion, she pounded the steering wheel and shouted, "Liar!"

She punched the accelerator and her car lurched away. The black sedan's lights came back on and it followed at a discreet distance.

Marion drove aimlessly through San Francisco until she reached Market Street. She swung the wheel sharply and the car shuddered to a stop, one wheel over the curb. She jumped out and hurried into a drugstore.

The black sedan parked up the street.

She ran to a phone booth in the rear, put a nickel into the coin slot and with a trembling finger dialed the one person in the world she could trust.

"Marion," said Lasch, "what's the matter?"

"Allen . . . Oh, Allen, I love you," she sobbed into the phone. "Please God, I love you . . ."

"Marion, what—?"

"Allen, it's all true."

He hesitated. "Where are you—at the hospital?"

"No."

"Where are you?" he repeated, now anxious.

"A drugstore . . . Allen, they're all dead—all of them!"

"Marion, please, you're in no condition to be alone. Where are you calling from?"

"San Francisco," she mumbled, wondering why he couldn't understand what she was trying to tell him. "They're dead!" she wailed, attracting the attention of the soda jerk behind the counter.

"We've been through this, Marion," Lasch said patiently. "Just give me an address and I'll come and get you."

"No," she sobbed. "You don't understand. I've found out the truth. I've been a fool, Allen. And I've hurt you terribly! Oh God, I'm so sorry . . ."

"Marion, an addr—"

She hung up on him, then stood quivering. What had she done to him? What had she done to herself? She whirled and stumbled out, ignoring the curious looks from the soda jerk.

She rushed back to the car, her mind a blur of confusion. Several thoughts clamored for attention. *Turn yourself in. Find a policeman. Go to the FBI.*

The starter whirred but the motor wouldn't catch. Out of

the corner of her eye she saw a broad, thick face lean into the window on her side. The man smiled and said, "Can I help you, miss?"

Marion looked around at his heavy build, at the mechanical smile beneath cold, impenetrable eyes. "My car won't start," she said, beginning to explain, too startled to move away when his hands snaked swiftly through the window and seized the base of her neck. His fingers tightened on the pressure point. She tried to bring up her arms to push him away but nothing worked. Her eyes bulged as a searing pain exploded in her brain.

She was dead within seconds.

The man kept talking in a soothing voice as he eased her body down a few inches until her head rested upright against the back of the seat. Then he left the window and went to the side of the car. He lifted the hood and reattached the distributor cap. He opened the driver's side and got in, sliding Marion's body across the seat.

He turned the key and started the car, then backed off the curb and drove away, followed closely by the black sedan.

Lasch stood still after Marion hung up, trying to think where she might be. He couldn't accept what she'd told him. Why would she be in San Francisco? He called Cowell Hospital.

"She's not in her room, Dr. Lasch," the night nurse said after going down the hall for a look. "And her clothes are gone. If you can wait, I'll see if she's checked out."

"Please," he said and clung to the phone a few more seconds, until he realized there was no point. He slammed the phone down and ran out of his apartment.

He stopped in the dark alley and stared at the one open garage door. Marion's car was gone. She had come back here after leaving the hospital, but to go *where* in San Francisco? Upset—frantic—suicidal? The Golden Gate Bridge?

He dashed up to Beth Martin's apartment and rapped on the door. Startled, Beth opened it a crack, surprised to see Lasch.

"Marion's in trouble," he blurted out. "She's left the hospital, taken her car and gone to San Francisco. She called me from a drugstore, terribly upset. I'm afraid she'd going to do something . . ." He couldn't finish.

Beth let him in and tried to calm him, but Lasch paced the room restlessly. "We have to find her," he kept saying.

Beth went to the phone. "I'll call Snyder."

"No! Don't do that. If he hears about this, Marion's finished for that mission."

"But we have to do *something!*"

"Call the police."

Beth got a desk sergeant through the operator and put Lasch on. He picked up the phone and continued pacing as he explained about Marion to a confused cop.

"We'll start looking right now," the sergeant promised.

Lasch gave him Beth's number as well as his own and said he would wait to hear back. He hung up.

"I really think you ought to call Snyder," Beth said.

"Not yet. The police will find her." He sank onto her sofa and stared anxiously out the window.

Beth went to the kitchen, put up water for coffee and came back out. "How about a drink?"

She stared at the empty sofa. Lasch was gone. Her door was open. She stuck her head into the hall and heard his footsteps retreating into the next wing. He was headed back to his own apartment.

Beth closed the door and glanced at the phone, tempted to call Snyder herself. But that would make Lasch furious. She decided to wait.

Keith Fulbright's eyes flew open as his phone rang. He was lying spread-eagled on his bed, being worked over by a prostitute who was nude except for a garter belt and torn black net stockings. She was flabby, tired and slightly drunk. He had picked her up in Oakland on his weekly trolling expedition. Part of his game was sneaking his women into the Nunnery. Usually he had them come in through a window. There was something about a woman climbing into his bedroom that pushed his excitement into high gear.

She was just getting to her specialty act when the shrill ring of the phone interrupted them. He cursed and pushed her head away, stumbled across the room and snatched up the receiver.

"Keith," Bowen oozed over the line.

Fulbright felt a surge of anger. Not again. The guy must be psychic.

"I have to see you right away. I'm parked across the street at the end of the block. I'll expect you in five minutes."

Fulbright cursed again as the line went dead. The son of a bitch had no right to be so high-handed. The hell with Bowen and his five minutes. The ache in his loins would only get worse if he didn't do something about it right now. Besides, he wasn't about to leave this woman alone in his apartment.

He plunged to the bed, flipped her over and tore into her savagely. She gasped but fell into his rhythm without protest.

When he was done, he paid her off, watched while she dressed, then shooed her out.

Down the block, waiting in his car, Bowen saw the prostitute leave the Nunnery and head down the street. A few minutes later Fulbright sauntered out and walked toward him. He slid into the car and flashed a little smile. "What's the trouble?"

Bowen's nose wrinkled at the aroma of cheap perfume. "I have a special assignment for you," he said.

"Christ, couldn't it wait till morning?"

"No, it must be done now." He passed Fulbright a ring of keys. "Go to Marion Cypulski's apartment. One of these keys will open her door. I want you to find some letters."

Fulbright stared at the keys, then looked at Bowen and laughed nervously. "Are you serious? What if she's there?"

"She's not. I'm quite sure of that."

"Really?" Fulbright said skeptically. "What do I do—go through her entire place?"

"If necessary. They're all written in Polish on one kind of stationery."

"What's it look like?"

Bowen pulled a piece of pale green paper from his coat pocket. "Like this."

Fulbright's eyes widened in astonishment. "Oh, God," he said, "you've got her on the hook, too!"

"Most perceptive, Keith. She's been supplying information for quite some time."

"But that's what I've been doing!"

Bowen eyed him objectively. "I've always found it wise to have a second source."

Fulbright felt his heart pound. He fingered the keys.

"You'd better go, Keith. There could be enough in those letters to incriminate both of us," Bowen lied.

Fulbright stuffed the keys into his pocket and slid out of the car. He looked back, frightened. "What if she comes home?" he asked.

Bowen closed his eyes, refusing to betray his annoyance. "Have you forgotten about the hospital?" he said patiently.

"Oh . . . yeah."

"Don't worry. I'm watching."

Fulbright trudged quietly up to Marion's apartment. Clutching the keys tightly so they wouldn't jingle, he went to work with them, fitting them one at a time into the lock, cursing each one that failed to turn.

In the apartment beneath Marion's, Allen Lasch was too upset to sleep. It was eleven thirty when he heard the noise from overhead. He got up, listened, then dashed out his door and headed for the stairwell.

Fulbright frantically slid one key after another into the lock. The next to the last one clicked over. He lunged inside and shut the door behind him, hoping the footsteps pounding up the stairs would go past into one of the other apartments. He backed into the living room, then whirled and stumbled in the pitch dark, looking for a place to hide.

He ducked into the front closet just as a key turned in the lock. The door opened and dim light from the hallway silhouetted a man in the entrance.

"Marion?" Lasch said quietly.

Fulbright recognized the voice and shrank back into the closet. Lasch called again, then snapped on a lamp. Light streamed through a panel of cross-hatched latticework built into the closet door. Fulbright cringed. He could see Lasch's back a few feet away. If he turned . . .

Lasch was puzzled, positive he had heard something up here. He went through the rooms looking for Marion. The apartment was empty, just as he had left it when he had taken her to the hospital earlier. He stood in the bedroom, more confused and worried than ever.

Fulbright peered through the latticework and saw the letters he had been sent to retrieve strewn over the coffee table and the couch. His excitement rose, overcoming his fear.

Lasch came back into the living room, switched off the lamp and left.

Fulbright stayed in the closet, screwing up his courage. Finally he opened the door cautiously, took off his shoes and slid his feet across the floor so it wouldn't creak.

When his eyes were attuned to the dark, he groped for the letters and stacked them neatly on the sofa. He spent ten minutes searching to be sure he had them all, remembering Bowen's warning of what they might contain. He lifted the sofa cushions, searched beneath the table, but finally his nerve ran out. He just couldn't stay any longer: Lasch might come back. He stuffed the letters into his shirt, picked up his shoes and slid to the door. He closed it carefully and held his breath at the sound of the latch clicking shut.

He crept downstairs, paused at the bottom to catch his breath and put on his shoes. He went to the entryway and was about to make a dash across the courtyard to the street when he spotted Lasch pacing the front walk.

Fulbright swore to himself and headed for the rear exit. He came around the alley and hurried past the garages to the end of the block.

He slipped into Bowen's car and opened his shirt. He handed over the letters.

"Is that all of them?" Bowen asked.

"Everything I could find. Lasch came in—almost caught me."

"Really?" said Bowen, almost sympathetic.

"Barely got out with my ass." Feeling a bit cocky, Fulbright said, "Never thought of myself as a burglar before. Bet I could have done it even if she was home."

"No danger of that," Bowen said calmly. "Marion is dead."

Fulbright's eyes widened. His hand instinctively sought support.

Bowen drew an envelope from his coat and put it on the dashboard. "This is for tonight," he said. As Fulbright reached shakily for it, Bowen grabbed him. "It should assure you of a generous supply of tarts," he snarled. "But if you ever keep me waiting again, they'll be looking for another source of income."

Fulbright went pale and nodded his understanding. Bowen released him and swept the envelope into his lap. Fulbright edged toward the car door.

"Go home, Keith."

Fulbright stumbled out of the car and hurried, half-running, back up the alley. He stopped and flung himself against the garage wall. *Dead.* Marion Cypulski, dead. He hadn't considered that anybody might die in this business. Suddenly he felt as if his own grip on life was weakening.

Bowen sat in the car and sifted through the letters, debating whether or not to burn them right away. They might still be useful—he would only have to figure out how. In the meantime, where to keep them? He thought about his shop and his desk in the rear . . .

Beth opened her door at the insistent knocking. It was Lasch again, wild-eyed with worry. "I haven't heard a thing," he said. "Should we call the police again?"

She stared at him. "We're calling Snyder," she said finally.

July 18: Sausalito

At 6 A.M., Snyder stood on a mist-chilled pier in Sausalito, watching a wrecking truck back up to the end. The driver revved his engine; the winch drum tightened; the cable strained. The rear end of Marion's car broke the surface and rose into the morning air, cascading water back into the bay. The driver's door sprang open and Marion's body half-spilled out, her head lolling on the running board, eyes staring into space.

An MP standing next to Snyder winced. Civilian police watched with them. A couple of beefy detectives took statements from the two sailors on liberty who had reported seeing a car go off the pier around 1 A.M. Snyder had been in touch with the MPs and the Shore Patrol ever since Beth's call and had been notified along with the police.

The car was lowered to the pier and the body moved to a stretcher. Snyder came in for a closer look with the coroner.

"Have to run an autopsy on this one, Major."

"Right away then. Let me know what you find out."

Snyder walked back to his car, wondering how to break the news to Lasch. So Marion had been disturbed enough to commit suicide? He stopped and looked back. But why should she come all the way to Sausalito to kill herself? And by drowning? Ugly way to go.

Beth let him in. She was dressed in a housecoat and looked exhausted. Lasch was asleep on her couch, his legs draped over the arm. Snyder's expression telegraphed the worst; Beth's mouth opened in horror.

"You better wake him," Snyder said.

Beth gently shook Lasch. "Snyder's here," she said, choking back a sob. She stepped back into the shadows. Lasch blinked away the sleep and sat up.

"There's no other way to say this, Dr. Lasch. Marion is dead."

Lasch stared at Snyder, then shuddered once. He rocked back, his eyes fixing on the ceiling. "How?"

"Apparently drove her car off a pier in Sausalito."

"Oh, God," Lasch moaned, his eyes filling. His head and shoulders fell forward and he buried his face in his hands. "Oh, God," he sobbed, and his body shook with grief.

Beth sank into a chair. Snyder stood by helplessly.

Bowen was at his desk before 8 A.M., checking the letters off against a master list of all his communications with Marion Cypulski. Feverishly he went through it again, then realized he had been right the first time: one letter was missing.

His heart started to pound. That stupid Fulbright. Professional burglar, indeed. Professional incompetent!

He heard Mrs. Beach come in the shop entrance. Angrily he shoved the packet of letters deep into the bottom drawer and locked it.

July 18: Potsdam

On his way to a late afternoon meeting with Stalin, Truman said to Byrnes, "Churchill doesn't want me to tell Stalin that we have the bomb."

"I have to agree," Byrnes said.

"Well, I don't want him coming back later, complaining he's been left out. We decided that I should tell him without really telling him."

"How are you going to do that?"

"Just watch me."

Stalin was waiting for them on his balcony, along with Molotov and an interpreter. After the amenities, Stalin gave Truman a copy of the message from Emperor Hirohito to Ambassador Sato, asking Stalin to act as referee in the peace negotiations. Churchill and Truman had discussed it—and the danger that if Stalin agreed, they could kiss off most of Asia—but Truman reacted as if this were the first he'd heard of it. He felt a twinge of discomfort, sure that Stalin was expecting a tidbit in return.

"Do you see any value in replying to the Japanese?" Stalin asked cagily.

"Not on the strength of this. They want to send Prince Konoye, but to do what? I don't see any evidence of good faith."

Stalin grunted and offered a solution. "Since they're making such a vague request, suppose we give them a vague reply?"

Truman thought it over. Since it was not directed to him, he could let the Russians handle it as they saw fit, or he could send back a refusal to accept any neutral negotiation.

That would never do—it would set everything back. He finally decided Stalin's idea was best—give them an unclear reply.

"I'll tell you my position, Generalissimo," said Truman. "I would not be interested in anything less than unconditional surrender. Now if you can make that stick, go right ahead."

Stalin chuckled. "You're very determined, Mr. President."

Truman grinned broadly.

Stalin turned to Molotov and said, for the benefit of the interpreter, "This message is too vague. Reply in kind."

July 18: Berkeley

Snyder entered Marion's apartment, using the key Lasch had given him. He closed the door and switched on a light. The place was a mess. At first he was afraid somebody else had gone through it, but a second look told him this was the way Marion had left it.

He stood in the living room, not knowing what to look for. He chuckled to himself. Old security man's habit: when something goes wrong, make a search. But for what? Marion had come back from the hospital to get her car. Had she come upstairs? For what? To take something? Leave something? Maybe a suicide note. Where would she put it? His eyes swept the room—coffee table, desk, side table—nothing jumped out at him.

He went through the kitchen, then the bedroom. Nothing . . . Maybe she hadn't left a note. Why did it stick in his mind that he should look for something written? Of course: *letter*. Not a note, a letter! What was it she'd said in the hospital? *"The letters. They count for something . . ."*

What did that mean? Where would she keep letters? He went back to the living room and checked all the desk drawers. He found personal papers, stationery, but no letters. He lifted the blotter: there was nothing underneath. He opened the lid of a carved box and peered inside.

A single pale green envelope lay on the bottom of the box. He pulled it out and stared at the name written across the face: M. CYPULSKI. He opened it and drew out three sheets of stationery the same color as the envelope, covered with a thin handwriting in a language he didn't recognize. The last page was signed "Mama."

A letter from her mother. He looked for a date. 15.2.45. February 15th of this year. Snyder frowned. So this was how Marion knew her family was still alive. Letters. But where were the others? Marion had distinctly said *letters.* He stared at the one in his hand. What was in it?

There was a knock at the door. Snyder stuffed the letter back into the envelope and shoved it into his trouser pocket. He opened the door and let in Captain Browne, who seemed shaken.

"Christ, Major, this is the first suicide we've had since I've been here. What do you want me to do?"

"How many men did you bring?"

"Two—in civvies."

"I want one at the street door and the other up here with you. Go through this apartment thoroughly."

"What do I look for?"

"Letters—particularly anything on light green stationery. She probably hid them."

"Okay. Where are you going?"

"I'll be in Miss Martin's apartment." Snyder picked up the phone and called the San Francisco coroner, found out they hadn't completed the autopsy on Marion yet and left word where he could be reached. He waited for Browne to return with his man, then hurried downstairs.

Lasch was slumped at Beth's breakfast counter, a steaming pot of coffee on a tile in front of him. He looked up at Snyder with red-rimmed eyes. Beth offered to fix breakfast.

"Thanks," Snyder said. He sat on the stool next to Lasch. "Are you up to answering a few questions?"

"Yes . . ."

"What was all that business about Marion's family?"

Lasch spoke slowly. "She'd always told me they were missing. She didn't like to talk about it."

Snyder laid the envelope on the counter. Beth looked at it. Lasch touched it, slid the letter out and shuffled the three pages.

"Recognize it?" asked Snyder.

"I guess it's one of her mother's letters. She had a whole

pile of them spread out on the coffee table when I got back yesterday."

"What did she do with them?"

"Still up there as far as I know." He saw Snyder frown. "I saw them when I went to check last night. I thought I heard her come in—" He broke off and his eyes filled again.

Snyder watched him closely. "What time was that?"

"Don't remember . . . ten . . . eleven."

"You were back here at quarter to twelve," Beth offered.

"I waited outside for a while."

"Are you the only other person who had a key to Marion's apartment?"

Lasch looked at him slowly, then nodded.

"And you went up there *after* she called you?"

"Yes. I told you. I thought I heard her—"

"Okay," said Snyder. "Her security report lists her mother and brothers as missing, presumed dead. Are you aware of that?"

"I never looked at those things."

"Well, that's how it reads," said Snyder. "Which brings us back to this letter. How does someone missing since 1939 write a letter in February 1945?"

"I don't know," Lasch said weakly.

"But you saw more than one letter."

"I didn't look at any of them," he said sharply. "She was distraught—she said they were from her mother—I took her word for it."

"Apparently we all took her word. But you told me she had just learned that her brothers were dead. Considering the state she was in, it must have been a big shock. So that means she thought they were alive." Snyder paused. "Wouldn't you agree, Dr. Lasch, that she probably lied on her security clearance?"

Lasch stared at his empty cup. "What do you want me to say, Snyder? She must have had her reasons."

"I'd like to know what they were."

"Shall we play a guessing game?"

Snyder picked up the envelope and showed Lasch the front of it. "What do you see?"

"M. Cypulski," said Lasch.

"Why no address? No canceled stamp. Where did this letter come from?"

Lasch leaned back heavily then told Snyder about the phone conversation with Sikorski. Snyder listened quietly. Just before Lasch finished, Beth put out a plate of buttered toast. Her eyes met Snyder's, pleading for a little understanding.

But Snyder stood up and gazed intently at Lasch. "From Russia?" he said. "Her mother wrote regularly *from Russia*?"

"From a place called Sobinka. At least that's what Marion believed. Sikorski insists she was mistaken."

"Misled," Snyder corrected him.

"I don't care. That man is responsible. It was his information that set her off. Cruel and unnecessary . . ." Lasch's eyes burned with anger, then he sagged again in defeat. "I wish I hadn't made the call."

"Did she write back to her mother?"

"I suppose so."

"*Well, who delivered the mail, Dr. Lasch?*" Snyder's voice rang with displeasure.

Beth stared at him. "Major, can't you wait?"

"No."

Lasch jumped up. "For God's sake, what do you want? She's dead! Leave it alone!"

"It's not that simple," Snyder said.

"She killed herself! It's not simple, it's tragic!"

"I agree with you. Sit down."

Lasch stood breathing hard for a moment, then obediently sank back into his chair. Beth came around the counter and angrily faced Snyder. "I've heard enough. Can't you understand that he loved Marion? She was a tormented woman. Now we know what was bothering her for so long! Nobody could help because she wouldn't breathe a word about it! And you're trying to turn her life into something ugly! Well, *it wasn't!*"

Snyder nodded. "I'm willing to accept explanations. Suppose you tell me—how did those letters cross the ocean, from Russia to here and vice versa?"

"What difference does that make?" Beth said in disgust.

"Because I'm forming a nasty theory."

"Which is?"

"A diplomatic pouch." Snyder looked at Lasch. "How kind of the Russians to think so highly of Marion Cypulski, a Polish emigré working on the Manhattan Project, that they would go to such trouble just to see she had letters from home. Do you see a pattern emerging?"

Neither of them replied. The door buzzer broke the tension. Beth went to answer it and brought Captain Browne in.

"I couldn't find anything," Browne said. "Not a sign of a letter—" He spotted the one on the breakfast counter and pointed to it in surprise. "Is that what you meant?"

"Yes," said Snyder, glancing at Lasch. "According to Dr. Lasch there should have been more. On the coffee table, was it, Doctor?"

Lasch didn't reply. Browne scooped up the letter and perused it. "What language is this?"

"Polish, we think," said Snyder. "Captain, I want to see you outside a moment."

Snyder led Browne out to the hall and closed the door. Browne still held the letter. "I want you to locate the San Francisco office of the Polish Government-in-Exile," said Snyder. "Find me a man named Sikorski. I want him to translate this letter."

"Why not our own people, sir?"

Snyder took back the letter and said, "Finish your investigation, write your report and give it to me. Then forget about it."

Browne's eyes widened. "Sir, that's pretty damned irregular—"

"It's an order."

"Would you put it in writing?"

"As soon as I get back to the Rad Lab."

"Very well, sir." Browne swallowed.

Snyder heard the phone ringing in the apartment and opened the door. "Leave a man on guard upstairs. I may want to go through it again."

Browne left and Snyder went back into Beth's. She held out the phone for him. It was the coroner's office with the results of Marion's autopsy. "No water in the lungs, Major.

She didn't die from drowning. We found a bruise at the base of her neck . . ." He went on in technical terms, which Snyder only half-heard. "And that appears to be the cause of death," he finished. "What do we do with the body?"

"Send me a copy of your report and I'll make arrangements at this end."

He hung up and faced Lasch and Beth. "It wasn't suicide," he said, "or an accident."

Lasch went to the couch and dropped on it, dazed, immobile. Beth pulled Snyder aside and said she would keep Lasch here, maybe call down to Cowell dispensary for sedation. Snyder nodded and said quietly, "Look, I'm sorry I had to be rough, but it's possible we've been compromised."

"You think she was . . . murdered?"

"Probably. The Russians had a hold on her. God knows what she was coerced into doing to get word from her family. Why else would she have kept it secret? I've got to figure out what she might have been passing. If she's compromised S-1, that's one thing, but if she's also revealed Big Stick, we're in a lot of trouble."

Beth couldn't look at Snyder for a long moment. "If there's anything you want me to do . . ." she said finally.

"Yes. Make funeral arrangements."

He turned and walked out.

Sikorski was upset to hear of Marion's death. "Oh, my God, Major—this is terrible. I feel responsible. I never meant to hurt the woman."

Snyder was unable to tell him the truth and had to let him believe that Marion had taken her own life.

"It would be a great favor," he said, "if you would help us by translating a letter from her mother."

"Yes, yes, of course," said Sikorski. "When is the funeral? I would like to attend. Perhaps we can meet at that time."

"That will have to do," said Snyder. "A Miss Martin will be in touch with you. And I'll bring the letter. We can talk afterward. And Mr. Sikorski—don't blame yourself. She had a lot of problems."

"I thank you for that assurance, Major," Sikorski said hollowly.

Fulbright responded to the buzz and came into Snyder's office. "Keith, I've got an unpleasant job for you. Marion Cypulski has died. I want you to let everybody know."

Fulbright managed a stunned look, then sat down heavily in a chair. "What happened?"

"Just say she was in an automobile accident. Went off a pier in Sausalito. Don't answer any questions, because you don't know any more than that."

Fulbright nodded, uneasy at Snyder's hard attitude.

"One more thing. We're going to tighten up security. From now on nobody comes in early or works late without my written authorization."

Fulbright stiffened. "Is that aimed at me?"

"No. Just enjoy the extra hour's sleep."

"Is it somehow connected with Marion?"

Snyder studied him a moment, then said, "I'm going to confide in you, Keith, and I want you to keep it to yourself. Marion's death was no accident, and it's possible she might have been passing information to the Russians."

"I don't believe it," Fulbright said after a moment.

"Did she have access to sensitive files?"

"They're all under lock and key up here, and she worked down in the labs. Of course . . . there's no telling what was in her head . . . But I can't believe she would—do you really think . . . ?"

Snyder shrugged. "That's why we're tightening up."

Fulbright got up slowly, looking bewildered. He dabbed at his forehead with a handkerchief. "This is just awful," he said. "Is there anything else?"

Snyder didn't have a chance to answer. Escorted by an MP, an Army courier walked in with a sealed package. Snyder signed the receipt and glanced at Fulbright. "Stick around, Keith. I want you to help me catalog this stuff."

After the MP and the courier had left, Snyder broke the outer wrapping and laid out the contents of a cardboard box. Eyes widening in astonishment, Fulbright helped him list photographs, spectrographic analyses, radiation measurements, and a reel of movie film—a wealth of sensitive material on Trinity.

Fulbright was awed by the photos. Snyder stuffed them into a manila envelope.

"I can lock them up in my office," Fulbright volunteered.

Wordlessly, Snyder packed everything back into the box and opened his triple-locked safe. "I think it'll be fine right here," he said. He shut the door and spun the locks, then looked up. "No one else is to know about this until I'm ready to show it. Not even Lasch. For a while I'm your boss, Keith. I need your help: you're the only one who isn't emotionally involved."

Fulbright smiled wanly. "I'll do my best, Major."

Snyder closed the door after him and reached for the scrambler phone. While he was waiting to get through to Bud Veneck, he thought about Fulbright. It couldn't hurt to butter him up. Right now he was more useful than Beth and more trustworthy than Lasch. Odd that it should turn out that way.

He thanked Veneck for getting the Trinity material out so promptly, then he took a deep breath and quickly explained the Cypulski development. "Stimson has to be told," he said. "Can you handle it?"

"Don't worry, Major. Nobody reads our mail. I'll get on it right away."

Snyder hung up and sank back into his chair. From now on he would have to split his efforts—half into getting the mission on its way, and half into discovering what Marion had been up to. The letters were the key. Where had the rest of them disappeared to? And how had they been delivered?

Layton Mullen, head of the FBI's San Francisco office, was a tall, broad-shouldered ex–football player with a crew cut and a broken nose. He waved Snyder to a chair and looked him over quizzically. "I've just seen your name," he said. He fumbled through some papers on his desk, pulled one out and dropped it in front of Snyder.

It was a coroner's report on Marion Cypulski's death. At the top of the cover letter was the statement: "Autopsy authorized by P.T. Snyder, Major, USA."

"Is that you?" asked Mullen.

"Yes."

"Working with Captain Browne?"

"Yes."

Mullen picked up the phone and dialed. He pulled out a stick of gum and wadded it into his mouth. Snyder heard the garbled query from the other end.

"This is Mullen. I've got a Major Snyder sitting here—" He stopped and listened, then glanced at Snyder. "Yeah? Okay, thanks a lot." He hung up. "Browne says give you anything you want or you'll take it." He smiled. "Afraid it stops short of gum, though. I'm fresh out."

He picked up the coroner's report. "Need our help?"

"Not yet," said Snyder. "Let's talk first and see where it leads." He put a finger on the report and said, "This is murder rigged to look like suicide."

"Agreed. Who did it?"

"If I knew that, I wouldn't be here. Look, the situation is complicated because the woman was working on a top security project and may have been passing information."

"I know she worked at the Rad Lab," said Mullen. "That's why I got this report. My office did all the background checks on those people. So if she wasn't kosher, I'd like to see some evidence."

Snyder showed him the letter. Mullen scanned the green pages carefully while Snyder explained. "This was probably written by her mother from a refugee camp inside Russia."

Mullen whistled softly.

"She got a lot of these. Now they're all missing but this one. I want to know how they got into the country."

"Letters, huh? There's a hundred ways—"

"How about by diplomatic pouch?"

Mullen nodded. "Possible."

"I think probable," said Snyder. "For more than one letter they would have to set up a regular delivery system with no danger of any outside interference like a random customs search. I can't think of anything safer than a diplomatic pouch. What's the Russian setup here?"

Mullen laughed. "Big! Everything revolves around the consulate at Divisadero and Broadway."

"Do you watch them?"

"Around the clock." He reached up to a shelf and pulled

down a heavy notebook, opened it and displayed a rogues' gallery of nondescript-looking men and women. "Take your pick," he said. "Consular officials, staff, attachés, cooks, chauffeurs, clerks, typists, janitors . . . they're all involved in some way. There must be at least fifty people there who are either with the KGB, NKVD or GPU."

"Who's the head man?" asked Snyder.

Mullen flipped a few pages and stopped at one with four photographs on it. "They're operating four divisions. This guy is a trade attaché, sniffs around defense plants. This one is a military attaché, always trying to get into the Navy yard at Mare Island. This one is cultural, a lover boy, uses women to make contacts among the consular corps. Pretty good at it, too. We've never been able to nail these fellows for anything. We chase them around a bit, but they're pretty obvious. Now Portiakov here is the mystery man. Doesn't have any assignment. They carry him as a vice-consul, but we know he's a colonel in the NKVD. They wouldn't send somebody like that out here to do nothing. And that's exactly what he does."

Snyder peered at the photograph of a distinguished-looking fat man with heavy features.

"We think he's the top control agent for this area. No proof. If we had it, he'd be on his way back to Moscow. But he's clean as a hound's tooth. A charmer, moves around with the big money. Leads a hell of a social life."

Snyder tapped the page. "Which one of these four could order somebody to be killed?"

"Portiakov for sure. And he's got the goons to back him up."

Snyder nodded. "Can you give me copies of these pictures?"

"If you want. Personally I wouldn't have them sitting next to mother."

"Will you step up surveillance?"

Mullen waved a hand. "We'd need a better line on what to look for."

"Well, somehow they passed the letters to Marion Cypulski and got information in return—"

"You think," Mullen corrected him. "Sometimes it doesn't work as neatly as that. In any case she's dead now.

That flow is cut off. But if you could tell me how she was doing it, where she might have been meeting her contact, things like that, we could help each other. Was there anyone she was close to who might have been involved? Someone she would trust?"

Snyder thought of Lasch, but there was no reason to suspect he had any prior knowledge of Marion's activities. "No," he said.

"Tell you what I'll do," said Mullen. "I'll concentrate on Portiakov. You let me know what you come up with on Cypulski." Snyder seemed hesitant, so Mullen added, "Hey, Major, if you hadn't come to me today, I'd have been out to see Browne this afternoon."

Snyder smiled, knowing he was right. He rose and thanked Mullen.

"I hope you're wrong, you know. About her being a spy. Means we slipped up. The Director doesn't like it when we drop one."

Snyder smiled. "He won't hear it from me."

Instead of returning to the Rad Lab, Snyder drove out to Hamilton Field, fifteen miles north of Sausalito. Colonel Wardell Lowe, the base commander, saw him right away.

Lowe was a career officer in the Air Corps—short, square-jawed and feisty. He glanced at Snyder with interest as he read a directive signed by General Groves, requesting full cooperation with Major P. T. Snyder.

"Okinawa," muttered Lowe. "When?"

"Don't know yet, but it might be on short notice. I'd like to make arrangements now: route, supplies, aircraft and crew."

"Goddamnit," Lowe said with a laugh. "You people from Washington think you can just come in here and we stop everything and get you a nice shiny airplane and a good crew, which I can't spare, so you can go anywhere you want."

"I'm not going to take anybody from Hamilton, Colonel," said Snyder. "I want a picked crew from around the country. No two men from the same base." Lowe looked at him in surprise. "For security reasons I can't have people talking about this in advance. I'd like to bring them in at the last moment. We'll set it up so that when it's near time to go, we pull these men from their bases and bring them in within twenty-four hours."

Lowe looked at him askance. "A little dramatic, aren't we, Major?"

"No, sir. Cautious. You get me some names and let me run a security check. Once we set the flight plan, I'll want you to establish open-ended clearances all the way to Okinawa."

Lowe nodded, impressed with the thinking. "Where can I reach you?"

Snyder gave him the Rad Lab number and the names of Keith Fulbright and Beth Martin. "Leave messages with either of them—no one else."

There was a long silence as Lowe waited to be told what it was all about. Finally he said, "You're going to pick up the Emperor, right?"

Snyder nodded gravely.

Fulbright stood out of the way, watching Mrs. Beach putter about Bowen's shop, using a small feather duster to flick imaginary specks off the bric-a-brac. Fulbright kept a nervous eye on the window as he moved behind a large credenza and ran a hand along the woodwork.

Bowen finally ushered his clients to the door with a promise to show them new merchandise next week. He beckoned to Fulbright and they went into the back room. "Something bothering you?" he said.

Fulbright licked his lips and paced. He couldn't sit down. "Snyder knows that Marion didn't commit suicide."

Bowen stared at him a moment and Fulbright had the satisfaction of seeing his discomfort.

"Really?" said Bowen, sitting down. "How did he come by that?"

"I don't know. He called me in and told me. He wants to put his trust in me. I get the feeling he's singled me out."

"What do you mean?"

"A box of material on Trinity came in. Really important stuff. Incredible pictures, full reports. You'd die to get your hands on this: it's the sort of overall stuff we've been looking for—complete coverage of the development of key areas. I helped catalog it. Snyder didn't want anybody else to know, not even Lasch. He said he needed my help because I wasn't emotionally involved, whatever that means."

Bowen's eyes closed in thought. "Where is this material now?"

"A safe in his office. I don't have the combinations."

"What else did he say about Marion?"

"He's convinced she was passing information." Fulbright stopped and looked directly at Bowen. "I want to know something. What was she giving you that I couldn't?"

"Some of the same material. It helped to have it from a second source, though. Verification."

"Yeah? Well, let me tell you something, Bowen. If I had known about Marion earlier, we could have protected ourselves."

"We? My dear Fulbright, lack of knowledge is the best protection of all. Frankly, it would be unhealthy for one of my friends to know about another."

"Did she know about me?"

"Of course not. You're perfectly safe, Keith. And I don't see why you're worried about Major Snyder. After all, he's showing confidence in you. That could be marvelous for us."

Fulbright dropped into the rocking chair and stared at the floor. Bowen leaned forward and said quietly, "Unless there's something you're not telling me."

"No—nothing."

"Keith, did you get *all* the letters last night?"

"Every one I could find."

"Suppose you missed one."

"Impossible. They were all on the coffee table."

"Let us say that one of them escaped your notice and fell into the hands of Major Snyder. What do you think he would make of it?"

Fulbright blanched. "I—I don't know. But I know I got all of them."

"Isn't that odd?" said Bowen. "Because I seem to be missing one."

"I haven't got it!" Fulbright protested.

"I didn't suggest that you did. But if Major Snyder does, couldn't that be what has led him to suspect Marion?"

Fulbright shrank back into the chair. "Oh, Christ," he said. "Christ, what was in the letter?"

"Nothing important. Just the fact that it exists is in itself unfortunate." He gave Fulbright a reassuring smile. "However, I think you're relatively safe."

"But now he's going to be looking for spies! And I happen to be one!" He felt a surge of anger at Bowen's amusement. "Look, if he gets too close . . ."

He left it hanging. Bowen continued to smile and said, "I had ghastly problems with Marion. I really don't want any with you. Just remain calm. When are these scientists arriving?"

"Tomorrow," Fulbright said shakily. "What are you going to do about the mission?"

"Oh, I think we've slowed it down a bit. Major Snyder is going to be quite busy trying to sort out the mess we've created, don't you think?"

Fulbright was unconvinced. He had come there nervous and had no reason to change his mind. Even when Bowen opened the cash box and passed him two hundred dollars, his concern wasn't relieved. Bowen took him to the front door, clapped him on the back and said, "Why don't you find a nice girl tonight, Keith? I promise not to interrupt."

July 19: Berkeley

Kirby, Bliss and Willard presented themselves separately to Captain Browne in the morning. Each had received travel orders to Berkeley for a "high-level conference." They were cleared through Security then taken to the conference room in the rear Quonset hut. Browne told them only, "Major Snyder will brief you shortly. Please be patient."

Willard sank into a chair. Kirby opened his briefcase and pulled out a battered diary. He turned to July 19th, opened a gold fountain pen and made a notation. Bliss paced nervously, worried that his presentation would fall short. They were all still under the impression Snyder had originally given them, that they would be speaking before a committee about the effects of an atomic attack.

They looked up as Keith Fulbright walked in lugging a 16mm projector. Without speaking he placed it on the conference table then went out and returned with a screen.

"Army training films?" Willard cracked.

"No," Fulbright said. "Major Snyder will be along in a few moments. Are you all comfortable?"

"Yes, and curious," said Kirby. "Do you know anything about this meeting?"

"Sorry," Fulbright said. "I can't discuss it." He glanced at the suitcases they had stacked in a corner.

Bliss stepped in front of him. "How many people are we waiting for?"

Snyder walked in with the Trinity box under his arm. "Just me," he said, placing the box on the table next to the projector.

"I hope you all had good flights," he said. "We're going

to be pretty busy this morning and nobody will be leaving till we're through, so if you want anything, speak now."

Willard tried to appear casual. "The directive said something about a conference."

"This is it." He reached into the box and pulled out a reel of 16mm film, handed it to Fulbright and asked him to thread it up. He sat down.

"Gentlemen, by now you all probably know that Trinity was a success. The first device was exploded on Monday. We're going to take a look at that test."

Bliss sat down heavily and turned to face the screen. Willard eyed Snyder curiously.

Fulbright snapped off the lights and flicked on the projector. There was scrabbled leader followed by a black-and-white shot of the desert test site taken in daylight. Another angle showed Oppenheimer and the group at the base of the tower, loading the explosives.

"The first few minutes were taken on Saturday," said Snyder. "It should give you an idea of the layout."

The camera panned up the thin steel girders to the corrugated shack at the top. "That's one hundred feet up," said Snyder. "The device went into that shack and was triggered by cable."

There was a cut to a new angle of the same tower seen from ground level. The people were gone. The tower sat stark and silent in the desert. Another cut showed the abandoned farmhouse and the steel cylinder. "That's two miles away from point zero," said Snyder. "The shack was already there; the cylinder was built to approximate a twenty-story office building."

The screen went black. "This is the blockhouse view of point zero shortly before the blast."

He fell silent. There wasn't a sound in the room except the grind of the projector as Bliss, Kirby and Willard stared intently at the flickering image. Suddenly light filled the screen for almost five seconds, then began to subside and they saw the enormous cloud boiling up from the desert floor.

"Jesus Christ," said Bliss.

Kirby leaned forward to study the image.

"Am I seeing more than one explosion?" asked Willard.

"Within the column, yes," said Snyder. "I'm sorry this isn't in color. There was an astonishing blue glow around it."

The image jerked up and down. "Blast wave," said Snyder. "The camera was behind a thick concrete wall, ten thousand yards downrange. Even from my position the heat and force were very evident, and that was twelve miles from point zero."

"You were *there*?" said Willard, without taking his eyes off the screen.

Snyder didn't reply. The image steadied and the scientists watched the mushroom cloud taking shape, filling the top of the screen.

Fulbright stared at the screen in abject wonder.

There was another cut: daylight again, the desert viewed from above. "This was taken later the same day from an altitude of six thousand feet."

Kirby stood up and approached the screen, studied the slowly turning picture of the crater. There were glints of light, sparkles where the sand had turned to glass. The image moved on and circled the area where the cylinder had been. Only a few stubby, twisted girders remained. The farmhouse was gone.

"Remember, that was *two miles* from point zero," said Snyder.

The film ran out. Fulbright switched off the machine and turned the lights back on. The scientists moved their chairs around and stared at Snyder.

"Any comments?"

"You run that film for your committee," said Bliss, "and we won't have to do any talking."

Snyder smiled.

"Julian has a point," said Kirby. "The film is your strongest argument. Why do you need us?"

"To answer questions. The people we're going to meet with will want to know how we reached that result."

Willard put his hands on the table. "Sensitive information, Major. How much can we tell——?"

"Enough to scare them."

Kirby looked at him suspiciously. "Scare who?"

"The Japanese."

The three scientists were taken completely by surprise.

"I got you here under false pretenses," Snyder explained. "This has nothing to do with the United Nations. We're going to Okinawa to meet with representatives of the Japanese government, to warn them what this is capable of. You've been selected because of your individual expertise—"

"Wait a minute," said Bliss. "Why don't you send the big guns—Teller, Szilard, Fermi?"

"There is an element of risk," Snyder admitted. "We simply can't afford to send the top echelon. If it's any comfort, we don't go unless I'm absolutely convinced of your safety."

Kirby smiled. "I'll sleep better tonight."

"I don't like it," Bliss muttered. "Since when did the Army develop concern for the Japs?"

"The mission has been authorized at the highest level," Snyder said.

"By whom?"

"As far as you're concerned, by *me*, Dr. Bliss. Beginning now, there's no backing out. You'll be staying here under guard until we're ready to go."

"For how long?"

"We should be leaving sometime in the next five days. Figure you'll be home in two weeks."

"What are we supposed to tell our families?"

"Nothing. There'll be no outside contact."

Bliss laughed. "Major, don't you think we can keep this quiet? At least let us tell our wives we won't be around for two weeks."

Snyder leaned back. "You'll each be allowed one or two phone calls, in my presence."

Willard snorted. "Sounds like we've been arrested."

Snyder smiled.

"I don't think it's so terrible," said Kirby. "We've lived this way before. I've gone months without seeing my family. However, Major, I only wish you would have given us a clue that we were in for it again."

Snyder shrugged. "Couldn't. Look, you're going to be so busy the time will race by. Just keep in mind what you're going to accomplish."

"Who do I get to call?" asked Willard. "I'm not married."

"I'm sure you'll think of someone," Snyder said. "So, gentlemen, from now on this is home."

"Is it just going to be the three of us?" asked Kirby.

"No. Allen Lasch helped select you and he would have been with us today, but his close friend and the fifth member of our team, Marion Cypulski, died yesterday."

Kirby looked up in surprise. "Wait a minute—I know her. I met her in Chicago a few weeks ago. What happened?"

"Automobile accident."

Willard broke the awkward silence. "Cypulski was in electromagnetic research. Who's going to replace her on this team?"

"Lasch, I hope." Snyder paused. "One other thing: we're taking along a Japanese POW with a background in physics. His name is Nakamura. You'll meet him later."

Snyder watched Bliss shift uncomfortably. He's the whiner, Snyder thought. Willard walks alone and Kirby is the steadying influence. He wondered how they would behave under pressure. He gave Bliss a solicitous look. "Anything wrong, Doctor?"

"We're not diplomats, Major. You're putting us in a hell of a position. This is a big responsibility."

"I think you'll live up to it—"

There was a knock at the door. Captain Browne let Beth and Lasch in, then backed out and closed the door.

Lasch was wan and haggard. He surveyed the other scientists with slow-moving eyes. "Sorry I'm late," he mumbled. "Don't let me interrupt. This is my assistant, Beth Martin."

The three men rose, then Kirby walked forward and clasped Lasch's hand. "I'm sorry about what happened, Allen."

Lasch nodded, then introduced himself to Willard and Bliss. Snyder saw Beth's eyes riveted on Lasch. He moved to her side and whispered, "How's he holding up?"

"I don't know," she said. "He changes every five minutes."

Snyder frowned.

"Are you thinking of scratching him, too?"

"If he doesn't snap out of it."

Beth faced him. "This means more to him now than it did before—because of Marion. Can you understand that?"

"I'll take it into account."

The afternoon turned gloomy as Marion's funeral got under way at St. Mary's Cemetery in Oakland. Lasch, Beth, Snyder and Fulbright represented the Rad Lab. Beyond them, Marion had only a handful of friends. They stood at graveside while the priest intoned prayers. Snyder repeated the litany and crossed himself.

Lasch stood rigidly staring at the casket. Beth had a firm grip on his arm and finally, gently, urged him away. She walked him to a tree and stood with him while he covered his eyes with both hands. His body shook with sobs.

Snyder watched from the grave site, then saw two men in dark suits step out of the small group of mourners and approach him.

"Major Snyder?" one of them whispered in a heavy foreign accent. "I am Michal Sikorski and this is Josep Wajda. May we talk?"

Snyder nodded and led them down the hill away from the others. "I know this sounds crass," he said, "but I need to see some identification."

Sikorski produced papers identifying him as a colonel in the Polish Home Army. "Which does not exist as such anymore, Major," he explained. "But it still carries some weight with the United Nations."

"I'm sure it does." Snyder reached into his jacket pocket and brought out the letter from Marion's mother. "Would you translate this for me?"

Wajda peered over Sikorski's shoulder and they studied it carefully. "The first paragraph is just conversation," Sikorski said, then read, " 'I have your last letter. How are you? The weather is very cold in Sobinka . . .' "

He frowned and glanced at Wajda.

"Go on," said Snyder.

". . . 'The camp committee has issued extra blankets and heavier clothing. The firewood allotment has been increased. I had a lovely surprise this week. Your brother Jan came home on leave. He is now a corporal and looks so grown-up in his uniform. Max is still in Moscow. I received a letter from him. He sends his love . . .' " Sikorski's voice trailed off. "This can't be," he said.

"Please read the rest."

He translated the other two pages, but it was more of the same. Toward the end, however, "Mama" almost gushed with praise for Mother Russia. Sikorski read this, shaking his head. When he finished, he repacked the letter and gave it back to Snyder. "Lies," he said. "All lies."

"What makes you sure?"

Wajda produced a folded document from his coat. He spread it open for Snyder and explained, "This is a copy of an SS execution order, listing 'criminals' shot by firing squad on three December 1944."

Snyder followed Wajda's finger down the list to two names: Jan and Maximilian Cypulski. "May I keep this?" he asked.

"Certainly," said Sikorski. "And if we can help in any other way, please call on us."

Snyder stuffed the list into his pocket, thanked them both, then returned to the parking area. He found Beth, Lasch and Fulbright huddled by the cars.

Beth broke away to meet him and said quietly, "I want to get Lasch home. I don't think he can hold up much longer."

"No. You take Fulbright back. The doctor and I have some things to do." He went past her, took Lasch by the arm and started toward his car.

Beth stood bewildered as the car sped away.

Late that evening she couldn't sleep. Curled up on her living room sofa, reading, her attention was distracted by the sound of drunken singing coming from the street. Annoyed, she went to the window.

Snyder and Lasch were in the courtyard, stumbling into the Nunnery.

She threw on a robe and opened her door. Down the hall

she saw Snyder bring Lasch upstairs then guide him into his apartment. He staggered out a few moments later then groped down the hallway. He saw Beth and stopped, slumping against the opposite wall. He tipped his hat slowly, a silly grin widening on his face.

"Waiting up for us?"

"You're disgusting!" Beth snapped, turning away from him.

Snyder tried to focus on her. "Ah," he said, "the office conscience."

"You should be ashamed of yourself."

"I am, madame, I am."

"Lasch can't take that kind of drinking."

"Like a duck to water. He led all the way."

"I don't believe it."

He shrugged. "If you'll just point me to the stairway and give me a shove . . ." She did nothing, just glared angrily at him. With a groan he pushed himself away from the wall—and dropped to the floor.

"What's wrong?" she said.

"Bottle fatigue."

"Oh, Christ." She yanked him into her apartment, dragged him unprotesting across the living room and dumped him on the couch.

"Thank you," he said. She ignored him, slammed the door to her bedroom and locked it. Snyder tried following her with his eyes, but the effort was too much. His head dropped onto the cushions and he passed out.

July 20: Berkeley

He woke to an insistent hand on his shoulder. Sunlight streamed in the window and he slammed his eyes shut against it. A cold glass was pressed into his fingers. He sniffed a pungent aroma: tomato juice spiked with Worcestershire. His nose wrinkled. He struggled to his feet and the blanket fell off. Snyder looked down in surprise: he was stripped to his shorts.

He struggled to wrap the blanket around his body and took a few tentative steps. His head rang like a tuning fork. He groaned as he saw his face in the mirror—bearded, bleary-eyed and shaggy.

He shuffled to the kitchen and stood in the doorway, arms folded tightly across the blanket held against his chest. Beth, dressed in a housecoat, looked up and saw him standing there. "You look like a debilitated cigar store Indian," she said.

"Please, no humor," he said quietly.

"Coffee and breakfast?"

He nodded and collapsed onto a stool, watching her fill his cup. He leaned over and let the steam rise into his face. Three cups later he felt able to tackle some toast. Beth watched him eat, at once amused and reproachful.

"You don't approve of the way I handled Lasch," Snyder said. "He needed it."

"I understand. You got your psychology training in a barracks."

"You mean out of a bottle. True. I graduated summa cum bar rag. Anyway, it works. After he recovers, he should snap right out of his depression. As for me . . ." He held his head.

"Why is it," said Beth, "that when something bad happens, a man's only solution is to drown it."

"Only if you're Irish. The two-man wake is an old tradition. You don't do it to forget, but to put things in perspective. The good doctor was in danger of letting grief destroy him. Life goes on."

Beth took his plate. "I see. You're a philosopher, too."

He looked over his shoulder at his uniform neatly folded on the end of the sofa. "Also observant. How did I get out of my clothes?"

"With my help."

The idea that she had undressed him was intriguing. He watched as she did the dishes. Using one hand to hold up the blanket, he shambled over to the sink and passed her a towel with his free hand. "I'd like to help you dry," he said, "but I've got to hold up my dignity here."

"I don't know why I do it," she said. "I'm constantly taking in drunken Army majors." She flashed a smile.

"Well . . . I do appreciate it," he said. He leaned over and gently nuzzled her neck. When she didn't object, he stroked the curls on her shoulder. Then he turned her, lifted her chin and kissed her softly on the lips.

"Why do they call it the Nunnery?" he asked between kisses.

"It's a failed sorority house," she said, kissing him back, her hand caressing his cheek. "Twenty-five girls . . . got caught . . . thrown out of school."

"Why?"

". . . broke their vows . . ."

"Oh . . ."

She pressed her lips to his as she let herself go in his embrace. Her fingers plucked at his other arm. She wanted it around her back. He dropped the blanket and obliged.

They walked to the bedroom, arms around each other. They paused for a kiss, then he lifted her up and placed her across the bed. Gently he opened her housecoat. She was naked underneath. Her eyes darted over him and she flushed with excitement. He was uncertain where to begin, so she took his hand and pressed it to her breast. He slid down beside her and she rolled into his arms.

His hand stroked her skin and he felt her nipples grow hard under his fingers. Her eyes closed and her mouth sought his. With one hand she caressed his side, moving back and forth along the skin, finally sliding into his shorts, pulling them down.

He gasped in surprise as she touched him. Her tongue probed his mouth and she began to moan. He pulled her leg up, then felt for the center of her.

Beth sucked in her breath as his fingers moved against her—pressing, spreading. She felt him withdraw his hand, then he was pushing into her. They rolled together until she was on her back; then she crushed her lips to his and moved with him urgently, whispering encouragement.

Snyder was surprised when she stiffened and groaned: It happened so quickly. Her fingers dug into his back as he felt his own sensations spreading. . . . He shuddered with pleasure as Beth covered his face with kisses and smiled at him.

Afterward he lay sprawled across the foot of the bed while she sat up and brushed her hair, still naked, at ease with him. He pushed up his chin with one hand and looked at her. "You didn't learn all that from one short, aborted marriage," he said.

She slid back to the headboard and rested against the pillows, toying with the brush. "You're the first man I've slept with since leaving home," she said.

"I see." His mind flashed back to her security file. "That's a long time," he said.

"I just didn't want to get involved. After my annulment, I went a little wild. I used sex to get back at my father."

He looked at her in surprise.

"You want to hear it . . . ?"

He nodded. She put down the brush and pulled up one leg, clasping the knee between locked fingers. "I wanted revenge. He had really hurt me."

"The guy you married?"

"No, my father. I decided to meet a lot of men without letting my community standing get in the way. So I signed on as a USO hostess. The local staff was very pleased to have me. They thought it was terribly patriotic for a New England debutante to come down and mingle with the enlisted men. After all, I could have had my pick of the officers. Of course, I paid no attention to the regulations about not dating the men. I went to bed with every guy who had a stripe."

She paused to see if she was shocking him. Snyder was impassive.

"For three months," she continued, "I took on everybody and anybody. I don't remember a name or a face but I made a hell of a reputation."

"Why did you stop?"

"The staff found out and asked me to leave. I refused, so they said they would have to tell my father. I told them to go ahead," she said with a smile. "That's what I wanted. He was furious and demanded to know if it was true." She paused again, relishing the memory. "I rubbed his nose in it. I let him have it both barrels, in detail. He slapped me, called me a slut, and said I had destroyed his name." Her eyes darkened. "*His name.* Isn't that typical? Well, I said, 'Good. We're even.' He knew what I meant. He didn't have anything else to say. And that's how we parted."

She stared into space and her belligerence faded. After a moment her eyes settled on Snyder. "What do you think?"

He looked at her a moment then, without warning, moved up the bed and took her in his arms. "I'm glad you told me," he said. He would never let her know how much of it he had already seen in her file.

July 21: Potsdam

Stimson found Marshall right after breakfast and showed him the cable he had received from Snyder via Bud Veneck.

"Marion Cypulski," said Marshall. "The Russians . . ." He frowned and sat down with it.

"This is real trouble," said Stimson. "If the Russians know about Big Stick, we're in a hell of a spot."

"One consolation," said Marshall. "They probably think it's legitimate."

"I don't want to wait around to find out. If this gets back to the President from another source, we'll have a hard time explaining. I say we tell him now, today. Let him make the decision to go or not to go. At least we'll have made the effort."

"That's the same as calling it off, Henry," Marshall said quietly. "We have to keep it alive. Let's advise Snyder to be on the alert and to throw a concentrated effort into discovering just what the Russians actually know."

"George, if they've murdered one of the scientists, then the situation is already out of hand."

Marshall waved the cable. "He's not saying that. He's giving us his suspicions. Let's give him a chance. And ourselves, too. Until the bomb is dropped, we have to keep trying."

When he returned to his quarters at Babelsberg, Stimson was given General Groves' full report on Trinity. After reading it carefully, he no longer doubted that Truman would use the bomb.

In midafternoon he went to the Little White House, sat down with Truman and Byrnes and read them the report.

Excerpt from General Groves' Memorandum for the Secretary of War:

"At 0530, 16 July 1945, in a remote section of the Alamogordo Air Base, New Mexico, the first full-scale test was made of the implosion type atomic fission bomb.

I estimate the energy generated to be the equivalent of 15,000 to 20,000 tons of TNT.

The light from the explosion was seen clearly at Albuquerque, Santa Fe, Silver City, El Paso and other points generally to about 100 miles."

Truman was elated. He shook Stimson's hand. "Henry, I appreciate everything you've done. A fine job. I think you can go home anytime."

Taken by surprise, Stimson left the President, more unsure of himself than ever.

Back in his quarters he pulled out his copy of the draft warning to the Japanese and, with a red pencil, scratched out the line pertaining to the Emperor's postwar role. Then he took a blank sheet of paper and composed a note to the President, offering support for all the Administration's aims vis-à-vis the bomb, including the idea of using it to impress Stalin, "but only," he carefully added, "if events at the conference leave us no other recourse."

He folded the note, inserted it in an envelope, then paused to analyze the consequences. He wasn't capitulating to Truman and Byrnes; he just wanted them to know that he, too, could be realistic, so that when he and Marshall went in to outline Big Stick, they wouldn't be dismissed out of hand.

He buzzed for a messenger.

July 21: Berkeley

Snyder sat by the window in Beth's apartment, sipping coffee and contemplating the day and a half he had spent with her. They had gone to work on Friday then rushed back to spend the night in bed like two frantic teenagers. They were exhausted Saturday morning and had planned to spend the day quietly together, but Beth had received a phone call from Lasch early in the morning, asking her to come in for some special work.

She went right out after breakfast, leaving Snyder in her apartment. He sat there, relaxed and at peace with himself for the first time in months, reflecting on how warm and comfortable he felt with Beth.

The phone rang and he hesitated before picking it up. "It's Beth," she whispered. "You better get over here right away." Before he could ask why, she hung up.

Snyder stared at the phone, wondering what could have gone wrong. He grabbed his coat and rushed out. He hurried into Le Conte Hall and went upstairs. Beth saw him coming and left her desk to intercept him.

"He's packing."

"What?"

She showed him a letter of resignation. "He's quitting."

Snyder took it from her and headed for the office. He could see Lasch inside, throwing his meager possessions into a cardboard box. Snyder was brought up short by the phone ringing in his own office. He whirled.

"Beth, would you get that? Whoever it is, I'll call them back."

She nodded and dashed off. Snyder walked into Lasch's

office and closed the door. Lasch looked up but didn't stop packing. Snyder held out the letter.

"What's this all about?"

"I've had enough. I'm leaving."

"Why?"

"Oh, come on, Major, do I have to spell it out? You'll do fine without me."

"Bullshit. You're more essential now than before. I'm expecting you to pick up Marion's end as well as your own."

Lasch glared at him. "I just can't oblige you, Major. This little venture has already cost me too much. And don't take me out for more bar crawling. It won't work."

Snyder faced him across the desk. "I never had you pegged for being selfish," he said.

Lasch threw up his hands. "Please, no more psychoanalysis. I'm human. Let me go away and heal my wounds."

"What are you going to do? Make believe none of it happened? Forget about S-1, Big Stick and Marion?"

Lasch stiffened and said in a low, threatening tone, "I'm not going to forget about Marion."

"Good. If you have such strong feelings for her, how can you turn your back on something she believed in?"

Lasch's eyes narrowed. "You're not going to change my mind, Snyder."

"I'm not trying to. But you don't get out just by writing a letter. You're going down to explain it to the others."

Lasch wavered. "I don't have to."

"If you want to walk out of here, you do."

There was a knock on the door. Beth stuck her head in. "It's Mr. Thyssen on the other phone."

"I'll take it in here," Snyder said. Beth ducked out. "How about it, Doctor?"

Lasch stared at him. "You're a son of a bitch, Snyder. You don't give a damn about anyone, so long as you get what you want."

"We can discuss my powers of persuasion another time. If you leave, we're stuck. I need you."

The intercom buzzed and Snyder picked up the phone. Thyssen's voice crackled with excitement. "We are only a few days away from having Okinawa firmed up, Major.

Probably by next Wednesday, the twenty-fifth. Anytime after that, we can start moving west."

"That's very good news, Mr. Thyssen. I'll pass it on to the team and see that Washington is informed."

There was a distinct sigh of relief at the other end. "You do not know what I have been through," said Thyssen. "Your Eastern allies threw up more barriers, but it all seems fine now. I shall be in touch during the week."

"Thanks." Snyder hung up and turned back to Lasch, who watched him with a trapped expression. He had stopped packing his carton. "It looks like we can leave anytime after Wednesday, Doctor. Still want to back out?"

Lasch gazed at him in confusion, then said, "Yes."

"Okay," said Snyder, opening the door. "Work up a good farewell speech."

Lasch stuck out his jaw and followed Snyder, who stopped to lean over Beth's desk. "Do me a favor. Go to the campus library; check out anything you can find by Dashiell Hammett and Raymond Chandler, then come down to Security. I'll leave instructions for you. Okay?"

"All right." She watched them go, puzzled.

Snyder led Lasch down the hall to the rear hut. The guard rose and unlocked the door. Nakamura looked up from his newspaper.

"Ah, Major," he said, indicating the sports page. "Yankees are doing better in the Pacific than they are in baseball."

"That'll change. Major Nakamura, I want you to meet Doctor Allen Lasch. He had something to tell you."

Nakamura stood up and pumped Lasch's hand. "This is a great pleasure. We have mutual friends at Caltech."

"Yes . . ." Lasch's eyes worked furtively. He couldn't face Nakamura's trusting smile.

"Go ahead, Doctor," said Snyder.

Lasch drew himself up but struggled for words. "Look, I'm in a rather tough position about this mission to Japan."

"Yes?" said Nakamura.

"I . . . I've just had a . . . a great loss . . . and I'm . . ." He stopped and sat down heavily on the cot.

Nakamura glanced at Snyder, who leaned patiently against the door.

Finally Lasch held up a hand and said, "Okay, you win."

Nakamura was bewildered but smiled as Lasch stood up and said, "Major, we'll be leaving very soon. A few more days. I think we can all hold together till then." He turned to Snyder. "I better get my office back in order . . ."

"Right." Snyder opened the door and handed Lasch his resignation letter. "And file that."

Lasch went out. Snyder closed the door.

"What was all that about?" asked Nakamura.

"Misguided emotions. How are you doing?"

"Is it really true? We'll be leaving in a few days."

"Looks that way. The rest of the team has arrived. You'll be introduced shortly. In fact, as we get closer to leaving, I'll put you in with them."

"Very kind of you, Major."

There was a knock at the door and the guard let in Beth, carrying an armload of books. She stopped in surprise when she saw Nakamura. Snyder took the books from her.

"Miss Martin," he said, "I want you to meet Major Shinichiro Nakamura."

He bowed. She was speechless.

"Some reading matter, Major," said Snyder, dropping the books one by one on the desk. "Couple of Chandlers, Hammetts . . . ever read *The Maltese Falcon*?"

Nakamura gazed at the books as if he were being offered a royal treasure. He turned to Beth and bowed again. "Thank you, Miss Martin. This is wonderful."

Beth glanced at Snyder. "My pleasure, Major."

Snyder took her to the door, leaving Nakamura to flip through the books. "Read fast," Snyder said. Nakamura smiled back.

They walked back up the hall. "That's the enemy," Snyder said. "What do you think?"

"He doesn't look too ferocious."

They stepped into bright sunlight. Beth shielded her eyes. "Why did you want me to meet him?"

He ignored the question. "He's nuts about detective stories. By the way . . . Lasch has changed his mind." Beth looked at him, surprised. "And I want to thank you for calling me about it. You did the right thing."

"I must tell you something," she admitted. "I wasn't so sure. I don't know about my loyalties anymore. You've mixed me up."

"I've made you rational."

"Oh?"

"Three days ago you wouldn't have called me. You'd have been on his side. He appeals to your maternal instinct."

Beth glared at him. "Keep talking, P.T. You're digging yourself quite a hole there."

He smiled. "Nothing personal. Sometimes I'm happy you react that way. But where Big Stick is concerned, I don't want anything but cold, calculating logic. That's what I used on Lasch. Makes me seem like a real son of a bitch, but it gets the job done." He nodded back at the hut. "Nakamura understands. It isn't easy for him to go back to Japan. They're not going to roll out the red carpet for a prisoner of war."

"What does that mean?"

"He's considered dead. Showing up alive means he's disgraced himself and his family. It might not seem reasonable to us, but that's the way they think. But he's willing to do it if it will help his country. So if I get a little impatient with your boss's emotional ups and downs, I think you can understand."

She looked at him dispassionately. "One question—are you using *me*, too?"

"No," he said. "I hope you believe that."

She gazed searchingly into his eyes, then smiled and shook her head. "I guess I'll find out the hard way."

He stared at her and a grin spread on his face. "Don't be pessimistic," he said.

"Realistic," she corrected him.

They walked back up to Le Conte. "Anything planned for the weekend?" he asked.

"No . . . just you. A little peace and—oh, damn! I just remembered."

"What?"

"I'll call Louise and tell her no."

He snorted. "Another of her soirees?"

She smiled. "Her contribution to the war effort. She's providing a forum for the Soviet vice-consul to make an appeal for donations. Russian War Relief. I think we can afford to miss that."

"What's his name—this vice-consul?"

"I don't know . . . begins with a 'P.'"

Snyder caught his breath. "Portiakov?" he asked.

"Yes! That's it. You know him?"

"When is it?"

"Tonight."

"Get out your party dress."

"Beth," Louise called, slipping away from her guests and coming to meet them at the archway. She took Beth's hand and pressed it warmly between hers. "Friends again?"

Beth nodded and Snyder noticed the strain between them.

"How are you, Major?" said Louise. "Delighted to see you again." Her eyes twinkled mischievously. "You should find this an interesting evening."

"I'm sure I will," Snyder agreed, looking up as Bowen cut a path between the guests and raised his glass in greeting. "Major Snyder, you are an island of hope in this sea of sedition." He shook Snyder's hand fervently and gave Beth a forlorn look. "You have no idea what I would give to be somewhere else."

"No complaints, Bernie," said Louise, wagging a reproachful finger. "At least you're not tending bar tonight."

"A compensation sorely missed," said Bowen. "Major, join me in a drink?"

"Sure."

Louise took Beth away and Snyder followed Bowen to the bar, scrutinizing the crowd. Different tonight, a more complex lot. Very few of the slick types from last time. More tweedy intellectuals and women with glasses. To Snyder, they seemed professorial and stuffy.

"Scotch, wasn't it?" said Bowen.

"Fine memory, Mr. Bowen."

"Please make it Bernard. But not Bernie," he added

with distaste. "One must maintain some dignity in this world, and I despise nicknames. God, what a depressing crowd. There's not an original idea in the room. Louise and her causes." He scowled. "She doesn't know what she's doing."

"What made her pick Russian War Relief?"

"Bundles for Britain was all sewed up."

They laughed together and Snyder asked, "Know anything about the guest of honor?"

"Can't even pronounce his name. I tell you, Major, there is nothing more foolish than a woman with a misguided sense of duty and the money to back it up. Do you know that Louise spends two days a week with underprivileged children? Commendable, eh? Hah—they're nothing but a pack of little monsters. So why does she do it? For them— or to salve her own conscience?" He clucked sadly. "Louise has good intentions, but she can't discriminate. She's such an easy mark."

"She seems to have a lot of friends who fall into the same category. Is everyone here expected to contribute?"

"I can't speak for the others," said Bowen, "but my hand stays in my pocket. And frankly, I can't see you kicking in much, either."

Snyder smiled, his attention drawn to the archway as a large man wearing a dark blue double-breasted suit made his entrance. Louise fairly flew to his side to make him welcome. Some of the guests drifted over and formed a line to be introduced.

Bowen nudged Snyder. "Shall we go together?"

"Why not?" said Snyder, allowing Bowen to lead him across the room. He watched the big Russian shake hands, beam jovially and exchange pleasantries with Louise's guests. He didn't look as villainous as Mullen had painted him. Louise stood at his side, an arm hooked in his, basking in triumph. Beth was behind her and waved as Snyder and Bowen came up.

Louise tapped the Russian's arm and drew him toward Bowen. "Bernard Bowen, I want you to meet Vice-Consul Alexei Portiakov. Mr. Bowen is one of the city's leading antique dealers."

"Ah," said Portiakov. "Pleased to meet you, Mr. Bowen. There is much to be learned from the study of objects d'art."

"Indeed," Bowen said coolly. "I would like you to meet my good friend Major Snyder."

Portiakov smiled and extended a beefy hand. "Delighted, Major. The American Army has much to be proud of. A distinguished fighting record. My country in particular is most grateful."

Snyder smiled back. "Appreciate the compliment, sir."

Bowen tugged on his arm and led him away. "That sticks in my craw," he said.

Beth joined them and whispered in his ear, "Bernard, Louise says behave yourself."

Bowen waved expansively. "I won't embarrass her, my dear. She's doing so well on her own."

Louise clapped for attention. "If everyone will please find a seat, I think we're ready to begin."

Gradually the guests settled into sofas and chairs. There weren't enough to go around, so Snyder stood next to Bowen while Beth slid into a chair in front of them.

Louise stepped to the center of the room and said, "As you know, we have all worked long and hard on behalf of the unfortunate Russian people. Our efforts have gone largely unrecognized in our own community, but we should feel honored when those we have helped send such an important spokesman to thank us personally. Will you all please welcome Vice-Consul Alexei Portiakov."

There was an enthusiastic round of applause.

Portiakov stepped forward with a smile and kissed Louise's hand graciously. He bowed to the gathering and waited for full attention. Then he clasped hands behind his back, cleared his throat and began. "Dear friends, your kindness is overwhelming. During these long, arduous years we have worked together with great dedication to one common goal, the defeat of Hitler's Germany and the liberation of oppressed peoples. Your generosity in aiding my country is something we will never forget."

Bowen whispered in Snyder's ear, "How much got to his people and how much is sticking to his fingers?"

Snyder forced himself to smile. He was growing weary of Bowen's attitude, even though it echoed his own.

"Through your efforts," Portiakov continued, "we have managed to relieve incredible suffering. Your donations have enabled us not only to aid our own people, but to supply necessities to displaced persons and refugees of all countries. We cannot thank you enough." He bowed to more applause.

"Here comes the pitch," Bowen muttered.

Beth gave him a withering look.

Portiakov grew serious. "However," he said, "there is still much to be done. Words cannot describe the devastation Russia has suffered. I'm sorry to say we will never know how many of our citizens were killed. Great areas of our country have been laid waste. The Ukraine, the wheat basket of Russia, was put to the torch and now must be reseeded. Homes and cities must be rebuilt. The real work lies ahead. And so, we come to you again, in the hope that you will continue supporting our cause, and do for us in peace what you so willingly did in war."

Portiakov bowed once again in response to the applause.

Louise came forward to thank him then turned to her guests. "Vice-Consul Portiakov will be happy to answer any questions."

A middle-aged woman with a purse tucked under her arm rose and waved a hand. Louise pointed to her. "Yes, Charlotte?"

"I just want to say that we all admire the courage of the Russian people . . ." She continued in that vein, followed by several other flatterers. It was almost more than Bowen could bear. He rolled his eyes and shifted uncomfortably from one foot to the other.

Snyder grew impatient, too, recalling vividly what Mullen had said about Portiakov. As he listened to more paeans of praise, he became determined to bring Portiakov down a peg.

A tall bald man boomed out, "We'll keep on supporting you, Mr. Portiakov. With this!" He waved a check high in the air and drew loud applause.

Snyder signaled for Portiakov's attention.

"Major Snyder?" Louise said happily.

"All this money floating around," he said, "is it really going to help everybody? Even the Poles?"

"You can count on that!" the bald man yelled back.

Snyder pushed away from the wall and fixed Portiakov with a thin stare. "It's a little late for the ones who died in Warsaw," he said.

Beth looked up in surprise.

Snyder's voice rose. "Maybe you people don't know what the Russians did there. When was it, Mr. Vice-Consul? Last summer?"

A hush fell over the crowd. Faces turned to see who the upstart was. Even Bowen gazed at Snyder in surprise. Beth tugged at his sleeve, but he pulled away from her, intent on getting a reaction from Portiakov.

The vice-consul stood his ground in the center of the room, a target. "I don't know what you're referring to . . . Major Snyder."

"Let me refresh your memory. Your country told the Poles in Warsaw to attack the Germans and promised to come in and help. But you didn't. You sat back and let them be massacred."

Portiakov stared at him, then found his voice. "Please, Major," he said with a bemused smile, "you mustn't be taken in by renegade propaganda."

"I wouldn't call the Government-in-Exile *renegades*, Mr. Portiakov."

"Nevertheless, that's what they are. And the only people who spread these stories are collaborators."

Snyder shrugged. "Maybe you're right," he said, catching a furious look from Louise. "After all, it's common knowledge how generously your government looked after Polish refugees in 1939."

At this everyone relaxed, assuming Snyder was backing down. Portiakov seemed relieved. "That's very kind of you, Major. This is one of the things we are trying to overcome, you see—this great confusion left in the wake of the war."

"I'm happy to stand corrected," Snyder said with a slight bow, "but I wonder if you could straighten me out on one thing."

"My pleasure."

"Could you tell me, sir, if the refugee center at Sobinka is still operational?"

Portiakov's smile froze on his lips. Behind Snyder, Bowen listened intently.

"The reason I ask," Snyder continued, "is that I haven't heard from a relative there in quite some time."

Louise tried to interject. "Major, that's a private matter. Why don't you speak to the vice-consul afterwards. I really think we should go on—"

"No, no, quite all right," Portiakov said quickly, smiling at Snyder. "If you'll give me the name, I'll see what I can do."

"Certainly," said Snyder. "Cypulski."

Beth stiffened and stared up at him. Portiakov reached into his coat pocket and pulled out a note pad. "How do you spell that?" he said calmly. Snyder spelled it for him. "First name?" asked Portiakov.

"Marion."

Beth swung her gaze to the Russian, beginning to understand why Snyder wanted to be here tonight.

Portiakov snapped the pad shut. "Thank you, Major. I shall do my best to help you. Anyone else?" He jabbed a finger at the first woman to raise her hand, effectively cutting Snyder off.

Snyder met Beth's curious look but didn't say a word. Bowen moved up with a sly grin. "Beth warned the wrong person," he whispered. "Tell me, do you really have relatives in Russia?"

"I come from a large family, Mr. Bowen."

"Evidently. You're the first Irish Pole I've ever met. Oh, my—" He stopped and nodded behind Snyder, who turned. Portiakov's session was over and the crowd was breaking up into small groups. Louise sliced through them like a petite juggernaut, her eyes glued ferociously to Snyder.

Beth rose. "He didn't mean anything by it, Louise."

"Yes, I did," he said. "I meant to needle the bastard."

Louise's eyes narrowed. "Really, Major, one thing I cannot tolerate is rudeness. You owe the vice-consul an apology."

"I didn't hear him deny anything."

Louise turned to Beth. "Make your friend understand that he has insulted my guest."

Beth bit her lip. "There's nothing I can do about it. But if it will make you happier, Louise, we'll go."

Bowen stepped between them. "Louise, you're manufacturing an international incident. I thought the Major handled himself extremely well—"

Louise whirled on him and snapped, "We all know how you feel—so stay out of this!"

Snyder took Beth's arm, put down her drink and said, "Mrs. Daniels, thank you for another charming evening. Nice seeing you again, Bernard."

"My pleasure, Major."

Snyder led Beth across the room. Portiakov bristled as they passed. Snyder gave him a dazzling smile. "Was it something I said?"

He walked down the front steps with Beth and led her to his car. "What was that all about?" she said.

"Vice-Consul Portiakov is no sweet, charming diplomat with the welfare of the world his chief concern in life. He happens to be a colonel in the NKVD, and probably the top Russian control agent on the West Coast."

Beth stopped him, bewildered. "What did he have to do with Marion?"

"If she was murdered by the Russians, I'm willing to bet he had a lot to do with it."

Beth looked up at the house. "Louise does some pretty foolish things, but you don't think she's part of this—?"

"Not at all. They're just using her."

"Maybe you should warn her."

"Are you kidding? And have it spread all over town?"

"But she might be in danger."

Snyder shook his head. "She doesn't know anything. She's a minor pawn. She's no threat to them."

Beth was quiet a moment, then said, "What are you going to do?"

"About Portiakov? Nothing. The next move is his."

She stared at him, then turned away. He opened the door for her. On the drive back she sat huddled away from him.

"What's the matter?"

"Nothing."

"Come on."

She wouldn't look at him when she spoke. "If he's that dangerous—if you knew that about him—why did you take such a chance?"

"What do you mean?"

"If he's having people—" She couldn't finish. Her hand went to her mouth.

"He wouldn't," Snyder said. "Too dangerous. In fact, maybe it was smart to hit him in public. If anything does happen to me, you and everyone else will know right where to look."

"Oh, Christ, that makes me feel so much better! What are you doing?" she quavered. "Playing a game?"

"Yeah. With tough rules."

She fell back into silence, angry with him. Nestled in bed a half-hour later, she wouldn't let him touch her.

"Why not?" he said.

"I just don't want it right now."

"Okay, but why?"

"Because . . ." She hesitated, then turned away and tried to forget he was there.

"Now cut that out," he said. "I want to look at you." She wouldn't turn back. "Because of what?" he said.

After a moment he heard a muffled voice. "You're the first man I've had in a long time."

"You told me that before."

"I don't want to get involved with someone who's careless about risking his neck."

"There's still a war on, Beth."

"I know that."

"What are you afraid of?"

"Losing you."

He sank against the pillows. He had thought she was more courageous; maybe he had just wanted her to be. She turned back to him after a while, tears in her eyes.

"Sounds selfish, doesn't it?"

"No," he said. "Human."

"You don't understand. I don't want to end up like *Louise*. Husband gone—no idea if he's dead or alive." She paused. "If you're going to take chances, then maybe we better keep our distance."

He frowned, then smiled as he realized what lay under the things she was saying. "You really care, don't you?"

"No. Yes. But I mean it. I don't want to lose you. I've kept away from men for so long. Now I've got one, I just—"

"You really want to be that safe? You'd throw me away just because it might be difficult? Cut yourself off? Be isolated? If you do it this time, Beth, you'll never stop doing it. Look at me. It's true, isn't it? You've been dreading that somebody might come along and you might have to care again." He took her face in his hands. "Take a chance with me."

She trembled for a moment, then moved against him. They kissed deeply. His hand slid up to her breast, then slowly stroked downward, pressing . . . She mumbled a protest then felt his fingers parting her thighs. She gave in and helped him.

July 22: San Francisco

Alexei Portiakov stood by a draped third-floor window in the consulate and looked down at the rain-washed house across Divisadero. Being watched by the FBI was an occupational hazard. But the stepped-up activity of the last few days was bringing grumbles of annoyance from others on the consulate staff. Snyder's badgering last night was another matter. Not furtive like those poor clods across the street, but brazen, daring. A man like that could be dangerous and should be handled accordingly.

Portiakov took the stairs to the first floor, ignoring the guard at the reception desk as he signed the duty roster, then walked to the end of the corridor. He went down another flight of steps to the basement, passed the radio room, glanced at the two horse-faced girls in the file section, then shrugged into his raincoat and entered a large storage closet.

He turned on the light and swung out the rear shelving panel. Behind it was a steel door with a combination lock, which he twirled quickly. The door swung inward and Portiakov stepped into a dank tunnel, hollowed out of the ground and disappearing into blackness. He picked up a flashlight, snapped it on, pulled the shelving panel back into place and pushed the door shut. He spun the combination from the inside, then turned and began the long walk that would let him out in the house on Pierce Street.

He played the light across his path in an alternating arc, checking to see that the shoring was tight, that there were no new slides or signs of stress. Several times he felt bits of dirt pelt his raincoat. His feet clumped on soft earth and once he stepped into a two-inch puddle, cursing as the water ruined his shine.

He reached the end, a thin wooden door at the top of a short incline. He hung the flashlight on a hook drilled into the wood, then rapped twice. He was let into the garage by his driver, who opened the rear door of the black sedan for him.

He rode in silence to the park at Telegraph Hill and walked quickly through the morning drizzle to the base of Coit Tower. Why the Americans had constructed a monstrosity in the shape of a fire hose nozzle was beyond his understanding. He shook his head as he trudged up the steps to the observation deck.

Bernard Bowen looked up as Portiakov came over to him.

"Lucky today," said Bowen. "No tourists."

Portiakov managed an appreciative grunt then leaned against the ledge, keeping an eye on the stairway. "I deeply resent last night's performance," he said. "It was not only embarrassing, but dangerous. This Major Snyder is more than a nuisance: he's a festering sore. The last few days we've had increased surveillance of the consulate. Now I understand why."

"You're sure there's a connection?" asked Bowen.

"Of course. The man knew exactly what he was doing."

"I don't think so. He was just probing. He can't touch you, Alexei, and I'm sure he doesn't suspect me. We're quite chummy now, in fact."

"Don't count on a long friendship."

Bowen shook his head. "You're overreacting."

Portiakov looked at him sharply. "Am I? I've enjoyed relative freedom of movement until now, but I have a feeling that your newfound friend is trying to restrict that. I should like to pay him in kind. But I would make it a bit more permanent. I want Snyder eliminated."

Bowen's patient smile faded. "This isn't Russia, Alexei. If anything happens to him, we'll really have problems."

Portiakov glared at him. "Like the ones you've caused by killing the Cypulski woman?"

"I've already told you that was necessary. She was about to turn me in. Let's not quibble. If our primary purpose is to stop this mission, then we must begin to work from a less noticeable direction."

Portiakov mulled over that. "What do you have in mind?" he mumbled.

"Another approach."

"What will it accomplish?"

"We will misdirect Snyder's attention."

Portiakov frowned and listened to Bowen's plan with grudging approval.

July 23: Berkeley

Snyder scanned the proposed crew list just sent over by Colonel Lowe, then buzzed for Fulbright. "Copy this list for our files," he said, "then return it to me."

Fulbright glanced at it. "Final crew?"

"After we run a security check, yes."

"Right away, Major," Fulbright said, turning on his heel and hurrying back to his office. He sat down at his desk and copied out the six names and serial numbers and committed them to memory for Bowen's use.

Snyder answered the phone and heard a gruff voice. "Snyder, this is Mullen. I need some information."

"Anything you want."

"Got a description I want to read to you. Male, six-two, hundred seventy pounds, black hair sprinkled with gray, thin face—"

"Wait a minute, Mullen. That could be anybody—"

"Drives a '39 maroon Buick with a Rad Lab sticker on the windshield."

Snyder controlled his impatience. "What are you getting at?"

"I'm calling from a stakeout house on Divisadero at Broadway. The car I'm looking at is parked in front of the Russian consulate across the street. The guy I just described has been inside the building for the last hour."

Snyder stood up. "Jesus," he said.

"Not likely, Major. He wasn't carrying a cross."

Snyder buzzed for Beth. "Hang on a second, Mullen. I'm checking it out."

"Take your time. Want the license number?"

"Yes." Snyder wrote it down as Beth walked in. He held the receiver to his chest and asked her, "Where's Lasch?"

"Out to lunch."

"It's after two."

"I never tell him when to come back."

"Do you know where he went?"

"No. He got a phone call from somebody and went out in a hurry."

Snyder frowned. "Does he drive a '39 Buick?"

"I don't know what make it is—it's maroon, though."

Snyder lifted the phone with a sinking feeling. "Mullen," he said, "his name is Allen Lasch. Bring him in."

"Okay."

"What's going on?" Beth asked as Snyder grabbed his hat and ran out the door.

He whirled back. "Stay by the phone." He rushed down to Security, his mind seething with suspicion. All that sobbing over Marion Cypulski—had it been just an act? He stopped outside the Quonset hut to catch his breath, and logic replaced his anger. He ran the events over in his mind. There was something very wrong about this. No spy would risk exposing himself by openly walking into the Russian consulate. That was stupid. And Lasch was not stupid. So why had he done it?

Snyder hesitated. What had first struck him as a major security breach now looked like something else. Conditioned reflex, he told himself. Somebody was counting on that. Now if they wanted to play a game, what would they expect him to do next? Confront Lasch? Arrest him? Search his apartment . . . ?

Snyder began to see the pattern. Coldly he decided to follow it through. He rousted Browne, told him him what had happened. Browne grabbed a set of passkeys and drove Snyder out to the Nunnery.

They entered Lasch's apartment and searched thoroughly. Just when Snyder was beginning to doubt the theory taking shape in his mind, Browne called him into the bedroom.

He was holding up the mattress, and there, resting on the box springs, were three pale green envelopes. Snyder picked them up and pulled out the letters, immediately recognizing the slight, spidery handwriting.

"What the hell is going on?" asked Browne.

Snyder stuffed the letters into a pocket and stalked out.

At three forty-five Lasch walked out of the Russian consulate and back to his car. He was picked up by Mullen without incident, then driven back to the Rad Lab. By four thirty he was standing alone before Snyder. Browne and Mullen waited outside as Snyder closed the door and sat on the edge of his desk. The letters were on top of the out box behind him, concealed for the moment by his body.

"All right, Dr. Lasch. Where have you been?"

"You know damned well where. You had your goon pick me up."

"Just so we both know. Now tell me why."

"A wild-goose chase. I got a call before lunch: a Mister Goroschnov of the Information Division asked me to come over right away. Said he had news about Marion's family. He kept me waiting over two hours. When I finally got in to see him, he claimed it was all a mistake, that he had never made the call. I argued with him; he was polite but insistent." Lasch shook his head in amazement. "I tell you, it was all very strange."

I'm sure it was, Snyder thought. He got up so that Lasch would have a clear, unobstructed view of the out box and the three Cypulski letters.

Lasch stared at the telltale green stationery, then looked up at Snyder. "Where did those come from?"

"Your apartment."

"Impossible."

"Captain Browne found them hidden under the mattress."

"That's ridiculous. I don't believe it."

Snyder took a step toward the door. "Want me to call him?"

"No! I mean, maybe you did find them there, but I didn't put them . . ." He trailed off, confused.

"I see," said Snyder. "Would you care to revise that story about the Russians?"

"Why should I? It's the truth." Snyder regarded him skeptically. Lasch reddened. "Look, Snyder, I don't have to sit still for the third degree—"

"Let's have another look at what's been going on between you, Marion and the Russians." Lasch stared at him. Snyder went on smoothly: "Marion was passing information because they had her family. You got involved with her romantically and she led you into it, too. Together you fed them what they wanted until Marion learned how she had been duped. She threatened to expose everyone and you were ordered to kill her—"

Lasch shot out of his chair with a scream of rage. "*You son of a bitch! I loved her! I never gave the Russians anything, and neither did she!*"

The door flew open behind him. Browne and Mullen burst in, followed by two MPs. Lasch whirled in surprise then threw out a hand to keep everyone at a distance. "What the hell is this?" he said, looking around wildly.

Snyder picked up the letters and waved them at Lasch. "How did you get these?"

"I don't know! Maybe you planted them!"

Lasch's shouting brought people out of their offices. A small crowd gathered behind the MPs, including Beth and Fulbright. Snyder's eyes flicked over them, then he shook his head at Lasch. "Nice try, Doctor, but it isn't working."

"What isn't working? What the hell have I done?"

"I'm not going to explain it again. It'll just embarrass you further. You can be Captain Browne's guest downstairs while we sort it out."

"You're going to lock me up?" Lasch said incredulously.

Beth stepped in. "What are you doing?" she demanded.

"Stay out of this," Snyder said sharply. He turned to Browne. "Get him out of here!"

Browne nodded to the MPs, who moved in. Lasch backed away and bumped into the desk. He turned to Snyder. "You're crazy!" His eyes became frightened. "This is a mistake!"

The MPs led him away. The people outside were stunned. Beth found her voice. "Have you lost your mind, Snyder? After all he's been through? You're treating him like a criminal!"

"Maybe he is."

"*What has he done?* Beth shouted. Fulbright moved up beside her.

Snyder's eyes flashed as he indicated Mullen. "This man is an FBI agent. He picked up Lasch a short time ago coming out of the Russian consulate. Browne and I searched his apartment and found these!" He held up the letters.

Fulbright blanched.

"Lasch and Marion saw a lot of each other," Beth snapped. "Maybe she left them in his apartment."

"Under the mattress? Look . . . I'm not interested in hearing any more emotional pleas. I've caught the man dead to rights and I'm going to hold him until I find out otherwise."

"You bastard," she said. "You see conspiracies everywhere. You don't trust anyone!"

Snyder grabbed her. "That's enough."

She yanked free and backed up, screaming at him, "Don't touch me! *Don't ever touch me again!*"

She stalked out. Several of the people outside glared at Snyder.

"Would you mind clearing the doorway?" he said, then watched them drift away. Fulbright stood his ground uncertainly, not knowing with whom to align himself. "Got anything to add, Keith?" Snyder said quietly.

Fulbright shook his head and moved away, deeply troubled. How had Bowen pulled this off? And what for? And more important, why hadn't he been informed?

Mullen closed the door and turned to Snyder and Browne. "You let it get out of hand, Major. I had you pegged for a professional."

Snyder leaned against the desk, glad it was over. "I had my reasons, Mullen. Tell you about them someday."

"Need me for anything else?"

"Not right away, thanks. And Mullen . . . seal your report."

The FBI agent glanced at him curiously, then said, "It's your show," and left.

Browne snorted. "Does that go for me too, Major?"

"Naturally."

Browne shook his head and walked out quietly. Snyder stared at the closed door, wondering if he had made the right moves. He had certainly made enemies.

July 23: Washington

General Groves finished preparing his first draft of the order to drop the atomic bomb.

TO: GENERAL CARL SPAATZ
CG
USASTAF

1. The 509 Composite Group, 20th Air Force, will deliver its first special bomb as soon as weather will permit visual bombing after about 3 August 1945, on one of the targets: Hiroshima, Kokura, Niigata and Nagasaki.

July 23: Potsdam

While brandy and cigars were being served after the sumptuous banquet hosted by Winston Churchill, President Truman gathered Marshall, Stimson and Byrnes together for a quick conference. Speaking in a low voice and keeping an eye on Stalin, who was only yards away puffing on a cigarette, Truman said that he had received a query from Chiang Kai-shek. The Nationalist Premier was concerned because the Russians were demanding heavier concessions from China in return for their coming participation in the Far Eastern war. Chiang was hoping Truman would use his influence to get Stalin to modify his demands. Truman wanted Marshall's final view on whether or not the Russians were needed at all in the war.

"So far, Mr. President, all they've managed to do is tie up Japanese forces along the Manchurian border," said Marshall. "If they do attack, they'll take what they want. The Japs can't stop them. But if we bring in S-1, sir, doesn't their involvement become a moot point?"

Truman said, "Let's put aside S-1 for the moment."

Stimson brightened.

"Then Manchuria is the only area where the Russians can be useful," Marshall continued, "holding down those troops. I can't see any need to get them further involved."

"That's in line with my thinking, General," said the President, turning to Byrnes. "Tell Chiang to keep up the negotiations. Say that we think the Russians will be flexible." Truman chuckled. "That'll keep them at the conference table till hell freezes over."

He thanked Marshall and strolled away. Stimson was ex-

cited by what Truman had said about S-1. Marshall said
soberly, "Don't be misled. He's going to use it, no matter
what he says in front of your or me."

Stimson's momentary elation faded. He sagged into a
chair and shook his head sadly. "I still don't see how we
can bring it off," he said. "We better forget about Big
Stick."

Marshall grunted. "On the contrary, I think we should
send it immediately."

Stimson blanched. "George, that's not what we agreed.
We have to tell the President."

"And we will. But wouldn't it be better to have the plane
sitting on the runway, ready to go, when we present it to
him? God knows what's going to come out of this conference, but I'll tell you one thing: once the ultimatum goes to
the Japanese, Big Stick becomes old news. We better think
of it as a wedge, not an end in itself."

Stimson looked at him wryly. "I see. A wedge, not a
club."

Stalin called for attention and offered a toast. "We cannot allow our American and British friends to spill their
blood on Japanese soil without the aid of their Russian
comrades. I drink to the day when we all stand victorious
in Japan."

Marshall reached for his glass and eyed Stimson pointedly.

July 23: San Francisco

Fulbright ducked into the antique shop and headed straight for the back room, ignoring Mrs. Beach's startled look. He found Bowen at his desk and dropped into the rocking chair. "We've had a hell of a day out at the Rad Lab," he said.

"Oh?" Bowen studied Fulbright's jittery manner. "How so?"

"Snyder had Lasch arrested, accused him of spying—" His voice dropped. "Threw the whole place into an uproar. He was shouting at Lasch; Lasch was shouting back. Christ, I've never seen anything like it. A goddamned circus!"

"Really?" Bowen said flatly.

Fulbright began rocking and gazed at Bowen suspiciously. "Come on. You had a hand in this, didn't you?"

"What makes you think so?"

Fulbright snickered. "I can see suckering him over to the consulate. That wouldn't be too difficult. But how did those letters end up in his bedroom?"

"Was that brought up?"

"Are you kidding? Snyder was waving them around like a flag. I've got to hand it to you, Bowen, everybody's upset. Is that what you wanted?"

"Perhaps."

"Then why wasn't I told?"

Bowen smiled. "My dear Keith, some things I can handle myself."

Fulbright was not comforted. Was Bowen really saying, Some things I *have* to handle myself?

"But don't worry," Bowen continued. "You haven't been left out. Now tell me exactly what went on."

Fulbright settled back and carefully related the afternoon's events. When he finished, Bowen frowned.

"What's the matter?"

"I'm not sure. But Snyder may have swallowed the bait a little too easily."

"I don't understand," said Fulbright.

"The idea was to cast suspicion on Lasch, slow them down even more. Snyder's loss of popularity is an added bonus, but it doesn't feel right." He paused. "I want you to get close to him. If he has to turn to anyone for support, I want it to be you. All right?"

Fulbright nodded then said, "There's something else." He asked for paper and pencil, then wrote out the names and current posting of the men Colonel Lowe had selected to be Snyder's crew. Bowen watched him, detached, already formulating a way to use this information. Fulbright handed him the paper, then looked him in the eye and said, "Bowen, I want to know what you're up to."

Bowen laughed and unlocked his cash drawer. "In good time, Keith. In good time. Just remember your part." He counted out a hundred dollars. Fulbright pocketed the money wordlessly. Bowen led him to the side door and gave him a reassuring pat on the shoulder. "Sometimes, it is best not to know everything that's going on. It makes you a better actor."

Fulbright hurried off. Bowen returned to his desk and made a long-distance call to a newspaper in Phoenix, Arizona. He placed an ad to run in the classified section the next day:

BERNARD BOWEN ANTIQUES—INTERESTED IN FRENCH PROVINCIAL AND EARLY AMERICAN FURNITURE—CONTACT P.O. BOX 10846, SAN FRANCISCO, CALIFORNIA—ATTENTION M. ANDRÉ.

July 24: Luke Field, Arizona

The C-54 came in nose high, and Captain Mark Gardner braced for the landing. There was a jarring crunch as the wing wheels hit the runway. The nose dropped and there was another bone-rattling impact. The student glanced sheepishly at Gardner sitting in the right-hand seat. "Not so good, huh, sir?" he said.

Gardner nodded. "Just take her in." As an instructor in multiengine flying, he was used to these landings. He went through them at the rate of five a week, and he'd guided dozens of young pilots in the problems of handling four-engine transports.

After the postflight Gardner dismissed his student and went to the PX. Standing in line to pay for his shaving cream, two packs of razor blades, a carton of cigarettes and a copy of the Phoenix *Herald*, he looked like the model American flyer: tall, well built and tanned, with close-cropped brown hair.

He walked to the Officers Club, found a corner table, then sat down and opened the newspaper to the classified section. He searched perfunctorily, as he had every day for the last eight months. He stopped at the middle of page fifty-two and scanned the little box again, then quietly ate his lunch and read the rest of the paper. When he was finished, he went outside to a phone booth.

He placed a call and in a few moments heard an answering voice. "Monsieur André," he said.

There was a slight hesitation, then Bowen said, "Early American or French provincial?"

"A little bit of both."

"I'd have to see them."

Gardner frowned, then said, "When?"

"Right away. Can you arrange it?"

"Yes."

Gardner hung up without another word, slipped out of the phone booth and went back to the BOQ. He put a DO NOT DISTURB sign outside his room, closed the door, then sat down and wrote a letter, careful to make his handwriting appear feminine. He dated it July twentieth, then stuck it in a pocket.

He left his quarters and went down to see the CO, Lieutenant Colonel Raymond Somkin, who sat behind his desk luxuriating in the sweep of his new electric fan.

"What's the matter, Mark? That's a helluva long face."

"Got a sick sister, sir." Gardner waved the letter and dropped it on the Colonel's desk. "What's my chance of getting some leave?"

Somkin absently fingered open the letter and glanced at it with a grunt of sympathy. "Got any time coming?" he asked.

"Yes, sir. Thirty days."

"Too long. Any special duty?"

"I checked, sir. I'm not up for anything but the usual."

"Well, God knows we got enough guys to handle that. Okay, I'll give you two weeks. Get your stuff together; we'll have orders cut by the time you get back here."

"Yes, sir. Thank you, sir. Is there anything heading east today?"

"No. We'll send you over to Williams. There's a courier flight in forty-five minutes. Get moving."

Captain Gardner packed a bag, picked up his orders and hopped the courier flight to Williams Field, just southeast of Phoenix.

At Williams he went to the Transient Desk and asked for a flight to San Francisco. An hour and a half later he was on a plane, wondering how Lieutenant Colonel Somkin was going to react two weeks from today when Captain Mark Gardner didn't return.

July 24: Berkeley

Snyder entered the tiny room at the back of the Security Section and closed the door. Lasch sat up on the cot and faced him sullenly.

"Let's talk," said Snyder.

"You mean like yesterday?"

"You were set up."

Lasch opened his mouth and raised an arm, pointing to the door, then his face clouded over. "What?"

"Set up," Snyder repeated. "Deliberately lured to the Russian consulate. For two reasons. One, to give somebody time to plant Marion's letters in your apartment, and two, because they knew I was having the consulate watched and would have you picked up after you were seen going in."

Lasch stared at him.

"I was expected to be too upset, suspicious and stupid to see what they were doing. But they overplayed it. Letters under the mattress—kid stuff. And if you were really working for them, why would you let us see that in broad daylight?"

"You—you mean that everything you did was an *act*?" His face contorted incredulously.

"A performance," said Snyder. "And you wouldn't have been convincing if you'd known about it."

"But why go through all that? For whose benefit?"

Snyder pushed away from the door and folded his arms across his chest. "The Russians were probably using Marion even before Big Stick came up. Getting rid of her could have been for any reason—it might have had no connection to us. But taking a shot at you indicates their real concern is the mission—and that's something we didn't know before."

"That doesn't answer my question. Why the act?"

Snyder smiled. "They've got somebody else in here besides Marion."

"A spy?"

"An informant at least. Somebody who could tell them how this little charade turned out. Think about it. Wouldn't they have to know? They couldn't expect to read it in the *Chronicle*. Somebody else here at the Rad Lab is on their payroll."

Lasch shook his head and his eyes narrowed. "God . . . the way your mind works. Commies under every rock. Pretty soon you'll be holding everybody in isolation. Then who'll be going to Japan?"

"All of us, I hope. I've just received orders to bring in the flight crew. They'll be at Hamilton tomorrow. If you want to back out now, I'll understand. But the rest of us are going."

"Everything works out fine for you, doesn't it?"

Snyder shrugged. "I'd still like to know who the inside man is. You know, you almost caught him the night everybody was looking for Marion."

"*I* did?"

"You said you heard something upstairs. You went to look. You saw the letters that Marion had left on her coffee table. Next morning when I went to look, they were gone. Now, either you were lying—"

Lasch broke in. "What if I was?"

"Then I've already got you, haven't I?"

Lasch scowled at Snyder. "Are you going to keep me here?"

"Well, there was actually another purpose to that, too. I got you out of the Rad Lab so that when we leave, nobody will be asking where you are." Snyder flashed a grin then checked his watch. "There are some people down the hall anxious to get started. Shall we?" He opened the door. "Don't worry—they don't know about any of this. And when the time comes, I'll clear your name upstairs."

"Wonderful."

The MP opened the door to the briefing room. Snyder went in with Lasch and Nakamura. Kirby, Bliss and Willard silently appraised the Japanese.

"Gentlemen," said Snyder, "this is Major Shinichiro Nakamura."

There was a moment's hesitation, then Kirby stood up and extended his hand. Bliss and Willard were full of questions about Nakamura's work, but he seemed reluctant to elaborate, explaining that he had been away from it for over three years. Lasch listened dispassionately. Finally Snyder rapped on the tabletop and asked them all to take seats.

"Major Nakamura worked with Dr. Yoshio Nishina at the Riken Lab. Nishina is one of the people we will be trying to impress, so Nakamura will coach you on your presentations. Any questions?"

Willard raised a hand. "When are we going?"

"Soon, so don't waste any time."

Bliss rose. "Can we have that box of material down here to coordinate our presentations with the paper work?"

"For the time being, no. But I'll send down a list of contents."

"I think we all know what's expected of us, Major," said Lasch. "We can get on with our work."

"All right," said Snyder. "If you need anything, see Captain Browne."

Snyder walked back to Le Conte, hoping Lasch would keep his feelings to himself. As he trudged up the steps to the third floor, he heard voices raised in anger. He came around a corner and they fell silent. A half-dozen people gathered at the coffee urn gave him hostile looks as he went by.

"Nice day, isn't it?" he said. Nobody replied. Snyder headed for his office, looking for Beth. She was not at her desk.

Fulbright came in. "I got through to Colonel Lowe. I told him the crew list was approved."

"Fine. Where's Beth?"

"Haven't seen her for about an hour."

Snyder caught his discomfort. "What's the matter, Keith?"

"There's a lot of talk, Major."

"So what?"

"I just want you to know . . . I think you did the right thing." Fulbright bit his lip hoping he wasn't going too far.

Synder eyed him curiously. "Does that mean you think Dr. Lasch is a spy?"

Fulbright's eyes widened. "No!"

"Then what?"

"Well . . . given the evidence, I think you did the only thing you could . . ."

"You mean I'm a hero because I threw your boss in the clink? How long have you worked for him?"

Fulbright threw up his hands. "Forget it, Major." He stumbled out, sure he had bungled it. Bowen would be furious.

Snyder moved to the door and watched him go. If there was a spy here, it could only be Fulbright, Beth or Lasch himself. They were the only ones who knew about Big Stick.

He went back to his desk and sat down. Fulbright? Not likely. Too much of a civil servant: always looking for promotion; jealous, envious, but hardly devious; and his loyalty blew with the wind. As a spy, he would need to have a better grip on his cover stories. Snyder shook his head: Fulbright did not seem to possess any of the requisite spy qualities, whatever the hell those were.

What about Beth? Her checkered past rose in his mind like a beacon, but so what? A briefly overactive sex life was no indication of a treasonous mentality. Had she done anything worthy of suspicion? Defended Marion, defended Lasch, scolded him for his callousness—he couldn't fault her for any of that.

Then what about Lasch?

Maybe he already had the right man.

He looked up as Beth walked in and slapped some papers down on his desk.

"What's that?" he said.

"Read and find out."

Snyder glanced through them quickly. It was a petition calling for redress, complaing that Lasch had been unjustly accused and denied due process, and it listed Snyder's "high-handed tactics" in detail. He turned to the signature pages and scanned the names.

"How come you didn't sign this?" he asked.

"I'm giving you more consideration than you gave Lasch. I'd like to hear your side."

He smiled, amused. "Why don't you hang up your crusader's outfit for a while and let me take you to lunch?"

"What makes you think I'd want to be seen anywhere with you?"

He stared at her then picked up a pen. "You want *me* to sign this?"

Angrily she snatched the papers out of his hand, grabbed the pen and scrawled her name in large, firm letters. Then she whirled and stormed out.

Snyder sighed to himself. Groves was right: these people were crazy. They needed babying, the kid glove treatment. Maybe he should bow out, ask for a replacement, someone with more tact. The group in Security weren't the only ones isolated: it looked like he was due for the silent treatment. He decided to go see his parents for a change. A little of his father's circular logic would seem tame right now. He called Browne, told him where he could be reached, then left.

The cars were backed up from the intersection at Turk and Market Streets. Snyder inched forward, ignoring the impatient horns. As he drew up to Turk, he saw the reason for the delay: a DeSoto convertible with its grille pushed in, and a black Ford sedan with a bent fender. The drivers were out on the street arguing. The one from the Ford was in a chauffeur's uniform.

A teenager walked out of the crowd and began directing traffic around the accident, hollering at the rubberneckers to move on. As Snyder drew abreast of the Ford, the back window rolled down and a pudgy face came into view. It seemed familiar. Snyder turned to get a better look and stared directly at the pug jowls of Vice-Consul Alexei Portiakov.

The car behind him honked, so he pulled into the nearest taxi zone, stopped and then turned to look through his rear window.

The Ford's windows were coated to prevent anyone from seeing in, but the license was a standard California plate, and there was nothing on it or on the car itself to indicate Consular Corps.

Snyder chuckled to himself. No wonder Portiakov was having trouble: he couldn't claim diplomatic immunity with standard plates. But why was he staying out of sight? Why didn't he produce some identification and get it over with?

Intrigued, Snyder pulled back into traffic, drove down to Golden Gate, turned right on Taylor and came out on Turk, one block up from the accident. He parked, looked back and waited.

Finally the drivers separated and the knot of people on the sidewalk drifted away. The convertible limped out of sight and the black Ford came up the street and rolled past. Snyder let another car go by before he pulled away from the curb.

He followed the sedan down Turk then up Van Ness to Broadway, staying well behind. The Ford made a turn off Broadway, went half a block down Pierce, then pulled into a driveway. Snyder stayed on Broadway, stopping at the corner. He watched as the driver got out to open the garage door, jumped back in the car and drove in, reappearing a moment later to pull the garage door down from inside.

Snyder waited another two minutes to see if either man would come out of the three-story stucco house, but no one appeared. He got out of his car and strolled up the street. Ducking into an alley on Pierce, he studied the house across the road. His gaze swept heavily draped windows. The little bit of front yard next to the garage was weed-choked and unkempt. Snyder frowned. This couldn't be the consulate: it looked deserted. Something was terribly out of place.

"Mullen, this is Snyder. Haven't you got a tail on Portiakov?"

"Round the clock."

"Where is he now?"

"At the consulate. Been there all day."

Snyder hesitated. "Have you heard about the accident?"

"What accident?"

Briefly Snyder described the car-kissing at Turk and Market. "Big goon driving a Ford, windows blacked out—"

Mullen interrupted. "Snyder, the consulate has three Packards and a Cadillac limo, no Ford. Did you get the license number?"

Snyder fumbled in the phone booth to get out the piece of paper he had written the number on. He read it to Mullen, who grunted and said, "See?"

"See yourself," said Snyder. "That's why I followed him. It was Portiakov in that car, but nothing indicated consulate."

"Where's the car now?"

Snyder told him about the garage on Pierce and the house that seemed vacant. Mullen was silent a moment then said, "Pierce and what?"

"Broadway."

"Shit. The consulate is two blocks away. Where can I meet you?"

Snyder was standing in the alley, his eyes locked on the house, when he heard footsteps behind him. He turned to see Mullen and three men in coveralls carrying toolboxes.

"I think he's still in there," said Snyder.

Mullen grunted and glared at the house. "Son of a bitch, I knew it was too neat. That guy practically lived in the consulate, almost never went out. And when he did, he made a big show of it, inviting us to follow him." He swore again, then his voice dropped. "We checked the license number. Registered to a David Tanner, who also happens to own that house. Ten to one Tanner doesn't exist. Here come some of my men."

They watched as a San Francisco Water and Power truck pulled around the corner and parked in the driveway of the "Tanner" house. Two men got out of the truck and went to the front door. They rang, then knocked; there was no reply.

Mullen was watching the windows for any sign of movement. Satisfied at last, he nodded to Snyder, and the group crossed the street.

The back of the truck opened and more men poured out.

A total of nine, plus Snyder and Mullen, stood in the driveway. Someone tossed Snyder a pair of coveralls and Mullen
said, "Better not show your uniform."

Snyder tossed his jacket and cap into the back of the
truck. As he shrugged into the coveralls, Mullen tried
the garage. Locked from the inside. Snyder followed him to
the front door, where one of the men went to work on the
lock. In a few moments the door swung open and everybody
trooped inside.

The foyer was dark. There was no furniture, just the
musty smell of disuse. Mullen tried the lights: no electric-
ity. Mullen had his men split up for the search. He led
Snyder and another agent through the kitchen and down a
stairway to the inner garage entrance. The door was
locked. They went down three wooden steps, then their
flashlights picked out the Ford. Snyder pointed to the
dented fender.

Mullen nodded. "Question is, where did they go?"

He walked around the garage, probing into corners with
his flashlight, poking at the black paper and chicken wire
between wall studs. He rapped the panels, searching for
hollow spots.

"What do you expect to find?" asked Snyder.

"You never know."

The men conducting the search upstairs began filtering
into the garage. "The upstairs hasn't been lived in for a hell
of a long time," reported one of the agents.

Mullen acknowledged without surprise. He was looking
toward the back wall, at a single old rusted monkey wrench
hanging on a nail. He went over and played his light on it.
Snyder joined him.

"Looks pretty pathetic up there all by itself, doesn't it?"
said Mullen.

"Uh-huh."

Mullen's hand closed around the wrench and he tried to
pull it off the nail. It wouldn't move. "What have we got
here?" he mumbled. Gingerly, he pushed the handle to one
side and felt unexpected pressure. He pushed harder and
the handle moved up, flush with the stud it was attached
to.

It swung on a spring lock and when it snapped into place at right angles, part of the wall moved inward.

"Aha," Mullen said, grinning at Snyder. "Want to bet where this lets out?"

The man at the security desk in the consulate jumped when the alarm sounded. The basement staff heard it and stumbled over themselves in their rush to get upstairs.

In his office Portiakov also heard the buzzer. As NKVD agents burst through his door, he was unlocking the wall cabinet and reaching for the submachine guns. "One of you at the top of the stairs," he ordered. "The rest come with me."

They hurried down to the basement and entered the storage room, snapping on the light.

Snyder trudged down the tunnel with Mullen and his men. Their lights swept cold, dank earth, shored up every ten feet by beams and planking.

They drew up to a steel door. Mullen bent down and stared at the combination lock. "We don't have time to horse around," he said. "Bust it."

The first blow echoed loudly in the storage room, startling the Russians. Portiakov unlocked the shelving panel, pulled it inward, then stared at the door, which rang from repeated blows. Angrily he slammed the butt of his weapon against it. The pounding stopped.

Cradling the submachine gun in one hand, he spun the lock, pulled down the handle and edged the door open slightly.

"You are trespassing on territory of the Union of Soviet Socialist Republics!" he shouted. "I advise you to leave!"

"FBI. Open this door."

Portiakov stood stock-still, weighing the consequences of defying the authority of his host government. Still hefting the submachine gun, he edged the door open and flinched as a brace of flashlights stabbed his face.

Mullen held up his ID case. "I'll bet you're just as surprised as we are, sir," he said. "We discovered a vacant house on Pierce Street with a hidden tunnel in the garage.

Naturally curious, we followed it to see where it came out and, to our amazement and yours, too, I'm sure, it leads right here. We've come to protect you, sir. I'm sure you wouldn't want any unexpected visitors. Now that we know of its existence, we'll see that it's watched day and night."

Portiakov scanned the bland faces of the men in coveralls. His eyes locked on Snyder. He choked briefly, then handed the submachine gun to one of his agents. Coolly he faced Mullen. "Thank you for telling me. We're grateful for your concern. We appreciate your taking the trouble to warn us."

Mullen motioned for his men to start back, then glanced over his shoulder. "By the way, you wouldn't happen to know who owns the car parked in that garage?"

"Of course not."

"Looks like it's been in an accident. We'll probably have to confiscate it."

"Do what you will," said Portiakov. "It's no concern of ours." His gaze slid from Mullen to Snyder and seemed to promise revenge.

"I owe you for this," Mullen said as he walked Snyder back to his car. "Did you see the look on his face?"

"Couldn't miss it. That's what I'd call a mad Russian."

Mullen's eyebrows worked. "Maybe it wasn't so smart having you along."

"I was just thinking that myself." Snyder worried that it might jeopardize Big Stick. He could only hope that Stimson or Marshall would give him the go-ahead quickly, so he could leave these troublemakers far behind.

"What are you going to do about the tunnel?" he asked Mullen.

"Just what I told him. I'll put a coupla guys with a card table up by his door. Either he's got more than one tunnel, or he'll be coming out the front entrance in the future."

Mullen opened the door for him. "Where you going now?"

"Home."

"You carry a gun?"

"What the hell for? I've got an Army to back me up."

"Just a thought."

"Good-bye, Mullen."

He parked on Dolores, got out and paused for a moment to watch the kids playing softball on the grassy center strip. An ice cream truck came along, bells tingling, and the kids broke and ran, squealing and digging in their pockets for change.

He went into the house looking for his mother and was surprised to find his father home early, sitting on the sofa in his undershirt, clutching a bottle of Irish. The old man started complaining the moment Snyder entered the living room.

"You know what those bastards did today? The great mucky-mucks that run the cable car company?"

"No, Dad, what did they do?"

"Threw me out on my ear!"

He took another healthy pull from the bottle and muttered an obscenity. Snyder pulled up a chair and straddled it. "Where's Mom?"

"Out shopping. Didn't you hear what I said?"

"Yeah—"

"I work me ass off thirty years for those bloodsuckers and this is the thanks I get!"

"What about the union?"

"Oh, they took care of that! Offered me a job in their cruddy wheelhouse!"

"Oh," said Snyder, relieved. "Then you weren't fired."

"Fired? I was *retired*! I'm not even at the age yet!"

"They give you any reason?"

"Never mind their reasons! It was dirty and underhanded, sneaky, like those rotten—"

"Wait a minute, Pop. There's more to it, isn't there?"

"There's nothin' more to it. The bastards gave me a choice—go out to pasture or work in the wheelhouse." He said "wheelhouse" as if he were spitting dirt. "It's the world," he went on, "the cruddy world that don't give you a chance. Take away your job, your dignity, your children . . ."

Here we go again, Snyder said to himself, but he listened patiently because it was easier that way.

"I'm tough!" his father said. "Tough as they come. I can take anything they throw at me. But Dennis . . . that nearly finished me, lad. And your mother, too, bless her soul. Those filthy yellow scum—they took away my boy—" He choked off.

"Pop," Snyder interrupted, "Dennis wouldn't want this."

The old man eyed him suspiciously then took another swig. "Wouldn't want it, you say? What's that supposed to mean, Patrick Timothy?"

"You're making a career out of feeling sorry for yourself and if you don't stop it, it'll kill you."

Stunned, the old man glared at him. "Don't go tellin' me what Dennis would want," he said. "He was *my* boy—"

"My brother, Pop."

"I raised him! I taught him everything—"

"Self-pity, Pop?"

Patrick Senior's mouth clamped shut.

Snyder went on. "You've turned the Japanese into scape-goats. You blame them for all your problems. Now you've got somebody else to hang it on—the cable car company. Where's it going to end, Pop?"

The old man staggered up from the sofa. His open hand flew out and caught Snyder across the cheek.

Snyder stared at his father then got up from the chair, turned his back and walked out.

He went down the steps and stopped to watch the kids again. Wearily he sat down on the porch and forced his mind to concentrate on them. He heard heavy footsteps behind him. His father stood on the porch a full minute before sitting down. They sat side by side, not looking at each other. Finally Patrick Senior passed the bottle. Snyder took a deep drink.

"You're right, you know," he said. "I have been carrying on too long about your brother. But maybe it didn't have much to do with him at all."

Snyder handed the bottle back. "What do you mean?"

"Gotta understand your own people, son. We don't run from fights. I could never tell you to duck one. But maybe I've just been trying to let you know it's you I'm worried about."

"Me?"

"Sure. I know I can't bring back Dennis. But maybe before *you* take risks you'll think of your mother and myself and be careful."

Snyder stared at him. "What risks, Pop? I'm not in a shooting war. Besides, I can take care of myself. I got my training from you."

The old man forced back a smile. "You wouldn't be handing me some blarney, Patrick Timothy?"

"Just get off your ass and go do something for yourself. Take the retirement and to hell with the cable car company."

His father thought about it a moment then sucked air into his chest. "Right," he said. "Who needs them anyhow?"

They sat on the stoop and finished the bottle. They were both drunk by the time Snyder's mother came home.

Captain Mark Gardner cleared through Alameda Naval Air Station late on the afternoon of the twenty-fourth. He hitched a ride to San Francisco, got directions to the downtown bus terminal, where he used the men's room to change into civilian clothes. Stuffing his uniform into his B4 bag, he checked it into a locker, pocketed the key, then went outside and hailed a cab.

He went straight to Bowen's shop and arrived almost at closing time. He stood on a corner as if waiting to be met by someone. After a while the door to the shop swung open and a frail, elderly woman stepped out. He watched her walk down the street until she disappeared around the corner, then he crossed at the light and went up to Bowen's display window. He studied a lamp.

Bowen opened the door and leaned out with a gracious smile. "Sorry," he said, "we're just closing."

"That's all right," said Gardner. "I was just admiring this lamp. Tell me, was it made by the André family of France?"

Bowen's smile deepened. "I'm not sure. If you have the time, I'll check the base for a signature." He held the door open and let Gardner step in. "Where did you hear about the André family?"

"Phoenix."

Bowen nodded and silently led Gardner to the back of the store. He closed the connecting door and said, "What shall I call you?"

"André will do."

Bowen filled two sherry glasses and fixed André with a penetrating gaze. "You've been activated because I understand you can fly a C-54. Is that correct?"

André nodded.

Bowen pulled out the Big Stick crew list and showed him the names. "Do any of these people know you?"

André scanned the list, then looked up. "No."

"Good. You'll be replacing the aircraft commander, Major Robert Macklin." In a low voice Bowen described Operation Big Stick, what it was expected to accomplish for the Americans and why it had to be stopped. He told André as little as possible about the atomic bomb.

"You will be a contingency," he explained, "if there is no other way to stop the mission leaving San Francisco."

"What about their security?"

"A major by the name of Snyder is running things from Berkeley. I must warn you, he could be dangerous."

"What about this crew—where are they coming from?"

"From all over—selected by the commanding officer at Hamilton, a Colonel Lowe."

"Wouldn't he know them—if he picked them?"

"That's a chance we'll have to take. I assure you, he's the only one who *might* know the real Macklin."

André grunted. "We'll see about that."

"You'll be there when Macklin comes in tomorrow. Find out if he knows Colonel Lowe. If he does, then you're out of it. Drop him off at Hamilton and return to Luke Field at the end of your leave."

"Wouldn't Macklin have some knowledge of the mission already?"

"I don't think so," said Bowen. "Just where to go and whom to see. It's really quite simple. They've handed us this opportunity on a plate."

André nodded. "Where do I stay tonight?"

Bowen picked up the phone. "We have a little house on Larkin Street."

July 24: Potsdam

Truman sat at the baize-covered table, listening to Stalin and Churchill bicker about the fate of Eastern Europe. The heat was oppressive and the lake breeze that swept through the open windows brought with it the usual swarm of mosquitoes. Truman was thinking about Stimson's latest request: if the ultimatum for unconditional surrender failed, the United States should offer some verbal assurance regarding the Emperor. That appealed to Truman's poker sense. If he could play it as a hole card . . .

He was roused by laughter. Stalin and Churchill had accomplished the rewording of a crucial clause by changing a couple of prepositions. Relief flooded the room.

Truman saw that the pot was right, the players primed. Now it was time to turn up the buried ace. He rose, left his interpreter behind and moved around the table to approach Stalin.

Churchill watched him through a haze of cigar smoke, slouched in his chair, fingering the tight bow tie under his bulldog jowls.

Stalin glanced up and smiled at Truman, who leaned over and said casually, "I just thought you'd like to know we've developed a new weapon of unusual destructive force."

Stalin listened to his interpreter, then nodded and replied, "This news is gratifying. I hope you use it well against the Japanese."

That was all there was to it. Truman was pleased at how easily he had discharged the obligation that he and Churchill had foreseen. The announcement had caused hardly a ripple. When the bomb was dropped and the results reported, Stalin would realize what he had just been told.

On the way back Truman passed Churchill, who asked how it had gone.

"He never asked a question," said Truman.

That evening Stalin met with Molotov and Marshal Georgi Zhukov, "the Conqueror of Germany."

Stalin had already received reports on Trinity from two sources: from Alexei Portiakov's unit and from Klaus Fuchs at the fest site. Fuchs was one of a small group of spies highly placed within S-1 and had been reporting regularly since the inception.

Stalin paced impatiently now, angered by the massive scope of the Manhattan Project and resentful that the expediencies of war had forced him to divert most of his own scientific effort into defeating the Germans. The Russian atomic program was pitiful: a total of twenty physicists and fifty staff members at one laboratory under the direction of Igor Kurchatov.

Zhukov and Molotov listened stonily as Stalin described his brief conversation with Truman.

Molotov was pessimistic, convinced the Americans were ready to use their bomb on Japan any day now, and that it would probably end the war.

Stalin lit a cigarette and rolled it between his fingers. "Anything else?"

Molotov was startled, constantly amazed at the Generalissimo's ability to sense when he wasn't getting complete answers. Molotov shrugged. "In light of what you just told me, I have some news that I no longer think is relevant."

"Let me be the judge of that."

"Our San Francisco group reports that a team of scientists is being prepared to warn the Japanese of what they can expect from such a bomb."

"Warn them?" said Stalin. "Is this true?"

Molotov nodded.

"But it doesn't make sense. Why would Truman tell me about it if he did not intend to use it? Did he think he could scare me with words?"

Zhukov had stood in silence, listening. He cleared his

throat and said, "It's obvious. He's playing a double game. On the one hand, he stands firm for unconditional surrender. On the other, he wants to go on record as having tried to warn the Japanese."

Stalin was pleased with that assessment. "So much for Western conscience," he said.

"Call it what you may," Molotov said grimly, "the Japanese position is hopeless. The Americans don't need this weapon."

"Yes, they do," Stalin said, "if they want to end the war before we come in. You can be sure they're going to use it, if for only one other reason—to impress me!" His eyes grew cold and he put out the cigarette. "See that Dr. Kurchatov is given all the help he needs. And find out more about this warning mission."

July 25: Hamilton Field

The first two crew members arrived by train, cleared through Colonel Lowe's office at 0700, and were installed in a special barracks. Three more trickled in via air transport. They all relaxed to wait for Major Macklin.

Snyder had received Marshall's latest communiqué, advising him that Big Stick should be prepared to leave on or after the twenty-sixth. From the morning of that date he was to be in constant communication with Thyssen and to notify Marshall as soon as the Japanese approved the mission.

He went down to Security to check on the scientists. He stood in the back of the briefing room and listened to Nakamura fire questions at Willard, who knew his information and was cool under pressure. Lasch jumped up as one of his answers became too technical.

"You're telling too much," he said. "You know the limits. If a question crosses the line, just say you're sorry, but you're not at liberty to divulge that. Okay?"

Willard threw up his hands in disgust. Nakamura turned. "Dr. Lasch, without being more candid, we're going to have difficulty."

Lasch looked at Snyder. "You know, Major, we're really groping in the dark here. Without seeing what's come from Washington, we don't know what to include."

Snyder unfolded his arms. "I'll send the Trinity box down after lunch. But it comes back every night. I'm holding you responsible."

Lasch smiled thinly. "Thank you so much. It'll make this a lot easier."

Kirby sat forward. "What's the word on when we go?"

"Any time after tomorrow."

The men glanced at each other. Bliss dropped his pencil on the table. "Jesus," he said, "we're nowhere near ready."

"Yes, we are," Lasch said. "We'll be fine, Julian." Bliss shook his head. "I suggest we break for lunch."

The men got up and stretched. Snyder cornered Lasch and Nakamura. "What's the verdict?"

"I think we can do it," said Lasch. Nakamura nodded agreement.

"And Bliss?"

"He's emotional," said Nakamura. "Always trying to make a speech. We have to force him to stick to the facts."

"Is he in over his head?"

"No," snapped Lasch. "He's afraid of fouling up."

Snyder watched Kirby and Willard go out. Bliss stood at the blackboard, hands shoved in his pockets as he anxiously studied a formula.

"Don't lean on him too hard," Snyder told Lasch. "This isn't a contest."

"I know that, Major. You just see that box gets down here. God knows what good it does sitting in your safe."

Snyder spun the triple locks on his safe and pulled open the heavy door. He set the Trinity box on his desk and instructed the two MPs on how he wanted it handled: inventory checked before leaving his office, checked again when the scientists were through for the day, same procedure every day. "Only Captain Browne and I have the combinations to this safe and that's how it stays."

The MPs repeated his instructions then took the box and left. Beth came in to say that Thyssen had called. "He wants to meet you at Sather Gate in thirty minutes."

"Thanks."

"You're welcome." She turned sharply and walked back to her desk. Snyder watched with a rueful smile. He still hadn't told her the truth about Lasch's arrest. He grabbed his cap and went over to her.

"Since we have a few minutes, let's go down to the faculty club for a bite."

Reluctantly she joined him, treating it as an order. She sat silently, toying with her sandwich.

"Do you blame me for doing my job?" he asked.

"No. That's all I expect of you."

"What the hell does that mean?"

"You do your job and let me do mine."

"I see. And *us*?"

She shook her head, indicating there was no more "us." Snyder scowled at her across the table, anger rising like a hot sword in his throat. He pushed away his plate. He didn't want to see this relationship end because of a misunderstanding, but he couldn't take her into his confidence yet. While he didn't believe she was the other informant, until he was dead certain, she would have to remain in the dark. And so would "us."

"I've got to go," he said, checking the wall clock. "We'll pick up again some other time."

"Why bother?"

He leaned over the table. "Because I still think it's worth it."

Their eyes met for a moment, both dark with anger. Snyder turned on his heel and stalked out. He marched down to Sather Gate alone, trying to drive her from his mind. He passed South Hall, the ivy-wrapped stone tower that reminded him of a Norman castle. He liked it here: Berkeley was more a park than a school, a grab bag of architectural styles mounted, no doubt, by some toga-draped Bohemian immersed in classical design.

He stopped under Sather Gate, a dark wrought-iron archway, the official entrance to the university. Thyssen was waiting for him, grim and disturbed.

"More trouble?"

"I have been going round and round with the Japanese. I thought it was all settled, then they started in with conditions. My country's foreign ministry says they might be trying to get the Russians to intercede for them."

"So what do we do?"

Thyssen sighed. "I have pushed them as far as I can."

Snyder uttered a curse. "That's not good enough. We're supposed to be ready from tomorrow on."

"Major Snyder, politics is economics—supply and demand. If the Japanese want to hear us, they will, as long as they believe it will help them."

"I don't need any more lessons," Snyder said angrily. "I need results. Can you deliver, or should we go another way?"

"You cannot go another way," Thyssen said quietly. "It is too late to change."

"Then you better bring it off!"

Thyssen's eyes went cold. He buttoned his jacket and said, "Of course." He turned and walked quickly back to his waiting limousine.

Snyder called after him. "Mr. Thyssen—I'm sorry."

Thyssen didn't look back, but he raised a hand and waved before he got into the car. Snyder deflated and leaned against Sather Gate, shaking his head, angry with himself for losing his temper. He felt completely frustrated.

André was on the platform of the Southern Pacific railroad station at Fourth and Townsend twenty minutes before the passengers from Reno were due in. He was in uniform; he had a car waiting, the driver an NKVD agent posing as a U.S. Army sergeant.

As soon as the train pulled in, André had Major Macklin paged.

Standing at the information desk, he saw an Air Corps major carrying a B4 bag step off the train and react to his name booming over the PA. He was tall, within a few inches of André's height, not quite as well tanned, but with the sinewy build common to most pilots. There was a superficial resemblance.

André intercepted him at the window. "Major Macklin?"

"Yes?"

André stuck out his hand. "Captain Grodin, sir. Orders to pick you up and drive you to Hamilton Field."

"Oh, that's very considerate. I was planning to take a cab."

"Yes, sir. You'll find this more comfortable."

André took Macklin's B4 bag and led him out of the terminal to the sidewalk. The driver took the bag and stashed it in the trunk alongside André's, which he had picked up earlier from the bus station locker.

André got in front with the driver, leaned over the seat, and chatted with Macklin as they drove uptown to the Golden Gate Bridge.

"Ever been to San Francisco before, Major?"

"No, I've been up at Stead Field, training C-54 pilots. Some job, but then I've seen my combat, so what the hell?"

"I know what you mean, sir. Family up there?"

"No. One good thing about Reno, though—the divorce capital of the world. And those ladies do love pilots."

"I'll bet they do, sir. Colonel Lowe, my CO at Hamilton, tries to get up there as often as possible. Ever run into him?"

"Sorry, don't recognize the name."

"Too bad. Nice guy."

André kept talking as the car swung onto Broadway and entered the tunnel through Russian Hill. In the darkness, André opened the glove compartment and pulled out a silencer-equipped .22 revolver.

He turned to be sure Macklin was sitting still, then swung his arm over the seat. Macklin had just a glimpse of the gun before it went off with a soft pop. The bullet slammed into his forehead. His eyes bulged from the impact, then he slumped sideways.

André dropped the revolver on the front seat then reached over the back, grabbed Macklin's body and rolled it onto the floor.

The driver sped out of the tunnel and turned up Larkin Street, pulling into the open garage of the third house from the corner. The door slammed down after him and two NKVD agents opened the car doors.

André stood aside and watched them work. They opened the trunk and hauled out the two bags. Macklin's body was stretched out on the cement and stripped of all identification. André traded his dog tags and insignia for Macklin's and took a silver ID bracelet from the dead man's wrist. He opened his own B4 bag and threw out everything with Mark Gardner's name on it, then stuffed the rest of his gear into Macklin's bag.

The driver found a photograph of a girl in a bathing suit, inscribed "To Bob with Love, Karen." André threw it on the discard pile then zipped up the bag.

Macklin's orders were in a manila envelope. André substituted the forged ID card the agents had made for him, then jammed Macklin's wallet into his back pocket.

Satisfied that everything was in order, André opened the garage door and slipped out with the bag. He walked up Larkin Street and hailed a cab.

One hour later the new Major Macklin reported to Colonel Lowe at Hamilton Field. Lowe called Snyder and told him his crew was assembled.

"Major Macklin wants to know what it's all about," he said.

"Keep everyone on ice," said Snyder. "I'll come out to brief them later."

Macklin faced one final test as he went to join the crew in a day room on the first floor of the special barracks. The men looked up from a pool table.

"I'm Macklin," he said, dropping into a soft chair. "How are you guys?"

"Fine," said the skinny one, waving a pool cue in greeting. "I'm Slocum—navigator."

The others introduced themselves: Grant, the copilot, Lefferts, the back up, and Beddic, the radio man. Whelan, the crew chief, looked up from his magazine. "Anybody tell you what's going on, Major?"

"Sorry, fellas," Macklin said. "I'm as much in the dark as you are."

He had coffee with them and talked, trading stories. They seemed amiable and in a short time everyone was at ease. Macklin was convinced he had successfully brought off the transformation.

He was still confident when he was called to Colonel Lowe's office. Snyder returned his firm handshake. Lowe volunteered to excuse himself but Snyder asked him to stay. "You'd better hear this, too," he said, then turning to Macklin: "Have you done much over-water flying?"

"Some. A tour in Europe. I was with Ferry Command at the beginning of the war."

Snyder checked that on Macklin's record, then said, "How well do you know the C-54?"

"That's all I've been flying at Stead." Macklin shifted his weight and smiled. "What have you got in store for us, Major?"

"You and your crew have been picked to fly a group of civilians and a Japanese POW to Okinawa."

Colonel Lowe's eyebrows went up; he stared at Snyder.

"I see. Where are the passengers?"

"They'll be brought here just before we leave. In the meantime you're on twenty-four-hour standby. Colonel Lowe has worked out the flight plan. He'll fill you in, but don't discuss it with the rest of the crew."

"Have we got a plane yet?"

"Yes," said Lowe, "C-54, just had its engines majored—best one on the field."

"I'd like to check it out with the crew."

"Fine," said Snyder. "But make it local. I don't want to be standing here with my thumb up my ass waiting for you to come back."

Macklin got up, smiling. "Don't worry. You shout, we'll be there."

Snyder turned to Lowe. "What about meals?"

"Major Macklin can requisition supplies from the In-flight Mess. How many are you taking?"

"Thirteen, counting the crew. I'd like food for seven days."

Lowe grunted. "Well, I can guarantee it'll be filling, but not sumptuous. Major Macklin can save his crew chief some work. All the Mae Wests, life rafts and chutes have been checked. They're well within the survey dates."

"Thank you, sir," Macklin said. "I'll pass the word."

"Don't be too disappointed if we don't use that stuff," Snyder said. "The idea is to fly to Okinawa, not row there."

Macklin's face broke into a grin. "I haven't lost a passenger yet, Major. I won't start now."

"Fine. Anything you need, tell the Colonel."

Macklin nodded and went out.

"What's all this about a prisoner?" Lowe asked.

"You were right," said Snyder. "We're going to snatch

the Emperor." He turned at the door and added, "Washington is sending out a Jap uniform for our POW. Would you see that it gets aboard the plane?"

Colonel Lowe stared after him, then shook his head slowly.

The C-54, serial number 229526, touched down gently, blue-gray smoke spurting from the wing wheels as they bit into the runway. Macklin chopped the throttles, then worked the brakes. The aircraft handled well, not like the ones from Training Command. He taxied to the end of the runway, swung onto the tarmac and turned the controls over to Grant. "What's the verdict?" he asked.

"All right by me," said Slocum.

"Runs like a fine Swiss watch," squawked Whelan in his gratingly high-pitched voice. Everybody seemed to agree with him.

"Okay," said Macklin. "Postflight critique in thirty minutes. I'll meet you guys in the day room."

They parked the aircraft and Macklin slipped away to a phone booth near Base Ops.

It was five thirty when Bowen answered the phone in his office. "Bernard Bowen Antiques," he said with an edge of hope.

"André," the voice said back.

"Where've you been?"

"Flying. You better tell me what you expect, because I've got a feeling we won't be here much longer."

"Our plans are not firmed yet. Just play along."

Macklin grew impatient. "Look, if they decide to leave before you get organized. what am I supposed to do?"

"We'll talk about that later."

"What if there is no *later*?"

There was a strained silence, then Bowen said, "Wait for further instructions."

Macklin heard the click and swore to himself.

July 25: Potsdam

Henry Stimson turned his bags over to Colonel Kyle and was about to leave his quarters when the phone rang.

"This is the President, Henry. I want you to know that I've just approved the bombing order. It's on its way to Tooey Spaatz."

Stimson sat down heavily.

"That order will stand," Truman continued, "unless I notify you that the Japanese reply to our ultimatum is acceptable. Understand?"

"Yes, Mr. President. Have the Chinese approved the draft yet?"

"We're still waiting for Chiang's answer. As soon as we get it, the ultimatum goes out." He thanked Stimson again and wished him a pleasant journey home.

Marshall was waiting at the car. Stimson motioned to him and they walked up the street to be alone. Stimson frowned angrily. "The man just won't understand. He's still playing politics like poker."

"What happened?"

"He sent through the bombing order."

"We expected that."

"I know, but . . ." Stimson turned an anguished look on Marshall. "Isn't there any word from Thyssen?"

"No."

Stimson sighed. "I hate leaving you holding the bag, but the President strongly *suggested* I go home. Let's face it: I'm not needed anymore. He listens to Byrnes, not me."

"Don't put yourself on a shelf so quickly."

Stimson managed a smile. "Nevertheless, I shall probably retire soon. But for now, George, we're caught in a squeeze. We can't tell Truman about Big Stick until Thyssen has Japanese approval. And if he doesn't get it before the ultimatum goes out, it's finished. We can't be at cross-purposes!"

Marshall nodded in agreement, then said, "There's still time. I'm staying here. I'll be close to it."

Stimson shook his head doubtfully. "Look, the conference has gone well in some respects, not so well in others. Stalin thinks he's got Europe by the throat. Clearly that's reinforced Truman's opinion of how to deal with him. He wants to use the bomb, now more than ever. If we're going to turn him around, we can't just walk in and say we've got this neat little mission. We've got to prepare him, get him thinking along the same lines that we have, make him aware of the larger issues."

"It's been tried," Marshall said.

Stimson struggled with himself for a moment, then reached into his coat pocket and drew out a fat envelope. "I'm not sure it's right," he said, "but will you see that the President gets this?"

Marshall held it a moment. "May I read it?"

Stimson nodded. Marshall opened it and scanned a lengthy memo addressed to Truman. Certain sections stood out:

> . . . I consider the problem of our satisfactory relations with Russia as not merely connected with but as virtually dominated by the problem of the atomic bomb . . .
>
> If we fail to approach them now and merely continue to negotiate with them, having this weapon rather ostentatiously on our hip, their suspicions and their distrust of our purposes and motives will increase . . .
>
> The chief lesson I have learned in a long life is that the only way you can make a man trustworthy is to trust him; and the surest way to make him untrustworthy is to distrust him and show your distrust.
>
> If the atomic bomb were merely another though more devastating military weapon to be assimilated

into our pattern of international relations, it would be one thing . . . but I think the bomb instead constitutes merely a first step in a new control by man over the forces of nature too revolutionary and dangerous to fit into the old concepts.

My idea of an approach to the Soviets would be a direct proposal . . . that we would be prepared in effect to enter an arrangement . . . to control and limit the use of the atomic bomb . . . and so far as possible to direct and encourage the development of atomic power for peaceful and humanitarian purposes.

Marshall looked up, sobered and moved. Even in the warm sunshine, he felt a chill of conviction.

"I'll make sure the President gets it right away," he said.

July 26: San Francisco

The double doors went up and two limousines pulled out of the garage, one behind the other. They turned out of the Russian consulate onto Divisadero. An FBI tail eased in behind them and the caravan drove south for several blocks. As they drew up to California Street, the first limo shot ahead and beat the signal. The rear one accelerated as if to follow, but at the last second the driver slammed on his brakes and fishtailed, blocking the intersection. His passenger was out of the car in a second, screaming at him in Russian and putting on a great show of disgust for the two startled FBI agents stopped behind him.

The first limo kept going, turning at Pine and pulling to the curb just long enough to let Alexei Portiakov out, then it sped off. Portiakov went into a small grocery store and stood by the window until the other limo drove past and the FBI tail scooted around it, continuing down California.

Pleased with his deception, Portiakov bought a bag of peanuts, walked out and hailed a cab.

The Fleishhacker Zoo was at the southwest corner of San Francisco, just above Lake Merced. Portiakov went through the turnstile and headed directly for the elephant enclosure. He found Bowen leaning against the concrete barrier, watching a wrinkled old gray bull snake his trunk out for peanuts. Bowen glanced up at Portiakov.

"Is this good enough?" he asked.

Portiakov looked around and nodded. "I had quite a time getting here," he said. "No thanks to your friend Major Snyder."

"What do you mean?"

Angrily Portiakov described Snyder's raid on the tunnel, then gave a short account of how he had just managed to outwit the FBI.

"How did he stumble on it?" Bowen asked.

"I don't know. But doesn't it strike you as odd that while we're trying so hard to stop this man, he manages to turn it around on us?"

"I'm sorry, Alex. I don't know what to say . . . Snyder is full of surprises."

Portiakov shrugged off his sympathy. "How did the Lasch affair end up?"

"He was thrown into solitary."

"Good."

"I'm not so sure. Snyder reacted just the way we expected him to."

"What's wrong with that?"

Bowen frowned thoughtfully. "It's too tidy. I think he's playing with us."

Portiakov said nothing. He reached into his jacket for the bag of peanuts, shelled two and popped them into his mouth. The elephant shuffled over expectantly, beady eyes fixed on him. Portiakov obliged, tossing nuts over the concrete wall, watching the trunk snake along the ground scooping them up.

"What do you plan to do next, Bernard?" he asked.

"I've already activated one of our deep-planted moles and brought him to Hamilton to replace the mission pilot."

"On whose authority?"

"Mine, but I want your approval now. The man is in place and nobody suspects him. I consider it a complete success."

"Which agent?"

"Phoenix. He's using code name André."

Portiakov nodded. "What is he supposed to do?"

Bowen took a breath. "If we can't stop the mission, he'll have to crash the plane in the ocean."

Portiakov crumpled the empty bag in his hand. "Does he know this?"

"I haven't told him yet. I consider it a last resort."

"Aren't you counting on the ultimate in loyalty?"

"No more than is expected of all of us," Bowen said neatly, taking the empty bag from Portiakov and dumping it in a trash barrel.

"Of course," Portiakov agreed. "And will Major Snyder be aboard this plane?"

"If they go, yes."

Portiakov was about to say something but cringed at the sound of a child screeching somewhere behind him. He glanced around with distaste and saw a large group of children, herded by several women, coming down a walkway to a hot dog stand.

As the children clamored for food, Portiakov nodded to Bowen and they walked around the elephant enclosure to the other side, away from the noise.

"I think you've overdone it," said Portiakov. "You've dropped a very important agent into a critically dangerous situation, risking his exposure, and it isn't even necessary."

Bowen forced a smile. "It's called initiative, Alex. If we don't need him, he simply goes back to where he came from and the man he replaced ceases to exist."

"But why go to so much trouble when all you have to do is eliminate Snyder?"

Bowen stared at him. "You can't be serious."

"I am. We're playing for time. If anything will slow them up, that will."

Bowen shook his head. "Alex, he would be replaced within a day. We've been over this before."

Portiakov balled one hand into a fist and his face reddened. "It's all different now, Bernard. We can't afford any more of his meddling. The longer we wait, the more likely it is that he will uncover you or your inside man."

"I'll take that risk. Now, what I want from you is authorization to instruct André."

Portiakov scowled. Distracted by the shouts of the children, he glanced up and saw two of them at the top of the slope playing with a small rubber ball. He turned back to Bowen. "I'll have to get approval from Moscow."

"What for? Alex, if we have no other way, it's got to be André! A crash into the sea will do it. Nobody wlil suspect us and—"

He was interrupted by a banshee wail. The ball had gotten away from the children and a little boy in shorts raced down the slope after it, screaming at the top of his lungs. The ball hit the corner of a bench and rolled past Portiakov and Bowen. The boy made his turn too wide and tripped on the edge of the path. He went sprawling and let out a shriek of pain.

Bowen reacted instantly, rushing over to help the child up. "Take it easy, little man," he said. "You've had quite a fall. Here now, no crying. Let's have a look at that knee." He pulled out a handkerchief to dab at the scraped flesh.

"Tommy! Tommy, are you all right?" a woman called, running down the slope.

"You'll be all right now," Bowen said to the boy. As the woman drew closer, he stiffened. It was Louise Daniels.

He shot a warning look at Portiakov, who had already seen her and replaced his glower with a cheery smile of recognition. She saw him first and slowed down. "Mr. Portiakov?" she said.

He tipped his hat. "How are you, Mrs. Daniels?"

"Bernard!" she said in surprise as Bowen rose from his crouch. The boy ran to Louise and buried his head in her dress, crying until she put her arms around him and picked him up. She held him close and patted his back.

"That's a brave little lad," Bowen said, smiling and stuffing his handkerchief into the side pocket of his coat. "Tommy, is it? How old are you, Tommy?"

"F-f-five," the boy stammered. His crying subsided with a sniffle.

Bowen felt for his wallet and fished out a dollar bill. "Such courage should not go unrewarded, Tommy. Here, I want you to have this. Maybe Mrs. Daniels will let you buy some ice cream with it."

"Oh, I think we might manage that," Louise said, smiling as Tommy reached for the dollar. It worked wonders. Louise put him down. "Run along, Tommy. Go back to the others. Make sure Charlotte sees that knee!"

She watched him scurry up the slope, his sore knee forgotten as he waved the dollar bill like a flag and shouted to his friends.

Louise turned back to Bowen, surprised and pleased. "Bernard, you have talents I never suspected." Her gaze swung to Portiakov. "And how nice to see you again, Alexei."

"My pleasure, Mrs. Daniels."

There was an awkward silence as Louise began to realize what an unlikely encounter this was.

Portiakov stepped forward with a wide smile. "You know, I'm very fond of children. I'm so pleased to see you putting yourself out for them. These youngsters remind me how much I miss my own family."

"Oh?" she said, eyeing the two men curiously. "How many do you have?"

"Three. Two girls and a boy. They are much older though. And I have not seen them in four years." He sighed unhappily.

"That's terrible." Louise shook her head.

Portiakov shrugged and tipped his hat. "I have to be going, Mrs. Daniels. Good-day to you. Mr. Bowen, we shall conclude our business at a later date. Thank you for your time."

"At your convenience, Mr. Portiakov."

The vice-consul shambled away. Bowen faced Louise. "Free for lunch?" he asked.

"I'm with the children till three."

"What a shame. Louise, you're so dedicated."

"Just doing my part. Bernard . . ."

"Yes?"

"Excuse me for saying it, but that is the last person I would expect to see you with."

Bowen was silent a moment, then smiled sheepishly. "I know. An unlikely match, isn't it?"

"Unlikely! *Incredible.* Since when have you changed your opinion of the Russians?"

"This is business, Louise. He called me, and I must tell you I was quite surprised."

She looked at him quizzically.

"Icons," he said. "The most beautiful I've ever seen." His eyes took on a reverential glow. "He has the most unique set of Russian icons for sale. Never seen in the Western world. Their impact will be stunning."

Louise looked confused. "Why is he selling icons?"

"The Russians have to raise money."

She sighed skeptically. "Bernard, how many times have you told me you would never handle anything that would help the Communists?"

"My dear, the icons are seventeenth century, quite a bit older than the Communist party. Besides, there's the commission . . ."

"Greed before principles? Since when?"

"Louise . . ."

"I see. And in order not to sully your reputation, you use the elephant pen for an office?"

Bowen's eyes rolled. "Portiakov's idea. I don't question these people and their methods. To them everything is a state secret."

She folded her arms across her chest and rocked back on her heels. She smiled then began to laugh.

Bowen reddened then forced himself to join her. "I know what you're thinking," he said.

"You do?"

"Bernard Bowen has shown his true colors: a businessman selling himself for profit. Louise, that is not the case. These are true masterpieces and I consider it an honor to put aside politics and bring them to the attention of the art world—"

Louise waved a hand. "It's all right, Bernard. I'm not judging you. But oh, my God, how you've lectured me about Russians! To find you dealing with them cheek by jowl is too funny for words!" She laid an affectionate hand on his arm. "I've never seen this side of you before. It doesn't fit your image."

She laughed again. Bowen kept his smile but she had struck a sensitive chord. More important, she had seen a connection that he had worked hard to conceal. What would she make of it? Would she keep it to herself or spread the news around? He was tempted to ask her to treat it as a confidence, but that would make him even more vulnerable. Should he let it pass and hope it would blow over? No, he told himself, you can't operate that way: you have to be sure. After all, who was the first person she would tell? Beth Martin, who might turn around and tell Snyder . . .

"I have an idea," he said. "Why don't you come home

with me now? Make your excuses to the other women. I see three of them up there: that should be enough to handle the children. Let me show you the photographs of these icons. Then you be the judge. If you don't agree that they transcend politics, then perhaps I shall let you do something wicked to me."

Her smug look faded. She regarded him with interest. "Such as what?" she asked.

"I leave that to your generous imagination. The photographs are in my bedroom."

Louise stepped closer to him. "You never stop, do you?"

"No," he said. "I'm always thinking of you."

She smiled, weakening. "I don't know. I've never been asked to judge works of art."

"It could be a delightful experience." He closed a hand over hers. She squeezed back.

"Where are you parked?" she asked huskily.

Snyder grabbed the phone on the second ring. Thyssen's voice crackled with excitement. "It is done," he said. "The party is set for the twenty-ninth. If you can get clearance, I shall be ready to leave this afternoon."

"Where are you, Mr. Thyssen?"

"My office."

"I'll call you back. Sit tight."

Snyder hung up, then picked up the scrambler phone. He called Bud Veneck. "I need a final approval for Big Stick," he said.

"Jesus Christ, when?"

"We have to be in Okinawa on the twenty-ninth."

"Damn. Stimson's en route home but not expected until late tomorrow."

"What about Marshall?"

"Still in Potsdam. Want me to clear it with him?"

"Yeah. Take this down and send it plain language: Big Stick jackpot twenty-nine July, await blessing soonest, signed Snyder."

"Got it," said Veneck. "It'll go right out."

Snyder called Hamilton and got Colonel Lowe. "Colonel," he said, "orders are going to be coming through. I want to leave in three hours."

"All right," said Lowe. "I'll pass it on to Macklin, unless you want to talk to him."

"I'll see him when I get to the field."

Snyder put down the receiver and turned to his safe, then remembered that the Trinity box was down with the scientists. He hurried over to Beth's desk. "We're leaving," he said. "Drop whatever you're doing for the next few hours. Go to my office. I'm expecting a call on the scrambler. You can reach me in Security."

He started down the hall. "Wait a minute," Beth called. "What about Dr. Lasch?"

He spun around and looked at her. "See if you can get all those petition signers up here on the double. As many as you can find." He turned again and opened Fulbright's door.

"What is it, Major?" Fulbright looked up from his desk.

"We've got to put the Trinity box into a protective casing. Can you dig up something that's watertight?"

Bewildered, Fulbright stood up. "I can try."

"Get on it, Keith. We're leaving." Snyder ran out.

Fulbright stepped into the hall, trying to think where he would find such a case. For a moment his mind wouldn't function. *Leaving. Christ, why so sudden?* He had to get hold of Bowen. He couldn't use his own phone: Snyder might return at any moment. He decided on the shipping department. He hurried down to the first floor, then across to the Rad Lab. He found the receiving clerk and told him what was needed, giving the approximate dimensions of the Trinity box.

As the clerk went off to his supply room to look for it, Fulbright took a chance and picked up the phone. He called Bowen's shop. Mrs. Beach answered.

"Hello," he said. "Is Mr. Bowen there?"

"No, he's not," she said in a cracked singsong tone. "May I ask who's calling?"

"Uh . . . Mr. Keith. It's very important that you get in touch with him and give him a message. Tell him the shipment he was concerned about will be leaving this afternoon. Be sure to tell him it was Mr. Keith who called."

"I'll do that."

Fulbright hung up just before the clerk returned carrying a metal container. "Will this do?" he asked hopefully. "It's aluminum with rubberized seals around the lip."

"That's fine." Fulbright grabbed the case and hurried out.

Bowen pulled into his garage and was about to get out of the car when he felt Louise's arms go around his neck. She pressed her body against his. He turned to slip into an embrace and felt her breasts thrusting against his chest. He kissed her deeply and his hand worked against her back. He came up for air. "Inside," he breathed.

"Haven't you ever done it in a car, Bernard?"

He smiled. "Come on." He slid across the seat and opened his door. Disappointed, Louise stepped out and waited for him to close the garage door. He unlocked his service porch entry and let her in.

"Under the circumstances," he said, "I think the icons can wait."

"Good. Right now I don't feel very religious." She held up her arms and motioned to him with both hands. "Come here."

They came together. She kissed him again and pushed her tongue into his mouth. He felt a surge of excitement and wrapped his arms tightly about her, grinding his hips against hers. He groaned and she laughed.

"At least there's one thing you're consistent about, darling," she whispered.

"Upstairs," he murmured.

She shook her head with a mischievous smile. "I want to be daring. Make love to me in the living room with all the curtains open."

"I see. We're on display?"

In reply she unbuttoned her dress and let it drop to the floor. He stared at her sheer silk slip and stood back to watch her remove the rest.

"In the living room," she insisted. He followed her.

Instinctively he went to the windows to pull the drapes.

"I want them open, Bernard."

He hesitated and looked back. She had the slip off and was stepping out of her panties. Naked, she walked right up to the big front window.

"God, Louise, have you lost your mind?" With three quick pulls he had the drapes closed. Before she could protest, he picked her up and carried her back to the couch.

Playfully she fumbled at his clothes, undressing him. She tugged at his belt, then slipped a hand into his shorts, fingers caressing him. He threw off the rest of his clothes, gently removed her hand, then pushed her back on the couch and braced himself between her legs. She pulled him down and thrust her hips to meet him. His arms crept under her back, one hand digging into the soft flesh of her bottom, the other edging upwards.

She felt fingers cup the back of her head and moaned passionately. "I like that . . ."

His other hand worked up until a circle of fingers surrounded her neck. She pumped harder, grinding into him. As she neared her climax, she felt the fingers tighten about her throat and for a brief moment her pleasure was heightened unbearably.

Her eyes popped open and she tried to tell Bowen how much she loved him. He was so good with her; Gary had never been this good. She saw Bowen's face contorted with effort. She felt his breath coming in great gusts. She wanted to beg him to hold on just a little longer. She struggled to get the words out, then found herself struggling to breathe. Pressure. Windpipe. His thumbs digging in. Blurred vision. Spots. Bright explosions of white sparkling over his face like stars.

She flung up a hand to grab his forearm, to let him know he was hurting. One finger dropped down her neck and pressed something at the base of her skull. She heard a roaring sound. . . .

Bowen held her pinned to the couch, rigid, his hands choking the breath out of her, his forefinger jabbed into her carotid artery. He tensed, then exploded in orgasm.

He fell on Louise's body, gasping for breath, his hands letting go. She lay still beneath him. He dragged himself to a crouch and looked into her face—blue, tongue distended, eyes wide open in terror.

Bowen crawled off the couch and staggered to the bathroom. He washed and stared at his face in the mirror. It wasn't the first time he had killed, but by far the worst.

Was it necessary? he asked himself. Too late now. Louise had been useful and pleasurable, but she had stepped in the way. He would console himself with the fact that her death had been swift, accompanied by pleasure until the very last.

He heard the phone ring and ran out to get it. It was Mrs. Beach. Carefully she repeated Fulbright's cryptic message. Bowen listened with growing panic. He thanked her in a hoarse voice and hung up, staring back at Louise's body on the couch. Shaking with anger, he cursed her aloud. She may have cost him everything. André. What the hell was he going to do about André? If they lost this chance, Portiakov would not hesitate to point the finger at him. He knew what that would lead to.

At Hamilton, Macklin went through the preflight checklist automatically, mentally calculating his options. He was furious with Bowen for not getting back to him with instructions. He was hamstrung. If it were up to him, he would take the initiative and sabotage the mission. But there was always the chance that Bowen had something else in mind. The only thing he could do was fly the plane to Okinawa and back, then shed Macklin's identity and return to Luke Field as Captain Gardner.

But suppose there were delays at the other end? Suppose somebody discovered he wasn't Macklin? He grew angrier. There was no way he could get to a phone because Colonel Lowe had forbidden the crew to leave the plane once they were aboard.

So he sat, cursing Bowen's lack of organization.

Snyder and Browne walked into the briefing room, calling a halt to the scientists' morning session. The Trinity box was open on the table and its contents spread among the men.

"Time to go," Snyder said.

There was a stunned silence. Nakamura stood up and began to collect the Trinity documents. One by one the others rose and helped him. Lasch turned from the blackboard and picked up the inventory.

"I'll do that, gentlemen," said Snyder, coming across the

room. "I'd like you to return to your quarters and pack. Be back here in thirty minutes, ready to go."

Wordlessly Nakamura walked to the door, his face furrowed in thought. The MP rose in the hallway and fell in behind him. Kirby touched Snyder's arm. "Thank you, Major. I never thought you'd pull it off."

Willard grinned. "He's happy because he just won fifty dollars from me."

Snyder chuckled then told them to get moving. Lasch was still checking things off on the inventory. Snyder took the clipboard from him. "I said I'd handle that, Doctor. Make a list of what you want from your apartment and we'll send an MP over to pack for you."

Bliss smiled nervously. "Any chance I could phone my wife?"

"Afraid not. If you get an extra minute, dash off another note. Captain Browne will mail it."

Bliss looked dejected. "God, I hope we're ready," he said.

"You'll still have time during the flight."

Bliss nodded uncertainly and hurried out. Snyder folded up the box and went over to Lasch. "Finished with that list?"

"Yes. What next?"

"Come and watch me eat some humble pie."

A murmur of surprise greeted them as they pushed through the crowd of lab people. Harris Emmett clasped Lasch's arm in a show of support. He was beseiged with questions. Snyder ducked into his office and put the box down on his desk, then he went out and asked for attention.

They grew quiet. Beth was perched on the edge of her desk, watching with interest. Fulbright joined the crowd.

"I have something to say," Snyder announced. "Everyone here signed a petition protesting certain actions of mine. For reasons known only to Dr. Lasch and myself, we've had to play a little game. At no time was Dr. Lasch suspected of anything. I can't tell you why you weren't taken into our confidence, just that it had to be that way. I hope now you can understand, forget it and just go about your business as if it never happened. Dr. Lasch appreciates your loyalty and so do I."

His speech deflated their anger. Slowly they seemed to grasp that everything would be getting back to normal. They looked at Lasch expectantly.

"Please return to work," he said quietly. "And thanks for everything."

Most of the group broke up and drifted away. A few remained, talking with Lasch.

Fulbright stood back, wondering what was going on. Why had Snyder taken Lasch away only to bring him back? Why had he been playing this "little game," as he put it? Unless he knew all along that Lasch had been set up . . . He was startled when Snyder called his name.

"Keith, I want you and Beth in my office right now." He turned to Lasch. "Doctor, you too."

When they were all inside, Snyder shut the door. "Beth, anything from Washington?"

"No, I would have told you."

His eyes flicked at her. She was still standoffish. Evidently his grandstand play hadn't affected her. He glanced at Lasch. "Fulbright will be taking over for you here. How fast can you brief him?"

"He knows it pretty well. Twenty minutes."

"Okay. Beth, you'll be assisting him. Keith, did you find something for the Trinity box?"

"In my office."

"See that I have it before you and Dr. Lasch get together."

Fulbright nodded and Snyder opened the door. They left, except for Beth. She confronted him with a suspicious glare. "What *were* you up to?"

"Can't tell you. It's not resolved yet."

"What isn't?"

"Sorry."

"Look, if there isn't going to be any trust at all between us—"

"This isn't us."

She glared at him. "I'm not asking about anything but Dr. Lasch. What was going on?" She waited for an answer and got only a blank look. Finally she understood. Her mouth opened. "My God, it's *me* you suspect, isn't it?"

"Don't go reading—"

"That's all right," she snapped. "Now I don't want to hear it." She turned to leave. Snyder slammed the door shut and grabbed her by the shoulders.

"Let go. That hurts."

"Listen to me."

"No."

"Damn it, I said listen! Don't you understand what we're dealing with? They murdered Marion and tried to discredit Lasch! They're cold-blooded, and that's what I have to be! Now, if you want to help, get off my back!"

She stared at him.

"No emotion, Beth. Use your head. Make an effort to understand."

Her lower lip trembled. Finally, she muttered, "Yes," and opened the door. She walked out quickly and Snyder swore to himself. He glanced down and saw the watertight case placed just outside his door.

July 26: Potsdam

Marshall and Byrnes arrived at the Little White House shortly before Truman returned from inspecting troops stationed in Frankfurt.

Byrnes waited for Marshall to get a drink then showed him a cable: Chiang Kai-shek's endorsement of the ultimatum, which would go out as the Potsdam Proclamation.

Marshall read it with a sinking feeling. In his own pocket he was carrying Snyder's latest message, informing him of the Japanese go-ahead for Big Stick.

Marshall quietly sipped his drink, examining his alternatives. He could tell Truman about Big Stick and plead for approval, or he could keep his counsel and let the proclamation go. What if he ordered Snyder to proceed? Stimson's warning echoed in his mind. The two efforts *could not* be allowed to cross each other.

Truman came in, mixed his own bourbon and soda and sat down to read Byrne's cable. "Fine," he said happily. "See that the press gets the proclamation after nine tonight."

Marshall cleared his throat. "What do you think the Russian reaction is going to be, Mr. President—considering they haven't been consulted?"

"Let them find out along with the rest of the world."

"But if you recall Stimson's memo, sir . . . he points out the dangers of taking—"

"We've been all through that, General," Truman broke in. "I appreciate your concern but this is how I want to play it."

There was nothing more Marshall could do. Big Stick was in limbo until the answer came back. Marshall stood up and took his leave.

July 26: Berkeley

Bud Veneck was sympathetic on the phone. "Sorry, Snyder, but the General was clear as a bell. You can't go yet."

"Did he say why?"

"No."

"Are you sure he understood?"

"Positive. Wish I could tell you more, but that's all I know."

Snyder hung up. What the hell was Marshall waiting for— engraved invitations? He got up and walked across the hall to Lasch's office.

"Long twenty minutes, Snyder," Lasch said. "We've been sitting here for hours."

"There's been another delay."

Fulbright groaned, put down a file and rubbed his eyes wearily.

"Is it off?" asked Lasch.

"No. Keith, would you call Colonel Lowe and tell him to have the crew stand down?"

"Right away." Fulbright got up painfully and left the office.

Snyder picked up the phone, called Thyssen and curtly explained the situation.

Thyssen could not keep the disappointment out of his voice. "This is very disheartening, Major. They must understand what this does to negotiations."

"I'll keep you posted," said Snyder. He hung up and Lasch wiggled a finger at him.

"How long are they going to run us around, Major?"

"Sorry, Dr. Lasch, but it's up to them, not us."

"Do I have to go back to Security?"

"No, but I'd appreciate it if you'd come along with me while I tell the others."

Lasch got up, shaking his head in frustration.

"Anything I can do?" Beth asked. Her sympathetic gaze settled on Snyder.

"I'll let you know."

Almost as one, they stood up when Snyder and Lasch walked in the door. Kirby closed his diary; Bliss snatched up his valise; Willard smiled knowingly. "We're not going, are we?" he said.

Nakamura was sitting with his back to the door and turned to stare at Snyder, who looked right at him and shook his head.

"Not just yet," he said.

"What the hell is it now?" Bliss demanded.

"Sorry to say. I just don't know."

Kirby looked at Lasch. "How about it, Allen?"

"We wait," Lasch said simply.

"How long?" Bliss snapped, his voice rising with irritation. He came around the table to Snyder. "I'll bet you find this amusing. Keeping a bunch of people on the string."

Snyder regarded him stiffly, then said, "Why don't you all go back to your quarters and unpack?"

Bliss decided further questioning was useless. "Come on," he said, leading Kirby and Willard out.

Nakamura stood up, his face showing the strain. "Major," he said patiently, "are you sure this is just a delay?"

"Yes. I'm positive we're going to go—and soon."

Nakamura closed his eyes and nodded. Snyder thought for a moment he might be praying. Then he said, "Excuse me," and went out.

"Major Snyder," Lasch said quietly, "if things keep on this way, we're going to be useless by the time we get to Okinawa."

"Well, what do you want me to do about it?" Snyder said, barely tolerant.

"Make sure your superiors know it isn't just *politics*." Lasch spun on his heel and walked out.

Snyder looked at the blackboard, still half-covered with calculations. That was how he felt: half-informed.

Bowen peered between closed drapes at the small moving van pulling into his driveway. He walked into the garage and swung open the door. The two NKVD agents dressed in coveralls followed him inside carrying a large wooden crate.

"In the living room," he said. "Take the couch, too."

Bowen poured himself another drink and sat by his kitchen phone, worried. If the plane was gone and André was over the Pacific, he was finished. He couldn't keep that from Portiakov. And without orders André would simply fly the plane as Major Macklin, carrying the deception as far as he could.

He looked up as the two men returned, guiding the crate through a narrow hall. Louise was now just a thing in a box. He watched it disappear into his garage and heard the bump as they loaded it aboard the truck. Then they came back for the couch.

The phone rang and he snapped it up. "Bowen," he said.

"This is Fulbright. Shipment's delayed." The line clicked off.

Bowen, still holding the receiver, was stunned by his good fortune. Delayed. Slowly he sank onto his kitchen stool. For some reason he was to have another chance. He had long ago stopped believing in a God, but there was still luck. Relief flooded through his tense body.

He got up and walked to the living room. He stood aside as the two men went out with his prize Victorian couch. "Anything else?" one of them asked.

"No."

He waited till he heard the garage door close, then opened his front drapes and stood looking out at the city. He was going to miss Louise—her parties, her body, her teasing conversation, her useful friends . . .

Her friends. He began to wonder who would notice her absence first. Of course, she would be missed. There would be questions. And too many people knew that Bernard Bowen was a *dear friend* of Louise Daniels. How many he could never guess. Prudence had never been one of her virtues.

The phone rang again. It was André, flat contempt in his voice.

"I called your shop. Let's get something straight. I don't want to have to go through an old lady to reach you—"

Bowen cut him short. "How long is the delay?"

"You tell me. I'm the one without information. I need instructions."

"You'll get them. This was unforeseen. We were all caught off guard. It won't happen again."

"What if they decide to leave in the next five minutes?"

"It won't happen that quickly, and next time I'll know in advance." He was thinking, Why hadn't Fulbright called sooner?

"You better come up with something because I'm out here hanging on a limb."

"Don't worry." Bowen hung up, frowning to himself. André was right. This was senseless. Why hadn't Moscow come through? Were they afraid to take direct action against an American mission? He thought Portiakov had understood it was a simple matter: sacrifice the agent— make the plane and its passengers disappear. Bowen tried to think like a politician. Maybe there was more to be gained . . . He would have to bend his mind to that.

July 26: Potsdam

At 7 P.M. Byrnes distributed copies of the Potsdam Proclamation to the press, with instructions to release it through the wire services at nine twenty. Promptly at that hour the text was radioed to Japan.

THE POTSDAM PROCLAMATION
BY THE HEADS OF GOVERNMENT,
UNITED STATES, CHINA
AND THE UNITED KINGDOM

We, the President of the United States, the President of the National Government of the Republic of China and the Prime Minister of Great Britain, representing the hundreds of millions of our countrymen, have conferred and agreed that Japan shall be given an opportunity to end this war.

Following are our terms. We will not deviate from them. There are no alternatives. We shall brook no delay.

There must be eliminated for all time the authority and influence of those who have deceived and misled the people of Japan into embarking on world conquest . . .

We call upon the Government of Japan to proclaim now the unconditional surrender of all the Japanese armed forces, and to provide proper and adequate assurances of their good faith in such action. The alternative for Japan is prompt and utter destruction . . .

At seven thirty, long before the release hit the wire services, Byrnes received word from Molotov. He had seen a copy of the proclamation and wanted a two-day delay. Byrnes did not reply; the proclamation went out on schedule.

July 27: Tokyo

Japanese radio picked up the transmission at 6 A.M. on the twenty-seventh. Foreign Minister Togo was the first to get the Emperor's ear and voiced the opinion that it was "not a dictate of unconditional surrender." He suggested that the Emperor view it with "the utmost circumspection."

The Cabinet went into session and spent the rest of the day arguing over what it meant. Admiral Toyoda said it was absurd and the government should not even consider it. But he had been vilified in the proclamation, characterized along with all the other Japanese military leaders as a "self-willed, unintelligent militarist."

The doves in the Cabinet pointed out that the Russians had not signed the document and might still be persuaded to negotiate on their behalf. Also, the term "unconditional surrender" had been used only once and applied specifically to the Japanese "armed forces."

They finally reached a compromise decision—to release to the Japanese press a truncated version of the proclamation with no endorsement by the government.

July 27: Potsdam

Stalin and Molotov conferred early in the morning. Stalin paced nervously, chain-smoking.

"There is nothing new in the proclamation," Molotov said, "I don't see how they can hope to succeed with such a document."

Stalin's face creased into a little smile. "That's not what Truman has in mind."

"Then why send it? They're putting the Japanese on notice that the terms of the Cairo Declaration can't be tampered with, and the Alantic Charter doesn't apply."

Stalin pressed his fingers together and gazed into space. "We know the American atomic test was successful. I assume they are manufacturing tactical bombs, which they are prepared to use as a lever. That is what this warning mission is all about. The Japanese will be told that unless they surrender under the terms of the proclamtion, they will be destroyed. So the proclamation is just a front—the real pressure will come through the San Francisco mission. Of course, the proclamation will fail. It will arouse Japanese ire. But the mission might succeed. The Americans are throwing all their eggs into that one basket."

"Is it possible," asked Molotov, "that they don't want to use their weapon?"

"What are you talking about?" said Stalin. "Of course they want to use it. They have to in order to impress me!"

Molotov stepped in front of the Generalissimo with a little smile. "*That's not what you just said.*"

Stalin stared at him, slowly realizing he was right. He had just outlined a version of American purpose that put a secret warning mission at the center of their peace offensive, but perhaps it really was what he had originally believed it to be: an attempt at self-serving moral salvation, to show the rest of the world, "We tried to warn them. We gave them a chance to surrender. They wouldn't respond to that. We showed them what our weapon could do. They wouldn't respond to that. So we had no choice."

Stalin gnawed the inside of his cheek. His brow darkened. "That's it, of course," he said. "They know the Japanese will reject their ultimatum. Then the warning mission. Two failures. So then they can use their bomb. Well, I'm not going to give them their moral crutch. *I want that mission stopped.*"

July 27: Berkeley

Thyssen called Snyder about the UPI release on the Potsdam Proclamation. "This is asinine," he said. "It is a foolish, unproductive move that will destroy any chance for Big Stick."

Snyder was uncertain. "You're convinced it's all over?"

"Major Snyder, as I once heard an American general say, I do not need to be hit with a tombstone to know when I am dead. Nevertheless, I shall remain here at the consulate, in case I am wrong."

The news dismayed the scientists. "They can't do this!" Bliss shouted. "It's a disgrace!"

"It explains the delay," Snyder said, raising his voice to drown out their protests. "Obviously the government wants a response from the Japanese *before* they send us."

"That'll take days!" Bliss sputtered. "We're being played for suckers! Why don't you tell them what we think of this—!" He snatched the newspaper from Snyder's hand and started to rip it up. Nakamura grabbed his arm.

"Please," he said, "may I read that?"

"Sure," Bliss said. "I'd like to hear what you think, Major Nakamura." His eyes blazed at Snyder as he surrendered the newspaper.

Everyone was quiet while Nakamura read it. Kirby opened his fountain pen and made an entry in his diary.

Nakamura finally looked up, quivering with emotion, and said quietly, "Japan will not bend to this."

"What's the matter with it?" Snyder asked.

"The people who have to approve it are the very ones being accused. The military still runs Japan."

"Well then, that tells us what to do," said Snyder. "Stay prepared. As soon as the Japanese reject it, we'll be reactivated."

Nakamura shook his head. "You don't understand. This could cause all negotiations to be broken off. Everything!"

"That wouldn't be very smart," Snyder said lamely, but he felt Nakamura was right. After all, Thyssen had said the same thing.

"You're not in their place," Nakamura said sharply. "This is not negotiation—it's an *ultimatum!*"

Bowen heard the sound of traffic over the telephone as Portiakov repeated Moscow's instructions: "It must be stopped, period. All other considerations aside. You are to instruct André, then I want you to give me his answer in person. It's a delicate matter and we must be sure he will cooperate. Tell him anything you feel is necessary. Where can we meet tonight?"

Bowen thought quickly, then gave him Louise Daniels' home address.

"Is that wise?" asked Portiakov.

"I have some details there that must be attended to tonight. We'll be quite safe. Go around the alley and come to the back door at eight o'clock."

Bowen hung up and wondered how he was going to get in touch with Macklin.

Slocum picked up the phone in the special barracks day room.

"This is Colonel André," said the voice on the other end. "I want to speak to Major Macklin."

"Right away, Colonel."

Slocum found Macklin in the washroom. "Major, there's a Colonel André on the phone for you."

Macklin dried his hands and hurried to the phone, glancing at Lefferts and Whelan playing cards a few feet away.

"Major Macklin, sir."

"Can we talk?"

"No, sir."

"Then just listen. We have to meet. There's a tavern in Novato called the Dewdrop Inn. It's right on 101. Can you get away?"

"I'll try, sir."

"Six o'clock."

Macklin put down the phone, turned to Slocum and said, "Goddamned brass. They're all the same. You got the keys to the Jeep?"

Whelan held up a hand full of cards. "I do."

"Let's have 'em."

He tossed them over and Macklin went out, muttering, "I won't be long."

He went down to the Jeep they had been assigned, took off the checkered flight-line flag and shoved it behind the front seat. He drove to the main gate and cleared off the base with no trouble.

He drove up 101 until he found Novato. The Dewdrop Inn was a ramshackle beer bar frequented by servicemen and local farmers. Inside, it was dark and smoky. There was sawdust on the floor and a stained mirror that ran the length of the bar.

Bowen was at a back corner table. They ordered a pitcher of beer and went through the charade of old friends getting reacquainted. Once they were sure no one was paying attention, Bowen got down to details.

"The mission must be stopped at any cost," he said quietly.

Macklin put down his beer. "What does that mean?"

"You'll have to crash into the ocean. There can't be any survivors."

Macklin stared at him without flinching. He was silent a moment then said, "That's my order?"

"Yes. I'm afraid there is no room for argument."

Macklin nodded. "Has anybody considered that maybe I can't bring it off?"

"Can't or won't? I need to know."

"Can't," Macklin repeated. "As in five other crewmen who aren't about to twiddle their thumbs while we take a dive. Can't as in can't guarantee no survivors."

"I don't see the difficulty," Bowen said.

"Naturally. You're not a pilot. However, I do have a better idea."

"Go on."

"Why wait till we're over water? As we take off from Hamilton, I just push the controls forward and we nose into the ground. Quick—no chance for interference—a big ball of fire and it's finished." He looked across the table calmly.

Bowen felt a chill. "Are you being serious?"

"As serious as you are."

Bowen poured another beer but was unable to drink.

Macklin's gaze narrowed in contempt. "Goddamned pack of idiots," he muttered angrily. "You people really come up with deranged solutions. You haven't been able to think of anything useful to do with these scientists, so now you want to destroy them. Let me tell you something, Bowen, there's a lot about this business that doesn't sit right."

"Are you questioning policy?" Bowen whispered threateningly.

"No. I'd just like to point out some things."

"Such as?"

"Why is a major ordering a colonel around?"

"I don't follow."

"Major Snyder, Colonel Lowe. That's not normal. If Big Stick is such an important operation, why isn't the rank there to beef it up? Why is it all in the hands of one man? And this Swedish diplomat who's running interference with the Japanese—what has he got to gain from it?"

"The Swedes have acquired a reputation as neutral negotiators—"

"In Europe," Macklin interrupted. "What are they going to get out of the Orient?"

Bowen shrugged.

"The only links in this whole operation are these two men. Well, who's sitting on top? Who's in charge? I'm telling you, Bowen, it's fishy. That's not the way the Army does things."

Bowen frowned. "What brought on all this suspicion?"

"Where's the State Department? Diplomats? Generals? I would expect at least three. Who are the Japanese going to surrender to? Snyder? Thyssen? The scientists?" He softened. "Look, I'm only bringing it up because there might be something about this whole operation that you haven't found out yet."

Bowen had nothing to say.

Macklin rose. "I have to get back. You come up with a better plan," he said with a smile. "I'm not going to commit suicide."

He left and Bowen stayed behind to think. Ordinarily he would have been furious at having his orders questioned, but André had brought up some vexing problems. He didn't have André's military experience, so he hadn't thought of the chain of command. But then he had never really explored below the surface of Big Stick. He had taken what it was for granted. Now that he thought about it, hadn't it always seemed peculiar that Snyder was the only visible authority?

Bowen got up, threw some money down on the table, and hurried out. He had a lot to tell Portiakov.

Bowen parked his blue Cadillac a half-block away from the Daniels home and walked up the side alley in the waning twilight. He slipped his key into the back door lock and let himself in. It was the maid's day off, but she was due in tomorrow and he had to do something about that.

He went to the kitchen and found Louise's bulletin board and a list of phone numbers that included household services. He picked up the phone and canceled both the newspaper and milk deliveries. He copied down the maid's number; he would call her after he'd spoken with Portiakov.

He went upstairs to the bedroom and packed a couple of large suitcases full of Louise's belongings, anything he could imagine she might take on an extended vacation. Then he hauled the bags downstairs and put them by the back door.

He checked his watch—five minutes to eight. He mopped his brow and stood waiting for Portiakov.

At two minutes past eight there was a soft knock on the door. Bowen opened it and Portiakov stepped in with a grunt of thanks.

"I could use a drink," he said. "Losing the FBI works up quite a thirst."

Bowen led him into the living room and mixed drinks at Louise's bar. "Remind me to wash these before we leave."

"Certainly," said Portiakov, luxuriating on one of the plush sofas. "Ah, rich Americans," he said. "They raise such a fuss when one of their number disappears. Have there been any repercussions on the loss of your lady friend?"

"No."

"I for one am sorry to lose such a charming ally. She was generous with her time and her concern for our people was laudable. Too bad," he said with a sardonic smile.

Bowen handed him a drink. "Alexei, you'll never be a sincere eulogist."

"Maybe not. I have been curious why you acted so drastically. It puts you in a dangerous position."

"I'm taking steps to see that there are no inquiries for a while."

"Then what?" Bowen didn't answer and Portiakov elaborated for him. "Then your usefulness to us is impared. I presume you've thought of that."

"Yes."

Portiakov's eyes narrowed piggishly. "It's not like you to act in haste, Bernard. This makes three times. The Cypulski woman, Mrs. Daniels and André."

Bowen sat down and calmly regarded Portiakov. "I think, as we talk, Alexei, you'll discover I've given this great consideration."

"I hope so. Now what about André? Will he cooperate?"

"There's something we should discuss first—"

The doorbell interrupted him. Both men stiffened in surprise and looked at each other. Portiakov's face twisted into an accusing glare. "Idiot," he growled.

Bowen put a finger to his lips, got up and walked silently to the window. He edged the drapes aside and tried to see the front door, but his view was obstructed by an enormous hedge. The bell rang again and was followed by an insistent knocking. Careful not to move the drapes, he stood and waited.

*   *   *

Beth hammered impatiently. She was fifteen minutes late, so Louise should certainly be ready. She stepped back and looked up at the darkened house.

She couldn't believe it. On Tuesday they had planned a dinner date for tonight, just the two of them, and even though their recent encounters had ended in squabbling, it wasn't like Louise to hold a grudge. Or to forget a date.

Beth shook her head in resignation. She walked down the steps and glanced up once more. She considered leaving a note, but finally decided to call from the restaurant. She turned and walked back to the waiting taxi.

The cabbie held the door open for her. She was about to get in when she caught sight of the blue Cadillac up the street. Didn't Bowen drive a car like that? She stared, gradually growing sure. She looked back up at the darkened house and felt a surge of anger. Were they watching together? Laughing at her? Suddenly she knew where she fit into Louise's scheme of things. Of course, Louise might have forgotten about tonight, but the idea that she was up there right now with Bernard Bowen was just plain repugnant.

Beth whirled and threw herself into the cab.

Bowen waited until the cab drew away before he released the drape. He turned to Portiakov. "Gone," he said.

"Who was it?"

"A possible complication."

"You see what you've let yourself in for?" Portiakov drained his drink. "Hadn't we better conclude this quickly? I would like to put some distance between us."

Bowen took the jibe calmly and went back to his seat. "That happens to coincide with my thinking, Alexei. Let's look at the situation. The Americans have been stalled once again. According to my informant they were ready to go and were called back at the last moment."

"Isn't that lucky—for you?"

"Yes. I'll admit a miscalculation, but I was waiting for instructions, which were not forthcoming. What we now have is one of two chances: either the mission is delayed permanently through no control of our own, or it goes and André sees that it never arrives in Okinawa. Correct?"

"Yes."

"I think it's a waste," Bowen said flatly. "We're throwing away a chance we've never even considered."

"What's that?"

"We have a highly trained operative planted as pilot. We have access to a group of very important nuclear physicists and some very important documentation on the American bomb project. It seems foolish just to let it all slip through our fingers."

"Access? I don't follow," said Portiakov. "What are you suggesting?"

"That we take them."

"Take them?"

"All the people and the information."

Portiakov stared at him. "But you've just told me the mission is not going."

"For now. But I'm convinced they will still try to send it. And if not, perhaps we can arrange things so that it does go."

"And Snyder is just going to stand still while you take his scientists away?"

"We'll get him out of the picture."

"But you were the one opposed to eliminating him!"

"I still am. We can sidetrack him."

"I presume you have a way of doing that." Bowen nodded. "And the scientists? Are they going to cooperate?"

"They can be persuaded. According to my source, they've been eager to go from the beginning. They're fed up with delays. All we have to do is convince them they're going on a bona fide mission."

Portiakov shook his head slowly. "It sounds risky."

"You haven't heard me out, Alexei."

Over the next half-hour Bowen outlined a plan that began to appeal to Portiakov. He ticked off details, requesting one thing after another: a team of the consulate's best forgers, a vacant building in the Marina district, an electronics expert and a cryptographer, underground cable schematics, vehicles, clothing and other supplies. "And we'll need official stationery. I'll see that you get a list of letterheads."

"That's easy," said Portiakov. "We have a man at the

Government Printing Office in Washington. But what about the time element?"

"We must have everything set up in the next seventy-two hours," Bowen said firmly.

"Of course," Portiakov said, musing to himself. "Most of it is no problem. We've done things like that before. I'll put people on it right away." Then he frowned and said, "Bernard, is there something you're not telling me?"

"What?"

"Well . . . suppose you do get Snyder out of the way. As you've said, won't they simply replace him?"

"That depends."

"But this is a terribly important mission for the Americans—"

"Is it?" Bowen said sharply.

Portiakov growled. "It's top level; we know that!"

"Do we?"

"What are you talking about?"

"Think for a minute. A top-level operation run by a single major? And one foreign diplomat? A negotiating team that consists of four scientists and a Japanese prisoner of war? How impressive does that sound to you?"

Portiakov stared at him then rose to his feet. "Not very."

"Precisely. André made some interesting observations. Snyder appears to be operating on his own along with Thyssen. It seems very odd."

"Then what do you think?"

"I don't know yet, but I want to proceed. Before we do anything that could backfire, I feel certain we will learn the truth about Big Stick."

Portiakov nodded and threw him a smile. "Once again, Bernard, like a cat, you've managed to land on all four feet. I'm overwhelmed. Naturally we shall share credit for this—if it's successful."

"That's only fair." Bowen smiled.

"And it certainly gets you off the hook and out of the country, doesn't it?"

Bowen didn't reply. He took both glasses into the kitchen with Portiakov following. The vice-consul shook his hand and said, "I'll be in touch as quickly as possible." He disappeared out the back door.

Bowen dried the two glasses and smiled to himself. There was a lot of work ahead, but the rewards could be staggering. He put the glasses away, folded the towel, and used it as he picked up the phone to call the maid. He identified himself and told her that Mrs. Daniels had been called out of town suddenly and would not be back for a few weeks. "Would you continue to come at least one day a week?" he asked. "Pick up the mail and see that the house is all right. Mrs. Daniels has left money for you in the kitchen."

The maid took it in stride and didn't seem troubled. Confident that he had gotten over that hurdle, Bowen hung up and left some cash on the kitchen counter. He picked up the two suitcases and took them down to the cellar. He hid them behind a woodpile then left the house, wondering how long it would be before Beth Martin started nosing around.

July 28: Tokyo and Potsdam

At 3 P.M. Prime Minister Suzuki called a press conference to straighten out what the Tokyo newspapers had done to the Potsdam Proclamation. The "truncated version" had been turned into a laughable matter by overpatriotic editors. Suzuki explained, "The Potsdam Proclamation, in my opinion, is just a rehash of the Cairo Declaration, and the government therefore does not consider it of great importance. We must *mokusatsu* it."

Makusatsu was a Japanese expression meaning "to kill with silence."

Suzuki's conference was picked up by the wire services and the American Intelligence network, which translated *mokusatsu* as "ignore."

When it got to Truman, he summoned Byrnes and Marshall to the Little White House and told them, "The goddamned Japanese are going to goddamned *ignore* the proclamation!"

He carried on at length about Japanese arrogance, then said, "We all knew they wouldn't knuckle under, but we tried. Now it's up to General Spaatz and the 509th."

"Mr. President," said Marshall, "perhaps you're forgetting what was discussed with Secretary Stimson."

"What was that?"

"If the Japanese rejected the terms, there was talk of modifying them with some guarantee of the Emperor's status."

Truman stared at him. "George, do you seriously believe that I should do that?"

"At least consider it."

"Why? We're not the ones losing the war. I won't negotiate from a position of weakness."

"But they don't know anything about the bomb: they're expecting an invasion. If we warn them what's going to happen and at the same time make a concession about the Emperor, won't we achieve everything we set out to get—a quick surrender, minimal loss of life, and keeping the Russians out?"

"No," said Truman. "It's beyond that. We're dealing with a nation of fanatics who've lost touch with reality. They don't know when they're beaten. They have to be shown. I don't want our forces involved in months of mop-up when we can handle it quickly."

"The end results could be the same," said Marshall, "if we do it with reason rather than force."

"No! We've got to make an impression that they won't forget! And we've got to do it before the Russians get involved."

"Mr. President," said Marshall, "who do you want to impress? The Russians? They weren't awed by the Germans, a far more direct threat. You'll only succeed in fostering mistrust for years to come."

"It's already there!" Truman said hotly. "On both sides!"

"But you'll force them to go out and perfect their own atomic bomb."

Byrnes said quietly, "They haven't the capability."

Marshall turned on him angrily. "Where do you get your information, Mr. Secretary? We don't know what they have and don't have."

Truman walked between them and went to the window. He turned and spoke with flat conviction. "General, forget the Russians. Think only of the Japanese. I refuse to dicker with those fanatics any longer. We're not going to warn them about the bomb, and that's final!"

Marshall stared at the President, holding back his anger.

"However," said Truman, "if there's a willingness to resume contact, then I'll take your suggestion under advisement. George, this is a terrible burden for all of us and I don't take it lightly. But you have to agree that our first objective is to win the war."

Marshall returned to the Army Communications Center, feeling drained and defeated. There was nothing left. He coded a message for Snyder, to route through Bud Veneck with a copy to Stimson:

> PUT BIG STICK ON ICE RELAX STANDBY BUT HOLD ALL GUESTS FOR SECURITY X INSTRUCTIONS WILL FOLLOW X SORRY MARSHALL.

July 28: Berkeley

Snyder listened to Bud Veneck on the scrambler phone, thanked him and hung up. Anything that ended with a general saying he was sorry usually meant the kiss-off was not far behind. But he couldn't tell that to the scientists. On the way over to Security he wondered exactly what he was going to say.

They were all together in the briefing room. It was hot; the windows were wide open. Beth and Fulbright had brought sandwiches and cold drinks. Snyder avoided looking at Lasch or Nakamura while he explained the latest news.

Bliss let out a bellow of rage. "Who the hell is making these decisions?" he yelled.

"It's just another delay," Snyder said halfheartedly.

"You don't believe that, Major," said Lasch.

"My instructions are to keep everyone ready. So it's not down the drain yet." His voice sounded unconvincing.

Nakamura trembled with anger but said nothing.

Bliss pounded the table ferociously. "I think we should make the flight—with or without approval!"

There was a stunned silence and before Snyder could say anything, Kirby and Lasch agreed.

"Now just a minute," said Snyder. "This is out of line—"

"Is that so?" interrupted Lasch. "I think it's a damned good idea."

Snyder looked for support. Beth hadn't said anything, but her shock had given way to wan helplessness. Fulbright was standing with his mouth open. The other faces were set.

"Who would you meet with?" Snyder said. "And where?"

"It's all arranged," said Willard. "We'll just go."

Snyder shook his head. "The last thing I need is a bunch of unauthorized heroes."

"I don't hear any suggestions from you, Major," Bliss said harshly.

"All I can tell you is to be patient. I said before that maybe they have another way of doing this and we just haven't been told. It's more important that the war ends than that we have a direct hand in it." They looked back at him vacantly. "If I'm wrong, say so."

Gloomy silence. He searched hostile faces—only Beth's seemed to offer compassion. Snyder reached for his cap and said wearily, "If there's another change in plans, I'll let you know immediately."

Lasch intercepted him at the door, his face drawn and angry. "When are you going to stop playing games? You were so quick to get us pumped up. Now you come in every day just to let out a little air. Why don't you do something useful? Like find out what happened to Marion!"

"The police—"

"—are doing nothing! To them, it's just an open case, because *you* won't give them any information, right? So they can't make a move. And nothing happens!"

"Dr. Lasch, *there are no leads.* Believe me, if I had one, I'd follow it."

"Like hell! You just want to sit on your duff until your mission is authorized. What about the Russians?"

Snyder grabbed his arm. "Outside!" he snapped, yanking Lasch into the hallway.

He slammed the door then shoved Lasch up against the wall. "What are you trying to do? I don't want them to know about that!"

"Then do something about it!"

"Where do you want me to start? We're dealing with diplomatic immunity! I can't touch them!"

"Then let me out of here."

"For what? A shoot-out on Market Street?"

The door opened behind them and Beth stepped out, concern etched deeply across her face.

Lasch struggled for self-control. "Look," he said finally, "you just can't do this to people. You act as if we don't have emotions."

"I know you do, Doctor. And that's the problem—they're constantly getting in the way."

Lasch pulled away, his face hardening ominously. He whipped around and stalked back into the briefing room. Snyder stood still a moment, then caught Beth looking at him searchingly. He walked out. She followed him.

She closed the door to his office and faced him.

"Go ahead," he said. "Get in your shot. Everyone else has."

She moved closer and reached for his hand. "I understand what you're going through."

He looked at her quizzically. "First time."

"Maybe. I've tried before and every time you've done something to make me furious with you. But now I see it's out of your hands. You're being whipped around just like everybody else."

"What about Marion? You think I'm sloughing that off?"

"If you could do anything about it, you would." She lifted his hand to her cheek.

"You told me once that you hoped it would never come off," she said. "Do you still feel that way?"

"I don't know. I wish it was over."

She wrapped her arms around him and pressed close. "So do I."

He finally gave in to her embrace and stood with her, silently rocking together.

Bowen returned to the back room, leaving the door ajar. "I sent Mrs. Beach to lunch, Keith. Now what exactly is going on?"

Fulbright relaxed and told him the latest development. "I don't think they'll ever go," he finished. "I think it's all over."

Bowen smiled. "Where are the scientists now?"

"Still in Security, on standby—but that's just to keep them under Snyder's control. They're really burned at him, too. You should have heard Bliss. He was all set to go anyway, without approval."

Bowen laughed. "I'm sure that didn't please Major Snyder."

"I think he wanted to strangle the guy. Everybody jumped on the bandwagon, though. Even Lasch. They all thought it was a terrific idea."

"I see. And the plane, the crew—have they been dismissed?"

"No. Still at Hamilton." Fulbright looked at Bowen, puzzled. "Why all the questions? I should think you're satisfied. They're not going."

Bowen stood up. "I'm quite satisfied actually. More so than usual." He reached into the cash drawer and slipped Fulbright an extra hundred.

"What's this for?"

"An advance payment—for continued information. It's important now that I'm kept apprised of every development. If any of these people are moved, I must know immediately."

Fulbright rose uncertainly and pocketed the money. "You mean there might be more to this?"

"Keith, please. Just do your part."

Fulbright walked to his car with an uncomfortable feeling about what lay ahead.

Beth lolled in the tub and gazed through the half-open door at Snyder, sprawled naked and asleep across her bed. She smiled, glad they were together again. Sitting in the briefing room listening to the others tear him apart, she had surprised herself by realizing how much she wanted to defend him. The poor guy was only trying to do his job. And she had made it as hard for him as the others had.

He *was* irritating—but not when he relaxed. She smiled again, thinking of their love-making. It would be wonderful if he could be not only her lover but her friend. Except for Louise, she didn't have many of those. . . .

Thinking of Louise made her angry. Why hadn't she heard an apology for last night? Louise hadn't even answered her phone when Beth called from the restaurant. She stood up and reached for a towel, deciding it was time to have it out. She slipped into her robe, closed the bedroom door and padded to the living room. She picked up the phone and dialed Louise's number. She let it ring, but there was no answer.

Determined now not to be put off, she called Bernard Bowen at home. He answered right away and seemed delighted to hear from her.

"When are you coming out to visit again, Beth?"

"Soon, I hope. Bernard, I was trying to reach Louise. Is she with you?"

"Of course not. She's out of town."

Beth sat down. "Really? Since when?"

"Thursday afternoon. I put her on the train to Chicago at two. Went to visit a sick aunt."

"Oh, I didn't—in Chicago?"

Bowen hesitated. "Yes."

"That's odd. I thought I knew all her family. I didn't think she had any relatives outside New England."

"Well . . . she got a telegram. She told me she got a telegram . . ." He trailed off, sounding confused.

"It's probably someone I've never met," Beth offered. Then the contradiction hit her. "Bernard, you said she left two days ago?"

"That's right."

"I was supposed to have dinner with her last night."

"Oh, dear. She left me a list of things to do, but let me . . ." She heard paper rustling. "Just checking . . . No . . . Nothing on here about calling you, but maybe I forgot to put it down. I've been so tied up with clients, I haven't been able to leave the shop until tonight. I'm terribly sorry—"

"Bernard, didn't I see your car outside Louise's house last night?"

"My car?"

"Yes—blue Cadillac, parked halfway down the block."

"You must be mistaken. I was at my shop until nearly midnight."

Beth sighed. "I guess I was wrong. Please do me a favor. When you hear from Louise, ask her to get in touch with me?"

"Of course."

* * *

Bowen hung up and sat staring at the phone. The car—she had seen his car! He cursed to himself. If Louise's disappearance began to attract attention, Beth Martin would certainly bring up his car. . . .

He could not let that happen.

July 29: Potsdam

Stalin had a cold. He sat in his bedroom, wrapped in a woolen dressing gown, sipping hot tea, his red-rimmed eyes watching Lavrenti Beria, chief of the NKVD, who had just arrived from Moscow. He was tall, plump and bland. The head of the largest and deadliest secret police organization in the world had the bearing and demeanor of a department store floorwalker.

Molotov joined them and sat down, uneasily greeting Beria.

Stalin blew his nose then said, "Tell him what you told me, Lavrenti."

Beria shifted in his chair and gestured with a pudgy left hand. "The American warning mission to Japan has been delayed. Our San Francisco agents have come up with an alternate plan for dealing with it, which, if carried out, would net us a group of high-level nuclear physicists and a large amount of technical information."

Molotov frowned, then said carefully, "You're talking about kidnapping them?"

Beria nodded and smiled.

Molotov glanced uncertainly at Stalin.

"You have reservations?" the Generalissimo said quietly.

"I can assure you the Americans will not sit by while we snatch some of their top scientists."

"My dear Molotov," said Beria, "the Americans will never know what happened. The plane will simply disappear."

"But if they even *think* we're involved—"

"There is no chance of that." Beria smiled enigmatically, removed his pince-nez and wiped it.

"The plan is very well worked out," Beria added. "Our risk is minimal."

Molotov finally shrugged. "You know best."

Stalin sneezed, wiped his nose and wiggled a finger at Beria. "Do it," he said, and leaned back euphorically.

July 30: Berkeley

Early Monday morning Fulbright ate a fast breakfast, packed his briefcase, then hurried down to his car in the rear garage. He slid behind the wheel and stuck the key into the ignition. A hand reached over from the backseat and closed on his arm. Fulbright gasped, then forced himself to turn slowly.

He saw who it was, then closed his eyes and sighed in relief. "For God's sake," he said, "don't ever do that to me—"

Bowen cut him off. "Be quiet and listen. There is a lot to be done."

"What do you want?"

"Your help. We must get Snyder away from the scientists, out of Berkeley, out of the mission entirely."

Fulbright grumbled. "Why don't you do your own thinking? Leave me the leg work."

Bowen stiffened, then relaxed and smiled. "You're closest to what's going on at the Rad Lab. Now use your head. There must be a way to get at this man. A weakness. A mistake he might have made."

Fulbright snorted. "Snyder's made nothing *but* wrong moves. Nobody trusts him anymore—"

Bowen held up a hand, clutching at a thought. "No one trusts him . . ."

"Well, Lasch sure doesn't. He'd just as soon have Snyder drop from sight. Is that what you want?"

"Why does he feel that way?"

"You know why. That business you rigged up against him—and Marion's death. He's nursing a grudge."

Bowen shook a finger excitedly. "I want you to exploit that. Play on it. Lasch can be manipulated. He feels wronged and he's in the best position to lodge a complaint.

"With whom? We don't have a complaint department—"

"Surely Snyder must have a superior."

"I don't know who it is. I've never seen an order. Come to think of it, Lasch hasn't, either."

Bowen felt a surge of excitement. All the plans he had put into motion might be based on something firm after all, something more than Macklin's hunch.

"Stay close to Lasch. Be sympathetic. Make him feel he's been played for a fool. Tell him you're disgusted, that he doesn't have to take it, that he should get in touch with General Groves and complain about Snyder."

"What about Thyssen?"

"Stay away from him. Don't even bring up the man's name. And don't let Lasch go near the Swedish consulate."

Fulbright scowled. "What in hell are you up to?"

"It doesn't matter," Bowen said, drawing bills from his wallet and handing them to Fulbright. "You're up to one thousand dollars—and more—if this works out to my satisfaction."

Fulbright stared at the wad of bills and said, "I'm not much of an actor."

Bowen patted him on the shoulder and opened the door. "Have faith in yourself, Keith."

He slipped out of the car and walked away.

Fulbright found Lasch having breakfast in the faculty lounge. Lasch had little to say. He toyed with his waffle and listened to Fulbright chat about what they were all going to do after the war.

"It's almost over," Fulbright was saying. "We're just marking time until the end. I wonder if they'll disband the lab."

Lasch shook his head. "I don't think so. We're going to be here a long time."

Fulbright fixed him with a worried frown.

"What's wrong?"

"You don't look well, Dr. Lasch. Feeling okay?"

Lasch shrugged. "Sure."

"You've had it pretty rough the last few weeks." Fulbright put his elbows on the table. "I don't see how you've put up with it. All the jerking around that's been going on—and for what? Operation Big Stick," he said contemptuously.

"You don't approve?" said Lasch.

"Of the idea, yes. But not the way it's been handled—or should I say mishandled." He looked around the room to be sure no one was listening, then he leaned over and spoke in a conspiratorial whisper. "It's Snyder, you know. He's incompetent."

Lasch washed down his waffle with coffee. "That's your opinion, Keith."

"I'm not alone. Everybody feels that way."

"Don't speak for me."

"Do you *like* having him disrupt everything?"

"Keith, drop it."

Fulbright pressed his attack. "Snyder was the wrong man for the job. You should have been in charge. I'll bet the meeting would already have come off."

Lasch stared at him.

"But we'll never know that, will we? I'm surprised at you."

"Me? Why?"

"You just sit here and take it. Snyder fouls up everything—even tries to smear you—"

"That'll do, Keith."

"No, it won't. I think you should call General Groves and tell him everything."

"You're forgetting something. Snyder works for Groves."

"So what? If he's inefficient, Groves would be the first one to have him out of here. Look, Snyder was damned quick to point the finger at you about Marion's death! Maybe *he* was the cause of it!"

Lasch stared at the table. Marion's death. Lasch had not yet reconciled his feelings about all the abuse Snyder had handed him: Marion a spy, used by the Russians, then disposed of when her usefulness ran out. What evidence did Snyder have to support any of it? He could have cooked up the whole thing, partly from what the London Poles had told him, and partly out of that inflexible willingness of a security man to believe the worst of anybody. As Lasch recalled the events of the past several weeks, he began to sense a pattern: Snyder had manipulated incidents and interpreted them to his own best advantage. Fulbright was right: Snyder was the bottleneck—in every way.

Lasch stood up. "Keith, you better come with me."

Back in his office and on the phone, Lasch was told by Los Alamos that Groves could be reached at the Pentagon. After thirty minutes of trying, Lasch finally got hold of him.

They chatted amiably for a moment, Fulbright sitting quietly on the couch, listening to Lasch's side of it with straining curiosity. Then Lasch inquired about Major Snyder.

"Who?" said Groves.

"I'm just trying to verify something," Lasch said, covering his confusion. "I'd like to know if he's on permanent assignment out here or if this is just temporary duty."

Groves was silent a moment before asking, "Would you repeat that?"

Lasch did, and added, "Frankly, there's been a lot of friction and I was hoping we could get someone else to head up the team."

"What's the nature of the friction?" Groves asked.

"Well, General, it's a delicate situation. One minute we're on, the next minute we're not. It doesn't help to have a military liaison whose only contribution seems to be disruption. I should think it would be in all our best interests to have this thing come off smoothly. Don't you?"

"Of course." More silence from Groves. And with every passing second Lasch grew more concerned.

"General," he said finally, "if he's so antagonistic to my group of scientists, can you imagine what he's going to be like with the Japanese?"

The next silence was ominous. Groves said carefully, "Dr. Lasch, tell me your story from the beginning."

Lasch briefly outlined Operation Big Stick and said that Snyder had claimed he was representing the highest authority.

Groves gave up all pretense. "Not mine," he said flatly.

Lasch glanced at Fulbright, who betrayed no emotion. "Frankly, General, he's never identified his superior to me. But he did clear with Captain Browne of our Security Section."

"I see. Where is Snyder now?"

"Here at the Rad Lab."

"Dr. Lasch, I don't want you to tell him about this phone call."

Lasch frowned. "General, you didn't know anything about Big Stick?"

"No."

Lasch watched Fulbright's eyes widen.

"Now give me the names of all the personnel involved," said Groves.

Lasch reeled them off, his concern rising. When he got to Nakamura, Groves stopped him.

"Would you repeat that last name, please?"

"Major Shinichiro Nakamura, a Japanese prisoner of war."

"At the Rad Lab?"

"Yes, under guard."

"How considerate. Why him?"

"According to Snyder we needed an interpreter. Nakamura's background was physics—"

"That's fine, but what does he know about S-1?"

"Snyder took him to Trinity to witness the test."

"*He what!*" Groves exploded. "Why?"

"So he would be able to give a firsthand account to the Japanese."

"My God."

Lasch quickly explained about the Trinity box and the aircraft assigned to them.

"This is incredible," said Groves. "Have you left anything out?"

Lasch told him about Thyssen. Groves muttered the name to himself, then warned him again not to alert Snyder. He finished with a promise: "You'll be hearing from me."

After hanging up, Lasch turned to Fulbright and said, "Groves didn't know a thing about this mission."

Fulbright felt his heart skip a beat as he wondered who was backing Snyder.

Fifteen minutes later, two Army six-bys drove through the gate into the Rad Lab complex and emptied out two squads of MPs. One squad fanned out to cover the Security Section where the scientists were quartered. The other entered Le Conte Hall and stormed upstairs.

An MP walked into Snyder's office and said, "Major Snyder, I'm Mayor Rovin. You're under arrest."

Snyder was dumbfounded. "On whose orders?" he finally asked.

"General Groves."

Before Snyder could say anything more, they pulled him to his feet and marched him out. Beth stood up and moved toward him. One of the MPs blocked her way.

"Sorry, ma'am, you can't speak with the prisoner."

"Prisoner?" Her eyes widened in shock.

"Just stay where you are, ma'am."

The MP took off after the others. They turned a corner and went downstairs. Beth whirled and saw Lasch in the doorway of his office, fidgeting uncomfortably. "You've got to stop them!" she yelled.

He shook his head. "There's nothing I can do."

She moved to the window and pressed her face to the glass. Down below she saw Snyder being put into the back of one of the trucks.

Major Rovin returned a moment later and strode up to Lasch. "Dr. Lasch, General Groves wants everyone here to maintain complete silence about this matter, including everything you told him."

"Where are you taking Major Snyder?" Beth asked anxiously.

"That's not your concern, ma'am."

She swelled angrily. "What right have you got to come barging in here? Major Snyder hasn't done anything wrong."

"I'm following orders, ma'am. I suggest everyone else do the same. Do I have your assurance, Dr. Lasch?"

Lasch nodded.

"One other message for you, sir. General Grove said you should have called a lot sooner."

Beth gaped at Lasch in disbelief, finally realizing why the MPs were here.

Lasch avoided her look. His voice cracked. "Is that a reprimand?"

"Just a message, sir."

Major Rovin turned on his heel and left. Beth faced Lasch, fixing him with an incredulous look. "What have you done?"

"What I should have done in the first place. I checked him out. General Groves never heard of Operation Big Stick!"

Confused, Beth choked out, "That's impossible."

"He suckered us, Beth—all of us—" His voice rose and he trembled. "And God knows what he did to Marion—" he broke off and lurched into his office, slamming the door.

Beth backed away uncertainly. Snyder . . . It couldn't be. There was some mistake. It couldn't all be lies. She bumped against her desk. Her hand went to her mouth; she felt sick. She caught sight of Fulbright at his door, peering at her with frightened eyes. She pushed away from the desk and stumbled to a bathroom.

The second squad of MPs went through security and burst in on the scientists, grabbed Nakamura and took him to an empty room, where they made him strip and submit to a body search. Breathing quickly, his muscles tensed against the indignity, Nakamura stood naked in the center of the room, the muzzle of a submachine gun waving ominously in his line of sight, like an impatient cobra.

The door opened and a major eyed him with calculated menace.

"Okay," said the major.

One of the MPs advanced on Nakamura and he backed away, terrified. Another one leaned over, scooped up his clothes and flung them at him.

"Let's go."

His heart didn't stop pounding until they had thrown

him back into his quarters and snapped the door shut behind them. He knew there were guards outside: he could hear them talking. He dropped his clothes on the bed, shuffled to the desk and leaned against it, unable to stop the sobs welling up from deep within.

He clenched a fist in anger and swore under his breath. If they wanted his life, they could have it. What was it worth if he couldn't get back to Japan with Lasch and the others? Then it hit him: he wasn't going, but now neither were they. Something had happened. They wouldn't come in and drag him away for no reason, not if Snyder was still around to stop it. Something had happened to Snyder.

He lifted his head and stared out through the bars, afraid.

Major Rovin walked into the briefing room.

"What's going on?" Bliss demanded, more indignant than frightened.

"I'll do the talking," said the Major. "If you people will guarantee full cooperation, you can stay here pending further instructions. If not, we'll all take a little trip to the Presidio and you can sit on your thumbs in solitary."

Willard faced him. "Is this another one of Snyder's ideas?"

Rovin ignored him. "I'm waiting for an answer."

"We'll cooperate," Kirby said, throwing a warning glance to his colleagues.

"Is that unanimous?"

Bliss nodded and so did Willard.

"Very well," Rovin said. He turned and walked out, taking the remaining MPs with him. Kirby dropped into a chair and automatically reached for his diary.

"Goddamnit," Bliss said. "Damnit! Damnit!"

Willard rubbed his chin and smiled philosophically. "Somebody doesn't like us."

"It's Snyder again!" Bliss bellowed. "I'm sick of it."

"We don't know what it is, Julian," Kirby said, "so let's just sit here and be patient."

"Sit here? You heard the man. We're prisoners! We don't have any choice!"

"Yes, we do," Willard said. "Solitary." He frowned, then brightened. "Not a bad idea, if it'll get you off my back."

Bliss turned on him, swelling up like a bloated frog. "You're so goddamned calm, Willard—because you don't care! You don't give a damn if we finish this thing or not!"

"I did," Willard said quietly. "Now I'm just numb. I'm not going to let it worry me."

Bliss puffed angrily for a minute, then slowly sank into a chair. He threw his hands to his face and rubbed his eyes. All three men were quiet for a moment, until Kirby cleared his throat.

"We'll go yet," he said.

Captain Browne stood up when Major Rovin walked in and curtly dismissed the two MPs he had left on guard. Cold eyes bored into Browne as the Major said, "Orders for you, Captain. Keep these people confined. Got it?"

"Yes, sir, but—"

"I understand that Major Snyder cleared Security with you. Is that correct?"

"Yes, sir."

"Did he have orders?"

"Yes, sir."

"Let me have them."

Browne licked his lips, remembering the explicit threat in Snyder's order against revealing their source. "I'm sorry. I can't do that, sir."

"Captain, either you do it or you're going to be in one shit-load of trouble with General Groves."

"Groves?" Browne was puzzled. He stood stiffly, his mouth working, then he blurted out, "But the orders *came* from him!"

"No, they didn't."

Browne stared at the Major, bewildered, then he sagged visibly. "I'll get them for you," he said, and turned to his safe.

Fulbright hurried up Telegraph Avenue to the Hotel Durant. He slid into one of the lobby phone booths, shut the door and called Bowen.

"This is Mr. Bowen speaking."

"Snyder's been arrested." Fulbright waited for a reaction but got nothing. "The MPs went through us like a bunch of wild men. They took Snyder I don't know where, split Nakamura away from the rest of the scientists—and you want the big news? *Groves did not know about Big Stick!*"

There was silence, then, "Are you sure?"

"Positive. I did just what you said—stirred Lasch up and got him to call the General, who didn't have the faintest idea what he was talking about. Do you know what that means? Snyder was not operating through proper channels!"

"Yes . . . Well, Keith, you've done marvelous work. Is the Trinity material still in Snyder's safe?"

"Far as I know. Wait a minute. Letters are one thing, but—"

"Relax. Just keep your eye on it."

"Okay," Fulbright said, relieved. "What else?"

"I'll be in touch."

Bowen hung up and folded his arms on his desk. He tapped his fingers thoughtfully and puzzled over what Fulbright had told him. It was more than he had hoped for, but it was confusing. Was Snyder really operating independently? Impossible. Although sometimes secrets were kept from commanding officers, Groves was not just any CO. He was the head of S-1 Security. He knew everything concerning the Manhattan Project. It was inconceivable that Big Stick could exist without the General's full knowledge and cooperation. Certainly no one under him would ever think of working around him—unless that person had friends higher up. But who could be higher up?

Bowen tried to imagine Truman's position in this: could Big Stick have originated with him? Why would he handle it this way—behind the back of his top project commander? André was right: if the mission was legitimate, a higher echelon would have been involved.

Was it possible that even Truman didn't know about it?

Bowen grinned ecstatically. The audacity of it was astonishing—if it was true. There was only one way to find out, and it required his boldest move yet.

*   *   *

Stefan Thyssen lumbered up the stairs and caught a wave from his secretary. She read him a message from Beth Martin: "Major Snyder en route to Hamilton, wants you to pack a bag. Will have you picked up outside the consulate at 3 P.M."

Thyssen grunted, went into his office, opened the closet and pulled out a worn valise that he had already packed. He checked his watch: it was fifteen minutes to three. Enough time to leave a few instructions for his secretary. He told her that he would be going away for at least a week and dictated two brief notes of apology for functions he would have to miss. He slung a coat over his arm, picked up the valise and walked out.

At exactly three o'clock an Army staff car pulled up to the curb and a smiling sergeant jumped out and opened the front passenger door. Thyssen handed him his valise and slid in.

There was another smiling sergeant in the rear, his arm stretched across the back of the seat. As the car pulled into traffic, Thyssen felt a pinprick sting at the base of his neck. His mouth opened in surprise, then he went numb.

He was conscious but immobile, sitting dumbly as they drove through the city. The car roared into the garage on Larkin Street and the door was shut. Thyssen was lifted out and carried into the house.

He lay on a breakfast table in an unused kitchen for what seemed hours. Then three men came in. His sleeve was rolled up and he saw one of the men lower a hypodermic needle to his arm. After another thirty minutes feeling flooded back into his body and his muscles protested with a dull ache. The pain at the back of his neck was intense. He swung his head from side to side and saw a dapper older man looking down at him impassively.

"My dear Mr. Thyssen," said Bowen, "I'm happy we have this opportunity to talk. How are you feeling?"

Thyssen wiggled his fingers to see if they would work.

"No gestures, please. I want to hear you speak."

"Uh . . ." Thyssen groaned.

"You are the Danish ambassador, are you not?" said Bowen.

"No . . ." Thyssen said hoarsely. "Got the wrong man . . ."

"There now," Bowen said with a pleased smile. "I knew you could talk if you tried. Now then—*Big Stick*."

Thyssen stared hard at him, memorizing the face against the day when he would have to describe it to Snyder.

July 30: Los Alamos

Snyder was flown to Los Alamos and taken to the Nuclear
Weapons Laboratory, a huge desert complex atop a broad
mesa. He was placed in an isolation cell.

At six the next morning he was wakened, fed, then
marched under guard to an office.

General Groves, Colonel Tully and a stenographer sat in
the only three chairs. Tully noded for the MPs to leave.
Groves leaned forward, his thick neck layering over his
collar as he regarded Snyder piercingly. Finally he nodded
to Tully, who lit a cigarette before beginning.

"We want to wrap this up quickly, Major. First of all,
what's been going on at Berkeley and who's behind it?"

"I can't tell you, sir."

"And what was the reason for the mission?"

"What mission, sir?"

"Big Stick."

Snyder remained silent, gathering his thoughts. How had
they found out?

"I'm waiting," said Tully.

"I can't tell you anything about it, sir."

"Why not?"

"Orders."

"Whose?"

"I'm sorry, Colonel."

"Major, do you know what kind of trouble you're in?
Setting up a clandestine military operation, conspiring to
consort with the enemy, failure to report the murder of
Marion Cypulski and bringing a Japanese prisoner of war

into the most highly restricted military zone in this country—"

"A physicist," Groves added sharply. "*A goddamned Jap physicist!*"

Snyder said nothing.

Tully added, "We're very curious, Major. We want some answers."

Snyder met their antagonistic looks and said simply, "Who tipped you off?"

"I'll ask the questions!" roared Tully.

Groves put his hands flat on the table. "Major Snyder, would you please tell me why I shouldn't convene a general court-martial, try you and send you straight to Leavenworth?"

"Sir, I'd like to help—"

"Good. Now, what is all this shit about a mission to warn the Japanese?"

Snyder didn't answer.

"Look, Snyder, Tully and I both know you didn't dream this up yourself. Just give us some names."

"I can't do that, General."

"Then I have to assume you acted on your own!"

Snyder felt that was a bluff. "Could we make a deal, sir?"

Tully flew out of his chair, livid. "Who the hell do you think you're talking to!"

"Just a moment," Groves interrupted. "What deal, Snyder?"

"Let me call and get permission to tell you what you want to know."

Tully started to object, but Groves cut him off. "You can make the call from my office."

"Sorry, sir. From a pay phone. It's the best I can do. I'd like to cooperate, but I'm under orders."

Groves eyed him squarely, then said, "All right."

"We should all go together, General. I'll pick the phone booth, and I'm going to need plenty of change."

Groves emptied his pockets of coins and handed them to Snyder, who looked down at the handful of silver and said, "I think we're short." He didn't look up, but he was sure this was getting to Tully. Groves, on the other hand, was faintly amused. He went out to the corridor and made the MPs contribute to the phone fund.

When they walked outside, Snyder's pockets were jingling. They got into a staff car and Snyder guided the driver around the base until he spotted a suitable phone booth out in the open near the motor pool.

"That'll do," he said.

They sent him into the booth alone, then surrounded it. Snyder nervously called the long-distance operator. Tully was too close: Snyder waved him back. He refused to budge until Groves snapped something at him.

Snyder's call went through to Washington and he fed the phone with coins. He knew they would trace it, but he also knew they wouldn't get very far. He got hold of Bud Veneck and told him, "We've got serious trouble with Big Stick. I have to speak to your boss right away."

"Hold on," said Veneck. "He's right here."

Snyder waited, watching his audience outside. They glared back at him. Finally the line crackled and Stimson's voice came on. "What is it, Major?"

"Big Stick is no longer a secret. I'm being held for questioning by General Groves in Los Alamos. They desperately want to know who and why."

"Oh, my God—"

"How do you want me to handle this, sir?"

"How did they find out?"

"Someone at the Rad Lab. Just a guess, sir."

He heard Stimson take a breath. "The mission is off, Major. I'm ordering you to keep silent about it until I come forward. Sorry to put you in this position, but you'll have to tough it out."

Snyder felt his knees going weak. "Very well, sir. Are you going to inform the people at the lab?"

"I'm going to do nothing, Major. Nothing. I will have no contract with those people. I'm certain General Groves will see they don't go anywhere or say anything. That should be sufficient."

"Yes, sir. I'm sorry it's come to this."

"So am I."

"I'm to take full responsibility, sir?"

Stimson was silent a moment. Snyder felt he was hanging by a thread. Then the Secretary's voice came back, softer. "We'll hash that out later."

"One more thing, sir. I'm calling from a pay booth. I would suggest you take steps to avoid a trace."

"Thank you. I will."

He hung up. Snyder stepped out of the booth and said to Grooves, "General, I'm sorry, but I still can't cooperate."

He handed the remaining silver to Tully, whose face fell in amazement.

Groves said, "Well, you'll have time to think about that. Tully, get in there and find out who he called."

Groves produced papers from his pocket and waved them at Snyder. "Recognize these, Major?"

"No, sir."

"The orders you fooled Captain Browne with. Any idea what you can get for forging the signature of a general?"

"I think so, sir."

"Good. Multiply it by ten."

Tully stalked out of the booth and whispered something to Groves, who whirled on Snyder. "The War Department!" he bellowed. "Who?"

Snyder shook his head.

"Get him out of here," Groves snarled.

August 1: Berkeley

Lasch came in late Wednesday morning and tried to resume his normal work routine. But other thoughts kept intruding: he had heard nothing further from Groves. Thank God he had been able to talk his way past the guards last night. He had gone in to see Kirby, Bliss and Willard to explain that problems had cropped up regarding Snyder's involvement and he had been forcibly removed. He did not tell them that he had been the cause. The less they knew, the better. They still wanted to know when the mission would leave, if at all. He had given them a vague answer. Then he had gone to see Nakamura and apologized for the way the MPs had treated him. "They weren't properly informed," he explained.

Nakamura was nervous about what was going to happen—not only to himself, but to Japan. He pleaded with Lasch for information. Lasch mumbled an excuse and left feeling depressed and guilty. Had he botched it for everyone?

Fulbright came in and closed the door. He stood before Lasch, fidgeting, waiting for him to look up.

"What is it, Keith?"

"I got the damnedest phone call just before you came in," he said. "Someone in the Swedish consulate, an aide to Thyssen . . . named Holbrecht."

"Sit down. What did he want?"

Fulbright dropped onto the couch. "Wanted to meet with you and Snyder today about Big Stick. I tried to cover but he insisted on speaking with Snyder. I had to tell him Snyder had been arrested and we were no longer sure that the mission was legitimate. He got awfully upset, said something about a terrible mixup. So I told him I didn't think we could go further until everything got cleared up. He said that would be too late. He wants to meet right away."

Lasch frowned. "Why didn't Thyssen make the call?"

"He's on his way to Japan."

Lasch sat up. Fulbright nodded and went on, "Listen, it shocked me, too. But according to Holbrecht, Thyssen flew on ahead to finalize arrangements and to be sure the Japanese don't get cold feet. He's going to meet you at Okinawa."

"Wait a minute," said Lasch. "What the hell is going on?"

"I'm not sure, but it looks like the Swedes and the Japanese believe we're going ahead. Holbrecht said that if we don't proceed, we're going to jeopardize everything."

Lasch shook his head in amazement. "What does he want us to do?"

He wants you and me to come to the consulate to hear him out. He said he would wait there all afternoon. I've got the address." Fulbright waved a piece of paper.

Lasch hesitated. "I better get in touch with Groves."

"No! That's what I said. But he asked that we hold off until he's had a chance to explain himself."

Lasch got up slowly, troubled. He thought for a moment: what harm could it do to listen? "Okay," he said. "Let's go."

They drove over to the Marina district in San Francisco, parked on Chestnut Street and walked over to a two-story stucco building. They went up a flight of steps and glanced at the bronze plaque to the right of the door, which read: CONSULATE, GOVERNMENT OF SWEDEN.

The lobby was small, dominated by a huge Swedish flag draped on the wall. Beneath it a blonde receptionist looked up and asked if she could help.

"Mr. Holbrecht is expecting us. My name is Fulbright, and this is Dr. Lasch."

"Just a moment, please." She smiled sweetly, picked up a phone and buzzed. A moment later she said quietly, "Mr. Holbrecht? A Dr. Lasch and a Mr. Fulbright to see you,

sir. Very well." She smiled at them and buzzed for a uniformed attendant. "The guard will escort you back."

They were taken down a corridor, past several offices.
Through an open door they saw a girl typing. On the wall
above her was a portrait of King Gustav. Two men in dark
suits came toward them, deep in conversation, and went
into one of the offices on the left.

The guard let them into an office bearing two name-
plates: STEFAN THYSSEN, OSCAR HOLBRECHT. The secretary
asked them to wait and stepped into the right-hand office.
The room on the left was open and Lasch peered inside. It
was neatly laid out with plush furniture but unoccupied.

The secretary returned and said, "Mr. Holbrecht will see
you now."

They went into the other office, which was a little
smaller, more functional, with two filing cabinets, a long
bookcase, a large desk, several chairs, a wall map of Sweden
and another picture of the King.

Bernard Bowen rose, extended a hand and introduced
himself. "How do you do, Dr. Lasch? I am Oscar Holbrecht."

Lasch shook the outstretched hand and introduced Fulbright. He studied Holbrecht's features, the engaging
smile, well-tailored suit, manicured hands . . .

"Please sit down," Holbrecht said. "Some coffee?" He
gave his secretary orders in rapid Swedish.

Lasch sat on the edge of his chair, nervous and wary, as
Holbrecht kept up a running patter of chitchat—about the
weather, the charm of San Francisco, the pleasures of
travel in general and his fervent hope that the war against
Japan would soon come to an end. By the time the coffee
arrived, Lasch had begun to relax.

Fulbright was amazed at Bowen's performance. He had
done nothing to his appearance, yet he seemed completely
different. And the Swedish—*where* had he picked that up?

Holbrecht smiled and said to Lasch, "I sense your discomfort, and given what Mr. Fulbright has already told me
over the phone, I can well understand. I'm sorry things
have turned out this way, but if I may be so bold, I would
suggest that your actions regarding Major Snyder might

have been a bit premature." He waved aside Lasch's protest. "What's done is done. Let me repeat what I said to Mr. Fulbright. Stefan Thyssen is already on his way to Japan. He will meet with representatives of the Japanese government, personally escort them to Okinawa and await our arrival. I assure you these negotiations are now quite crucial, and we must strive to bring your two countries together."

Lasch chose his words carefully. "I can understand Mr. Thyssen's anxiety to bring this off. I respect the motives of the Swedish government, but I am not a diplomat or a politician. I'm a scientist, employed by my government and bound by its regulations. While Major Snyder was running this operation, we were all under an umbrella of authority. Now there's some question as to whether it was genuine. My colleagues and I can't go off on the say-so of a foreign government."

"I would not ask you to. But you must have an open mind about this. It goes beyond just ending the war."

"I realize that. But without official approval I can't get involved."

Holbrecht frowned. "Surely you've seen the correspondence on Big Stick?"

"I saw one memo: Thyssen's proposal to form the mission. It seemed convincing at the time, but there was no approval attached. All I had was Snyder's word. That's no good anymore."

Holbrecht wagged a finger. "I understand your reticence. One moment, please."

He drew a folder from his desk and opened it in front of Lasch, disclosing a small stack of correspondence—some carbons, some originals. "Please examine these, Dr. Lasch." He flicked a warning glance at Fulbright, who was staring, astonished, at the top letterhead: the White House.

How had Bowen accomplished *this*? Fulbright wondered.

Lasch carefully combed through the papers—directives from the President, the State Department and the War Department. He picked up a letter from Thyssen to Truman, outlining the proposal for the mission; a memo from the

Secretary of War to the President with a copy to Thyssen, agreeing with the proposal and suggesting it be implemented right away; Truman's letter of approval, specifically launching Operation Big Stick; Stimson's recommendation of Dr. Lasch to head the scientific team; then a final letter from Byrnes to Thyssen, datelined Potsdam, urging the mission to go at all costs and reminding Thyssen that secrecy must be kept absolute.

Most of the letters were dated variously from late June through July. Lasch realized he had in his hands the complete official background of Big Stick. He returned it, saying, "Why wasn't I shown this before?"

Holbrecht closed the file. "I cannot account for it. Certainly Major Snyder has seen it. In fact, here is a letter sent directly to him."

Holbrecht handed Lasch a letter from Byrnes, informing Snyder that he had the authority of the State Department and the War Department, but he must not under any circumstance reveal either their involvement or that of the President. The letter was dated July 5th, just prior to Truman's departure for Potsdam.

Lasch sucked in a deep breath and sat back.

Holbrecht retrieved the letter. "I apologize for the nature of diplomacy, but sometimes this is how it has to work."

"What do you want me to do?"

"If you're agreed to go forward . . . ?"

"Under the circumstances, yes."

"Then I think you should tell your scientists that the mission is on again. And this time there will be no delays and no last-minute cancellation. However, you must caution them not to breathe a word. There are people in your own government who do not approve of this operation."

Lasch looked at him quizzically.

"No more contact with General Groves," Holbrecht continued. "He is one of the top proponents of use of the bomb and would be no party to this effort unless given an express order from the President. As you can see from Byrnes' last letter to Snyder, that could never happen. So General Groves must be left in the dark, along with everyone else not directly involved. Am I clear?"

"Very."

"Of course, we're sorry to lose Snyder, but he will have
to stay in Groves' hands to preserve our secrecy. Now, I
would suggest that you keep Mr. Fulbright completely informed, but no one else."

"My other assistant, Miss Martin—"

Holbrecht shook his head. "That would be unwise, Dr.
Lasch. Once the team leaves, it's only necessary for one
person at this end to know where they have gone. I don't
wish to dictate, but some common sense does apply."

"But she's known about the mission all along."

"Give her a holiday."

Lasch nodded. "Will anyone be replacing Snyder?"

"I've already been in touch with your State Department
about that. They feel that Major Macklin could take over
Snyder's duties in addition to being the pilot. Accordingly
Macklin will be getting new orders. He will handle all details from now on. All you need do is stay at your office
and be ready to go."

"What about Captain Browne?"

"Tell him nothing. He'll get orders, too."

"When?" asked Lasch.

"Almost immediately. We will pick you up at the Rad
Lab tomorrow morning at 3 A.M."

Lasch glanced at the wall clock and realized he had only
half a day left to get things in order. He stood up and
offered his hand. "Thank you, Mr. Holbrecht. We'll be
ready."

As soon as Lasch and Fulbright left, the Holbrecht mask
fell away and Bernard Bowen walked out of the office,
grateful that Thyssen, though under duress, had fed him so
many valuable links. The receptionist was packing her
purse. The uniformed attendant dropped into a chair and
lit a cigarette. Bowen stepped into an office where the two
men in dark suits were waiting.

"Cover that plaque outside," he said, "but keep the
building occupied and the phones open in case Dr. Lasch
calls back."

He returned to "Holbrecht"'s office, gathered up the
files and cleared out.

* * *

They drove back in silence, Fulbright not daring to interrupt as Lasch sat against the passenger door, lost in thought. Marion had died for this. And he had almost thrown it away in his zeal to get rid of Snyder. "Damn it, Keith," he said impulsively, "you almost cost us the whole thing!"

"Me?" Fulbright went pale. "How?"

"We shouldn't have called Groves."

"B-but we had to!" Fulbright stammered. "Besides, aren't we better off without Snyder?"

"I suppose," said Lasch. "At least we've got another chance, and this time we're going to see it through. Nobody will stop us now."

They entered through the Rad Lab gate, parked and walked over to Security. Captain Browne let them in to see the scientists but refused to bring out Nakamura.

"Why?" said Lasch.

"Orders from General Groves. He stays isolated."

"Where?"

"In his quarters, sir."

"All right, Captain," said Lasch. He would have to think of a way to get word to Nakamura. Browne left him alone with Fulbright and the scientists.

Lasch motioned everyone into a huddle around the table.

"Big Stick is on again," he said quietly. He was met with stunned silence.

"Don't play games with us, Lasch," Bliss warned.

"I'm serious." He stifled a barrage of questions and quickly recounted the meeting with Holbrecht.

"It's all true," said Fulbright. "I was there."

Bliss laughed excitedly. "I can't believe it," he said. "You mean we're going to do this under the nose of the Army?"

"In a sense," Lasch said. "The pilot, Major Macklin, will be in charge. He's replacing Snyder."

"Best move yet," Willard said.

Lasch cautioned them to be discreet. "Any leak can be fatal," he said, "because S-1 Security doesn't want us to make this mission."

"What about Nakamura?" asked Kirby.

"He's included. How we get him out of isolation is

Macklin's problem, I'm afraid. So sit tight until we're ready to go."

Bliss nodded and slapped a hand on the table. "Now that's more like it," he said, immensely pleased.

Lasch went upstairs and called Beth into his office. "I want you to take the rest of the week off," he said, cutting off her protest. "We've all been through a strain and I think I know what you're going through." She stared at him uncertainly. "Take a vacation. Visit friends. Do some shopping. But get your mind off what's happened and *stay away from the lab*. I don't want to see you here until next Monday."

"But—"

"That's an order. Now go home."

Beth went out, picked up her purse and left, very upset. She didn't know who to turn to. Snyder was gone, Lasch wanted to get rid of her, and Louise could not be found.

She went home, made a drink and sat in her living room, pondering what to do. She dialed Bowen's shop, hoping for news about Louise. Mrs. Beach answered and said Bowen was out. Beth left her name and number, then hung up and sat back, alone.

August 1: Washington

General Groves flew back to Washington on Wednesday morning, still seething. He had hit a blank wall in trying to run down Snyder's War Department contact. He called for a meeting with Stimson on his arrival, intending to apprise him of the situation and find out if he knew anything. To compound his annoyance, he was also bringing in a packet of papers from the Chicago protest group. To Groves it was a load of moralistic garbage, but he had to pass it on.

Sixty-nine of the scientists at Chicago had signed a statement to the effect that the first nation to deploy the atomic bomb could very well have to shoulder "the responsibility of opening the door to an era of devastation on an unimaginable scale."

Groves glanced down the list of names again while waiting to meet with Stimson. A secretary came out to say that Stimson was unable to keep his appointment and had left word for Groves to meet with Under Secretary Clark Rodeway.

Groves went to Rodeway's office and turned over the Chicago packet with a curt explanation. Rodeway studied the papers and agreed they were pointless at this late date. He gathered them together and put them into a drawer.

Then Groves detailed his problem with Major Snyder. "It looks like he's been dealing with someone here. Do you know anything about it?"

Rodeway shook his head. "Sounds like something State might cook up."

"Nevertheless, we traced Snyder's call to the War Department."

"What can I do?"

"Tell the Secretary and ask him to get in touch with me as soon as he can."

"Will do, General."

Groves stood up, eyeing Rodeway mistrustfully. "Clark," he said, "this could have been catastrophic. Don't let it end up in the same drawer with those papers. *I want to talk with Stimson, and fast.* Understand?"

"Okay, sir. Where can he reach you?"

"Pentagon today, but I'm flying back to Los Alamos tonight."

August 1: Potsdam

It was a week since Churchill had left Potsdam to go home for the British parliamentary elections, confident he would soon return. His party had lost and he had been reduced to head of the Loyal Opposition.

On July 28th Clement Attlee, the new Prime Minister, and Ernest Bevin, the new Foreign Minister, replaced him at the high stakes table chaired by Truman. Attlee sat quiet and aloof through the closing proceedings, deferring to Bevin, who had plenty of bluster but in the long run fared no better than Churchill had.

The conference had now narrowed down to give and take between Truman and Stalin and at the final evening session the last scrap of paper was signed and the Potsdam Declaration, covering the European settlement, was ready.

Truman rose and said, "I declare this conference adjourned. Until our next meeting, which, I hope, will be in Washington."

Stalin smiled and added, "God willing."

August 1: Moscow

At the Japanese Embassy in Moscow, Ambassador Sato received a new cable from Foreign Minister Togo. He studied it carefully, with a sinking realization.

> The battle situation has become acute. There are only a few days left in which to make arrangements to end the war. . . . Efforts will be made to gather opinions from the various quarters regarding definite terms . . .
>
> It is requested that further efforts be exerted to somehow make the Soviet Union enthusiastic over the special envoy (Konoye). Since the loss of one day relative to this present matter may result in a thousand years of regret, it is requested that you immediately have a talk with Molotov.

Sato called the Kremlin and asked for the Foreign Minister's office. Molotov was not available. "When do you expect him?"

"I'm not sure, Mr. Ambassador, but we will notify you as soon as he returns."

Sato hung up, positive the Russians were stalling.

August 1: Novato

At eight thirty in the evening Macklin walked into the Dewdrop Inn. He found Bowen in the back at the same table, slid into the booth and asked, "What's up?"

Bowen started chatting amiably about imaginary friends. He ordered drinks. They downed them quickly, then Bowen paid and they walked out together.

They got into Bowen's car and drove north to a dirt turn-off. It was only a five-minute ride, but Bowen was silent all the way. He parked under a tree, switched off the engine and listened a moment. When he was sure they were alone, he turned to Macklin and said, "Our plans have changed. How would you like to go home to Russia?"

Macklin said nothing.

"I said go home, man, a hero!" Bowen grinned and his eyes sparkled excitedly. "Not sneaking in the back door, but welcomed with open arms."

Macklin refused to be impressed. "What do I do to earn these honors?"

"You will fly the mission after all. But we are not going to destroy it. We're going to divert it and appropriate the cargo."

Macklin's eyebrows went up. "You mean the scientists?"

"*And* all their precious information."

Macklin let this sink in, then asked, "When?"

"Three A.M. tomorrow."

Macklin glanced at his watch. It was just nine o'clock. "Six hours," he said.

"You won't be in the air by that time, but you will be on your way to pick up the people."

"And how are you arranging that?"

"Orders are being drawn up by our specialists. All you have to do is follow them to the letter. The scientists will be handed over to you with no problem. There must be no coercion used in obtaining these people. To that end I have very specific instructions."

He spent fifteen minutes outlining his plan. At the end Macklin repeated it all back.

"One more detail," added Bowen, "and this I place in your hands. Can we delay any possible search?"

Macklin thought a moment then said, "Leave it to me."

Bowen returned Macklin to the Dewdrop Inn then went on alone, several miles south. He took another turnoff and drove through rolling farm country, then parked under a grove of trees beside a green telephone company truck.

Leaving his car, he joined two men that Portiakov had imported from Canada. Elgin was the electronics expert, a ferret-faced little man with a cigarette perpetually hooked in the corner of his mouth. Peel, the code man, was heavy-set and hard-breathing. He let Bowen have his seat in the back of the truck, then got out, climbed into the cab and started the engine.

The truck went back to the highway then turned toward Hamilton, stopping by the side of the road two miles outside the base.

Peel and Elgin, dressed in overalls, got out and set up a barrier. They rigged worklights, opened a manhole cover and dropped down beneath the road, dragging a line from the truck. Using schematics purchased from a telephone company draftsman, Elgin singled out the cable he was looking for, made his splice and clamped off the other side. All teletype communication with the base would now have to pass through Peel's keyboard.

Peel hoisted himself back into the truck, puffing with the effort. He slid into a chair, pulled the tarp off his equipment and turned it on. Bowen handed him a model sheet then took up a position as lookout. Elgin remained in the manhole to be sure the connection held.

Peel rapidly typed a message through in the proper code:

TO COMMANDING OFFICER HAMILTON FIELD CAL 012150A X MACKLIN ROBERT MAJOR USAAC SERIAL NUMBER 0733103 TO PROCEED ON 2 AUGUST AT 0300 TO BERKELEY RADIATION LAB WITH MP ESCORT TO PICK UP FOLLOWING CIVILIANS DOCTORS LASCH KIRBY WILLARD BLISS AND POW NAKA- MURA X RETURN HAMILTON FOR IMMEDI- ATE DEPARTURE PER PRIOR INSTRUCTIONS X ACKNOWLEDGE X LESLIE GROVES GEN- ERAL COMMANDING.

The orders were received and acknowledged by Colonel Lowe's headquarters. The duty officer personally notified Macklin, who woke his crew and headed for the hangar.

By 0130, the preflighting was complete. Macklin gathered his crew together and explained that they were involved in a highly secret operation and they would be required to follow some unusual procedures. "To start with," he said, "I want the aircraft identification number changed. All our clearances through to final destination have been set up under this new number for security reasons."

He handed a sheet of paper to Whelan, the crew chief, and told him, "Get into the paint shop, cut a stencil and change the numbers on the tail surface and nose wheel door. And don't let anybody see you do it."

Forty minutes later Aircraft Serial Number 229526 disappeared, replaced by ASN 297271.

August 2: Berkeley

At 0245, the Teletype started clicking in Security Head-quarters at the Rad Lab. The Charge of Quarters tore off the strip, read it, then went to wake Captain Browne, who scanned it hurriedly.

TO COMMANDING OFFICER SPECIAL SECU-RITY DETAIL BERKELEY RADIATION LAB 020245A X RELEASE DOCTORS LASCH KIRBY WILLARD BLISS AND POW NAKAMURA TO CUSTODY MACKLIN ROBERT MAJOR USAAC SERIAL NUMBER 0733103 FOR IMMEDIATE TRANSPORT LOS ALAMOS NEW MEXICO X RELEASE CLASSIFIED MATERIAL CUSTODY LASCH X ACKNOWLEDGE X LESLIE GROVES GENERAL COMMANDING.

Browne grumbled to himself as he threw on a uniform. First Snyder taking over, then accommodating a Jap POW, then playing nursemaid to a bunch of cranky scientists, then Snyder's arrest . . . and now, in the dead of night . . .

Bowen's phone company truck was parked in a dark spot between street lights on Telegraph Avenue in Berke-ley. The barrier was up and lines had been strung down into another manhole.

In the back of the truck, the keyboard clacked as Browne's acknowledgment came in. Peel waited a discreet minute then sent back a coded confirmation. Bowen grunted in satisfaction. He told Peel to keep the line monitored until 6 A.M., then climbed out of the truck and walked around the corner to his car.

Browne read the confirmation, then gave orders to get the scientists ready. He sent a man to the Nunnery to pick up Lasch, then called him.

Lasch was sitting in his kitchen, sipping coffee, packed and ready to go, when Browne's call came.

"Sorry to wake you, Dr. Lasch," said Browne, "but I've got orders to send you and the others to Los Alamos."

Lasch felt a stab of panic—why Los Alamos? Then Browne made it clear.

"A Major Macklin is going to be taking everyone back. I know it's short notice, but can you—?"

"Don't worry about it, Captain," Lasch said, relieved. "I'll be ready."

"Fine. An MP will pick you up shortly."

Lasch hung up, finished his coffee and waited.

Browne was at the gate at 0330. Headlights stabbed through the campus and two Army staff cars wound up South Drive and stopped.

"I'll handle this," Browne said to the gate guard. He went over to the lead car and peered inside. An MP was driving and an officer sat on the other side. "Major Macklin?"

"Yes."

"Captain Browne, sir. May I see your orders?"

Macklin handed over a paper prepared by Colonel Lowe's exec, identifying him and calling for the scientists to be released into his custody. There was nothing about eventual destination, but that didn't bother Browne.

"Okay, this checks out." Browne opened the back door and slid into the car. "Around to your left," he told the driver.

The cars pulled up outside Security. Browne led Macklin back to the briefing room. Kirby, Willard, Bliss and Lasch were there, with their valises lined up by the door.

"Where's the Japanese prisoner?" Macklin asked.

"Be right out, Major," said Browne.

Lasch stepped forward. "Excuse me, Major, but what about the Trinity material?"

Macklin looked at Browne. "Where is it?"

"In Major Snyder's safe," Lasch volunteered. "Captain Browne should have the combinations."

"Yes—in my office," said Browne.

Macklin glanced at his watch. "Let's go then—we're wasting time."

Browne took them up to Le Conte Hall, turned on the lights on the second floor and entered Snyder's office. He opened the three locks with Lasch and Macklin hovering over him. He hauled out the box and the watertight casing. Lasch checked the contents quickly. Everything was there: papers, films, photographs. He lowered the box into the aluminum casing and sealed it.

They returned to Security just as Nakamura was brought out. He had been hurriedly wakened and dressed in plain black trousers and a white shirt. No one had told him where he was going and he was once again in handcuffs.

Macklin asked for the key and removed them. The group picked up their luggage and marched out to the cars. Nakamura got into the backseat next to Lasch. Macklin slid in and the two-car caravan started off.

When they were past the gate, Nakamura turned uncertainly to Lasch, who smiled and said, "We're on our way."

It wasn't until they had crossed the Bay Bridge into San Francisco that Nakamura relaxed enough to feel the excitement. Then his face broke into a broad grin.

"We have one stop to make, gentlemen," Macklin said. "The Swedish consulate—to pick up a Mr. Holbrecht."

Bowen had been watching from the dark upstairs window. As the cars drew up, he hurried downstairs, back to the office he had used posing as Holbrecht.

"They're here," he said clamly.

Fulbright got up and watched Bowen shrug into his overcoat.

"Well, my friend, it looks like this is good-bye. I shall never forget all you have done," Bowen said, reaching into the desk drawer and pulling out a silencer-equipped .38 revolver.

Fulbright went pale and stared at it.

"I have one last job to entrust in your care," Bowen said, enjoying Fulbright's discomfort. "Go back to Berkeley and take care of Beth Martin."

"W-what are you talking about?" Fulbright stammered.

"She knows something that could be dangerous to all of us, Keith. We must keep her from using it."

Horrified, Fulbright slowly comprehended. "You want me to *kill her?*"

Bowen held the revolver out, barrel first. "Keith, if your life is threatened, you defend yourself—correct?" Fulbright nodded. "Good. Take it." He thrust the revolver into Fulbright's hand, then gave him a passkey and an envelope. "The key to her apartment . . . and ten thousand dollars."

Fulbright's gaze shifted to the packet of money. "H-how do I escape?"

Bowen relaxed. "Look, my boy, it's quite simple. You go to her apartment—"

"Now?"

"No. I want you at the lab today in case anyone tries to get in touch with Lasch. You'll fend them off as we discussed. But tonight let yourself into her apartment and do the job. Afterwards, come back to this building and you will be taken out of the country . . . with ten times the amount in that envelope waiting at the other end."

"*A hundred thousand?*"

"Come on, Keith. I haven't got all night."

There was a knock at the door. Bowen let Macklin in. Fulbright held the gun in one hand and picked up the envelope with the other. Finally he stuffed both into his coat pockets. "Just make sure somebody's here waiting for me," he said.

"Don't worry about that." Bowen smiled at Fulbright then put out his hand. They shook, then Bowen picked up his valise and walked out with Macklin.

They hurried down to the car. Macklin thrust the valise at the driver, who dropped it into the trunk. Bowen slid into the car on Nakamura's side and beamed at Lasch.

"This is Major Nakamura," said Lasch.

"Pleased to meet you, Major. I am Oscar Holbrecht. This is a great moment for our countries."

The cars drove north across the Golden Gate Bridge and up toward Hamilton Field.

The *Della B*, a small fishing trawler, was ten miles out of the Golden Gate, in open sea. A winch chugged on her deck and slowly pulled in the first catch of the morning. The net came up in a rain of sea water. The boom swung over and the trap dropped away. A silvery cascade of fish spilled into the open hold.

The body landed with a resounding splat and was nearly obliterated by more fish before the net tender had the sense to stop staring and yell.

They dragged it out. Unusually heavy because of chains wrapped tightly about the legs, it was clothed in a dark blue suit and had been in the water at least twenty-four hours.

The captain of the *Della B* radioed the Coast Guard, his eyes glued to the bloated corpse on his forward deck. For Stefan Thyssen, the war was over.

August 2: Los Alamos

Tully let Snyder cool his heels for a day. Groves called from Washington Wednesday night to say he would be delayed: he was still trying to meet with Stimson. "Damnit, I think he's avoiding me," he said.

"Do you want me to do anything about Snyder?" asked Tully.

"Yeah, draw up charges for a court-martial. Lay it on thick and let him stew over it. That ought to get results."

"Yes, sir. With pleasure."

Tully spent most of Thursday morning with a legal officer, preparing a list of the many offenses committed by Snyder. In the afternoon he brought a copy over to the detention cells.

Snyder was stretched on his cot, arms folded behind his head, staring up at the ceiling, trying to make sense of recent events.

"Present for you."

Snyder jumped up in surprise.

Tully was standing at the bars. He handed through some papers and said, "I'll bring you a list of officers so you can select an attorney. But don't make any plans for the next twenty years."

Snyder sank back on his cot and examined the charges. The case looked airtight. What kind of defense could he put up without Stimson's help? The one man who could clear him was obviously willing to leave him holding the bag. After all those assurances back in Washington that he and Marshall would stand behind the operation—Sure, Snyder thought, *way* behind it.

August 2: Berkeley

Except for a quick trip to Oakland to empty his safe deposit box, Fulbright spent the day in his office, on edge for fear that Groves might call and start asking questions or, far worse, want to speak to Lasch or one of the scientists. And then there was tonight. He was fluctuating between exhilaration at the thought of all the money he was going to get and sheer horror at what he had to do to get it.

He got through the day without incident, cleaned up his office, stuffed personal papers into his briefcase and stopped to consider if he should walk off with some more sensitive information. But what if someone noticed the extra bulge in his briefcase?

Reluctantly he rejected the idea. He walked out of the lab for the last time and drove home.

He parked right in front of the Nunnery so he could get away quickly. As he walked the brick pathway between the hedges, he glanced up at Beth's windows. Trying to remain calm, he went around to the garages. Her stall was empty. He blinked thoughtfully and stood in the alley, wondering what to do. What if she didn't come home? Should he wait? Should he go out and find her? How? Where?

Then another idea occurred to him. Why do it at all? Why bother killing her? If he went back and said it was done and collected his money, would Bowen ever know the difference? He didn't want to kill Beth: he didn't want to kill anyone. He thought of the revolver hidden under his shirts in the bedroom of his apartment. On the way back to the "Swedish consulate," he could fire off a couple of rounds just to make it look good. Would that convince them? They wouldn't be expecting to hear anything about the murder in the papers or anything, because Security would keep it quiet. Long enough for him to be paid and taken out of the country.

As he got up to his apartment, doubts flooded in. How could he fool them? Had he ever fooled them before? They wouldn't just take his word that he had killed Beth. They would check.

He clasped his breast pocket and felt the money Bowen had given him. He thought of his own savings safely stashed in his briefcase. He had enough right now to make a run for it if he wanted to. But the idea that there was 100,000 dollars waiting for him was too tempting to pass up.

It came down to one simple choice: it was her or him.

He sighed. Should he go over there now, while she was out, and let himself in with the passkey? Surprise her when she walked in? He quivered involuntarily, remembering that night at Marion's apartment, hiding in the closet, his heart pounding while Lasch prowled around. . . . No, he didn't want to repeat that experience. Too nerve-racking. Why not stay here? Be comfortable in case it turns into a long wait. He could always get in: just pretend he had to tell her something. He might not even need the key. As usual, Bowen had underestimated him. He clasped the key. Still, it would be better, he thought . . . better if he used it. He didn't want any conversation at the door.

He played the probable scenario over in his mind. The idea of threatening this woman appealed to him. But when it came to the moment of truth . . .

He was too nervous to fix dinner. He sat at his kitchen table and stared through the window at her apartment. As it grew dark, he dragged out a bottle, drank bourbon and ginger ale and listened to comedy shows on the radio, but he couldn't find anything to laugh about.

Where was she?

He kept checking his watch. Once he tried calling. If she answered, he would just hang up. He heard the phone ring across the courtyard, but it wasn't picked up.

He dropped back into his chair and waited in the dark, pouring another drink and staring at the revolver on the table before him, illuminated by the glow of his radio dial. He was tired of comedy. He switched to a quiz show. He listened to the questions and joined the game, trying to answer before the contestant. But he wasn't fast enough: the alcohol had dulled his thinking.

"For forty-six dollars, Mr. Isaacman, name the volcano that erupted in 79 A.D., and the city that it buried."

Fulbright jerked upright. "I know that," he mumbled. "It was Vesuvius!" He tried to think of the city.

"Vesuvius," said Mr. Isaacman.

"And the name of the city?" prompted the moderator.

Fulbright had it on the tip of his tongue, but he was distracted by the musical clock from the show, counting off the seconds while Isaacman struggled for the answer.

"P," he said to himself. "It starts with a 'P'." He stared out the window, as if he could find the answer in the night sky, but a light across the way burned for his attention.

"Pompeii!" shouted Mr. Isaacman, snatching victory away from Fulbright. The radio audience erupted in applause.

But Fulbright was rising to his feet, staring at the light. It was her window. She was *home*.

"Congratulations, Mr. Isaacman! You've just won forty-six—!"

He switched off the radio and groped for the gun. His fingers closed over the butt, then he hesitated, still turning over his options. Should he go now or wait for her to settle in a bit? What if she was going right out again?

Another light went on—in her kitchen. He watched, fascinated, as the top of Beth's head moved back and forth above the curtain line. She had lace half-curtains in the kitchen windows, covering the bottom panes.

What was she doing? Preparing dinner? That meant she would be in for a while. His hopes rose. He wondered if she would stick something on the stove then take a shower or a bath. If he waited, he could go over and perhaps catch her naked—that might make it worthwhile. It took the edge off his anxiety.

Her head disappeared from the kitchen window and he thought he saw movement in the bedroom. Was she getting undressed?

He steadied himself, woozy from the bourbon. His shirt was soaked through with sweat. He felt the gun to be sure the silencer was fully screwed in, then he jammed the barrel down into his pants. He shrugged into his jacket, made certain that Bowen's money was still there, then headed for the door. His bag was already packed, next to his briefcase. Should he load the car now? No. He would take care of Beth first, come back for a last drink and then leave.

He went out, then up the stairs and down the hall toward her apartment. He fumbled for the passkey. The hallway seemed to bob around him and the walls moved as if alive. He made it to Beth's door and stood weaving in front of it. He pressed his ear to the wood and listened. He could hear nothing inside. She was such a quiet girl. She was going to get a lot quieter, he thought, and couldn't help a chuckle. He hoped she was in the bath.

He felt excited again as he moved the key toward the hole and missed. He struck metal several times then focused all his attention on the key and the hole. Come on, you son of a bitch, stop moving. Get in there.

It slid in. And without a thought of caution, he turned it in the lock.

Beth heard the tumblers from the kitchen, then the door opened with that telltale squeak the landlord had never got around to fixing. She heard it even over the water running in the sink. She wondered who—?

No one else had a key. She stood very still.

Fulbright stepped into the living room and closed the door quietly, paying no attention to the water running in the kitchen. All his being was focused on the bathroom, which he knew would be to his right, next to the bedroom. All the layouts were the same in these apartments. He pictured her in the bath, then pulled the gun, hooking the barrel for a second on his waistband, softly cursing.

Then he heard the water go off in the kitchen, followed by a gentle drip-drip-drip—

She was still cooking. Disappointed, he changed direction. His hand tightened on the revolver.

Instinctively Beth pulled open the knife drawer. She picked up the biggest one and backed across the kitchen, through the open door into her breakfast nook. She stood out of the light from the kitchen and called out tremulously, "Who's there?"

No answer. She felt a stab of fear and moved around the door, which swung inward from the kitchen. Stepping behind it, she peered through the crack between the hinges.

She caught a glimpse of movement. The gun came first, the silencer barrel nosing stealthily into the kitchen archway like a predator testing the scent. To Beth it looked as big as a cannon. She stiffened in fear, then looked to see who was holding it.

Fulbright's eyes were wide, his face flushed as he stepped cautiously into the kitchen, confused because she wasn't there.

Beth recognized him and gasped in horror.

Fulbright heard the sound but wasn't sure where it came from. He whirled around and backed up, expecting her to come through the same way he had. He stopped. His woozy mind remembered the door behind him.

Through the narrow slot, she saw him turn and start toward her. In panic, she slammed the door and threw her weight against it.

From the other side, Fulbright lunged and forced the door part way open.

"Go away!" she yelled, terrified. "Fulbright—what are you doing?"

He lunged again. Beth slipped on the linoleum and fell against the door. She crouched and pressed her weight against it, holding it closed. She yelled, "Go away!"

Fulbright stepped back, remembering the gun. He raised it, drew back the hammer and fired at chest level.

There was a *phfft* from the silencer and the smack of a bullet tearing through wood.

It went by inches above Beth's head. She slid to the right, away from the door, then scrambled to her feet. The second shot ripped through. She screamed.

Fulbright snarled, "Shut up!" He fired twice more then flung his weight forward.

She held the knife out with both hands as he burst through the door. He saw the gleaming blade only an instant before impaling himself. The point sliced into his heart, and he loomed over her, blood spurting from the wound, his eyes bulging in shock, the gun half-raised.

She screamed again and pushed him away. He staggered backward. The gun came up and he got off a wild shot. He reeled and collapsed on his face, driving the blade in to the hilt.

Beth fell back and screamed.

Neighbors poured in. Fulbright hadn't closed the front door all the way. Harris Emmett found Beth on the floor of the breakfast nook. He stumbled over Fulbright's body and shrank back in surprise. He grabbed for the wall switch and snapped on the lights. The others crowded in behind him to stare at the corpse on the floor.

Beth slid to the farthest corner of the nook, her hands and slip drenched in blood. "He tried to kill me!" she sobbed.

"Who is it?" someone said.

Dr. Emmett shakily pulled up the head. "Fulbright!" he said, and dropped it in horror. He stared at the revolver.

They had the good sense to call Security rather than the police. Emmett muttered something about getting Dr. Lasch.

Beth rose, clutching the door for support, and said, "No! Get Snyder!"

Forty-five minutes later Snyder was taken from his cell, hustled into a Jeep and driven to headquarters. General Groves was waiting for him with Colonel Tully.

Snyder looked at the clock. "Midnight interrogation?"

"Sit down," Tully said, closing the door.

"Where's the stenographer?"

"Shut up."

Groves took over. "Can you think of any reason why Keith Fulbright would attempt to kill Elizabeth Martin?"

Snyder's whole body froze. Somebody tried to kill Beth? Was she hurt? He had to get to her. Protect her. Why would anyone—?

Did he really say Fulbright?

Groves' face swam back into view. Snyder leaped up and demanded, "What happened?"

Groves eyed him levelly. "According to Captain Browne

this Fulbright broke into her apartment. She managed to get him first—with a knife—"

"Then she's all right?"

"Yes. When they searched Fulbright's body, they found ten thousand dollars cash in an envelope. That and a key to her apartment. Plus the gun he was carrying—silencer-equipped. What do you make of it, Major?"

Snyder's brain was whirling. Fulbright after Beth with a gun? Why? It didn't make sense. A silencer. Money. Had he been paid to do it? By whom? Oh, Christ, how could he have missed it?

Fulbright was the inside man.

And he had risked Beth's life by suspecting her, by failing to catch on to Fulbright. "What about Lasch and the other scientists?" Snyder finally asked. "Are they okay?"

"Why should they enter into this?" Groves asked calmly.

"Because I think Fulbright was working for the Russians."

Groves stared at him then leaned forward. "I've been assured of their safety," he said slowly. "It might interest you to know that Captain Browne was ordered to send them all to Los Alamos."

Snyder didn't reply, sensing something wrong.

Groves' eyes bored into him. "The order was signed by me. And goddamnit, I never sent it!"

Tully tapped a pencil as Snyder managed a weak reply. "What's that supposed to mean, sir?"

"You tell me," Groves hissed back. "Someone I never heard of—a Major Macklin—picked them up—"

"Macklin, sir?"

"You know him?"

"Yes. Have they arrived here yet?"

"No. And they're not expected, either. Now who the hell is Macklin?"

"The pilot for the mission. Sir, I think we'd better get in touch with Colonel Lowe at Hamilton and find out where Macklin and those people are."

Groves scowled then snapped, "Tully!"

"Right away, General." Tully reached for the phone. In a few minutes he raised Hamilton and was connected to Colonel Lowe.

"Give him the phone, Tully," said Groves.

Snyder spoke briefly with Lowe then covered the mouthpiece and told Groves, "Macklin left. He's taken off in the C-54 assigned to Big Stick, along with the four scientists and Nakamura. They cleared the field at 0600 this morning."

"That's eighteen hours ago," said Groves. "What destination?"

"I can't—"

Groves grabbed the phone. "Colonel, this is General Groves. Did you get an order to release that aircraft? And who signed it?" He paused, then snapped, "No, I did *not*, Colonel! Now where are they going?" He waited again. "Okinawa? What the hell for?" He looked up at Snyder. "All right, Colonel, you'll be hearing from me."

He slammed the phone down and glared at Snyder. "Browne says Los Alamos. Lowe says Okinawa. Who's right?"

"I-I don't know, General—"

"Quit fucking around, Snyder! Do you want me to let Tully wring it out of you?"

"Sir, I'd like to make one more phone call."

"Why?"

"Sir, I don't know where they've gone. Okinawa is a possibility, but—I've got to make that call."

Groves blew out his breath. "All right, Major. But no more nickels! We're running out of small change—and *time!*"

Snyder snatched up the phone and called the War Department. He asked for the night duty desk at Stimson's office. Groves and Tully exchanged looks. The duty officer came on the line and Snyder requested Henry Stimson's home phone number. Groves took a deep breath.

When the duty officer refused to give out that information, Snyder motioned to Groves for help. The General flipped open his personal phone book and slapped it in front of Snyder. His finger jabbed down on the page. "Try this one," he snapped.

Snyder called again. He had no idea what he was going to get from Stimson, but one thing was certain: there was no more time to "tough it out," as Stimson had suggested.

Snyder had to go through a butler and a three-minute wait before Stimson's voice came on. "Major Snyder, sir. Sorry to bother you, but did you authorize Big Stick to proceed?"

Stimson was silent a moment, then said, "No."

"Well, they're gone, Mr. Secretary. All the scientists, our handpicked crew and the plane."

"Are you certain?"

"Yes, sir. We know they're airborne. And now it appears there might be Russian involvement."

"Russian?"

"There was an attempted murder at the Rad Lab. The names don't mean anything to you, sir, but it directly involved Big Stick."

"Who's with you?"

"I think it's time, sir, that you speak with General Groves."

Stimson groaned.

Snyder added softly, "If you don't, sir, I will."

"Put him on."

Groves listened for five minutes, his anger visibly rising to a pitch as he paced impatiently, unable to get a word in. When he began to calm down and get in a few "I understand, Mr. Secretary's," Stimson let him speak. "Henry, you should never have gone around me."

"Would you have supported me?"

"Never."

"Of course. So now you understand what Major Snyder's position has been. I strongly urge you to give him every cooperation. Get this matter cleared up—for all our sakes."

Groves grudgingly agreed. When he hung up, Snyder was back on the other phone. "Who are you calling now?"

"Trying to reach somebody at the Swedish consulate—"

"Stefan Thyssen?"

"Yes, sir."

"Missing. Nobody's seen him for two days. I've had people crawling all over San Francisco looking for him. You don't think I'd leave that stone unturned."

Snyder put down the phone. His mind raced. "He could be with them. He and the scientists might have cooked up a plan to complete this mission on their own. They were all pretty determined to go. But I don't see how they could have roped in Macklin and the crew."

"Now wait a minute. Macklin gets two conflicting sets of orders. Okinawa—Los Alamos. You'd think he'd stop and ask somebody—"

"Browne got the Los Alamos orders, not Macklin," said Snyder.

Groves was exasperated. "Has anybody checked out this Major Macklin?"

"He was picked by Colonel Lowe and cleared through the War Department."

Groves whirled. "Tully, you get Macklin's 201 file—in fact, get the files on every member of that crew. Snyder, you've really screwed thing up. Cooperating with a half-assed plan that runs counter to every security regulation I can think of—"

"Sir—"

"Don't interrupt me!"

"I was just going to suggest, General, that you save the chewing-out for later. We don't have time. And please remember, sir, I was operating under direct orders from the Secretary of War. As far as I know, I still am."

"Damned lucky," Groves growled. "Well?"

"Get me to San Francisco, sir, and have Macklin's file sent to the FBI up there, attention Layton Mullen." He picked up the phone again.

"Now what are you doing?" Groves demanded.

"Calling Colonel Lowe again, General. And you're going to issue a directive to stop that plane, wherever the hell it is."

Groves blinked at him, then said, "That's more like it."

August 3: En route to Hamilton

By the time Snyder left Los Alamos at 0100 aboard a B-25, Groves had already issued orders to every Allied military base in the world to hold Army 9526 if it landed.

Snyder switched on a gooseneck lamp and began making notes on a large pad. Tully had threatened him again before putting him on the plane, promising a quick trip to Leavenworth if he didn't show results—and fast. Snyder had ignored him; he had only one thought: Beth. Fulbright had tried to murder Beth. He wanted revenge for that. Fulbright was beyond his reach, but somebody else had ordered the murder, probably the same somebody who had taken care of Marion Cypulski.

He bent over the pad, wrote down names and began connecting them with thin lines, trying to establish relationships.

Why would Lasch go along with an unauthorized mission? Certainly he knew better. Was he so filled with zeal that he would risk his life and those of his colleagues to fulfill an imaginary obligation to Marion Cypulski? Had someone told him the mission *was* authorized? Who would he believe—Thyssen? Snyder drew a line from Lasch to Thyssen.

Then how did Macklin fit in? He wouldn't take Thyssen's authorization. And who had sent the order to Hamilton? Colonel Lowe had been fooled—along with Macklin, it would seem. Snyder traced a line back to Thyssen but it didn't seem right.

Beth was out of it: she had almost become a victim.

Then there was Fulbright. Snyder looked around for a name to connect him to. There wasn't any. He drew the line away, off to a corner of the page and ending in a blank circle. There had to be a name he didn't know yet.

The silencer on Fulbright's gun was professional equipment, spy equipment. The money—ten thousand dollars—a payoff for killing Beth? But again, why? What did Beth know that would make her a target?

Fulbright didn't make his move until after the C-54 had left Hamilton, which meant he wasn't planning to go with them. What was he supposed to do? Go back to the unknown man? And then what? Come to think of it, if it was the Russians, what possessed them to use Fulbright as a hit man?

Snyder put his pencil down. Someone had tentacles long enough and plans well prepared enough to think all this out ahead of time. Fulbright was nothing more than a cog—he couldn't have dreamed this up in a million years.

Portiakov? The big Russian wasn't the sort to do things himself. He would have plenty of others to do his dirty work. But who?

The Trinity box. He could bet that it was gone. Then he began to see the implications. If the scientists were off on their own, maybe it wouldn't come out badly if they got through. But if they were being used, manipulated?

Snyder landed at Hamilton and was whisked off to see Colonel Lowe. With him was Master Sergeant Bayless Tucker, the line chief. Lowe showed Snyder a copy of the orders authorizing Macklin to pick up the scientists.

"Here's his flight plan. He filed the one we laid out for him: Hamilton to Hickam to Wake to Okinawa."

Snyder stared at it.

"He didn't clear through base weather," Lowe added.

"What does that mean?"

"Usually a pilot wants to know what he's flying into."

"Couldn't he get that along the way?"

"Yes—when he makes his position checks."

"You mean if," Snyder said. He checked the names of the crew on the flight plan: they were the ones he and Lowe had cleared. But were they really heading across the Pacific? Why had Browne received different orders?

"We have to assume they're following this flight plan," Snyder said, "and concentrate our efforts along this route, but we can't neglect any other areas. Will you keep General Groves informed?"

"He'll hear it before God does. I guarantee it," Lowe said.

"What about the passengers?"

Lowe nodded to Tucker.

"Six of them, sir," he said.

"Can you describe them?"

"Not really, sir. It was dark. They drove right up to the plane and boarded. I think one of them was an Oriental."

"Did you notice anyone carrying a package?"

"Sir, they all had luggage, mostly small suitcases. I didn't see anything unusual."

Snyder turned back to Lowe. "Can I speak to the drivers?"

"Sure." He walked Snyder down the hall and opened a door. Two MPs came to attention.

"At ease," said Lowe. Snyder asked them to recount their movements. They described the drive from Hamilton to Berkeley, picking up the scientists, the one Oriental—

Snyder interrupted, asking about the package again. One of them recalled an aluminum box.

Snyder was silent a moment then asked grimly, "Then where did you go?"

"To the Swedish consulate in San Francisco. We picked up the last passenger."

Snyder frowned. Thyssen. "Was he waiting outside or did you have to go in to get him?"

"Major Macklin went in, sir."

Macklin. Snyder mulled that for a moment. Macklin didn't know Thyssen—but what the hell could he make of that? Macklin was in charge of everybody as senior military officer. . . . Now Thyssen was in this up to his eyeballs. He had to be the sixth man. Son of a bitch—why would he take part in something so crazy?

Snyder walked out with Colonel Lowe, who demanded to know what was going on. "General Groves said I'd be hearing from him, Snyder. And I'll be damned if I'm going to sit and twiddle my thumbs while he's asking questions."

"I wish I had the answers, Colonel. Just keep after that plane."

Snyder borrowed a car and drove to the Rad Lab. Captain Browne nervously greeted him outside Security. Snyder snapped out questions. "How did the orders arrive?"

"By teletype."

"Didn't you ask for confirmation?"

"Yes, sir, and I got it. Direct from Los Alamos."

Snyder stared at the single lamp over the porch, swarming with fluttering moths. Teletype. Damn, they had to be wired in! Now that didn't sound like a group of amateurs going off on their own: that took organization.

"What about Fulbright?" he asked. "Where's the body?"

"On ice up at Cowell. We're still trying to keep the police out of it."

"And the money that was on him?"

"Inside . . ." He took Snyder into his office and showed him the envelope.

"Did you find anything else on him?"

"No, but when we checked his apartment, we found this suitcase by his door." Browne lifted it onto his desk and snapped the catches open. "He was all set to go."

Snyder went through the clothing, found another envelope and opened it. More money. He shook his head in disbelief.

"That's real," said Browne.

"What do you mean?"

Browne indicated the first envelope. "Counterfeit."

Snyder frowned. "All of it?"

"The whole ten grand."

Snyder whistled. So they had set Fulbright up. He was to kill Beth and then disappear, though probably not in a way he would have liked.

"I've got to see Beth. Where is she?"

Browne took him to the rear Quonset hut. Beth was in Nakamura's room with an Army nurse. When she saw Snyder, she rose from the cot, threw her arms around him and buried her face in his shoulder.

"Are you okay?" he asked.

"Yes . . ."

Browne and the nurse left the room. Snyder kissed Beth then held her head in both hands and looked into frightened and confused eyes.

"I'd give anything to have prevented this."

"I know that."

"Beth, I'm sorry."

"For what?"

"For being stupid. My God, I even suspected you."

"You felt that way about everybody."

"But I should have seen . . ."

She touched his lips. "Forget it."

They sat down on the cot and looked at each other. "I'd like to make it up to you," he said.

"How?"

"By staying with you. Being with you."

She pressed his hand.

"I'm an idiot. It took a shock like this to make me realize what I felt."

She smiled. He pulled her to his chest and they rocked quietly together, and for a moment there was no war, no mission, no death . . . nothing but each other. Then the bars on the window caught his eye and he was brought back to reality.

"We're over our heads in trouble," he said. Quickly he explained what had happened since his arrest. When he got to Lasch and the others taking off without authorization, Beth couldn't believe it.

"He didn't tell me anything," she said, "except . . ."

"What?"

"He insisted I take the rest of the week off."

"Why?" She didn't answer. "Because he wanted you out of the way," Snyder said. "Or someplace where Fulbright could get to you."

"No! You're wrong!"

"Then who paid Fulbright?"

"I don't know, but it couldn't have been Lasch. If he was planning to go ahead with the mission, he might not have wanted me to know about it because of my relationship with you, but that wouldn't lead him to murder."

"Why not?"

"It was Lasch who turned you in to General Groves."

Snyder winced.

"Don't you see? He wouldn't do something like that and then try to kill me. It doesn't make sense."

So Lasch had blown the whistle! Why? Was he so fed up that he called Groves to get the thorn in his side plucked out? Or was it more sinister? Had he and Thyssen cooked up some way to get the other scientists to believe they were going on the real mission? Was Lasch a Russian plant after all? But what about Fulbright? Beth was right: Lasch wouldn't have to murder her to buy time. He accomplished that when he sent her home. So Fulbright was working for someone else. And had been all along, Snyder told himself.

Captain Browne walked in with a box of personal effects taken from Fulbright's apartment. Beth leaned against the window while Snyder sifted through it.

"Only thing interesting is this address book," said Browne. "Guy sure knew a lot of strange ladies. There must be twenty professionals in here. But one of his girl-friends doesn't check out. He had a number listed for some-one named 'Bibi.' Phone company ran it down for us. Turns out it's not a name at all. It's initials. Bibi stands for B.B., an antique dealer named *Bernard Bowen*."

Beth let out a cry.

Snyder's mind groped for identification.

"Bowen," Beth said. "My God, how did he know Bowen?"

Then Snyder remembered the charming older man who was having the affair with Louise Daniels, and who had protested so vigorously about the presence of Vice-Consul Portiakov at the last party.

"Louise!" Beth gasped. "She's been missing for days! I had a dinner appointment with her. She wasn't there and I couldn't reach her. I called Bowen and asked if he knew where she was. He said she had gone to Chicago—someone in her family was ill." She paused. "She hasn't got any relatives in Chicago! *He lied to me!*"

Snyder swore out loud. He grabbed the phone and called Mullen. "I need your help," he said. "How fast can you set up a raid?' "

"Tell me about it first."

Briefly Snyder explained, and when Mullen heard the Russians might be involved, he leaped to cooperate. Snyder gave him Bowen's business and home address, which he got from Beth, and asked him to call back when he was ready.

Then he called the Swedish consulate and got Stefan Thyssen's office. The secretary's voice seemed strange, choked with emotion. Snyder asked for Thyssen, was greeted with silence, then a mumbled, "Just a moment, sir."

A couple of minutes later a man's voice came on, introduced himself as Vice-Consul Lindquist and asked what Snyder wanted.

"I'm with U.S. Army Intelligence and it's important that I reach Mr. Thyssen."

"I'm sorry, Major, but Stefan Thyssen is dead."

Snyder was unable to speak for a moment.

"It appears he was murdered," Lindquist continued. "His body was fished out of the sea yesterday morning."

Snyder mumbled a shocked apology and hung up, surprised to find his hand quivering. If Thyssen was dead, who was the sixth man on the plane? Who had Macklin picked up at the Swedish consulate? Bowen's face rose into view.

Mullen called back and said the raids were scheduled simultaneously for eight forty-five at both addresses.

"I'll meet you at Bowen's shop," Snyder said.

Beth was at the door before he got off the phone. "I'm going with you," she said.

At eight thirty Mrs. Beach opened Bernard Bowen's shop. Fifteen minutes later, the FBI stormed in, scaring her half to death. Snyder, Beth and Browne followed. The agents fanned out for a search. Snyder and Mullen questioned Mrs. Beach. She hadn't seen Bowen in a couple of days, but that was not unusual: he often traveled.

For twenty minutes, the agents combed through the shop, peering behind stacks of furniture, going through cabinets, dressers, desks and ornate boxes, looking for hiding places.

Mullen drifted to the back, urging Snyder and his people to stay out of the way. He and another agent went through everything on Bowen's desk—bills, statements, canceled checks and correspondence—but found nothing incriminating.

The bottom right-hand drawer was locked and they couldn't find a key. Mullen asked Mrs. Beach to open it.

"That's private!" she said, horrified at what was going on.

Mullen called over an agent carrying a toolbox. Snyder came in and asked what they were trying to do.

"Open that drawer," said Mullen.

Snyder checked his watch and said, "This is taking too much time. Have you got a crowbar?"

The agent had his picks inserted in the lock and was already working them around. "Have it in a minute," he said.

"Shoot it open," Snyder suggested.

"Please," groaned Mullen, "we don't do that sort of thing."

The lock clicked and the agent slid the drawer open. It was empty. "So much for that," said Mullen.

"Why would he keep an empty drawer locked?" queried Snyder.

Mullen shrugged. "Force of habit."

"Exactly. That means he kept something in there." Borrowing a flashlight, Snyder got down on his knees and peered inside. His searching fingers found a piece of paper wedged tightly in the back. He pulled it but it wouldn't budge. He opened the drawer above and the paper fell out.

Snyder held it up to the light: a two-inch shred of pale green stationery. "Jackpot," he said, showing it to Beth and Captain Browne. "A piece from one of Marion Cypulski's missing letters."

Mentally Snyder saw all the lines on his pad converging on Bowen's name. He looked at Beth.

Her eyes filled with tears as she sank down heavily into a chair. "Louise," she muttered, staring across the room with a lost look.

Mullen dialed Bowen's house. One of his agents answered and reported that the house hadn't been occupied for several days; clothes and toilet articles were missing. Mullen repeated everything for Snyder, then added, "One of our boys showed up there with an envelope addressed to you. He's on his way over here now."

While they waited, Snyder called Colonel Lowe for a report on the plane.

"Our weather people say there's a storm system in the Pacific, and it's screwing up communications. We haven't been able to contact Hawaii at all. And they haven't received the order to hold 9526."

Snyder made a quick decision. "I may have to get out there myself. Can you figure the best way, sir?"

"Let me work on it."

The FBI agent arrived with the envelope and turned it over to Snyder. Inside was a teletyped facsimile of Major Macklin's 201 file along with a wirephoto of his ID picture. The face was not the Macklin that Snyder had been dealing with.

Now he had two suspects. Bowen and Macklin. He was sure Bowen was the extra man on that plane. And somebody posing as Major Macklin was flying it.

At nine forty-five Snyder arrived back at Hamilton. Browne had returned to Berkeley. Snyder left Beth at the Officers Club while he went to see Colonel Lowe, who said, "We've got two ways to get you to Hawaii. Either by C-54—"

"Too slow."

"Or the Navy has a squadron of F-7Fs about to leave Moffett to rendezvous with a carrier en route to Pearl. They'll divert one plane to pick you up. How's that?"

"Am I going to be stuck out there?"

"No, they'll leapfrog you across."

"Fine."

While Lowe called Moffett to make arrangements, Snyder contacted General Groves at Los Alamos and briefed him on the latest developments. As he unfolded Bernard Bowen's role, Groves listened patiently, waited for an opening, then said, "I'm not interested in speculating on his motives. You believe he and the pilot are Russian agents. I think you're right, and they have to be stopped."

"Yes, sir," Snyder said.

"Do you understand what I'm saying? We've always been afraid of something like this. I'll be damned if I'm going to let them pull off a stunt at this late date!"

"General, we don't know exactly what they're trying to do—"

Groves bellowed over the phone, "It doesn't take a genius to figure it out! Russians with *our* information and *our* scientists! I'd rather make the wrong assumption than wait to ask! I want that plane stopped! Now, what are you going to do about it?"

Snyder took a deep breath and tried to sound confident. "I'm not waiting to hear that some airfield has grounded them, General. I'm going after them myself."

"You know where they've gone?"

"They might be following the original flight plan."

"Why would they do that?"

"Because they're cleared across the Pacific and they don't know we're looking for them." Groves was quiet. Snyder added, "It's a theory, General, and right now it's the only one we've got. I have to get airborne. If I find out they're going somewhere else, I can change direction, but not if I'm sitting here."

"All right, Major. Follow your nose, but I meant what I said: *stop them.*"

"Would you clarify that, sir?"

"Divert them if you can. But if they won't cooperate, do what you have to."

"Sir," Snyder mumbled, catching his drift, "those are our people . . ."

Groves was quiet a moment. "Don't you think I know that?"

Snyder felt a surge of anger. Once again it was being dumped in his lap. "I understand, sir."

"Keep in touch through Colonel Lowe. I'll give you all the support I can."

Snyder hung up. Lowe caught his eye and said, "Forty-five minutes. You'll have to check out flight gear."

"Any word on the search?"

"Weather's still bad."

Snyder hurried out, sickened by what he might have to do and worried that he might be going off on a wild-goose chase. The plane could be anywhere—he could only hope they would be over the Pacific.

He returned to the Officers Club and joined Beth. He couldn't eat or speak, just stared at his plate, lost in thought.

"What's wrong?" Beth asked.

"I'll have somebody get you back to Berkeley."

"Where are you going?"

"To find that plane."

"How?"

"Follow them. With their head start, I may not have much of a chance, but if I don't try, you'll be writing letters to me at Leavenworth."

"They can't hold you responsible," she said.

"Can and will."

"But that's not right."

"Who said anything about being right, Beth? That's the Army. Look, Macklin is a phony, probably a Russian agent. There's an extra man on that plane and I'm almost sure it's Bernard Bowen. The trail of bodies is getting longer by the minute. Before anyone else gets killed—" He choked on his words. "I have to stop that plane."

She stared at him. "What does that mean?"

He couldn't answer.

Her lower lip trembled as she gazed at him, horrified. "Are you going to shoot them out of the sky? Is that it?"

He shook his head. "It won't come to that."

"It won't?" She didn't believe him. Her face darkened. "Allen Lasch is my *friend*! Are you telling me you're prepared to kill him? And the others, too?"

"Beth, this is not like stealing paper clips—"

"Why can't you give me a straight answer?"

He looked at her painfully. "Shooting them down is a last resort. I promise I'll do my damnedest to see it doesn't come to that."

She stared at him, her anger turning to trembling uncertainty.

"Beth, I don't know where they've gone, or even if I can

catch them. I don't know, but I have to try. Just pray
they're held on the ground someplace. Then there won't be
any shooting."

He grabbed her hand and she tried to pull away. He
tightened his grip. "I don't want anybody to get hurt," he
said. "Especially you."

"Let me go."

"No. Listen to me."

"You've said all I want to hear."

"You're too quick to judge. I'm just trying to clear up a
mess. It's important that you understand."

She looked at him a long time, not allowing herself to
weaken. "Why?"

"Because I love you."

"That's beside the point right now."

"Is it?"

"It is for me." She glared at him.

"Excuse me, sir." Snyder looked up at a clean-cut lieutenant standing hesitantly next to the table. "Are you Major Snyder?"

"Yes."

"Only a few minutes left to check out your gear, sir.
Could you come with me?"

"In a minute." The lieutenant went to the exit and waited.
Snyder got up and pulled back Beth's chair. He walked her
to the door. "You better go to Colonel Lowe's office," he
said. "He'll see that you get home."

He caught a glimpse of her face wrinkling with emotion,
then she broke away from him and hurried out.

At 1030 the F-7F landed at Hamilton and taxied to the
flight line. Painted blue-gray, its twin engines ticking over,
it looked out of place among the larger transports.

Snyder shrugged into his parachute harness and Sergeant
Tucker buckled it across his chest. The seat pack weighed
heavily against his rear. Colonel Lowe and Beth were beside him as he watched the fighter roll up and stop. The
front canopy opened; the pilot climbed down and walked
toward them.

Snyder turned to Beth. She was tense as he took her face
in his hands and kissed her.

"I still mean it," he said.

"Then come back with those people." She backed away, her arms clasped across her middle, her shoulders hunched against a morning breeze.

Snyder nodded to Lowe, who said, "I'll be coordinating with Groves, Major. We'll let you know anything that happens."

"Thank you, sir," Snyder said. "For everything. I'm sorry I got you into this."

"Finish it," Lowe said.

Snyder turned and found himself face-to-face with the Navy pilot. "Lieutenant Commander Dave Scheff, Major. If you've finished your farewells, we better get moving." He motioned toward the plane and Snyder followed. Scheff was a smallish man with a slight build and a fair complexion. There were crinkly laugh lines around his eyes.

"Ever been in a hot plane before?" Scheff asked.

"No."

"Do you get airsick?"

"No."

"Good, you'll love it." They reached the F-7F, a sleek fighter with a long nose and two cockpits. "The big nose is for radar," said Scheff. "The monitoring gear is in your compartment; it'll make you cramped and uncomfortable. Just thought I'd warn you. Now, put your feet exactly where I put mine or we'll be all day getting into this thing."

He climbed up, using hand- and foot-holds, and waved Snyder into the rear cockpit. Snyder stopped to stare at a painting on the nose—a large salami with Hebrew lettering over it, and around it the words, in red and white, *The Deadly Deli*.

"What's that?" Snyder asked.

"A salami," said Scheff. "My pop owns the best deli in Cleveland." He pointed to the rear cockpit. "Get in."

Snyder threw his leg over and settled in. Scheff was right: it was cramped. Radar equipment was bolted directly in front of him. He buckled in and Scheff closed both canopies. He couldn't see forward: the canopy lay flush against the fuselage. His only view was out the sides. He heard Scheff yell for him to put on his helmet. He found it under the seat and strapped it on. Through the built-in headset, Scheff's voice droned instructions: how to be sure he was buckled in, how to use the throat mike, etc.

"Any problem, Major?"

"No."

"Okay, now wave good-bye to your girlfriend, 'cause here we go."

He fired up the engines. Snyder, caught in midwave, instinctively grabbed the side of the cockpit. The sound was deafening.

He heard Scheff's voice over the headset again, a tinny crackle. "Commend your soul to God, Major, 'cause your ass belongs to Rabbi Scheff!"

They took off in a thunder of vibration and noise. Snyder grimaced as his teeth rattled.

They joined the rest of the F-7F squadron as it rose from Moffett Field and headed out to sea. A radio message from Colonel Lowe informed Snyder that they had finally gotten through to Hawaii, and there was no report at all on Army 9526. Its ETA at Hickam would have been between 1300 and 1500 yesterday. But it had not arrived, nor was it expected.

Snyder stared back at the receding coastline, then out at the ocean. The C-54 had vanished.

PART 4

August 3: The Pacific

Snyder readjusted the leg straps of his parachute harness, easing the tightness. He glanced to his right as one of the other planes edged closer. Fascinated, he watched the wing tips attract each other like magnets. When it looked as if they might overlap, he jabbed his throat mike in a strangling motion. "Scheff," he squawked, "if your buddy gets any closer, he's going to come right through us."

"Not used to formation flying, Major?"

"No. Is this how you get your kicks?"

Scheff laughed. "Back off, Dorward, you're making my passenger nervous."

The other pilot grinned—he was so close Snyder could see that his teeth needed work—then eased his plane away. Hotshot, Snyder thought, looking down at the Pacific. Out of sight of land, the vastness of the ocean was overwhelming. How was he going to find that plane out here?

Scheff's cheerful voice cut through his gloom. "How you doing back there? Enjoying the view?"

"Just what I always wanted—a window seat."

"Too bad we don't have a stewardess."

"Can I ask a question?"

"Nothing tough, Major. I'm just a lowly pilot."

"I'm looking for a C-54 that was headed for Hawaii. It left Hamilton at 0600 yesterday, and it hasn't been seen or heard from since."

"Army crew?"

"Yes."

"It figures."

Snyder ignored that. "If you were the pilot and you wanted to evade pursuit, how would you go about it?"

"First of all, get rid of that crew——" Snyder had to wait for Scheff to dish out a good dose of malarkey since he had the comm line. When he was through:

"All right, Scheff. That was a serious question."

"Oh—one of those! Well now, let me see. The C-54 has a range of thirty-eight hundred miles. With a top speed of three five zero miles per hour, they can fly a little over ten hours before refueling. So by now they would have to put down someplace."

"Right," said Snyder. "Where?"

"I don't know. Mexico, Canada, Alaska . . . ? You'd have to tell me where they don't want to go, see?"

Snyder frowned to himself. They could have flown north, up the coast of Alaska, refueling at any base along the way, then continued across the Bering Strait and into Siberia. But if they did land at an American base, he would have heard by now. Mexico was out of the question. It made no sense to go south.

"If you really want to find out," said Scheff, "get hold of some general with a lot of clout and have every C-54 in the Pacific grounded. If there's one still flying, then that's your baby."

Snyder seized on that. "Thank *you*," he said.

"No extra charge. You want I should get somebody on the radio?"

"Colonel Lowe."

Snyder repeated Scheff's suggestion to Lowe, who reminded him there was a war on. He agreed to relay it to Groves, then grudgingly admitted it was a good idea.

"Thank you, sir," Scheff said, cutting in. "The Navy is always happy to assist people who *need* help."

"Likewise," said Lowe.

Snyder relaxed, confident he had made the right move. But an hour into the flight he heard back from Lowe: Groves was overextended on clout and could not ground every C-54 in the Pacific without putting a serious crimp into the war effort. Plus the fact that it would take an inordinate amount of time to implement the order.

"However," Lowe continued, "we're checking everything that's landed in the islands during the last twenty hours."

"Very well," said Snyder. "Let me know the results, sir."

"Will do."

Snyder signed off and sat back, worried again. Scheff clucked sympathetically, "Too bad, Major. Say . . . how does one go about losing a plane anyway?"

"Scheff, shut up and fly."

Eight hours after leaving Hamilton on August 2nd, Army 7271 had touched down at Hickam Field on Oahu.

It was noon in the islands as the plane taxied to the transient area and Macklin requested refueling. He unstrapped, picked up his briefcase and went aft. "Holbrecht" rose to meet him as he came through. "Do we have any time to get out and stretch our legs, Major?" he said.

"Sorry. Orders are, no passengers leave the plane."

They were groans from the scientists. Bliss pulled himself out of his seat and complained, "It's already hot as hell in here. How long are we going to be on the ground?"

"I'll do this quick as I can. Just have to make a weather check."

Whelan opened the cabin door and waited for the rollaway steps to be brought into place. Then Macklin walked out into the humid air. He handed the line chief a copy of Form 23 that he had forged earlier, identifying the plane as Army 297271 and listing Pago Pago as final destination with a refueling stop at Hickam.

The line chief signed the yellow sheet, tore off the receipt and returned it to Macklin. "All in order, sir."

"Sergeant, I'd like to be out of here in twenty minutes."

"Can do, sir."

"One more thing—see that nobody gets off that plane."

"Yes, sir."

Macklin stepped into a flight-line Jeep and was driven to Base Operations. He walked in and requested a weather report for Pago Pago. The clerk gave him a teletype tear sheet and Macklin went over to the pilots' desk.

He filled out a fresh flight plan, using 7271 as the aircraft number but listing a dummy crew. He entered the weather report and signed his own clearance with a false name, then took it back to operations.

"Your ETA, Major?" asked a sergeant.

"1700 today."

"Okay, sir. Have a good flight."

Macklin returned to the plane; the cabin interior had become an oven. Holbrecht and Lefferts, the backup pilot, were passing out canned juices. Nakamura fanned himself with a magazine.

"How soon can we get out of here?" asked Lasch, stripped to shirt-sleeves, his jacket slung over a seat.

"Right away. Mr. Holbrecht, I have some sealed orders but I can't open them till we're airborne."

"Really, Major?" Holbrecht gave him a big frown and made sure Lasch saw it. "Who are they from?"

"We'll know in a few minutes."

"Oh, Christ," said Bliss, mopping his brow. "They're canceling."

"Not necessarily," Holbrecht said. "Let's wait and see."

Ten minutes later Army 7271 took off. Macklin climbed to 12,000 feet, leveled off, then turned the controls over to Grant. He went aft with Slocum, bringing the briefcase with him.

He handed Holbrecht a thick manila envelope and watched him break the seals and draw out a sheaf of papers. They were introductory letters for each of the scientists, to be presented to the Japanese upon arrival. There were sheets of instructions under Thyssen's signature with State Department verification signed by James Byrnes.

Holbrecht read quickly and expressed amazement. "We've been given a change of route and final destination," he said. "They now want us to go to Midway, instead of Wake, and from there on to northern Japan, not Okinawa."

"Where in northern Japan?" asked Nakamura.

"Karafuto. Do you know it?"

"Yes."

"There's a map here." Holbrecht opened it. Nakamura pointed to a large island mass north of Honshu.

"Karafuto is the Japanese name for the southern half of

Sakhalin," he said. "The northern part is occupied by the Russians."

Bliss murmured his displeasure. Kirby opened his diary and made a notation.

"Whose bright idea was that?" asked Willard.

"It would seem to have been a consensus," said Holbrecht. "Let me read you something from Thyssen's letter. 'Because of the deteriorating situation in Japan—mistrust of civilian government by the military and vice versa—the Japanese representatives feel it would be wiser to meet in an isolated area where the delegations would not attract undue attention. Meeting on Okinawa, they feel, is too dangerous. Despite all precautions, there is the serious fear that the Japanese team might meet interference from their own forces.' "

There was silence except for the drone of engines. Kirby stopped writing in anticipation of the next development.

"Where exactly is the final destination?" asked Lasch.

Holbrecht scanned the sheet then leaned over the map. "Taraika Bay." He pointed to it. "There's an airstrip along the inside here."

Nakamura nodded. "That's isolated all right. Nothing up there but a few fishing villages. Unless they've fortified it."

"Is it safer than Okinawa?" asked Lasch.

"Probably," Nakamura said.

Bliss jumped up. "Now just a minute, damnit. How close will we be to the Russians?"

"What do you mean?" asked Holbrecht.

"I mean the southern half of this island is Japanese and the north is Russian! He just told us that!" He pointed to Nakamura.

Holbrecht glanced at Macklin. "What difference does that make?"

"They'd give their back teeth to get hold of us—and what we're carrying!"

Holbrecht laughed. "Dr. Bliss, you're traveling under the protection of the Swedish government, a neutral nation respected by all the combatants. The Russians would not dare to interfere with us. Besides, they know nothing of this mission."

Bliss's eyes narrowed suspiciously. "You're sure?"

"Utterly confident. But I leave it in your hands." He glanced around at all of them. "Are there any serious objections?"

Bliss looked around, expecting support, but there wasn't any.

"When is the meeting?" Lasch asked.

Holbrecht checked. "August fourth."

"Then I suggest we concentrate on our presentations. The flight and landing we can leave to Major Macklin."

"That's okay with me," said Willard. Kirby nodded. Bliss sank back, grumbling to himself.

"Okay," said Macklin. "I'll take that map." Nakamura passed it over and Macklin handed it to Slocum.

"There's something else in here," said Holbrecht, sorting through the papers. "It's for you, Major. It has to do with making some radio checks." He pulled out a sheet and gave it to Macklin, who scanned it briefly, nodded assent and returned to the cockpit with Slocum.

The scientists relaxed. Bliss sat by himself, stewing silently. Holbrecht opened his briefcase and pulled out a set of stickers, reproductions of the Swedish flag, which he began affixing to the Trinity box. Lasch asked what he was doing.

"Turning this into a Swedish diplomatic pouch in case there's trouble. Mind you, I don't expect any, but . . ."

Bliss nervously watched the stickers go on.

Lasch relaxed, rubbed his legs to keep the circulation going and wondered about this Russian business. Holbrecht had said the Russians knew nothing of Big Stick, while Snyder had believed they were responsible for all the misfortunes to date. But Snyder was gone and here they were on the plane. Of course Snyder had been wrong. Where could the Russians have gotten any information? Not from Marion—he still couldn't believe that. And when they called him to the consulate, that could have been Snyder trying to frame him. The letters, everything—all Snyder. Yes! Snyder had been against the mission from the start! So he had systematically sabotaged it. Why didn't I see it before? Lasch asked himself. But it was all right now. Snyder couldn't touch them. They would get through. Okinawa or Karafuto—did it make a difference?

In the cockpit Slocum had already plotted the course change to Midway. Macklin explained the radio check to Beddic: he was to tune to 9400 kilocycles on CW at the prescribed time and listen for a steady tone, followed by a four-digit time check in Morse code, then reply with their ETA on Karafuto using Greenwich Mean or Zulu Time. The checks were to be every four hours starting at 0030 Zulu.

Macklin asked Beddic to get weather information for Midway then returned to the controls, relieving Grant. He asked Lefferts for a sandwich then smiled to himself. It was all working.

August 3: The Pacific

With the rest of the F-7Fs *The Deadly Deli* dropped through the clouds into bright sunlight, and Snyder got his first glimpse of an aircraft carrier.

"We're going to land on that?"

"First time for you, too, huh?" said Scheff.

Snyder growled, "Will you cut out the jokes?"

"Who's joking? I got my wings at Sears Roebuck."

"Scheff!" Snyder protested.

"Okay, Major." Scheff broke into the singsong tone of a tour guide. "We are now approaching CV-24, *Belleau Wood*, an aircraft carrier of the *Independence* class, with a six-hundred-eighteen-foot flight deck."

"Is that short or long as these things go?"

"Oh, very short. Very short indeed. Excuse me, gotta concentrate on landing now."

Snyder released his throat mike and pressed his cheek to the Perspex canopy, craning to see the elongated postage stamp pitching in high green seas below. She was surrounded by escort vessels, which Snyder presumed were there to pick up survivors of bad landings.

The F-7Fs changed formation and came in single file at two-mile intervals. Snyder realized his plane was going to be first in. He pictured the others piling up on top of *The Deadly Deli*.

"Hold on," Scheff said. "It's a little lumpy."

Snyder clutched the sides of his cockpit. Just before the plane straightened out and cut off his view, he saw a man standing on the incoming edge of the flight deck, waving what looked like orange Ping-Pong paddles.

The man stood his ground as the plane swooped down and at the last second he pulled the paddle across his throat. The wheels touched down and Scheff cut his engines. Too fast! Snyder thought, sure they would go shooting right through the barrier and into the sea. But the tail hook grabbed and they were yanked to a stop. Snyder was pitched forward and grabbed by his seat harness.

Men from the deck crew rushed over to disengage the tail hook. Scheff taxied down to the barrier, which lowered so that he could pass into the parking area.

"Howdja like that?" Scheff asked.

"I can't wait to take off," Snyder mumbled.

"Oh, much better. Much more fun."

They got out of the plane. Snyder thanked Scheff for the flight and said, "Listen, I don't know what arrangements they've made for my next hop to Hickam but—"

"Would I like to see Hawaii? You bet, Major. Just tell them you got used to me and you'd hate to switch."

"Thanks," Snyder said gratefully. "Thanks a lot."

"Jesus," said Scheff, "and here I did all I could to scare the shit out of you."

"Yeah, but you flew the plane just fine. The next guy might not be so good."

"Anything you cook up, Major, is okay by me. But it has to include *my* plane. I don't go anywhere without *The Deadly Deli*."

"Fair enough."

Snyder followed a Marine up to the communications bridge and reported to the Executive Officer.

"I'm aware of your priority, Major," he said. "In order to give you the needed range to Hawaii, you'll have to steam with us for at least an hour. Then you can take off again."

"I'd like the same pilot, and he'd like to keep his plane."

"No problem. I've got a message for you from Colonel Lowe at Hamilton. Information you requested is waiting with G2 at Hickam."

"Can we get them on the radio?"

Snyder spoke to a Lieutenant Mardeen there, who gave him a rundown on C-54 transits in and out of Hickam and all other Hawaiian fields. Of fifty-seven landings in the last twenty-four hours, the first forty-nine had all arrived before the probable ETA of Army 9526. Of the remaining eight, only five had come into Hickam. The other three were Navy transports carrying only Naval personnel. Of the five at Hickam, one was down with an engine malfunction and the other four had already left. There were crew complements available but no passenger manifests.

"Major, it looks like Army 9526 didn't land here."

Snyder thanked Mardeen, signed off and stood up.

"Is there anything else you'll need?" asked the Exec.

"Yes. A backup plane and crew."

At 1430 PDT, two F-7Fs left *Belleau Wood*, Snyder and Scheff in one and two new pilots in the other. Snyder was no closer to finding the C-54 and hoped that Groves' directive to hold the plane would turn up something, he didn't care where. But he was worried now that he could have been completely wrong about general direction. What if they had gone to Siberia? What if Macklin and Bowen, maybe even Lasch, had seized control of the crew—?

He stopped spinning stories in his head. He couldn't anticipate everything. He needed a clue, at least one solid clue.

August 3: Midway

There was a severe storm when Macklin landed at Midway on the night of August 2nd. The plane was immediately grounded. Nothing was getting in or out and, despite Macklin's radio efforts with Base Operations, Army 7271 was ordered to stay on the ground.

The plane was towed to a parking area awash with water. Heavy winds buffeted the aircraft as it sat there, with Macklin refusing the tower's requests to deplane and send his people to shelter. But after five hours of rain pelting the fuselage, the scientists had had enough. They sent Holbrecht up to the cockpit to tell Macklin they wanted off.

When Macklin relented, they were taken to VIP quarters, which turned out to be nothing more than a large room in a Quonset hut. Macklin had insisted they be kept isolated because of the sensitive nature of their mission.

By noon on August 3rd the storm was still raging. Visibility was nearly nonexistent. The C-54 sat on a swamped tarmac with other planes waiting to get off.

The confined scientists had grown restless and anxious. Even Holbrecht's placid patience was giving way. The lead he had built up was rapidly shrinking and he was tired of playing nursemaid to these men. He did his best to keep them calm, urging them to accept the delay with a philosopher's tolerance. He helped them use the time by pumping them for their presentations. For Bernard Bowen it was an excellent opportunity to discern who would be most useful to his superiors in Moscow, who might be the most cooperative and who might be superfluous. He had already decided that Bliss was impossible.

The door banged open: it was Macklin returning from another trip to Base Operations.

Bliss jumped up. "Well? How long are we going to be stuck here?" he demanded.

"Don't know," said Macklin, turning to Lasch and Holbrecht. "There's no change in the weather yet. This could last forty days and forty nights."

"Perhaps we should build an ark," Willard suggested.

Bliss swore at him; Kirby told him to shut up.

"Fine for you!" Bliss bellowed. "You just sit there and scribble away in that stupid book. What the hell are you writing, anyway, the history of World War Two?"

"Julian," Kirby said with great patience, "we're all concerned. Shouting isn't going to help anything."

"Who the hell are you—?"

Holbrecht stepped between them. "Gentlemen, please. This is not suitable behavior for the stature of our mission. Please sit down, Dr. Bliss."

"Goddamnit, Holbrecht—!"

Holbrecht stiffened and Bliss realized he had overstepped himself. He looked around at the others, who were all doing their best to ignore him. He apologized in a whisper and sat down.

Holbrecht laid a comforting hand on his shoulder, then went back to Macklin. "Major, may I have a word with you?"

"Certainly."

They moved away from the others. "How many radio checks have we missed?" Holbrecht asked quietly.

"Five."

"What if we go aboard the plane and try—?"

Macklin shook his head. "There's a complete communications wipeout. Nothing's getting through—in or out. One advantage, though, if there's any sort of pursuit, they're being held away by the same storm. We're at a standoff. Let's hope your people at the other end will still be waiting for us."

Holbrecht sighed. "We'll find out when we're back in the air. I assume we can get out of here just as soon as the storm clears, and before they start receiving radio messages again."

"We'll see. How are the eggheads holding up?"

"Well enough," Holbrecht said distastefully.

Macklin grinned. "They're all yours, nurse. I'm going back to Base Ops."

"Why?"

"Just in case something does get through about us, I'd like to be the first to know."

He banged out the door and dashed through the rain.

August 3: Hickam Field

Snyder's two-plane flight landed at Hickman in midafternoon. Leaving Scheff to handle refueling, Snyder took a Jeep to G2 headquarters.

Lieutenant Mardeen turned out to be a very young, alert, serious officer with the pale face of a zealous workhorse. He handed Snyder a piece of paper. "A list of the planes that landed here yesterday," he said. Before he could explain further, he was called away and left Snyder promising to return quickly.

Snyder examined the list of seventeen planes but could glean nothing from it. He kept glancing at the clock, measuring the minutes ticking away. Damn, if Mardeen had any news, why didn't he come back and say so? Snyder couldn't afford to waste time here.

Twenty minutes later Mardeen returned, followed by a staff sergeant. "Might have something for you, Major," he said. "One of those planes doesn't check out."

"In what way?"

The sergeant showed Snyder a clipboard with a list of numbers. "This one came in yesterday at 1200 and cleared at 1245 after routine refueling," he said. "But the number belongs to a plane based at Luke Field."

Snyder stared at the number, puzzled. "Did you contact Luke?"

"Yes, sir," said the sergeant. "297271 was not airborne yesterday. In fact, it's not going anywhere for a while. It's sitting in a hangar with two engines out for overhaul."

"No mistake?"

"We just double-checked," said Mardeen.

"Holy shit," said Snyder. "They switched numbers!"

"That's what it looks like."

"Where's it going?"

"Filed a flight plan for Samoa," said Mardeen.

The sergeant pulled the white copy of Form 23 off his clipboard and handed it to Snyder. "ETA Pago Pago was 1700 yesterday," he said.

Snyder stared at the crew list—none of the names was familiar. But if Macklin changed the number, what was to stop him from changing names? "Have you checked Samoa?"

"We're waiting to get through right now," said Mardeen.

Snyder went back to Base Communications with them. As a final destination or even a stopover, Samoa made no sense. Where could they be going? Australia? New Zealand?

The radio man motioned them over. "Got Base Ops at Pago Pago," he said.

Mardeen did the talking. "Did you have a C-54, ASN 297271, land yesterday anytime after 1500? Over."

"Have to check. Stand by, Hickam."

It took two minutes for the information to come back. 7271 had not arrived nor was it ever expected. Mardeen thanked him and signed off.

"It's a diversion," Snyder decided. At least now he knew the plane was over the Pacific. Everything jibed: the arrival time at Hickam, the use of deceptions.

"Did anybody get off that plane?" he asked Mardeen.

"Just the pilot—to file this plan."

"What about passengers?"

"According to the line chief," said the sergeant, "the pilot gave orders that nobody was to leave the aircraft."

"Any idea where they're going, Major?" asked Mardeen. "G2 is very interested."

"Wake Island," Snyder said quickly, then wondered if Macklin would stick to the original flight plan. Maybe all the deceptions were to hide that fact. In any case, given 7271's speed and time of departure from Hickam, they could already have landed at Wake and gone.

"Can you raise Wake?" he asked Mardeen. "Find out if

7271 landed there. And can you patch me in to Hamilton?"

The radio hookup took more time. He filled in Colonel Lowe and suggested he alert all stations in the Pacific to be on the lookout for 7271. "How fast can you get me top-priority use of Naval facilities, sir?"

"What do you have in mind?" asked Lowe.

"I need the location of aircraft carriers between here and Wake Island, and permission to land two planes and refuel about a thousand miles west of Oahu."

Lowe sighed. "See what I can do. Groves will have to be in on this."

"Thank you, sir. I'll wait for your reply."

Snyder turned to Mardeen. "Can you have my pilot brought over to get maps and coordinates?"

Mardeen sent the staff sergeant out in a car.

The radio man said he could not get through to Wake. "There's a huge front in from the north and it's fouling up communications."

"Keep trying," said Snyder. "As soon as you get through, contact me in the air. I've got to know if they've been there."

He went back to Base Ops and met Scheff. "We're going on," he explained. "If they can set up a carrier stop for us, we'll go through to Wake." He explained about the switched numbers and the other gags Macklin had been pulling.

Scheff laughed. "Boy, he's got balls."

"Let's see if we can cut them off."

Five minutes later, while Scheff was getting weather information, a message came in from CINCPAC at Pearl, advising that the carrier *Princeton* was proceeding west from Hawaii and was still within range to take Snyder's flight aboard, but only if he got in the air right away.

Scheff grabbed maps and a scribbled note with the carrier's estimated position. Snyder followed him out and they were whisked back to the flight line.

The two F-7Fs roared out of Hickam, Snyder flying with the backup pilot, Ensign Lang, while Scheff rode passenger with Ensign Terwilliger and tried to catch some sleep.

They were within fifty miles of the *Princeton* when Snyder's headset crackled. The carrier had made contact with Wake. The weather there had temporarily cleared but was expected to worsen again.

"What about Army 7271?" asked Snyder.

"They don't have it, Major. All C-54s that touched down in the last ten hours have been held and searched. And before that, no sign of Army 7271."

Snyder frowned in disappointment. *Where were they?*

"Wake advises that conditions will be so bad you'll never get in there. They say that if you must continue west, divert to Midway, as the front is moving south and is expected to clear there in a few more hours."

Snyder slowly came alert. *Midway.* That's why 7271 never showed at Wake. *It went to Midway.*

Snyder twitched impatiently while the *Princeton's* Communications Officer drawled information about the carrier's position. As soon as the line was free, Snyder cut in:

"*Princeton,* did anybody try to raise Midway?"

"No, sir."

"I think 7271 might be there!"

"You're coming in on final now. We'll get Midway on the horn once you're aboard."

As soon as Scheff killed the engines, Snyder opened the canopy and climbed down. He was rushed to the *Princeton's* bridge. The Communications Officer met him and said, "We haven't gotten through yet, Major. The weather is still screwing things up."

"How long has that storm been going on?" Snyder asked.

"It's a polar front, swept out of the north on August second. Been stationary over Midway ever since and now it extends as far south as Wake."

Snyder paced. "Isn't there any way we can find out if 7271 got to Midway?"

"Only by contacting them. We'll keep trying."

Snyder returned to the flight deck. Scheff had barely enough time to visit the head before they climbed back aboard the refueled plane and took off again, followed by the backup plane with Lang and Terwilliger.

Once they were at altitude, Snyder talked himself hoarse

trying to raise Midway. All he got was hash and static. Scheff finally interrupted.

"Are you sure you want to go to Midway, Major?"

"Don't give me any crap, Scheff."

"You're in it already. Take a look ahead."

Snyder peered past the starboard engine and saw an enormous gray-black mass of clouds ahead of them. "What the hell is that?"

"That, mine boy, is what is known as an occluded front. We can't go around it or under it, and I hope to hell we can get through it. I'm willing to bet you that fucker extends right up to Midway. The next couple of hours are going to be pretty damned hairy. You buckled?"

Snyder checked his straps and stared through the Perspex. It looked ominous. Ten minutes later they found out it was. They were sucked up into a wrenching, blinding gray mass that slowed their airspeed to a crawl and buffeted them like a canoe going down the rapids.

Snyder felt his stomach rise and fall with the plane. He couldn't see the other F-7F and prayed that Scheff knew where it was. Then he heard singing over his headset:

> *"She flies through the air*
> *With the greatest of ease,*
> *Alice, the goose-girl*
> *With warts on her knees . . ."*

"Scheff, if we ever get out of this, I'm going to have you committed," Snyder growled between gasps.

"Having a little tummy problem, Major? I thought a short musical interlude would take your mind off it, eh what?"

"Spare me. Just fly the plane."

Scheff left him alone and Snyder tried Midway again. Still no reply. The radio was worse than ever—almost steady hash. He closed his eyes and did some thinking.

Macklin was the key. Snyder had completely discarded the idea that 7271 was headed to complete its peace mission. That might be what the scientists and Nakamura thought was going to happen, but they were pawns in a larger game. And the players appeared to be Macklin for

sure, Bowen if he was aboard, and possibly Lasch. Macklin
seemed to be running the deception, which had started the
moment he had reported to Hamilton. And Bowen, whose
hooks were into the Rad Lab through Cypulski and Fulbright, was probably Macklin's boss. As for Lasch, his involvement was unclear, but he *had* told Beth to take the
week off, and he *had* willingly supplied the flight with the
Trinity box.

But even if he was right about Russian involvement,
what was their ultimate purpose? And their final destination? Okinawa was out—the last place Russian spies would
want to go. And as for weather having pushed them to
Midway, that he doubted. It seemed more like a deliberate
move. That's where they'd been headed all along. But from
there . . . where? General direction: northwest.

"Scheff, where's the nearest Russian territory northwest
of Midway?"

"Wanna give me that again, Major?"

"Russian territory."

Scheff fumbled with a chart and a flashlight. A moment
later: "There's all of Kamchatka and a whole lot of territory north of Japan. Sea of Okhotsk, Sakhalin, Khaba-
rovsk . . ."

"Give me ranges from Midway, comparative to Okinawa."

Scheff sighed. "Just looking at the chart, I can see that
from Midway, they're all closer than Okinawa."

Snyder ignored a rising surge of nausea: the plane was
still taking a beating and his head felt like an overweight
watermelon teetering on a fence. He gulped down air,
managing to fight the sickness and trying to think at the
same time. He would have to get planes in the air to intercept the C-54. It would be a huge operation covering a
tremendous amount of territory.

He wondered just how "overextended" Groves' clout
was.

Their airspeed knocked down from 450 to 300 mph,
thanks to furious head winds, the 600-mile flight from
Princeton took two hours. Conditions were still bad at Midway; they had to be brought in by radar. They landed in

heavy rain and nearly skidded off the runway. Lang and Terwilliger were far behind.

As soon as Scheff pulled the engines, Snyder said, "Get them started refueling, then meet me at Base Ops."

Scheff grumbled to himself as Snyder dropped off the fuselage and looked around in the rain for a Jeep. There was none. He saw the lights of the flight line buildings through the hammering darkness and took off at a run. He was soaked within seconds.

As he neared the hut marked BASE OPS, he saw the Jeep and heard the driver trying to start it, cursing. It tore away just as Snyder came up behind it.

He stumbled into Base Ops and was met by a Navy lieutenant commander name Kranzler. "We've been expecting you, Major Snyder." He rubbed his hands happily, reminding Snyder of an unctuous funeral director. All he needed was a black suit. "Just got word from CINCPAC," Kranzler continued. "We're to give you whatever you need." He beamed with pleasure.

"Swell," said Snyder, stripping out of his flight gear. "Start with some dry clothes."

"Yes, sir." Kranzler sent a clerk off for fresh gear.

"I'm looking for a C-54, Army 7271," Snyder said. "Did it land here?"

Kranzler threw his head back in contemplation, then went over to the operations board. "Yes," he said triumphantly. "It came in yesterday and left here one hour ago."

Buck naked, Snyder took a step forward. He couldn't believe it, but there it was in white chalk on a big blackboard.

"Destination Hickam," added Kranzler, beaming again. "Bullshit!"

Kranzler blinked uncertainly as Snyder checked his watch. A one-hour head start. By the time he and Scheff got in the air again, it would be an hour and a half lead. And they'd have to fight weather.

"They were stranded here twenty-six hours," Kranzler offered. "Had them overnight in transient quarters. A strange bunch: six crew, six passengers. And one was an Oriental."

Snyder hardly listened. The C-54's top speed was 350—
the F-7F was a hundred miles faster. But the C-54 had the
range to make it from here to anywhere on the Russian
mainland without refueling. The F-7F had to make 1200-
mile gas stops, and that range would be cut down because
of weather and weight. It would take a miracle to catch
7271 now. It was all going to hinge on search planes between here and the mainland.

The clerk reappeared with a complete change of clothes
and a new flying suit and jacket. Snyder dressed quickly,
still calculating. Until they cleared the weather front, neither aircraft would make top speed, but it would still take
him a good five to six hours to get within visual range of
7271, assuming he was not a thousand miles off.

Scheff came in, wearing a poncho supplied by the Jeep
driver. He spread his chart on a desktop and studied it with
Snyder. It was 2500 miles from Midway to Hokkaido. The
Russian mainland was only a couple of hundred miles farther. Given comparative speeds and F-7F fueling stops,
they could not catch up to 7271 until it was in Japanese
airspace. If it was going to Kamchatka, same problem.
They would be over land when they converged.

Scheff shook his head. "I don't think they're going to
Kamchatka. Too close to the Aleutians. We've got an advanced air base up there."

"Yeah, but do they know that?" asked Snyder.

"They seem to know everything else."

Snyder grunted. "The problem is going to be where we
take them—assuming we find them. If it's over Japan, we
risk their falling into Japanese hands. If it's over Russia—
worse. That's what we're trying to prevent."

"So where do you think they're headed for?"

"The mainland the other side of Hokkaido."

The logistical problems were monumental. He had to arrange to have carriers in place for his own refueling and he
had to find them in midocean. And would the Navy cooperate to that extent?

Snyder asked for paper and pencil, then carefully wrote
out a message:

REQUEST AIR SEARCH PACIFIC ROUTE TO
NORTHERN JAPAN AND ALEUTIAN CHAIN
TO LOCATE ARMY 7271 X NEED CARRIERS IN
POSITION TO REFUEL US AND SUBMARINES
TO COVER NORTHERN APPROACHES X SNY-
DER.

He handed it to Kranzler and asked him to have it coded
and sent top priority to CINCPAC, with a copy to General
Groves at Los Alamos. "And when you get answers," he
said, "get them to me within an hour and a half, because if
they can't supply a carrier, we'll have to turn back."

"You're learning," said Scheff in admiration.

"Did Lang and Terwilliger come down in one piece?"

"Three pieces. Two guys and a plane. They should be
through refueling by now. I think I'll take a rest. Let them
fly the next leg."

Snyder thanked Kranzler and headed for the door.
Scheff tossed him an extra poncho as they rushed to the
Jeep. "Listen," he yelled, "we're heading for the dateline.
From here on in, everybody operates on GMT, Zulu time."

Snyder popped into the Jeep. "Okay, what time is it?"

Scheff checked his watch. "1700 Zulu."

"You got it," said Snyder, setting his watch. "Now stop
bothering me with frigging details."

August 4: The Pacific

Army 7271 left the storm system behind a thousand miles west of Midway, flying at 10,000 feet above a carpet of clouds that stretched unbroken from horizon to horizon, blanketing the sea below.

Beddic stirred in the radio compartment. "Coming up on the radio check, Skipper," he said, turning to his set and switching over to CW at 9400 kc.

"Roger," Macklin said, finishing the last of his sandwich. "Slocum, is our ETA still the same?"

"1300 Zulu, Major, plus or minus ten. I don't know what kind of wind we may be flying into."

"That's close enough. Send 1300 Zulu, Beddic." Macklin shifted in his seat and was surrpised to see Lasch come up behind him, a wide grin splitting his face.

"I understand we've just crossed the International Dateline," he said, excited.

"We're all a day older, Dr. Lasch. As long as you're up, maybe you'd want to hear something. Grant, give him your phones."

The copilot took off his headset and handed it to Lasch, who put it on and listened to the open line.

At first all he heard was static. Then there was a click followed by a tone that grew louder in his ears as Beddic tuned it. The tone finally stopped and Lasch heard a rapid series of dots and dashes.

"Zero-eight-three-zero," Beddic sang out, reaching for the CW key. He sent *one-three-zero-zero* in reply.

A few seconds went by, then there were two more clicks and the line reverted to static.

Macklin breathed a sigh of relief. "Close up shop, Beddic. Dr. Lasch, we should be on the ground in approximately five hours."

Lasch nodded happily and turned to look over Slocum's shoulder at the chart. He grunted after a moment. "Snyder would blow a gasket if he knew how close we're going to be to the Russians."

Macklin chuckled. "A miss is as good as a mile." He opened the intercom. "Gentlemen, your attention, please. We have resumed contact with Japan and everything is in order."

In the passenger compartment a ragged cheer went up. Kirby pushed himself out of his seat and stretched.

Bliss jumped up anxiously. "Damn, when will it end?"

"Soon, Julian," Kirby said.

Bliss paced between the seats, screwing one fist into the other palm and muttering to himself.

"What now, Bliss?" Willard said.

"We've got to make the right impression," Bliss said. "That's very important."

"What do you want us to do? Bow and scrape?"

"Don't be a smart-ass. It's a serious matter. Look at us! Are we a bunch of rag pickers? We've been in these clothes since we left. We're rumpled and we stink!"

"Speak for yourself," Willard said.

Bliss shot him a dirty look then turned and rummaged in the luggage rack for his toilet kit. "The rest of you can be slobs if you want, but I'm going to get cleaned up."

"Don't worry so much about how you look," Willard said. "Worry about how you're going to sound."

Bliss whirled on him. "I'll be fine—just fine!" He lurched aft and disappeared into the head.

"Christ, he's impossible," muttered Willard.

"Leave him alone," Kirby warned.

Lasch returned from the cockpit and smiled at Nakamura, who sat huddled against a window. "Won't be long now, Major. Five hours."

Nakamura barely nodded. He was staring out, his mind far away.

Holbrecht motioned to Lasch. "Anything we can do to ease the tension, Dr. Lasch?"

"Bliss again?" Holbrecht nodded. "We're all feeling the strain, Mr. Holbrecht. Julian just shows it more."

"So be it. But I wouldn't want him to act this way when we land."

"He'll be fine."

"That's what *he* said."

"Hey—what's this?"

The shout came from aft and everyone looked around. Bliss had come out of the head and opened one of the lockers. He held up a pair of shiny black boots. He put them down and reached in again, pulling out a complete uniform on a hanger. "What the hell army is this?" he bellowed, wrinkling his face.

Nakamura's eyes fixed on the green trousers, green tunic and tan shirt and he felt an unpleasant rolling sensation in his stomach. "Japanese," he said.

"Well, what's it doing here?" Bliss stopped and looked at Nakamura.

Holbrecht rose, gravely eyeing the uniform, damning Snyder under his breath, for it must have been Snyder who had placed it in the locker. He thought fast, then cleared his throat. "Actually . . . we thought it would be a good idea . . . for Major Nakamura." He glanced at Bliss with a slight deferential bow. "To make the right impression, as you were suggesting, Dr. Bliss. I was going to wait until we were closer to our destination, but I see our little surprise has been found out. Major Nakamura, please try it on."

Nakamura bristled as Bliss brought it forward and held it out to him. He shook his head, saying, "It's a mistake."

"What do you mean?" Holbrecht said cautiously.

"I can't wear it."

"Why not?"

"I'm still a prisoner of war, not a returning hero. It would be an insult."

"What are you talking about?" Bliss said sharply.

"Please, Dr. Bliss," said Holbrecht. "Major Nakamura, Mr. Thyssen was quite explicit on this point. He felt it would show that you had our respect and confidence."

"It wouldn't."

Bliss pushed himself between the seats. "The way you're

dressed now isn't too impressive," he said. "Make us all look good and put this on."

"You don't understand," said Nakamura. "You're not Japanese."

"Look," Bliss said thinly, "maybe things have changed in Japan. Maybe they've got some sense now! We're trying to bring you people out of the thirteenth century, but if you don't change your ways, we might as well turn around and go back home!"

Nakamura jumped up, barely controlling his anger. "Dr. Bliss, you're a fool."

"I've been saying that all along," Willard muttered.

Bliss reddened. Lasch stepped between the two men and took the uniform from Bliss. "You're out of line, Julian."

"Did you hear what he said to me?"

"Yes. Now why don't you go sit down?"

Bliss stalked back to his seat. Lasch pressed the uniform into Nakamura's hands. "Mr. Thyssen must have had a good reason, Major. You're more than an interpreter, you know. You may be the key to this mission. Holbrecht is right: we've got to show that we respect you, that in our eyes at least, you're not disgraced at all. Please . . . put it on."

Nakamura listened, his anger diminishing, replaced by quivering agitation. He held the uniform away from his body, feeling his heart fill with anxiety as he stared at it. He pushed past Lasch and plunged down the aisle to the head, trailing the uniform after him.

He slammed the door and locked it, then leaned against the wall to catch his breath. Sweat broke out on his forehead. He saw his face in the mirror; he had turned pale. He laughed and it quickly turned to terror. Why had he agreed to this? He was already dishonored. Why compound the crime? Why risk what was left of his family's honor? For an ass like Julian Bliss?

He reached for the towel and pulled it off the rack, wiping his face. When he could look at the uniform again, it didn't seem so bad. There was a lot at stake. So what if he had spent the worst months of his life wearing that uniform and fighting for things he didn't believe in? If it could now be turned to better advantage—if he could make wearing it a kind of redemption—then maybe it was worth it after all.

When Nakamura came out, everyone stared at the transformation. He stood proudly erect in the black boots, cavalry-cut trousers, tightly fitted tunic over the shirt open at the collar. He knew he looked every inch the soldier. He knew he could make exactly the impression they wanted, but still he felt self-conscious under their scrutiny, wishing somebody would say something, how silly he looked, anything.

Lasch moved toward him and smiled. "Looks great, Major."

Nakamura choked out a laugh of relief, then tears flooded down his cheeks. He made no effort to control himself. He looked around at them and said, "You are all good men. But it's so tragic—if Japan had this weapon, would we send somebody to warn you . . . ?"

He returned to his seat and stared out the window, conscious of a sobering pall that had settled over the cabin.

August 4 (0830Z)

"Snyder."

The voice crackled over his headset. Snyder pressed his throat mike and answered. "What is it, Scheff?" He glanced through the canopy at the other plane. All he could see were the wing lights. But Scheff was there, in the rear cockpit.

"We're almost at the point of no return."

"I know that."

"I see. Well, I wanted to take a nap, but not if it's going to end with a swim. What do you say?"

"We keep going."

"My pilot's getting nervous. How's yours?"

Terwilliger cut in. "Have you ever ditched a plane, Major?"

"No," Snyder said.

"These waters are fucking cold."

"Look—we'll hear something soon," Snyder said. "Now get off the line so they can call us."

The two F-7Fs droned westward through the night sky. Midway was more than ninety minutes behind them. Snyder was angry, almost ready to give in to the pilots' demands and turn back. The radio crackled again.

"Pluto One, this is Mickey. Pluto One, this is Mickey. Over."

Snyder sighed. He heard Scheff take the call. "Mickey, this is Pluto One. Over."

"Pluto One, you'll be taken aboard the carrier *Sangaman*. Change heading to three-one-six and proceed to rendezvous. Your ETA is thirty-five minutes."

"Roger, Mickey. Anything else? Over."

"We have a message for Major Snyder. Over."

"This is Snyder. Over."

"Stand by. We're going to patch you in to Pearl."

Snyder waited until a familiar voice cut through the heavy static. "Lieutenant Mardeen, Major, with a little piece of news. Over the last couple of days of monitoring Pacific radio traffic, we've picked up some strange signals on niner-four-zero-zero kilocycles, a low traffic frequency—a sequence of transmissions at four-hour intervals. Sounds like a time check, keyed to Zulu. Starts with a constant tone, then four digits in Morse, then a short wait. If there isn't any answer, the sender goes off the air. Fifteen minutes ago, he got a response and acknowledged with two clicks."

"What was the response?"

"Different numbers. The sequence went like this: sent, zero-eight-three-zero; response, one-three-zero-zero."

"That sounds like time, too."

"Roger," said Mardeen. "That's what we think."

"How many transmissions were sent before you got this response?"

"Seven."

Snyder did some quick mental arithmetic. Four-hour intervals. Four times seven made twenty-eight hours. 7271 had been on the ground at Midway for twenty-six hours, the crew off the plane, unable to receive or send radio messages. It fit.

"Have you pinpointed the source?" he asked.

"Not yet. There was no response for so long, we really didn't know what to make of it."

"*Can* you pinpoint it?"

"We can try. We'd have to triangulate with radio compasses, pick it up in two different places, lock onto the angle of strongest signal, then bisect on a chart. Where the lines meet is where it's coming from."

"Do it," said Snyder.

"But they're not giving us much to work with. That much air time might not be enough for a radio compass to lock onto a signal."

"Then use more than two. Use every one you can dig up."

"That won't be necessary, Major. We feel it's coming from a stationary source. It won't require a lot of equipment, just very good operators."

"Okay, do it your way, but be ready for the next transmission."

Mardeen promised to follow through. Snyder felt at last he was onto something. Now if only Groves would come through.

At 0915Z the F-7Fs were down aboard *Sangaman*. By now Snyder was so numb from hours of noise and vibration that even the jarring carrier landings didn't faze him. He climbed out of the plane stiffly and waited for Scheff to join him.

They followed a duty officer up to the Combat Information Center. There was a message from General Groves:

SANGAMAN AND BUNKER HILL WILL AID IN SEARCH FOR ARMY 7271 X SUBMARINES AVAILABLE FOR SPOTTING ONLY UNTIL DAWN.

Snyder met with Commander Peters, chief of the CIC, who had received separate instructions from Groves and had already put his planes into the air. "But night visibility makes it tough," he said. "I can't guarantee results."

"How many?"

"Twenty in constant rotation." He steered Snyder and Scheff to the air plot board, a clear Plexiglas sheet on which was drawn a grease-pencil map of the Far East coastline. "We're running spreading circles across six hundred miles in three directions from our position. Your plane should fly through one of those sectors if he's in the area."

"He hasn't been spotted yet?"

"No. We're holding at twelve thousand feet, but the ceiling varies from five to eight thousand. *Bunker Hill* is five hundred miles east of Hokkaido, following the same search procedure. She'll be your next stop, unless you want to go somewhere else."

"No. How long will you keep your planes up?"

"Don't know. It's beginning to look as if they've slipped past us, isn't it?"

"Yes," Snyder said unhappily.

"Then it's up to *Bunker Hill*."

Snyder decided he wouldn't need Lang and Terwilliger anymore. Scheff felt he could handle the rest of the flight and at this point would not permit Snyder to cheat him out of it.

When they arrived back on the flight deck, *The Deadly Deli* had already been refueled and placed in position for takeoff. In all they were aboard *Sangaman* fifteen minutes.

Scheff banked west and headed for Japan. Snyder studied the map carefully. If the C-54 was going to Russian territory, it would fly north of Hokkaido to avoid possible Japanese or even American interference. For a moment he wondered again about Kamchatka, but finally realized why that was out. Macklin was going to great pains to keep up a deception. He had done it at Hickam and at Midway and, in order to make the journey free from worry, he would probably carry it as far as possible. If he wanted to go to Kamchatka, he would have trouble with the crew. Why pull a gun when he didn't have to? The crew and the scientists would cooperate as long as they believed they were heading for Japan. Of course, he had Bowen and Lasch to help keep things under control, but it would be so much easier and smarter to play the game right up to the end. . . . But Snyder was still having trouble fitting Lasch into all of this. It was hard to believe that Lasch could put on a performance. He didn't seem the type. Frankly, Snyder realized, he wasn't clever enough.

Maybe Bowen and Macklin were on their own, Lasch an unwitting accomplice. Snyder felt more comfortable with that assessment. But what was happening? Was Macklin going to fly toward Japan until the last possible moment then swerve and go somewhere else?

Snyder aimed the flashlight at Hokkaido on the chart. What if they overshot? Flew right on toward the Russian mainland? That wouldn't be too smart either. Flying over Japan would expose them to a terrible risk.

But if they made a run through the southern tip of the Kuriles, they could fly across the La Pérouse Strait and into Russian airspace. Snyder had to make another decision: was this the route he wanted to gamble on?

He radioed back to *Sangaman*'s Combat Information Center and asked Commander Peters to relay a message to Lieutenant Mardeen:

CONCENTRATE RADIO TRIANGULATION ON ANGLE BETWEEN KURILES AND HOKKAIDO FOR TRANSMISSION SOURCE.

With any luck the search patrols would locate 7271 before it could reach that area. Doing some more math, Snyder figured the C-54 to be anywhere from four to six hundred miles ahead of his present position. Then something else occurred to him.

"Scheff, radio ahead to *Bunker Hill*. Tell them to have another F-7F ready so we don't have to wait for this one to be refueled."

"This one!" Scheff growled indignantly. "Isn't that like chucking out the car when the ashtrays are full, Major?"

"Come on, Scheff."

"Now just a minute. You intend for me to leave *The Deadly Deli* behind so some miserable asshole can have her? This is my plane, Major."

"Tell that to the Navy."

"Look, Snyder, it takes fifteen minutes to refuel, ten minutes to transfer to a new plane. Are we desperate for five minutes?"

"Possibly."

Scheff was mad. "I'll make it up in the air! Hey, Major, I've flown you across the Pacific. Gimme a break. I know this plane will hold up; I don't want to take a chance with a new one."

Snyder's head swam. "Can we transmit on 9400 kilocycles?"

"Sure."

"Okay—because I want to have words with 7271."

"Fine." Scheff's tone eased. "Just reverse the charges."

August 4 (1030Z)

Macklin swiveled his head and rolled his shoulders, trying to work out the stiffness. 7271 was three hours from Kara-futo. Macklin was flying at 10,000 feet, scanning for signs of pursuit. It was nine thirty at night and there was a full moon.

In the passenger compartment Holbrecht was holding court. He had successfully kept the scientists awake the last couple of hours and now they were thoroughly exhausted, exactly as he wanted them. When Macklin's voice came over the intercom to announce they were only three hours from landing, Holbrecht rummaged in his briefcase, producing a bottle of brandy and a set of silver cups.

"Time for a little celebration," he said, pouring one shot per man. When everybody had a drink, Holbrecht raised his cup in a toast. "To the success of our mission. Big Stick."

"No," Lasch said. "To you, Mr. Holbrecht, and to Stefan Thyssen."

"Thank you."

Holbrecht watched them drink. He brought the cup to his own lips but was careful not to swallow any of the liquid. He saw Kirby open his diary to make a note. "Our official historian," Holbrecht said with a smile.

Kirby grinned sheepishly. "Something for my grandchildren."

"You'll have much to tell them, Dr. Kirby. Any refills?"

Bliss stuck out his cup. "I can't wait to get off this goddamned plane," he said, belting back the second brandy then sitting down. A strange expression came over his face.

His eyes fluttered. He put a hand to his head. "Hope to God we take a boat back . . ."

"You'd rather be seasick?" said Willard.

Bliss couldn't answer. His mouth worked but no sound came out. His head slumped to his chest. Sitting behind him, Willard also found it hard to stay awake. He drained the last of his brandy and looked out the window. The cup dropped into his lap and he made a halfhearted stab at picking it up before his eyes closed.

Kirby's pen rolled off the page and slipped out of his grasp. He stared with dulled comprehension at the mess he had made of his notation. He tried to rise and found his muscles had gone rubbery. He couldn't focus. He began to panic, then a warm sensation flooded through his body. This is very odd, he thought, then passed out.

Lasch had been sitting down, unmoving, when the drug began to take effect. He noticed only a strange soothing warmth and an overwhelming urge to rest. He closed his eyes and slumped in his seat.

Only Nakamura showed tolerance. He wanted to ask Holbrecht a question but found that his voice wouldn't co-operate. He looked around and slowly realized that every-one had fallen asleep. But Holbrecht was awake, sitting across the aisle, holding his cup and watching.

"I'm sorry," Nakamura heard him say through a tunnel, "I didn't quite catch what you said, Major."

Cobwebs veiled his eyes. He saw Holbrecht rise, come across the aisle and look down at him curiously. His body felt heavy, so heavy. . . . His hand slid off the armrest and he couldn't move it. The cup fell from his fingers and rolled down the aisle. He heard Holbrecht's voice again, deeper in the tunnel, growing high-pitched: "Can I get you a blanket, Major?"

The voice faded and with it the light.

Holbrecht waited for Nakamura's eyes to shut, then turned to be sure all the others had gone under. Quickly he gathered up the silver cups and tossed them into his brief-case. He reached into another compartment and drew out a snub-nosed Smith & Wesson .38. Stuffing it into his waist-band, he went around again to make certain that all the scientists were securely buckled into their seats.

In the cockpit Macklin reacted to a distant twinkle of light in the northern sky. Quickly, before any of the other crew caught a glimpse of it, he pushed the control column forward, nosed the plane down and dove into the cloud cover.

"Hey, Major," Grant complained, "next time say something, will you?"

"Sorry, buddy. I want to make sure we get a visual on Karafuto. We don't know how far the clouds extend, so we'll go in low."

"What the heck is that all about?" said Slocum. "We're dead on course."

"I know we are."

"Then thanks for the vote of confidence, Major."

"You're welcome."

Macklin said nothing more, just kept punching downward until he came through the clouds and leveled off at 4000 feet. He flew at that altitude for another minute then decided that the lower he was, the harder it would be for someone to spot him. So he dropped down even farther.

The cabin door opened and Holbrecht stepped in. "Anything wrong?" he asked.

"No," said Macklin. "Just thought I'd change the scenery. You may as well stay up here for a while, Mr. Holbrecht."

"Thank you." Holbrecht moved to Macklin's side and peered over his shoulder, pressing his arm in a prearranged signal to let him know the scientists were out of the way. Through the windshield Holbrecht could see moonlight streaming through holes in the cloud cover and reflecting off the ocean.

At 1100Z the crew chief said, "Major, we've got a problem."

"What is it, Whelan?"

"I don't know if our dive had anything to do with it, but we're losing oil pressure in number four. We're below eighty and dropping."

Macklin checked the instruments. Whelan was right; the needle was dropping steadily. He ran a few checks with no results, then finally said, "Have to shut her down."

He killed the engine and feathered the prop.

Holbrecht glanced over the instrument panel and his eyes locked on the airspeed indicator. He watched it fall from 330 to 260.

Macklin met his grim look. "Don't worry about it," he said coldly. "We'll do fine on the other three."

"Won't it slow us down?"

"A bit," Macklin said, a warning tone in his voice. "Slocum, work out a new ETA."

Holbrecht backed through the cabin door and went aft to check on his sleeping beauties. They were still slumped in their seats. He peered out a window at the dead engine and saw the propeller locked against the slipstream.

Slocum finished calculating from his map. "From our present position we have about seven hundred-plus miles to the southern tip of Karafuto, the little part that looks like a heel. If we maintain an airspeed of two-six-zero, our ETA should be 1345 Zulu."

"Okay, save it for the next radio check."

"Yes, sir. That'll be in an hour and a half."

August 4 (1150Z)

The submarine USS *Bowfin* was surfaced, charging batteries 150 miles east of the Kuriles, when its radar picked up a distant blip and informed the deck watch. From the bridge, lookouts scanned the night sky and caught a glimpse of moonlight reflecting off a distant moving object. Then they heard engines droning. The plane was low, estimated altitude 3000 feet, coming in well to the east, but it would pass close by. It did, about a mile off their starboard side. A lookout spotted three jets of exhaust flame.

Using night glasses, he was able to identify the plane as a C-54 with one engine feathered. The Officer of the Deck tracked it with the Target Bearing Transmitter, then relayed the information below. The Captain sent off a radio message to *Bunker Hill*.

Scheff made his final approach to *Bunker Hill* with Snyder frantically calculating on his map. *Bunker Hill* was 600 miles from the La Pérouse Strait. If Scheff could hold an airspeed of 435 mph, they could make the mainland in another hour and a half.

They landed and got out quickly. Scheff sent to the galley for sandwiches. *The Deadly Deli* was refueled while the carrier swung into the wind and prepared to relaunch.

A Commander Ross met Snyder at the air plot board. "This might interest you, Major. Message from one of our subs." He picked up a piece of paper and read, " 'Spotted C-54, one engine down, proceeding northwest on heading three-one-five.' "

Ross turned to the board. "Given the sub's position, that

would put 7271 about here," he said, grease-penciling an "X" on the board. He drew in the heading as an arrow, picked up a yardstick, laid it over the "X" and the arrow and ran a line across the map. "That makes their probable route straight up between two of the Kuriles, Iturup and Urup. If they keep going through there, they'll fly over Karafuto. Now, either that's their final or they're going on. You tell me."

"I don't know yet," Snyder admitted. But he was delighted that 7271 had one engine out of commission. That might be the break he needed. He studied the board and decided that either they were going to the Russian part of Sakhalin, the half of the island above latitude 50°, or straight on to the Russian mainland. He turned back to Ross.

"Can we concentrate all the search patrols into this area?" He swept a hand across the board, indicating the Kuriles and the sea just west of them. "We should be able to intercept them somewhere in here."

"That presents a problem," said Ross. "If they go beyond the Kuriles, it's six hundred miles to the next landfall, Karafuto, which is past the extreme range of any F-7F sent from this carrier. We've already got our planes out there in rotation, concentrated along this route. As soon as we heard about the sub sighting, I instructed them to move in, but it's damned hard to find one C-54 running at night without lights."

"Any of these planes equipped with radar?" asked Snyder.

"No. Yours is the only two-seater. And you'll have to operate it. Ever done that?"

"Of course," Snyder lied, then changed the subject. "How many planes can you put in the air behind me?"

"Maybe ten."

"How soon?"

"Fifteen minutes. We'll try to give you as much support as possible, Major. We'll bring *Bunker Hill* in closer to provide return capability for that extended range. But if you stay up too long, you're going to be in trouble. The only land bases in that area belong to the Japanese. And there are no other carriers available. Keep that in mind."

"Okay," said Snyder, intending to worry about it later.

"Also, we've received word from Army G2 at Hickam to cooperate with you in pinpointing some sort of broadcast on ninety-four hundred kilocycles. We're monitoring right now—our unit and two of our escorts. If they transmit again, we'll get a fix and send it on to you. Your designation is Peashooter One. *Bunker Hill* is Long Tom. Okay?"

"Fine with me." Snyder stood thinking a long moment. "Anything else, Major?"

"Yes. I'm not armed. Just in case we have to force them down somewhere, I'll need a persuader."

"Not much room in your plane for anything bigger than a handgun."

"That'll have to do then."

Snyder copied the information from the air plot onto his own chart, while Ross sent for a weapon. An ensign came back with a .45 and a shoulder holster. Snyder strapped it on under his jacket. He thanked Ross and rushed out.

Scheff was already buckled into *The Deadly Deli* when Snyder climbed aboard. "What took you so long?"

"Had to get a gun."

"What for? Target practice?"

"Get going, Scheff. We're Peashooter One and *Bunker Hill* is Long Tom. And you're going to have to check me out on radar."

"How much do you know?"

"Nothing."

"Great. As soon as we're airborne, I'll switch to my professor's hat."

Scheff started the engines and revved up to top rpm. He watched for the launch signal, then slammed the throttles forward. The wind shifted suddenly and *The Deadly Deli* lurched sideways.

"Son of a bitch!" Scheff yelled as they roared down the flight deck.

Snyder's heart pounded. He had visions of them tumbling off the deck into the sea and sinking like a stone.

Somehow Scheff got the plane into the air and they soared off to the west. Snyder looked down at his feet and saw that one of his boots had crushed the bag of sandwiches.

He sighed and checked his watch. 1205 Zulu. The last round was about to begin.

As soon as they were at altitude, Scheff began Snyder's crash course. Up to now the radar scope and accompanying gear had been just a large nuisance cramping Snyder's movement; now he had to grasp the idea of blips and sweeps with a mind dulled from fatigue. Scheff kept testing him, making him repeat everything several times until he seemed to understand.

At 1225Z, Snyder called a recess. He now knew how the equipment functioned, how the electrical impulse that bounced back from a distant target registered the location of the bounce on his scope grids. Reading the grids was still a problem, but he felt he would catch on.

He asked Scheff to tune 9400 kilocycles. Scheff turned up the gain and hissing filled their headsets.

At precisely 1230Z there was a loud click, and a tone nearly blew out Snyder's eardrums. Scheff dropped the gain and they waited an agonizing eternity until they heard a series of dots and dashes.

Snyder clamped the headset tighter and listened. The response finally clicked in. There were more dots and dashes, than two clicks of acknowledgment before the line reverted to static.

He switched back to the intercom. "Scheff, what did you get?"

"Numbers. One-two-three-zero first, then one-three-four-five."

1230 was current Zulu time. Then 1345 had to be ETA. So Army 7271 had only another 75 minutes of flying to get where they were going.

"What's our position?" he asked Scheff.

"Coming up on fifty miles southwest of Iturup."

Snyder checked the chart and made a notation. Three minutes later Long Tom came on the line. Aboard *Bunker Hill*, Commander Ross had worked out the location of the sending station.

"It originates above the fiftieth parallel—" Snyder fumbled with his chart. "—from the Russian side of Sakhalin. I would say in the general vicinity of Aleksandrovsk on the western coast."

Snyder's finger stabbed down at that location—sixty miles north of the border separating Japanese-held Karafuto from the rest of Sakhalin. Was this the final destination—not the Russian mainland? Although the sending station didn't have to be the landing point, it seemed a likely choice. If Macklin and Bowen were still playing their charade, they might tell everybody they were headed for Karafuto and then at the last moment make a dash across the border. Ingenious.

"Did you get a fix on 7271?" Snyder asked Ross.

"Negative, Peashooter One. They weren't transmitting long enough."

"Can you move all the planes ahead of us into a picket line off the southeastern coast of Karafuto?"

"If we do that, we'll run into fuel problems."

"Long Tom, I need help. Can you come in closer, cut down the range—?"

"Peashooter One, if our planes go beyond extended range, they will have to ditch because they won't make it back. Is that clear?"

"Perfectly, Long Tom. I still need anything you can give me."

Scheff cut in. "Long Tom, haven't you got any dumbos in the area? Flying boats? Hey, anybody on this line?"

"We read you," said Ross. He was silent a moment. When he came back, he announced, "Can do, Peashooter One. We'll hand a few planes off to you. We've got some submarines already on station for lifeguard duty, in case anybody goes into the drink."

"Thank you, Long Tom. Over and out," said Snyder, exhausted from the strain.

August 4 (1315Z)

Army 7271, still flying in darkness at 3000 feet, was about twenty minutes from the heel of Karafuto. Slocum verified their heading and Macklin asked for the chart. To outward appearance, he was scanning it lazily, but actually he was calculating the distance to the Russian border.

Taraika Bay, the landing point he had designated for the benefit of the scientists and crew, was another ninety miles up the inside of the heel. It was sixty miles from there to the airstrip on the other side of latitude 50°. All he had to do was keep the crew at bay for an extra thirteen minutes.

He handed the chart back to Slocum and pressed the intercom switch. "Mr. Holbrecht, would you come to the cockpit, please?"

In the aft compartment Holbrecht made one last check of the drugged scientists, buttoned his coat over the revolver in his waistband, then went up to the cockpit, closed the door and stood to the rear.

Macklin glanced back at him. "Thought you might want to be here for our first glimpse of land."

Holbrecht grunted, too tired to keep up the pleasantries. He moved behind Macklin; his eyes swept the crewmen, fixing their positions in his mind: Grant on the right, the navigator and crew chief in their open cubicle behind him, Beddic on the left at his radio and Lefferts, the backup pilot, asleep in the jump seat.

In Peashooter One, Snyder watched his radar intently, aware of the time: 1325Z. He watched the outline of Karafuto spread on the rim of his scope with every new sweep.

He craned his neck for a glimpse of land ahead, but it was too dark. His eyes went back to the scope.

The sweep came round slowly and a blip popped up way over on the right at three o'clock. It faded then appeared again on the next sweep, millimeters closer to the outline of Karafuto.

"Son of a bitch, there he is!"

"Where?" said Scheff.

"Off to our right. Get on the horn!"

Scheff switched to channel one. "This is Peashooter One. All other Peashooters in range, acknowledge!"

Three disembodied voices answered. Scheff gave them his heading and ordered them all to converge on him. Then he banked to the right and flew straight for Karafuto.

"Watch your scope," he told Snyder. "When you see that blip on a line that will take it to twelve o'clock, that means we're on the same heading. Let me know."

"Okay," said Snyder. Over the next two minutes he fed Scheff course corrections until they were locked on the heading.

Snyder caught a flash of light off to one side and looked around. Another F-7F was coming up alongside. Two more approached from different angles.

Then Scheff barked, "Damnit, we should be within visual range now, and I don't see anything!"

Peashooter Three suggested the target might be at a lower altitude.

"Right," said Scheff. There were no clouds ahead. For the first time he saw the island in the distance. "Peashooter Two, follow me down. Three and Four, fly high cover."

Scheff nosed over and dove down from 14,000 feet. He stared ahead, looking for the target. Snyder still had it on his scope, traveling on the same line and close to center screen.

Suddenly, Scheff announced, "All Peashooters, form on me. Target's in sight."

Snyder pressed his face to the canopy, staring at the moonlit water below. Then he saw it, a glint of silver suspended above a sea of tossing whitecaps.

"Scheff," he said, "I want to come up on his left. Then have everybody else box him in. Okay?"

"Don't you think we better be sure this is the right plane first? We could end up scaring the shit out of some poor Jap." He paused. "What am I saying? We'll *shoot* the shit out of him!"

The four F-7Fs swept down and closed on their target. "One point for us," said Scheff. "It *is* a C-54."

Snyder got a glimpse of the number on the tail: 297271. He was about to let out a whoop when Scheff called out, "All Peashooters, drop airspeed to hold target." He throttled back and Snyder was jerked forward.

"What are you doing, Scheff?"

"What are *you* doing is the question, Major," said Scheff. "What's the plan?"

"We want to get him to turn back."

"To where? He can't land on a carrier and the nearest territory is Japanese."

Snyder glanced at his chart. "Could he make it to Okinawa?"

"Probably."

"Then that's where we'll take him."

"He has the range—we don't."

"We'll have relief planes meet us and take over."

"Suppose he doesn't cooperate?"

"Get up alongside and let them know they've been found. We're faster than they are and we're armed. We don't have to *use* any muscle, just flex it a bit."

"That depends," said Scheff. "How desperate are they?"

That was the question that had been worrying Snyder. What had started out as a million-to-one shot at finding the C-54 had turned to hard reality. There it was; he couldn't shirk it anymore. Images tumbled through his mind: Thyssen and Marion, both dead; Louise missing; and Beth almost a victim . . .

If they had already gone that far, how could he hope to reason with them? And all Groves had said was, Do what you have to—leaving Snyder the guilt.

Maybe if he could force the plane down in Japan, it wouldn't be so bad. Even if the men were caught, what use could the Japanese make of their information? But suppose he couldn't even do that? The only other choice was to stop them. The idea of it sickened him.

"Scheff," he said.

"Right here. What's the decision?"

"The pilot is a Russian agent. He's kidnapped a group of American scientists. If we can't get them to change course, we may have to shoot them down."

Scheff was silent a moment then said, "That's a little final, isn't it?"

"If I give the order, will you obey it?"

"It's your party, Major." Scheff switched to the command channel and transmitted to the other planes, "Peashooter One to all Peashooters, we're going to try to get that C-54 to turn south and head for Okinawa. If he won't, we may have to shoot him down. Acknowledge."

The other pilots acknowledged quickly. Scheff growled back at Snyder, "Hell of a way to run a war—knock down your own planes."

"That's enough, Scheff."

Aboard 7271, Grant sighted the surf line off the southeastern heel of Karafuto. The black land mass jutted up in the moonlit darkness, whitecaps breaking on a reflective sandy beach.

Macklin flicked on the intercom and said, "We're within fifteen minutes of arrival, gentlemen."

In the aft cabin the scientists were still in a drugged stupor, oblivious to everything.

Holbrecht stared through the windshield with mounting excitement. He missed seeing the F-7F come creeping up alongside. But Slocum saw it—a sleek reflection of blue-gray metal just off the left wing tip.

"Jesus!" he said. "We've got an escort!"

Macklin and Holbrecht looked around in surprise, followed his pointing finger and saw the fighter ease up even with them. The man in the rear cockpit waved a flashlight, then shined it on himself and tapped his headset.

Slocum broke the stunned silence. "They want to talk with us, Skipper."

"I know that!" Macklin snapped.

"This is very irregular," Holbrecht said. "There was no call for an escort in our orders, Major. It may be a trick."

"I don't know," said Grant. "He's sure sportin' the right insignia."

"The Japanese are masters at camouflage," Holbrecht insisted. "We have no reason to believe that's an American aircraft. It should not be here." Desperation built in his voice.

In Peashooter One, Snyder had Scheff tune to 9400 kilocycles, then pressed the sending button and called, "Army 7271, come in, please. Come in, 7271."

He released the button and waited. There was no reply.

"Why don't we fire a warning burst?" suggested Scheff. "Peashooter Four is in position. He could just lay one over their nose. That oughta wake somebody up."

"Do it," said Snyder.

Scheff gave the order.

A second later a line of tracers arced through the night, falling in front of 7271 and causing Holbrecht to jump nearly out of his skin.

"My God, it *is* the enemy!" he shouted. "Can we get out of here?"

Grant peered to the right and saw another F-7F off that wing tip. "Looks like they have us boxed."

Holbrecht stared at the plane on the right.

"He's tapping his headset again, Skipper," said Slocum.

"I see it," Macklin replied. "Beddic, turn on the radio but stay on ninety-four hundred. Let's see if we can raise our friends."

"Morse?" asked Beddic.

"No. Plain language."

"Roger." Beddic switched on his receiver and tuned 9400.

Snyder's voice boomed over his headset: "7271, come in. Come in, 7271 . . ."

"Voice message!" Beddic exclaimed. "I think it's our escort."

Holbrecht's hand crept toward his hip. He watched Macklin stare uncertainly at the F-7F on his left, then hit a switch on the instrument panel and press his throat mike.

"This is Army 7271," said Macklin. "You are not authorized to be in this sector. You are endangering a diplomatic mission."

Snyder's voice came back in a low growl. "Cut the shit, Macklin, or whoever the hell you are. Change course and head south—immediately."

Macklin was calm as he pressed his mike again. "Who am I speaking to. Identify yourself."

"Major P.T. Snyder. Now what's it going to be?"

Macklin paused, glancing around at the crew. They were listening in frozen silence.

"What does he want, Major?" Holbrecht asked anxiously.

"Wants us to turn back. It's Snyder."

"Snyder?" Holbrecht gasped. "Can you stall?"

"I'll try." Macklin turned to Grant. "Keep on this heading until I tell you different." Then into his throat mike: "Where do you want us to go *to*, Snyder?"

"Okinawa. You'll follow our lead. We'll put a plane in front. I want your answer, Macklin."

"Just a moment, I have people on board to consult."

"No, Macklin! If you don't comply, we'll start shooting!"

"You'll have to wait until I inform my passengers. Sorry, Snyder, but I don't really believe you want to endanger their lives."

He didn't give Snyder a chance to retort. Without releasing his throat mike, he said, "Beddic, shut that receiver off."

Slocum started to get up. "Major, maybe he's legitimate—"

"He's bluffing," Macklin said.

Aboard Peashooter One, Snyder heard the click as the line went dead. "Shit," he said, "son of a bitch wants to test us."

"Then we'll oblige him," said Scheff.

"Holbrecht, brace yourself," said Macklin. Holbrecht grabbed the back of his seat as Macklin pulled up and banked to the left. Slocum was thrown across the deck, cracking his skull against the aft bulkhead.

* * *

7271 came across the top of Snyder's F-7F. In order to avoid collision Scheff dropped down and to the right. Macklin slid the C-54 over him and dove for lower altitude.

Scheff yelled into his throat mike, "All Peashooters—follow him but don't shoot!" He pulled around and the other three F-7Fs flashed by. Scheff straightened out and came down fast behind them.

Aboard 7271, Slocum was sprawled on the cabin deck. Beddic was trying to reach him but had to hang on during the dive. He was shouting at Macklin to pull up. "Slocum's hurt!" Beddic screeched.

Holbrecht clung to the seat for support and struggled to get the pistol out of his waistband. Macklin leveled off at 2000 feet and came up along the southeastern heel of Karafuto.

Holbrecht regained his balance and trained his gun on the crew. "Everybody stay where you are!" he said sharply as Beddic unbuckled and started to rise.

They looked up, mute with surprise, glancing at the snub-nosed .38.

Holbrecht aimed at Beddic. "Sit down. Keep your hands where I can see them."

Beddic slowly eased back into his seat, finding it odd that Holbrecht made no effort to cover the Skipper.

Macklin turned the C-54 on a heading that would take them north along the Karafuto coastline. "This'll take fifteen minutes," he said, ignoring the copilot's bewildered, frightened look.

"What can you do about the planes behind us?" Holbrecht asked.

"Not too much. Let's hope they didn't mean it."

Beddic finally realized there was something terribly wrong. Slocum lay at his feet with a split skull, perhaps already dead, and this Swedish maniac was using a gun to keep order. Enough of that, Beddic thought, his adrenaline rising. Holbrecht's eyes slipped to the windshield for a second and Beddic lunged at him.

Holbrecht saw him, wheeled and fired once. Beddic felt

a blow against his chest. Blood spurted through his flying suit as he collapsed in a heap.

"Any other foolish moves?" Holbrecht said, glancing at Lefferts and Whelan. Rigid, they just stared at Beddic's body next to Slocum's.

The F-7Fs caught up with 7271 and took positions wing-to-wing astern. Scheff called for another warning shot and this time tracers from all four planes lit up the sky ahead of 7271. Snyder watched the trails of light arcing over the C-54's nose.

Suddenly the air was alive with answering fire. Flame erupted to Snyder's left. His plane rocked and pitched. More vivid colored bursts went off around them. For a second, Snyder thought Macklin was shooting back, but how could that be? They didn't have any guns.

"Jesus Christ!" yelled Scheff. "Flak! Ground fire! The Japs!"

Searchlights stabbed up from the ground and one of them locked on 7271, bathing the cockpit in a blinding glare. Macklin pulled the controls back and took the plane up. Holbrecht lost his balance and slid to the aft bulkhead. Lefferts, strapped in, took a swipe at him, trying to get the .38. Holbrecht brought the barrel down hard on Lefferts' hand. He screamed in pain.

Holbrecht looked up through the windshield and saw explosions ahead. Macklin banked to the right.

The F-7Fs kept on his tail, matching his moves, even through the flak. Macklin was throttled down and having trouble maneuvering.

Scheff yammered orders to keep after him, then said to Snyder, "Last chance, Major. We can't stay in this much longer. You want to shoot him down?"

Snyder hesitated, petrified. Lasch, Kirby, the others—he had gotten them into this, had made himself responsible for their lives, had told them if it wasn't safe, they wouldn't go. Now . . . ? Nakamura—that hurt the most. Nakamura had trusted him, believed him, depended on him to bring the mission off. Snyder found himself shaking: the last thing he wanted was that man's blood on his hands.

Scheff yelled for an answer as their plane was bracketed by two bursts. "Come on, Snyder, that's not fireworks out there!"

Snyder opened his mouth to reply, then he heard Beth Martin's voice: *"Allen Lasch is my friend. Are you telling me you're prepared to kill him?"* Angrily he pushed her from his mind. "Scheff—" he said.

He was shocked into silence as he saw the C-54 take a hit on the port wing. Number one engine burst into flames and wreckage spun away in jagged pieces.

As the plane shuddered from the first hit, Holbrecht ducked, saving his life. A second burst ripped open the left rear of the cockpit, spewing shrapnel everywhere. Lefferts was killed instantly. Parts of the fuselage blew across the deck, shearing off Whelan's right leg.

7271 yawed violently and surged upward, pressing Holbrecht against the door to the passenger compartment. Whelan was next to him, bleeding and screaming. Lefferts' body was impaled on his jump seat.

Holbrecht smelled rubber burning. Smoke swirled around the cockpit then was sucked out into the slipstream through the cavity where the radio equipment had been. Terrified, Holbrecht grabbed Lefferts' seat and held on to it.

Macklin fought the controls. Grant was busy hitting the CO_2 valves and handles in a vain attempt to put out the fire in the left wing. Of the two engines still working, one was laboring badly. Oil pressure was dropping fast out of the port side. The plane dipped and started losing altitude.

As it continued to nose down, Holbrecht released Lefferts' seat and reached up, straining to pull the latch on the cabin door. He forced it open and with a cry of effort heaved himself into the passenger compartment, rolling out of the way as the door slammed shut behind him.

He struggled toward the seats, pulling himself along the aisle with one hand, fighting the nose-down angle of the deck. His other hand still clutched the .38. He worked himself up to a crouch and glanced at the scientists.

Bliss was sprawled between the seats, blood streaming from his face where his glasses had been crushed in a fall. The others were still buckled in, aware that something was desperately wrong but still so groggy they couldn't raise to help themselves.

"The Japs have done the job for us, Major," Scheff said. "How bad's the damage?"

"There's a big hole in the cockpit. She's losing altitude. Another engine gone."

As if to punctuate his words, their plane was rocked by a blast close to port. The F-7F next to them trailed smoke from its starboard engine and went down in a screaming dive.

Snyder concentrated on the C-54 ahead. It was wobbling badly. Scheff was still pacing it, directly behind. The flak let up as they flew out of the area.

"He hasn't got a prayer," Scheff said. "He's going down."

"Let's hope it's in the ocean."

Macklin fought the control yoke, teeth clenched from the strain. His muscles screamed for relief. Out of the corner of his eye he saw tracers streaming up out of the darkness below. He tried to evade them but the plane wouldn't respond. He braced himself.

Something slammed up beneath him. His seat jumped. There was no pain, just a weakness that filled his body. He tried to ignore it and concentrate all his efforts on controlling the plane, but his muscles wouldn't cooperate. His arms fell from the controls. He screamed but had no voice. He tried to get Grant's attention but when his mouth opened, he spat blood.

Grant saw Macklin start to slump forward and reached across to pull him back. Macklin sagged; his head lolled to one side.

Grant took over, trying to fly parallel to the coast. He had to keep the plane in the air until he could find a landing spot, maybe a long stretch of road with no bends. He had to keep the nose down or they would stall and drop like a stone. No radio, no way of communicating with those fighters—he was all alone, and scared.

Holbrecht crawled over Bliss and back to his own seat, where he grabbed the Trinity box. Then he made his way as far aft as possible. Kirby watched him with frightened, glazed eyes, his arms dangling over the armrests. Cradling the box in his lap, Holbrecht sat down on the floor of the cabin with his back to the last seat. He caught his breath and waited.

The scientists were still groggy. Lasch felt the plane bucking. Uncooperative fingers fumbled for his seat belt release but something told him not to touch it. He fought the haze in his mind . . .

Nakamura struggled for consciousness. He smelled something burning and panic welled up inside him. Instinctively he doubled over to protect his head.

Scheff couldn't risk staying on the C-54's tail any longer: it was losing altitude rapidly. "We've got to get out of here!" he said.

"No, I have to see what happens!" Snyder insisted.

"They're gonna crash—that's what's gonna happen!"

Snyder watched 7271 lumber downward along the coastline, then with great strain bank out again to miss a jutting promontory in its path. Come on, you bastard! thought Snyder. Put that thing down in the sea!

But the pilot still had some control and banked the plane around the promontory.

"Follow him!" Snyder yelled.

Scheff told the other pilots what he was going to do. The three remaining Peashooters whipped around the promontory and saw the C-54 settling on a run across the beach. The flaps caught moonlight as they lowered. The pilot was slowing up, trying to soften the impact.

"He's going in!" shouted Scheff.

In, yes, thought Snyder. But where?

He had his answer almost instantly. The C-54 dropped suddenly and plowed across the dunes, kicking up sand. One wing was sheared off at the fuselage. The plane slewed around and skidded into a forest, crashing into the trees, demolishing the cockpit.

The fuselage broke into three sections; the aft portion wheeled around and slid down a dune. The remaining wing burst into flame.

Scheff banked then tore upward for altitude. "That's it!" he yelled.

"Wait a minute, Scheff! I've got to see if there are any survivors!"

"From that?"

"Yes, damnit! Quit fighting me!"

"Anything you say."

Scheff dropped down to treetop level. The flames from the burning wing lit up the wreckage and started fires in the woods. The other F-7Fs came in behind Scheff, each making a pass.

"Anybody spot anything?" Scheff asked.

The last plane through reported movement on the ground. "Looked like at least one man," said the pilot.

Snyder felt his heart start to pound. This time did he have a choice? He couldn't go back to Groves with the job half-done. If there was any chance the Russian agents were still alive and the Trinity box intact, he had to make sure they never left the wreckage. But how?

He could strafe it.

He could order Scheff to make another pass and blaze away. But what about the scientists? He could almost hear the angry chatter of the machine guns, see Nakamura's face just before he was obliterated by bullets.

"Come on, Snyder!" Scheff said. "We can't hang around!"

"Make another pass!" Snyder ordered.

"Bullshit! There's no time!"

"God damn you—do it!" Snyder shook with anger, which faded only when he heard Scheff repeat the order. All three remaining planes flew back for the run. One by one, they roared over the wreckage. Peashooter Three reported lights coming up the coast road. Snyder asked again if anybody had seen survivors.

"One positive," called Peashooter Two.

Scheff said tightly, "Look, Major, if we want to make it back, we've got to leave now."

"Let the other planes go, Scheff. I've got to be sure."

"What are you going to do, Major? Ask the Japanese?"

Snyder was staring out his canopy window at the burning plane below, letting a decision well up inside and grip him with a certainty he had never felt before. It had been staring him in the face the last ten minutes—the only solution, the obvious one.

"I'm going to bail out, Scheff. Find out who survived. If it's the Russians, I'll have to kill them."

There was a silence, then Scheff yelled at him, "*Meshuganah!*"

"What's that mean?"

"Fucking crazy! The Japanese are practically *there!* What in hell can you do?"

"Finish my job. Now how do I get out of here?"

"Have you ever jumped before?"

"Not exactly."

"Don't get cute! It's your life!"

"Not at all, then."

"All right, pay attention."

Scheff ran through parachute procedure. When Snyder was able to repeat the instructions in order, Scheff asked if he felt he could do it. Snyder said yes.

Scheff ordered the other two planes to "head for the barn." Then he banked and made a run back up the coast toward the crash site.

"Do something else for me, Scheff. Radio for a submarine to stand off this position to pick me up, using that promontory as a landmark. Tell them to stay in position several days if they can. I'll take the flashlight for signaling at night."

To be safe, Scheff radioed those instructions on to the other two F-7Fs. "I can't let you drop in there unprotected," he explained. "I'll hang around and give you air cover as long as I can."

"Thanks."

"I hope you live to mention it."

Snyder checked his gear: the flashlight tucked into his flying suit, .45 snugly strapped in the shoulder holster, sur-

vival knife in a sheath at his waist, parachute tightly
strapped to his body in a seat pack, inflatable raft below
that. He was ready.

"Okay," said Scheff. "Here we go."

Snyder looked ahead and saw the promontory go by,
then beyond it a glow on the ground—the burning wreckage. He pulled the canopy release and opened it, letting
wind rip into his compartment—cold, forcing the breath
from his body. Scheff didn't give him time to get used to it.

"This is good-bye, Snyder. I'll turn the plane over, then
you unhook and drop out. Make sure you pull the earphone
jack before you go or your head will stay here and I'll have
somebody to talk to on the way home."

"Scheff—thanks."

"Stop thanking me, will you?"

He throttled back and flipped the plane over, then said,
"Anytime."

Snyder ripped out the earphone jack then unbuckled. He
shot out of the cockpit, tumbling in air. The sensation
wasn't as bad as he'd thought it would be. He fell, wind
whipping against his flying suit. He gathered his wits,
counted slowly to five, then pulled the ripcord.

The seat pack blew open and the pilot chute steamed up,
dragging the main chute behind it. In a few seconds he was
floating down, his body sore from the opening snap. He
looked down to see where Scheff had dropped him. It was
hard to judge. The crash site was north of his position. He
could be as much as a mile or two off the coast. He
couldn't tell. He wriggled his bottom to be sure the raft
pack was still strapped on. The weight of it reassured him.
He ran the instructions through in his mind again, watching the smoke and flames from 7271 billow up into the
night sky.

Then he picked up the sound of an engine roar. Scheff's
plane streaked across from the north and made a run along
the coast.

Scheff banked and looked down at the lights on the
road: vehicles, probably trucks from a nearby Army camp.
His hand slid to the firing button and he went lower. He

strafed the convoy, tearing up the road with machine gun fire.

He flew past and continued on down the road, hoping to get whatever else was coming. He roared over the promontory and realized too late that he was coming up on a fortified position.

A searchlight stabbed him in the eye and locked on him. He pulled up hard and gritted his teeth. Tracers streaked up from the ground and the sky exploded in front of him. His plane shuddered. He ducked just before the cockpit glass blew apart.

The F-7F rolled, trailing smoke and flame, then dove into the sea.

Still floating down, Snyder saw it happen—the burst of tracers, the hit, then the arc of fire down into darkness. Then nothing. And he was alone.

August 5: Karafuto (12:15 AM)

Snyder hit the water hard. He bobbed to the surface and, following Scheff's instructions, twisted the chest release then smacked it. The straps popped free and he shrugged out of the harness then inflated his Mae West. It kept him afloat as he fumbled for the raft pack with hands growing numb in the cold water. He worked it free of the harness, found the CO_2 ring and yanked it. The raft blossomed like a flower. Snyder heaved himself into it from the rear and lay panting in the darkness until the motion of the sea urged him to his senses.

He sat up, his back to the high end. Unsnapping the paddles, he slid his hands through the straps and dug the blades into the water. He was about a mile off the coast and being carried south by a strong current.

He looked toward shore and saw the fire from the C-54 wreckage illuminating the beach, part of the coast road and the tree line. The wreck was surrounded by shadowy vehicles and he could barely make out running figures.

Drawn gradually south, past the promontory, he struggled with the paddles and tried to angle the raft in, but after a while he stopped and just let the current carry him.

Hooded lights came around the bend behind the promontory, heading south from the wreck. One truck and a car moving slowly down the coast road. The truck was loaded with Japanese soldiers, but it was the car that drew Snyder's attention: a stretcher was strapped to the roof.

He couldn't tell whether the sheet-wrapped body was alive or dead. Was it someone from the crash or one of the Japanese wounded in Scheff's strafing attack?

Snyder wanted to get to the wreck to see what had happened, but if survivors had already been removed, he would be better off following that car. He kept his eye on what he could see of the road and the receding headlights.

Finally they disappeared. Snyder made a mental note of where he last saw them then again started paddling toward shore. The last two hundred feet were the toughest. A groundswell heaved the raft up and down. He heard the sound of breakers ahead, then suddenly he was in them. The raft stood up on one end and Snyder was dumped overboard.

He tumbled in the surf until he was washed ashore. He fought to grab the raft before it was swept out by the backwash, finally managed to haul it out of the surf, then carried it to a clump of rocks under a cliff.

He rummaged through the raft pockets and pulled out emergency rations and water tins, stuffing them into his jacket pockets and zipping them closed. He didn't dare use the flashlight, so he tucked it into the canvas folds of the raft. Using the paddles, he scooped out a hole in the sand behind the rocks, dragged the raft over and buried it. Then he picked up a clump of seaweed and wiped out his footprints leading from the surf. He memorized landmarks before climbing up the rocky embankment.

At the top he was about twenty yards from the road, a narrow ribbon of potholed blacktop. He crouched for a few minutes, protected by the darkness, listening and watching. The cold penetrated his wet clothing and he shivered. When nothing came along, he got up and ran across the road into the dunes on the other side. The only way to find the car was to stay close to the road and move south, so he began walking.

After fifteen minutes of slogging through dry sand, his legs ached in protest and the going was too slow. He risked exposure by moving closer to the hard-packed dirt that shouldered the road, but he followed the angle of the tree line—a thick stand of fir that rose up on the other side of the dunes like a black wall—so he could make a quick dash for cover if need be.

The whine of an engine crept up on him. He wasn't aware

of it until nearly too late, then he dashed through the dunes and into the trees, turning to see what was coming.

A sedan with flags on the front bumpers sped down from the north, bouncing among the potholes, then disappearing into the night.

Some curious CO, Snyder thought, just had to go take a look at the remains of the American plane. What a feather in his cap! That crash was probably the biggest event of the war for Karafuto.

Snyder waited until the car was long past then resumed plodding south, keeping to the trees. He rounded a bend and reached a crest where the road dropped almost to beach level. Far in the distance he saw the receding taillights swing away from the coast and blink intermittently as the car moved inland. Why blinking? he wondered.

The trees. The car was going into the woods. The lights disappeared completely. But now he knew what to look for: a turnoff, a road leading away from the beach.

He was exhausted—twenty hours of flying, the chase, the battle, bailing out, rowing ashore and now a seemingly endless walk. He forced himself to go on, but every step was an agonizing effort.

He unzipped one of his pockets, pulled out an emergency ration kit and examined what was inside it. Four small flat bricks wrapped in heavy foil, four tins of A rations and a can opener. He tore open one of the bricks and stared at the contents. It looked like an ordinary chocolate bar, so he broke off a piece and put it into his mouth. He sucked on it, letting it dissolve slowly as he kept walking. In a few moments he had devoured the bar. After a while he felt a surprising surge of energy. What did they put in those things?

Stuffing the rest of the rations back into his pockets, Snyder's thoughts returned to the stretcher and what he would learn when he found it. Was it a survivor? If so, who? Were there any others? How ironic—a mission shot down by the very people it had been designed to benefit.

An hour later he found the turnoff: a dirt road leading away from the blacktop. He stopped and peered into the trees. It was so dark the moonlight could barely penetrate.

The dirt road was narrow, less than ten feet wide, ribboning into blackness.

Cautiously Snyder moved forward, staying off the road, hugging the trees. He went nearly a hundred yards, then found himself going up an incline. At the crest he stopped, smelling a tantalizing aroma not far off.

Cooking.

He edged between the trees and pressed forward until he had a dim view of an expanse of land below—a depression, a bowl-shaped valley covered with more forest. Between the branches and the thick trunks he saw points of light. He was looking down into an encampment.

There were guards at a barrier gate where the road led into the camp. He wondered if sentries were concealed in the woods. Moving cautiously, he slipped from tree to tree and made his way down into the depression, stopping for long stretches of time to look and listen.

Something rough scraped his face and he fell back, grabbing a tree trunk for support. He groped ahead and touched netting. Tugging on it, he followed movement upward with his eyes. There was a camouflage net over the entire camp, supported on guy wires wrapped around trees.

Snyder peered into the camp and saw that the Japanese had cleared out a great number of trees from the area. From the crest overlooking the camp it had seemed a continuation of the woods but was actually a blanket of fabric patches and strategically placed foliage.

Huts were clustered among the few trees still standing on otherwise barren ground. There was no perimeter fence, no wires to cut or crawl under. The few visible lights were carefully shaded just to illuminate doorways. They helped Snyder get the layout.

The huts were all wooden, their roofs piled high with dead foliage. Smoke curled from what had to be the cook shack. Snyder's eyes took in the slit trenches and the sand-bagged antiaircraft gun emplacements. The barrels loomed out of the darkness at the camp perimeter. They must have been the ones that had hit Scheff. Snyder stared at them and tried to push Scheff's face out of his mind. He didn't need an added dose of guilt to complicate his job.

Moonlight filtered unevenly through the canopy and illuminated a few moving figures—soldiers on sentry duty. There was a parking area to the right under an overhang of branches and a separate netting. Snyder saw the truck and the car with the bumper flags.

He stayed behind a tree, scrutinizing each hut, trying to determine where the survivors, if any, would be held. The command post was obvious: larger than the rest of the buildings, it was up on a raised foundation and had a long porch. Two guards stood on either side of the door.

A soldier banged out of the cook shack carrying a tray. He crossed the compound briskly and went up the steps. One of the guards opened the door for him. He was inside only a moment, then came out and returned to the cook shack.

Snyder looked across to the other buildings. Guards were posted at only two other huts, both small and run-down, made of corrugated tin against a wood frame. They were at the opposite end of the camp, backed up against the trees.

The door to the command post opened again. Another soldier stuck out his head and said something to the guards. They took off at a run to one of the tin huts. They came out a moment later, pushing a limping man ahead of them.

Snyder watched with rising anticipation as they came across the camp. Only when they got up the steps to the command post and the door opened, spilling light from inside, did he get a glimpse of the prisoner, dressed in a torn Japanese uniform.

It looked like Nakamura.

The guards pushed him in and closed the door.

Snyder waited twenty minutes before the door opened again. The two sentries double-timed to the other guarded hut, entered and came out with another man, this one dressed in a suit.

What kind of parade is this? Snyder wondered. They climbed to the porch and the door swung open again. Light poured out and Snyder stiffened. The man in the suit was Bernard Bowen.

He held his head high, his face impassive and grim. His forehead was bandaged, the clean white dressing contrasting starkly with his soot-streaked face and torn clothing. He was shoved unceremoniously through the door, which closed behind him.

Snyder stared after him. Of all the people to survive—Bernard Bowen. He bent low and moved right up to the netting.

"Oscar Holbrecht"'s eyes flickered over his surroundings. The command post was divided into two large rooms. He was standing in what he took to be the headquarters office: two desks, three file cabinets, little else. The door in the back opened and he was propelled into the second room.

The commandant's section was partitioned into office and living quarters. On Holbrecht's right was a half-open sliding door and beyond it a tatami mat and a small Shinto shrine. In front of him, at an angle to the corner, was the commandant's desk, and on it the battered Trinity box. Holbrecht eyed it eagerly, relieved to see that the seals were still unbroken.

Behind the desk was a short, stocky Japanese officer, about forty, with a sword strapped to his waist. He eyed Holbrecht sternly. Holbrecht took in the flag on a floor stand, the Emperor's portrait on the wall and the row of cabinets.

Nakamura was in front of the desk, barely able to stand up, a jaundiced pallor to his skin.

The officer snapped out a command in Japanese, startling Holbrecht. The guards turned on their heels and stamped out.

The officer snapped again. Nakamura turned and in a hoarse and laboring voice said, "His name is Captain Gohra. He wants to know who you are."

Holbrecht bowed deeply and said, "Good evening, Captain."

"He doesn't speak English," Nakamura said.

Holbrecht grunted annoyance. "Captain Gohra must know my name because his men took my passport when they rescued us. Please tell him that."

Nakamura translated into Japanese. Gohra did not respond, just continued eyeing Holbrecht suspiciously. Finally he sat down and picked up the passport from his desk. He studied it coldly then spoke to Nakamura again.

"I told him you're a Swedish national. He wants to know what you were doing on an American plane."

"What else have you told him?" Holbrecht asked.

"Nothing that he'll accept. He said I was lying about our mission, that if anyone was going to Taraika Bay, he would have known about it. I had to beg him to bring you in here."

Gohra rapped sharply on his desk and barked a string of Japanese at Nakamura, who rocked back on his heels then stared at the floor. When Gohra stopped talking, Nakamura said meekly, without looking up, "He wants an answer."

Judging the effect Gohra was having on Nakamura, Holbrecht took advantage of it. "We can't deal with these people," he said. "We have to be very careful. I will tell you some things that are not true, but I want you to translate exactly what I say."

Nakamura nodded.

"I am a Swedish diplomat," Holbrecht began, then pointed to the box. "That is a diplomatic pouch, property of the Swedish government, a neutral country." He waited for Nakamura to translate, then stepped forward and showed Gohra the seals and the Swedish flag stickers. "I have been brought here under duress—"

Nakamura stared at him. Holbrecht gave him a tiny insistent nod and went on: "I demand to be taken to the nearest neutral country."

As Nakamura translated the word "demand," Captain Gohra stiffened. His eyes bored into Holbrecht, then he told Nakamura in Japanese, "This does not support your story."

Nakamura gazed at the floor again. "What are you doing?" he muttered to Holbrecht.

"We cannot let our information fall into this man's hands."

"He's already got it. You could get us killed."

"I know what I'm doing."

"Why not ask to see Dr. Nishina?"

"The mission is over, Major. We're too late. They know something's wrong. They won't wait." Holbrecht gave Gohra a big smile and continued talking. "This is the military. If they knew why we were here, to force their country to surrender, they would never allow the information to get through. I can only use what's in that box if I get to neutral territory."

Nakamura's brow furrowed as he struggled to absorb Holbrecht's reasoning. Gohra looked at him expectantly, waiting for the translation, a curious glint in his eye.

Nakamura drew himself up, faced Gohra and said in Japanese, "I have nothing more to say." Then he repeated it in English for Holbrecht.

"You're making a mistake," Holbrecht hissed.

"I'm sorry."

Captain Gohra rose again, waved Holbrecht's passport and spoke in Japanese. Nakamura translated: "He says he will contact the Swedish embassy in Tokyo to verify your credentials. He asks that you be patient, as it may take some time."

Holbrecht didn't react. Gohra barked out another order. The door opened and the two guards returned, one to either side of Holbrecht, who jabbed a finger at the Trinity box and said, "Tell Captain Gohra that box must remain with me."

Reluctantly Nakamura translated. Gohra picked up the box and shook it carefully. He asked if there were any weapons in it. Nakamura said, "On my word, no."

Captain Gohra snorted contemptuously then handed the box to Holbrecht. A nod to the guards and Holbrecht was pulled around and roughly shoved out of the office.

Snyder's eyes followed Bowen as he was pushed across the compound, clutching the Trinity box to his chest. Snyder eased back behind his tree and cursed to himself. How did that slippery bastard get the box? And what were the Japanese going to do with him?

Nakamura was alone with Captain Gohra, watching him pace. Gohra turned suddenly and said in very clear English, "Why was that man lying?"

Nakamura stared at him, astonished, then felt his knees buckle. He closed his eyes for a moment, cursing Holbrecht.

"Why was he lying?" Gohra repeated.

"I don't know. As I told you, the information in that box is intended for very high authorities in our government. Mr. Holbrecht is only trying to protect the security of our mission. If you would just get in touch with the Swedish embassy or Dr. Nishina. . . . We were supposed to meet him at Taraika Bay. . . . I am a former colleague of his."

Gohra's eyes blazed. "*And what are you now?*" he screamed. "How can you speak of *our* government? You *have* no government!"

Nakamura's eyes filled. "Captain, this goes beyond what you think of me." He tried to harden his voice. "I am a major in the Japanese Army, your superior. You must listen to me."

Captain Gohra slapped him. "You are nothing!" he yelled. "There is only one course for you!"

"Deal with me later!" Nakamura shouted back. "But for the sake of the Emperor, do as I say!"

Gohra reddened. In a sudden move he drew his sword. Nakamura shrank back. The blade flashed and he felt something tug at his collar. In two quick strokes, Gohra cut away his insignia, then stepped back.

"Now you are no longer a major. You *are* nothing."

He shoved the sword back into its scabbard and yelled for the guards.

Nakamura stumbled to the porch and heard a laugh just before a rifle butt thudded into the small of his back. He tumbled off the steps and sprawled in the dirt. The guards prodded him with their bayonets and screamed at him to get up. He tried but his legs refused to work. Rough hands grabbed him under one arm and jerked him to his feet. The arm was twisted behind him and he was pushed across the camp to his hut.

The sentry opened the door and Nakamura was thrown inside.

* * *

Snyder watched them shut the door and shove a bar into place. He was startled by the way they treated Nakamura. Why was Bowen handled so differently?

At least now he knew about two survivors. But what about the others? Could he assume they were all dead? Lasch, Kirby, Willard, Bliss . . . the crew . . . Macklin. Macklin he'd like to be sure about, though.

He rubbed aching muscles and stared at the two huts. He wouldn't mind killing Bowen, but how was he going to help Nakamura? Somehow he had to get across the camp to the two huts, but not tonight. He was too tired; he wouldn't be sharp enough. He needed to find a place to sleep.

He backed into the forest, turned and moved at a crouch, heading deeper into the woods. Climbing the side of the bowl-shaped valley, he found a hollowed-out center under some shrubs—an animal's lair. He moved in, lay down and covered himself with leaves.

The last thing he remembered before falling asleep was the salty tang of sea air coming in with the first wisps of early morning fog.

Snyder woke with a start. Diffused light streamed through branches. The sky was thickly overcast with light gray and blue patches. He brushed off the leaves and rolled out of the hollow, ears straining to be sure no one was around. Something skittered into his line of sight then shot away in a brown blur. An animal, probably the former tenant of this burrow. He crawled to a tree and instinctively glanced at his watch. It had stopped. He looked up at the dim sun and gauged the time to be about midday. Had he slept the whole morning? What about Nakamura and Bowen? If they had been moved, he would have no way of tracing them. He had to get back to the Japanese camp.

He reached into one of his zippered pockets and pulled out another chocolate bar and a ration tin. He ate on the move, hurrying quickly down the slope, using the trees as cover. In daylight the camouflage appeared much phonier, but now he saw how immense an area it covered. He heard voices drifting up, the sound of a motor starting.

Snyder peered around a tree and had a full view of the

camp, filled with Japanese soldiers hurrying into formation. They were streaming out of what looked to be a mess hut.

There were more vehicles than he had seen the night before. Three additional trucks. There was a driver in one of them, warming the engine. The men below came to attention, then at a shouted order turned as a unit and double-timed to the back of the truck and got in. An officer climbed up to the cab and the truck took off in a cloud of dust. As it passed Snyder, he looked into the back. All he could see were soldiers. There was no sign of any prisoners.

When the dust cleared, Snyder gazed across at the two tin huts. Both were still closed, barred and guarded. He relaxed: Bowen and Nakamura were still being held.

He gazed around the camp again. There were still plenty of soldiers around: crews in the gun emplacements, a few men outside an armory cleaning machine guns, and others on work detail. He studied the layout. He was at the north end; the road came in from the east. Immediately on his left was a supply hut, then clockwise around the camp were the radio shack, the gate, the armory, the two guarded huts, then a medical hut, cook shack, mess hall, two barracks structures, the command post and the vehicle area.

Another officer stepped out of the command post and the two sentries snapped to attention. The officer marched across the camp to Bowen's hut.

It was dark. The sentry prodded Holbrecht to his feet then stepped out of Captain Gohra's way. Gohra studied the Trinity box. His eyes flicked up to the prisoner, who watched him warily.

"Mister Holbrecht," Gohra said in English, "I have contacted my superiors about you."

Holbrecht's mouth opened in surprise, as he slowly comprehended the blunder he had made last night.

"They will consult with your embassy in Tokyo," Gohra went on, acting as if it made no difference. "I hope you will be patient. Communications are difficult."

Holbrecht recovered, closed his mouth and nodded. "Thank you," he said, smiling wanly.

"You are welcome." Gohra turned to the door, then paused to look back. "The man Nakamura—does he also claim the protection of the Swedish government?"

Holbrecht saw a ray of hope. Maybe all this bastard wanted was one scapegoat. "No, Captain. He is an American prisoner of war."

"Ah," said Gohra. "Too bad."

He left. The door was shut and barred, and Bowen realized that the charade he had been playing would shortly come to an unpleasant end, just as soon as this clever, English-speaking Jap got his answer from the Swedes. Bowen cursed out loud then sank back onto the mat and leaned against the wall.

How was he going to get out? His head throbbed. He felt the bandage. It was still in place. He had been thrown against the aft bulkhead when the plane had crashed and it had knocked him senseless. He had recovered to find himself in wreckage about twenty yards behind the rest of the plane and away from the fires. Kirby had lain mangled at his feet, Bliss crushed between the seats, Willard nowhere in sight, nor Lasch. He had grabbed the Trinity box, stepped out on the sand and staggered into the trees. He remembered hearing engines roaring by overhead. He had dashed as far and as fast as he could to the south, keeping to the woods.

If he hadn't left the trees to find the road just as the Japs came roaring up, he wouldn't be here now. He would have regained his good sense and headed north. A long walk to the border, but better than a shallow grave.

There wasn't much time left. But how could he escape during the day? His one hope seemed to lie in the inadequacy of Japanese communications.

Snyder watched the officer's polished boots cross from the hut to the radio shack. He disappeared inside for a few minutes then returned to the command post.

Snyder stayed behind the trees and watched the camp for the rest of the day. In midafternoon a patrol of three soldiers walked the perimeter, and Snyder had to scramble deeper into the woods. When he was able to return, he heard motor noise then saw the truck come down the road, bringing the men back from wherever they had been. From then till dusk the camp was alive with activity.

Snyder watched as food was taken to the two tin huts. A medic visited each of them and came out of Nakamura's hut with a tray full of bloody dressings. Snyder frowned. That couldn't be from Nakamura. Was somebody else in there with him? He recalled the stretcher on top of the car last night. Who could it have been? A scientist or one of the flight crew? If it was anyone in uniform, he was probably safe as a prisoner. But if it was one of the scientists, an American civilian, he stood a good chance of being shot as a spy.

The officer who had taken the men out in the morning was now busy posting the guards. He relieved the gun crews and sent them to mess.

Snyder crawled back into the trees, opened a tin of rations and a can of water and relaxed. He felt more confident today, not quite so far out of his element, and he was beginning to work out a way to get to Nakamura. All the huts were on raised platforms supported by foundation blocks. Each had an open crawl space underneath. If he could get around to the south side, he could crawl in under Nakamura's hut and not be seen.

As dusk settled, Snyder checked his .45, hoping there had been no damage from his dunking in the sea. The only way to find out was to fire it, which was the last thing he wanted to do.

Twilight seemed to last forever. When it was completely dark, Snyder rose and flexed his muscles to get the circulation going again. Then he moved stealthily through the trees and made his way slowly around the camp perimeter.

He passed behind the barracks, the mess hall, the cook shack and the dispensary, staying well outside the net, until he was even with the two tin huts. The guy wires for the net were sunk into the earth behind them.

Snyder dropped to his belly and slipped under the net. He stopped at the edge of the trees, realizing he had miscalculated: there were fifteen feet of open ground to Nakamura's hut. He flattened and peered under the structure.

He couldn't see through the crawl space, but he was sure the sentry would be standing on the other side.

He inched forward, clutching the.45, pulling with his elbows and pushing with his feet, expecting to be discovered at any second. His heart thumped and his breath came in shallow gasps until he rolled under the edge of the hut and into blackness.

He lay on his back, stiff and silent, listening. Across the crawl space he could see the guard's shoes ten feet away. He looked up at the floorboards then became aware of a horrible smell. There was a hole in the corner at one end and he knew immediately what it was for—the prisoner's toilet. He wasn't going to try communicating from there.

He crawled to the center of the hut and turned belly up. The guard was ten feet from his head. He looked up through irregularly spaced floorboards into a dark room and heard someone moaning.

Then Nakamura's voice, quietly: "You want the doctor?"

Another voice, badly cracked: "No . . . too late . . ."

Snyder strained, trying to put a face to the voice, but he couldn't. And it presented another problem: if the other man was Macklin . . .

He would have to chance it. Slowly he reached down and unsnapped the sheath at his belt, drew out the knife and slipped it between the floorboards over his head. Moving it along until he found the widest opening—about an inch—he pushed the blade up to the hilt then tapped the sides.

Two taps . . . pause . . . two more . . . someone sucked in a breath . . . stop tapping . . . silence . . . wiggle the blade again . . . two . . . two more . . .

The boards creaked over Snyder's head. Footsteps approached cautiously and Snyder drew the knife back slowly. A thump of knees hitting wood, then a shadow moving across the darkness above.

Nakamura whispered in Japanese.

Snyder hissed back, "English—it's Snyder."

A gasp of surprise, then Nakamura stretched out on the floor and peered down through the boards. Snyder grinned up at him. They could barely see each other.

"How did you get here?" Nakamura whispered, astonished.

"Followed you across the Pacific."

In the dimness Snyder thought he saw a grateful smile on Nakamura's face, and tears glistening in his eyes.

"Who's in there with you?"

"Lasch."

"Is he hurt?"

"Badly—I don't think he'll make it."

"Who else?"

"Just Holbrecht—in the next hut."

"Holbrecht? No, that's—" Snyder hesitated. "Who's he?"

"Works with Thyssen. Flew over with us."

Snyder felt angry again. He saw it all clearly now. Bowen wouldn't use his real name, but he had to choose a believable, even useful alias. Holbrecht. He had killed Thyssen and taken his place, posing as another Swedish diplomat.

"Snyder . . . Hsst!"

"I'm here."

"Can you get us out? Thyssen is waiting at Taraika Bay for the meeting."

"No, he's not."

"Yes—what do you mean?"

"Thyssen is dead. He's not waiting anywhere."

"But Holbrecht—"

"—is a phony. His real name is Bernard Bowen. He's a Russian agent."

Nakamura sucked in his breath and muttered something in Japanese.

"Nakamura, what about the others?" There was no answer. "Hey, Major!"

"Dead . . . all of them."

"Macklin?"

"Yes—the whole crew."

Snyder was relieved. With Macklin gone, there was one less problem. There was no time to feel remorse for the others.

"Holbrecht has the box."

"I know," said Snyder. "I've been watching. What happened last night?"

Nakamura whispered a brief account of his visit to the commandant. "Holbrecht was brought in to verify my story. He asked me to lie. Demanded to be taken to the nearest neutral territory . . ." Nakamura's whisper trailed off as the truth struck him. "The Russian part of this island!"

"You're getting the idea," Snyder said.

Nakamura grunted angrily. "What are you going to do?"

Snyder sank back, resting his head on the ground. He looked over at the crawl space under the other hut. "I'll have to kill him."

"How?"

"Go under his hut. Get his attention the way I got yours. Then use the knife—or my gun."

Nakamura was silent a moment then whispered, "They'll catch you!"

"He's got to be stopped."

"Listen—Captain Gohra is checking his identity with the Swedish embassy. If there is no Holbrecht, then shortly there won't be any Bowen, either."

"What about the Trinity box?"

"Maybe I can get it to Dr. Nishina."

"Don't be a fool," said Snyder. "I've been trying to tell you, the mission was called off long before you left. Bowen switched it back on again with the pilot's help. Macklin was in on it."

"But why?"

"My guess is, they were trying to take all of you and the Trinity material to Russia."

Silence a moment, then, "The mission was called off?"

Snyder felt the horror in Nakamura's voice and said softly, "Yes. I'm sorry. There's no support for it. No one is expecting us."

Nakamura lapsed into Japanese again. His tone was one of defeat, not anger.

"Look, Major, we have to get you out of here. Can Lasch travel?"

"No."

"Then it's just you."

"I can't go."

"Why not?"

"I have to warn my people."

Snyder wanted to throttle him. "If they don't believe you, they'll kill you."

"I'm already a dead man."

Snyder refused to argue that point anymore. He was past caring about Japanese logic. "What'll you do? Try to convince this Captain Gohra?"

"Yes. Once he finds out about Holbrecht, he might believe me."

"Might!"

"Snyder, you have to give me this chance . . . or everybody died for nothing."

Snyder was about to reply when he heard the sound of feet on wood. "The guard," he warned, rolling away from the hole and crawling to the far edge of the hut.

The door opened and the guard poked his head in. He saw Nakamura hovering over Lasch's broken body on the mat. In Japanese, he asked who had been talking. Nakamura indicated Lasch and said, "Delirious."

The guard gave a staisfied grunt, then turned and left, closing the door and replacing the bar.

Snyder rolled back to the hole. Nakamura was waiting for him. "I can't do anything more tonight," Snyder said, "but I have to tell you, I don't like leaving Bowen alive another minute."

"If you touch him now, we're lost!"

"All right. You'll have through tomorrow to make your pitch to Captain Gohra."

"There is another way," Nakamura said.

"What?"

"You surrender."

Snyder was stunned. "Are you crazy?"

"To support my story. That would impress Captain Gohra."

"Well, you can forget it! I don't need to impress anybody!"

"Think about it, Snyder. It would be a display of honor, and that may be all we have left."

"We'll see about that," Snyder said tightly. He rolled away.

* * *

Nakamura rose from the floor and saw Lasch's feverish eyes burning into him. He had overheard Nakamura's end of it and, in his delirium, had desperately been trying to piece it all together. He was stretched out on a straw mat, conscious of little else beyond his own agony. Both his legs were broken; one lung was punctured. When he breathed, his throat rattled and he felt stabbing pains in his rib cage.

Nakamura's face swam in and out as he bent close and whispered an account of the conversation. Lasch's attention wavered, his eyes frequently closing in pain. When he learned who Holbrecht really was, Lasch let out a sob of anguish.

There was a sharp rap on the door. The guard said something in Japanese. Nakamura answered quietly, then whispered to Lasch again, describing their problem. Snyder could not do anything for them until Bowen had been taken care of. If the Japanese didn't handle it, Snyder would have to. "And if he gets caught, that may be the end for us."

Lasch stared at the ceiling with sad, liquid eyes, then turned them on Nakamura. "You've got to try . . . to finish the job," he said. "Got to."

He sank back with a moan. A dark stain spread on the dressings wrapped around his chest. Nakamura watched it helplessly. Lasch didn't have long to live. Soon it would all be up to him.

Lasch lay on the mat, listening to the strained rattles coming from his own throat and thinking of Marion. So good, so pure—all she wanted in life was to rescue her family. He would do it now. He would save them for her. Nakamura would help. Snyder . . . He struggled for breath and the pain shot through him like a sword in his chest. He pushed it from his mind and forced himself to see only Marion . . . For you, darling, he said, we'll do it for you . . . finish the job. God help me, he cried in a voice that echoed in his mind, God help me, let's finish it! Finish it! So Marion and I can rest . . . together . . .

August 6: Karafuto

Snyder woke up shortly before dawn. The morning fog was low in the trees above him, concealing the uppermost branches, seeping down toward the camp. He shook away the cobwebs of sleep and fumbled in his flight suit for another tin of rations. He ate slowly, savoring every bite.

He made his way down to the camp perimeter, peered out from behind a tree, looking into the camp. It was still dark; the only activity was at the cook shack. Two sentries stood at the gate, stamping their feet to ward off the morning chill. Snyder's gaze settled on the two huts at the far side. Gradually he sensed something wrong.

Where were the guards?

And Nakamura, Lasch and Bowen: had they been taken away while he slept? In a car? A truck? His eyes turned to the parking area and he counted the vehicles. They were all exactly where they had been since yesterday afternoon. He stared at the huts again.

Both doors were closed and barred. He glanced at the gate sentries, wondering if they had noticed, but their view of the prison huts were blocked by the armory. Sndyer looked up at the fog, trying to calculate how much time he had until sunup. It was already getting light above him: he had to move fast.

Bending low, he scurried through the trees, trying to move noiselessly. Keeping back from the perimeter, he circled around to the south until he arrived behind and above the two prison huts. The fog diffused the first rays of sunlight and sank lower, blanketing the compound.

Snyder dropped to his belly and crawled down the slope,

slithering between the trees to the edge of the clearing. Again he had fifteen feet of open space to get across. And this time there was light; he would be exposed. He rose behind a tree, watched for signs of movement, then dashed to the rear of Nakamura's hut.

Flattening against the wall, he pulled out the .45, eased back the slide and jacked a round into the chamber. Hugging the side of the hut, he wriggled around the corner and slid along the wall to the front.

He stopped, fully exposed to the west side of the camp. He pressed an ear to Nakamura's hut but heard nothing from inside. He moved to the corner of Bowen's hut. From there, he could not be seen. He swiveled around for a look at the door. It was closed and barred. If Bowen was still in there, Snyder finally had his perfect opportunity.

He glanced once more at the camp building. Still no activity. He slipped from hiding and in two bounds made it to Bowen's door, went up three wooden steps and paused, lifting the bar off and swinging the door inward.

It stopped, blocked by something soft and yielding. He pushed with his shoulder to the wood. The heavy object behind it gave. Snyder peered inside and saw the empty mat to the left.

He pushed harder, forcing the thing on the floor back. His heart beating furiously in anticipation of what he would find, Snyder stepped inside, holding the .45 straight out in front of him. He closed the door quickly and peered through the gloom. Silence—not even the sound of breathing. His eyes dropped to the floor and he saw what had blocked his way: two uniformed bodies sprawled on the boards.

The guards.

He dropped to one knee and examined them. They couldn't have been dead long: they were still warm. There was blood all over the floor. One of them had been stabbed in the back and his throat had been slit. Fighting nausea, Snyder moved to the other one—a much cleaner job, strangled with a bandage, probably the one Bowen had worn around his head.

Snyder had no trouble imagining what had happened. Luring in the first guard, Bowen had garroted him; then, when the second guard came looking for his companion, Bowen had killed him using the other man's bayonet. One rifle still lay in a corner on the floor. The other one was gone. And there was no sign of the Trinity box.

Snyder whirled, cursing Bowen under his breath. Edging open the door, he peered out. A soldier came out of the cook shack, crossed to a row of garbage cans and dumped his load of trash. He turned, looking right at the prison huts. Snyder inched the door closed to just a crack and watched him stomp back into the cook shack.

No time to warn Nakamura. The camp could come alive at any moment. Snyder slipped out the door, replaced the bar, then jumped off the steps and dashed back between the huts.

He was into the woods in seconds, running east through the trees, following the road out of camp. Bowen would undoubtedly try to get to Russian territory with the Trinity box. That would mean traveling north as fast as he could. To be sure of direction, he would have to stay along the coast.

Snyder reached the edge of the woods and saw the coast road ahead through the fog. A dull glow rose in the east over the ocean: the sun was coming up. He dashed across the road, reached the dunes and dodged between them at a crouch, heading down a long slope onto the firmer sand near the water.

He looked both ways through the fog then down at the sand for any trace of footprints. Nothing. Had he been wrong? Could Bowen have taken an inland route? Maybe he wasn't going north after all. Questions tumbled through Snyder's mind. Finally he started north along the beach. He would go on until he found something . . .

He kept up the pace for half an hour, head down, eyes sweeping left and right, the fog obscuring his view beyond twenty yards. He was almost ready to quit when he spotted a small depression in the sand close to the tide line. He found a few more farther on, trailing into the water. Footprints. Snyder felt a surge of energy. Bowen *was* going this way, letting the water obliterate his tracks.

Snyder stopped about a hundred yards farther on to examine a row of irregular footprints ending in disturbed wet sand, as if someone had stumbled and dropped something. Bowen and the Trinity box? Snyder hurried along the water's edge, watching to see that the footprints did not veer off. An hour later he reached the promontory south of where the C-54 had crashed. It was past dawn. The fog still hung heavily over the beach but was beginning to thin out. Snyder had no idea how far ahead Bowen was, or whether he would encounter any towns or fishing villages. And how long would it be before the Japanese discovered the escape and began pursuit? Would *they* guess which way Bowen had gone?

He passed the promontory, which jutted out to sea and ended in a cluster of rocks. As he was climbing over them, Snyder heard two flat reports.

Gunshots. But from where?

The wreck of 7271 was a short distance ahead up at the tree line. The Japanese would have left it guarded. Had Bowen stumbled on it and been caught? Snyder jumped off the rocks and ran up the slope.

Nakamura woke from a fitful sleep, jarred by a strangled sound. He rolled over and stared at Lasch, who was half off the mat, his head jerking on his arm as he retched blood and groped feebly at his chest. His eyes met Nakamura's an instant before they rolled back into his head.

Nakamura leaped up and hammered on the door, yelling in Japanese for the guard to fetch a doctor. He pounded relentlessly but got no response. He glanced back at Lasch, who had rolled off the mat and was spasmodically heaving, covering the floor with blood.

Tears streaming down his face, Nakamura bellowed for help.

At last there was an answering shout. The bar was ripped off the door and two soldiers burst in, bayonets pressing Nakamura back against the wall. He yelled at them to get a doctor.

One of the soldiers covered him while the other ran out. But no one moved to do anything for Lasch. The remaining guard impassively watched him struggle for breath.

Then Lasch shuddered twice, stiffened and went limp.

Nakamura stared down at him, slowly becoming aware of a commotion outside.

More soldiers ran up, some coming into his hut, faces drawn and frightened. Captain Gohra stalked in, his rage obvious. Barely glancing at Lasch's body, he ordered it removed.

Nakamura stood against the wall and watched two men cart the body outside. He tried to comprehend how Lasch's death could make Gohra so furious. Gohra snapped an order and Nakamura was roughly pushed out of the hut.

He saw the soldiers drop Lasch on the ground next to two other bodies with bloody uniforms. The door to Holbrecht's hut was open and grim-faced soldiers stood around the steps.

"What's happened?" he asked.

Captain Gohra's fist shot out, knocking him to the ground. "I ask the questions!" said Gohra.

Through a haze of pain, Nakamura saw a truck slew around in the center of camp. An officer ran across his line of sight with a squad of men, yelling at them to get into the truck.

Captain Gohra waited for the truck to move out and the noise to lessen, then he turned and dragged Nakamura to his feet.

"Your Swedish diplomat has escaped," he said, "and killed two of my men."

"How could he—?" Nakamura started to ask.

Gohra slapped him. "Now tell me why you came here!"

"To warn the government." Resolutely Nakamura clung to the same story he had told before. Gohra was not satisfied. He paced back and forth, listening, then held up a hand for silence.

"Thank you for your cooperation," he said evenly, then he turned, nodded to the soldiers and walked away. Nakamura was caught by surprise when a rifle butt smashed him to the ground. He tried to cover his head. One soldier held him down with a foot while the others kicked him. He groaned in pain. They hauled him up. Fists tore into his middle. As he lost consciousness, he thought how useless this was. There was nothing left to beat out of him. Lasch was dead, Holbrecht had escaped and where was Snyder?

* * *

Captain Gohra stalked back to his headquarters. A communiqué was waiting for him from Second General Army Headquarters in Hiroshima, datelined 6 AUGUST 0530 HOURS:

SWEDISH EMBASSY DENIES ANY KNOWLEDGE OF DIPLOMAT NAMED OSCAR HOLBRECHT STOP HOLD FOR QUESTIONING STOP LIEUTENANT COLONEL KATUMIYA INTELLIGENCE SECTION WILL LEAVE 1200 TODAY TO TAKE CHARGE STOP.

Crumpling the paper, Gohra went into his office and shut the door. He stared at the Emperor's portrait a long moment, but it had long since lost whatever inspiration and comfort it projected. This war would end soon and it would not end well for Japan. What future was there for the officer corps? He frowned angrily at the passport on his desk. He would pursue this slippery "Holbrecht" with a vengeance. And if he was lucky, he would capture him and have his own chance at torture before Lieutenant Colonel Katumiya arrived.

But how could he have been so stupid as to let "Holbrecht" keep that box? Now it was gone, and if it wasn't recovered, Gohra knew he would be the one to pay for it. He felt a certain dread about the contents he had failed to examine. Why had he let "Holbrecht" 's lies impress him at all? Stupid.

Well, there was still time. Katumiya had to come all the way from Hiroshima.

Snyder lay flat across the crest of a dune, looking at the wreckage of the C-54 strewn out over a hundred yards. The broken-off tail section was some distance away from the fuselage, the cockpit a mangled remnant twisted into fire-blackened trees like a metal sculpture, the center of the fuselage a burned-out hulk of torn and jagged aluminum. Fog hung thick, bleak and surreal over the crash site. No sign of sentries other than a wisp of smoke from the opposite side of the wreck.

Snyder crept closer. Around a dune he saw a body lying on the near side of the belly section of the plane: a dead Japanese soldier, his back a pulpy red mass where it had been blasted at close range.

A puff of wind blew smoke in Snyder's direction and he recoiled from the smell. What the hell were they cooking?

Gripping his .45, Snyder went around the wreckage and spotted a second body sprawled over the campfire, smoking like a barbecuing steak. He had been shot through the head and had fallen into the embers.

So Bowen had passed through and left his calling card—more bodies. For a charming Old World antique dealer, he was showing considerable aptitude for another profession. But why? Snyder could not figure the logic. Why should Bowen leave the safety of his beach path to come up here and murder two Japanese soldiers? That was the act of a psycho, not of a methodical killer.

He made a quick search of the area and behind the remains of the cockpit found the reason: a smashed radio covered with Japanese markings. Coming up from the beach a few minutes ago, Bowen must have heard one of the men broadcasting and figured it was only a matter of time before someone at the camp alerted these guards to watch for him. So he had saved them the trouble.

He couldn't be too far ahead now, probably back on the beach again. Snyder took off after him.

Ten minutes later he picked up the trail again. Bowen's intermittent footprints at the edge of the water. He followed them north, watching the breakers wash up and fill the depressions. A dark mass loomed through the swirling fog ahead: a rock outcropping that disappeared into the water. While Snyder stood figuring the best way to get around it, he thought he saw movement at the crest and stiffened, caught in the open.

It could be anybody—a fisherman, a soldier, Bowen or his imagination. He started climbing cautiously, pausing before he reached the top. As he came over the rocks, there was a dull flash in the fog ahead, followed by a sharp crack.

The bullet whizzed past his head.

Snyder dropped to the sand and dragged the .45 around,

lying motionless, staring into the fog, unable to see his attacker, hoping the situation was mutual. If it was the Japanese, he wouldn't have long to wait. But if it was Bowen, would he waste valuable time checking on his handiwork?

Snyder edged slowly toward another clump of rocks then froze when he heard the roar of an approaching engine. He rolled quickly behind the rocks then scrambled up the slope till he had a view of the road.

A truck drove by and shuddered to a stop a hundred yards north of Snyder's cover. The tailgate slammed down and a dozen soldiers jumped to the ground. Fanning out on either side of the road, they walked back toward him, their eyes sweeping the ground.

Snyder stayed wedged behind the rocks, watching as two of them came down to the beach and headed his way. He cocked the .45. One of the soldiers stopped abruptly, staring at the sand near the water. Calling to his buddy, he ran over and together they examined something. Bowen's footprints, Snyder guessed. He cringed as a shout brought more soldiers running. They zigzagged down the slope, crossed the beach, then trotted up the waterline. They stopped and one of them pointed north, then they all scrambled back to the road.

Snyder watched the truck start up and roar on ahead. He sagged in relief: they would probably keep going until they found no more footprints, then they would sweep back from that point. He would have to catch Bowen before they did. He got up and climbed to the road, hoping there wouldn't be any other search parties coming up behind him. He would make better time on firmer ground. As long as the Japanese stayed ahead of him, he could assume Bowen was still traveling along the coast. Let them be his eyes, he thought. All he had to do was listen for the sound of their truck.

As he trotted along the hard shoulder, he imagined himself in Bowen's place. With the Japanese now hot on his trail, Bowen could no longer afford to travel openly on the beach. He would have to go overland. And if he had already made his move into the trees, he could be anywhere by now.

Snyder stopped, his gaze caught by something in the sand ahead. He saw the vague trace of an irregular pattern along the hollow between two dunes, as if something had been dragged up from the beach. Wind wouldn't make such a pattern, nor would an animal or a bird.

He followed it then stopped again. The track wound along between the dunes, not once coming up over a crest where it could be seen from the road. Snyder felt a burst of interest. There in the dip between two dunes was a slick strand of seaweed, still damp when he picked it up. This far from the tide line?

He followed the drag marks until they curved between two dunes and came up to the road. Then he found a larger clump of seaweed, half-buried and encrusted with sand, as if it had been thrown there, then someone had kicked sand over it to hide it.

Bowen had used it to conceal his tracks, then had pitched it away.

Snyder looked at the road. Bowen would never risk running down the blacktop. He must have crossed into the trees *here*.

Snyder cut across the road. After five minutes' running, he spotted footprints going up to the tree line. He followed, slipping into the woods.

Tracking became easier. Bowen was getting careless, leaving broken branches and footprints in his wake. Snyder grunted, grateful for the trail. Sound was muffled under the canopy of thick green branches cloaked with gray mist. He moved through the silence, his feet squishing on damp ground.

He stopped and leaned against a tree, tired. Bowen, carrying that box and being older and more desperate, had to be a lot worse off. Snyder was too deep in the forest now to know whether the road was still below and to his right. Because of the fog, he couldn't tell direction by the sun. He stopped, hearing something up ahead.

Another branch snapped . . . then silence. The sound resumed a moment later—branches whipping back and forth. Snyder tried to locate the noise. It was off to his left, ahead and above, moving away fast. He took off, climbing quickly.

The thrashing stopped but he picked up the echoing sound of distant shouts. He edged down toward the tree line. It seemed an eternity before the trunks and branches thinned out and he could see the road below. Up a little to the north the Army truck was coming back, moving at a snail's pace. The soldiers were stretched out like a line of jungle beaters from the forest to the beach, pacing the truck, shouting to one another as they searched, coming slowly toward Snyder.

He backed into the trees and scrambled up the slope, as far away from the road as he could get, his muscles aching with fatigue. He looked for a place to hide, hoping Bowen would do the same and not try to outrace the soldiers.

Finding a huge fallen tree, black with rot and half hollowed out from an old fire, Snyder dove behind it and rolled into damp, mushy wood. The smell of decay was awful, but it gave him good cover. There was a jagged crack in the trunk, and he peered through it into the forest.

The first soldier came through the trees, rifle extended, the flat of his bayonet glinting dully. He padded cautiously across the carpet of fir needles. Another men appeared about twenty feet away from him.

If they kept on in this direction, Snyder's hiding place would be between the two of them.

He huddled closer to the wood and pulled his head away from the crack, then held his breath and waited. Finally one of the soldiers came around the jagged stump on his left; the other passed the broken end to his right. Neither looked back. If they had, they couldn't have missed seeing him.

Slowly he eased out his .45 but didn't pull back the hammer. In this hollow, he knew the click would be amplified. As the soldiers disappeared into the trees, eventually swallowed up by fog, he shoved the .45 back into his shoulder holster.

A moment later he slid away from the log, his flying suit caked with mushy growth. He slapped off a few bugs and looked around. At least now he would have no trouble getting back on a northerly course. He just turned in the direction the Japanese had come from.

* * *

Bowen, too, had found a hiding place, deeper in the woods, to the west and higher up, where the fog was low and thick. He had crouched behind a broad tree trunk, clutching the Trinity box, exhausted and cold and afraid that his shortness of breath would give him away. The point man of the patrol had passed by just twenty yards below him.

As the Japanese moved on, Bowen waited to be sure they were out of earshot. The rifle slung across his shoulder bit into his collarbone, pinching painfully. Slowly he eased it off and turned it butt down, using it as a crutch to pull himself erect. He had squatted too long: his legs had gone to sleep and when he rose, they wouldn't hold him. He pitched forward and smacked into the ground, losing his grip on the rifle. It clattered against a rock.

Bowen stiffened, pulled the Trinity box against his side and glanced around, terrified that any second he would hear a Japanese voice shouting and footsteps running his way. But there was nothing.

He closed his eyes and breathed deeply, then rolled over on his back and rested a moment, his chest heaving. His eyes moved to the box; he stared at the Swedish stickers. Was it worth it? Or had his people across the border already given up on him? So what? he told himself, because when he did show up, he would be met with even greater appreciation. It would boost his stock enormously. He would be on a plane to Moscow tonight, and tomorrow— who knows? It was enough to give him strength.

He pulled himself to a sitting position and listened again, his senses sharpened in anticipation of reaching his goal. Not a sound. He stood up, picked up the box and the rifle, then turned to move on.

And stopped, staring at the tree he had hidden behind and the others around it. Suddenly, they all looked alike.

He realized with growing panic that he had lost his sense of direction. He was at the top of a crest and the ground fell off in two directions, the trees sloping down on both sides. Which way had he come up? Which way was north? He couldn't see the road: the branches and fog obscured his view. He had to take a chance.

He stumbled along the crest and a few minutes later

came up between a pair of trees and stopped again. Had he heard a noise ahead—or was it from his left? Sound was swallowed up in this fog.

He stumbled backward then turned and started running. His shoes pounded the needle carpet, beating a tempo of deadened thuds. He whipped around a brace of trees then staggered to a halt.

Half-concealed by the fog, only a few yards ahead, someone was standing next to a tree.

"Bowen," said a disembodied voice.

Bowen gasped, dropped the box and brought up the rifle, his fingers groping for the trigger.

The figure ducked behind the tree and called out quietly, "Fire that and we're both dead."

Bowen's finger stopped on the trigger, the warning echoing in his terrified mind. The man was right, but who was he?

Bowen dipped and scooped up the box. He backed behind a tree then turned and ran.

Snyder raced after Bowen, following him by sound more than sight. Their feet thudding on the damp ground, slipping more than once on the slick carpet of needles, neither man knew which way he was going, both afraid they could be heading right back into the arms of the Japanese.

How could he move so fast carrying all that weight? Snyder wondered. He heard Bowen panting with the effort, the fog ahead throwing back sound like an acoustical wall.

Bowen lost his footing on the fir needles and slid against a tree. The rifle flew from his grasp, hit a branch then caromed down the slope. He stopped for a split second, deciding whether to go after it, his breath coming in rasping wheezes. He pushed away from the tree and lurched onward, stumbled again and felt his grip loosen on the box.

A weight slammed into his legs and he crashed to the ground. The tackler slid with him, off the crest and down the slope.

They rolled to a stop and fell apart. Bowen looked up into Snyder's face.

"You!" he said, the recognition bringing with it an acute sense of terror.

Snyder lost all reason, wanting his hands around Bowen's neck. Forgetting his knife, he lunged into Bowen's outstretched hand, caught the blow badly and tumbled backwards. Bowen kept that hand out; the other one cradled the Trinity box close to his chest. Snyder lashed out and grabbed Bowen's leg, jerking it upward. Bowen fell back, his arms flailing wildly. The box flipped over and rolled end-to-end down the slope, coming to rest against a tree.

Bowen stared after it a second then switched his attention to Snyder. They went at each other like Sumo wrestlers, shoulders cracking, hands grasping for strangleholds, probing for weak spots, clawing at each other.

Bowen's weight shifted and he flipped Snyder beneath him. His right hand groped for Snyder's throat, fingers searching for his windpipe. His eyes were wild as they fell to Snyder's chest, to the open flight jacket and the shoulder holster. The butt of the .45 was within easy reach if he could just dare to relax his grip and make a grab for it.

Snyder felt the grip on his neck loosen. A hand shot downward and Snyder's knee came up at the same instant, jabbing Bowen at the base of his spine. Bowen grunted, missed his grab for the pistol, and Snyder shoved with both hands.

Bowen flew backward. Snyder staggered to his feet, hardly getting his wind back before Bowen was after him again, swinging a heavy dead branch he had picked up. Snyder dodged and maneuvered for position. Sidestepping a vicious swipe, he grabbed Bowen's arm and pulled him around, smashing him nose first into a tree.

Bowen's hands flew up to his face and he stumbled back. Snyder picked up the branch and watched Bowen, convinced he was now in command.

But Bowen lowered his head and charged, crashing into him.

Before Snyder could protect it, he felt his knife jerked out of its sheath then saw the blade swing back as Bowen went to drive it into his side. Using both hands, Snyder shoved the branch upward. The jagged end punched into Bowen's throat, snapping his head back.

Bowen staggered back, slashing maniacally with the

knife, the sharp end of the branch embedded under his jaw. Snyder watched him stumble and fall. The knife dropped from his hand and he slid across the needles, groping for the branch, his face contorted in surprise and pain. The branch came away and his throat gushed blood. His head jerked spasmodically and his hands thrashed for support. Then he stiffened and collapsed.

He lay on the slope. Snyder listened to the strange whistling sound as Bowen tried to breathe. At last that diminished to silence.

Snyder sank to one knee, bruised and out of breath. Waves of pain shuddered through him as he stared at the lifeless body a few feet away. He sucked in his breath and held it, listening to see if the Japanese had been attracted by the noise.

He waited interminably, but not a sound came back to him. His eyes shifted to the .45 at his shoulder. It would have been so much neater, he thought, but then the Japanese would have heard.

He rose painfully and looked around for the Trinity box. He found it under a tree and had to crab-walk down the hill to get it. How many lives had been lost for it? He sat down, his back to the tree, pulling the box to his side. He didn't care if the Japanese found him: he just couldn't move.

He stayed there a long time, watching the fog lift. Soon bleak sunlight appeared through the branches and he began figuring which direction would take him back to the road.

Snyder traveled south along the beach, twice eluding Japanese patrols. He went past the promontory near the wreck of 7271 and on down the coast until he came to where he had buried his raft.

Digging into the sand with cupped hands, he uncovered the rubberized canvas. He found the flashlight and a ration tin he had missed. Eagerly he opened it and devoured the contents. He buried the raft again then tested the light— the beam lit up his hand.

He sat on a rock and gazed out to sea. All he had to do was wait for night then blink the light at regular intervals. If Scheff's request had gotten through—if the submarine was out there and somebody was watching through a periscope—he would be spotted.

He sat for a full hour, the flashlight in his lap, the Trinity box wedged between two rocks, thinking of Nakamura and Lasch. Could he just leave them like this? Their faces hovered in front of him like accusing ghosts—and behind them appeared Bliss, Kirby, Willard, Marion Cypulski and Louise Daniels. Had he forgotten Thyssen? Poor Stefan Thyssen. . . . Then the other faces, the ones who had survived and who still expected something of him: Stimson, Marshall, his father, Beth . . .

Something inside kept telling him to forget them, push them out of your mind. You've done all you can. Don't let them force you further.

But he knew Nakamura was right. It was worth trying.

Finally he got up, reburied the flashlight next to the raft and picked up the Trinity box.

August 6: Karafuto (1730 HRS)

Snyder left the main road and walked into the trees just north of the turnoff. He maneuvered across the slope and down into the bowl. Stopping behind the trees, he shrugged out of his shoulder holster and left his .45 and the knife on the ground. Then, cradling the Trinity box in front of him, he looked into the camp, deciding on the best way to make an entrance.

The grounds were nearly deserted. There were the usual two guards at the gate, another on the commandant's porch. A single soldier walked across to the parking area, reached into one of the cars and drew out a clipboard, then went into the armory.

Where was everybody else? Snyder wondered. Out looking for "Holbrecht"?

That left only one man between him and the Japanese commandant: the guard on the porch, who stood staring straight at the main gate. Snyder hoped he was asleep with his eyes open. As he watched, the door banged open and the guard's shoulders snapped back. An orderly stuck out his head and said something; the guard turned and went in with him.

Now the way was clear. Snyder sucked in a deep breath, ducked under the net and walked cautiously into the camp.

He took even, measured steps and kept telling himself he wouldn't be spotted. He stopped ten feet from the porch, set the box down and backed up two steps, then waited for someone to appear.

He resisted looking back to see what the gate guards were doing. If he was going to get a bullet, he would rather not see it coming.

Nothing happened. He stood still for an endless two minutes until he began to feel ludicrous. Christ, he thought, what does it take to get captured around here? He shifted his weight and glanced around. It was like a western street deserted before the big shoot-out.

He didn't see the first men emerge from the mess hall, but he heard laughter, clumping boots, a door swinging, chatter . . .

He turned just as they became aware of him. An ominous silence fell. Twenty Japanese soldiers stood across the open space, staring at him. He managed a halfhearted glare of defiance.

There was a loud grunt of surprise. The guard had just returned to the porch and stood gaping at him.

Snyder threw up his hands and yelled, "Don't shoot!"

The guard swung up his rifle and shouted something back into the office. Pandemonium erupted. The men coming out of the mess hall surged across the open ground and surrounded Snyder, who held his hands high in the air.

Captain Gohra burst through the door, yelled in Japanese, and the unarmed soldiers fell back to give Snyder room.

Hands still upraised, Snyder looked up at the commandant, whose eyes went to the Trinity box.

Gohra muttered a command to the guard, who came off the porch, moved behind Snyder and pushed him toward the steps. Snyder bent down slowly to pick up the box.

Gohra wheeled and disappeared inside. Snyder followed, ignoring the stunned looks on the faces of the two clerks in the outer office. He was ushered through to the rear.

Gohra stood behind his desk, his face flushed and his stance a bit shaky. Snyder studied him, surprised at the lack of poise. In fact, Gohra looked drunk. Snyder groaned inwardly. That was all he needed: trying to explain a complicated story to an unstable Japanese officer who had lost four men within twenty-four hours and had permitted a prisoner to escape.

With a curt nod Gohra dismissed the guard. Snyder set the Trinity box down on the desk, wondering how he was going to communicate. Gohra stared at the box, growing visibly upset.

"I am Captain Gohra," he said finally in English. "Who are you?"

Surprised, Snyder said, "P.T. Snyder, Major, United States Army."

Gohra grunted then pointed to the box. "That was in the possession of a prisoner at this camp," he said. "A man calling himself Holbrecht, who claimed he was a Swedish diplomat."

"He lied."

Gohra did not seem surprised. "And how did you get it?"

"I killed him." Gohra looked up, fixing Snyder with a wary gaze. "He was trying to shake your patrols and get to the Russian border."

"I see. Were you also aboard the plane that crashed?"

"No, I was pursuing it in another plane. We knew what Holbrecht was trying to do. I parachuted in to stop him."

"And to recover that box?"

"Yes. It must get to Dr. Nishina, along with Major Nakamura."

"Then why did you bring it here?"

"To convince you that Nakamura told the truth and Holbrecht didn't."

Gohra studied him. "No credentials—you could be anything."

Snyder ripped open the top of his shirt and displayed his dog tags. "Don't even think about it, Captain. I'm an American officer, entitled to certain protections."

Gohra grunted a laugh.

Snyder smiled grimly. "Do you think I walked in here for my health? Captain Gohra, thousands of Japanese lives are at stake."

Whatever remained of Gohra's poise seemed to drain away. His eyes drifted to the box again. He became distraught, almost as though he were going to cry. But after a moment he straightened, walked to the door, opened it and said something in Japanese.

He returned and circled Snyder. He stopped and fumbled a pack of cigarettes from his tunic and held them out.

"No, thanks. I could use some water, though."

Gohra poured a glass from a carafe on his desk and gave

it to Snyder. Then he moved back to the box. "I have a message confirming that Holbrecht was not Swedish," he said. "So these diplomatic seals mean nothing."

He looked up expectantly. Snyder said nothing. Gohra broke the seals and opened the aluminum box. He pulled out the carton and set it on his desk. Unfolding the flaps, he stared at the contents. He pulled out the can of film, then drew out some of the papers and glanced at them. The mathematical equations meant nothing to him. He set them aside and dug deeper. He found a fat manila envelope and opened it, drawing out the Trinity photographs.

He sat down and studied each of them in turn, the detailed eight-by-tens of the atomic test. Two in particular caught his attention: one showing the farmhouse and the tower before the blast, and the other showing their vaporized remains afterward.

Gohra held them up. "Where were these taken?"

"At a test site in New Mexico."

Gohra picked up another print and for almost a full minute stared at the mushroom cloud. "What is it?" he asked hoarsely.

"An atomic bomb. It's very powerful. Major Nakamura was part of a group coming to warn your people that this will be used on them if they don't surrender."

"Why Nakamura?"

Snyder pointed to the photographs. "We were there, together. I took him to see this."

The door opened and Nakamura was brought in, his face puffy with cuts and bruises. He moved with a painful limp and stopped when he saw Snyder. Then his eyes moved to the open box, the papers and the photos. A flicker of hope crossed his face. He looked quizzically at Snyder, then caught Captain Gohra's penetrating gaze. He bowed his head and stared at the floor. A lifetime of tradition still dictated his actions, compelling him to feel shame and dishonor.

Gohra got up slowly and came around the desk. He put a hand on Nakamura's shoulder. In Japanese he said, "You are not yet of the dead."

Nakamura looked up in surprise.

Gohra switched to English so Snyder would understand.

"Your efforts come too late," he said, reaching back to his desk and picking up a cable. "This came from Army Headquarters in Tokyo a short while ago."

In a voice trembling with emotion, he read: " ' Hiroshima was completely destroyed at eight fifteen this morning in an attack by one American plane and what is believed to have been one bomb. Casualties are reported to be unusually high, perhaps as many as one hundred thousand.' "

Silence hung heavily in the room for a long moment. Nakamura stared at Gohra. Snyder felt sick with anger. The delays, the double-dealing, the weather, selfish interest, espionage—all of it led to this—a moment too late . . .

"We should still try to reach Dr. Nishina," Snyder said. "Let him know exactly what the weapon is."

Gohra shook his head. "Your President has already informed the world." He handed Nakamura another cable. "This is the text of an American announcement."

Nakamura translated from the Japanese: " 'It is an atomic bomb. . . . The force from which the sun draws its power has been loosed against those who brought war to the Far East. . . . If they do not now accept our terms, they may expect a rain of ruin from the air, the likes of which has never been seen on this earth.' "

Gohra walked to the door and snapped out an order in Japanese. The guards reappeared. He turned his back on Snyder and Nakamura while they were taken out. Nakamura glanced into Gohra's quarters on the way and saw the tatami mat and the Shinto shrine. There was a sheathed knife laid out on a ceremonial altar mat.

In silence they were escorted across the camp and back into Nakamura's hut. As soon as the door was closed and barred, Snyder sagged against the wall.

Nakamura said quietly, "They're not going to kill us . . . yet."

"That's comforting. Where's Lasch?"

"He died this morning."

"Oh, Christ." Again Snyder saw the faces lined up like tenpins. Would they ever go away?

"Captain Gohra won't be with us much longer, either."

"What do you mean?"

"He's going to commit hara-kiri."

"Why?"

"He's disgraced. Because he didn't listen to me, Hiroshima is gone."

"That's crazy! He's not to blame."

"He thinks so."

"Where does that leave us?"

Nakamura shook his head uncertainly then looked up, interrupted by sounds outside: soldiers running and shouted commands.

"What's going on?" Snyder asked.

Nakamura moved to the front wall and pried loose a rusted edge of corrugated tin. Snyder peered through the hole with him and saw two soldiers hurrying from the parking area carrying what looked like cans of gasoline.

An orderly came out of the command post with the Trinity box. He placed it on the ground and the soldiers poured gasoline over it. The orderly struck a match and threw it on the pile. There was a loud *whump*, then flames shot up and consumed the contents.

Nakamura backed away from the sight, leaving Snyder to watch the fire until it died down. One of the guards poked at it to be sure everything was destroyed. Fine ash floated up and was wafted away in the breeze.

It was twilight. Snyder glanced at Nakamura. Would their fate be similar? Would they too be wiped away like a bad dream? Expunged with fire?

Snyder sat down and waited.

After a while they heard footsteps crunching toward them and rose in anticipation. The bar was removed and the door opened. A soldier stepped in with a tray of food. Another stood at the door, covering them with a rifle. The first man set his tray down and withdrew without a word. The door was closed and barred again.

Snyder hesitated, but Nakamura squatted down and uncovered the dishes. Bean paste, rice, a little meat and a carafe of sake with two cups.

"Just be careful of the sake," Nakamura cautioned. "Strong."

"Right now I could use a wallop."

A short time later they heard more commands outside and moved back to the hole in the wall. A double rank of men was drawn up in front of the command post. A lieutenant came out and stepped off the porch, followed by the clerks and the orderly. They took up positions facing the porch and stood at attention in absolute silence.

Nakamura whispered, "Do you understand what's happening?"

"Not exactly, but if anybody comes over here, I'm going to put up a fight."

"Listen."

Two minutes later a single gunshot echoed across the camp. The soldiers bowed deeply in unison.

Snyder looked at Nakamura, surprised. "Gohra?" he said hoarsely.

Nakamura nodded.

"I don't understand. I thought it was done with a knife."

"Someone finished it for him."

Around ten o'clock they heard footsteps again, marching to a halt in front of the hut. They stood up. Snyder flexed his knees, got into a half-crouch and balled his fists, ready to fly at whoever came through the door. The bar was lifted, the door opened and the lieutenant they had seen earlier stepped inside.

He disregarded Snyder's stance and spoke to Nakamura in Japanese. "Major Nakamura, I am Lieutenant Korukai." He bowed slightly then said, "You will come with me now. Both of you."

Nakamura nodded for Snyder to follow. Snyder hesitated, then stepped outside cautiously.

They were marched out of camp quietly, between four soldiers and behind Lieutenant Korukai. They went all the way back to the main road, Snyder expecting either a bullet or a bayonet and furtively looking for nearby cover he could dash to . . .

They had crossed the coast road when Lieutenant Korukai called a halt. They stood in the open, the chill night wind sweeping over the dunes. Snyder felt his breath coming in short gasps as he eyed the soldiers' bayonets.

Lieutenant Korukai ordered the soldiers to stay where

they were then led Snyder and Nakamura down to the
sand. Snyder tensed to make a break, thinking, How stupid
this guy is. How dumb. We'll go around that dune and I'll
jump him——

He felt Nakamura's restraining hand squeeze his wrist.

They stopped at the edge of the beach, Snyder staring at
Korukai's holstered pistol. Then he saw Korukai hand
Nakamura a note written in English. "My instructions are
that you read this to Major Snyder," he said.

Snyder could have made his move at that moment, but
he watched, fascinated, as Nakamura angled the note to
catch the moonlight, then read haltingly, " 'When you read
this, I will have passed into the next world . . .' " He
looked up.

"Captain Gohra?" Snyder asked.

"Yes. 'My soldiers know nothing of Hiroshima. They
will learn soon enough. If the information came while you
were still prisoners, they would be hard to restrain. Lieutenant Korukai has been told that you are honorable men. He
knows I would not say so if I did not believe it. Your effort
was valiant. However, it is best that it die with all of us.
You in your time and I in mine. I assume Major Snyder
has made arrangements for rescue. So I have ordered Lieutenant Korukai to release you tonight. Your lives are the
only gift I have left to bestow. Major Snyder, I salute your
courage. Major Nakamura, you and I will meet one day at
the Yasukuni Shrine, where the souls of all true warriors
find eternal rest.' "

Nakamura hesitated over the last words. His eyes filled.
Honor, which meant more than life, had been returned to
him. "May I keep this?" he asked in Japanese. Lieutenant
Korukai nodded. Nakamura folded the note and stuck it
into his tunic.

Korukai saluted them both, then turned and walked
back up to his men. They disappeared down the road.

"Can you beat that?" said Snyder.

"I don't think so."

Snyder and Nakamura trudged along the sand until Snyder located the spot where he had buried the raft. They
dug it up. Snyder switched on the flashlight and began signaling out to sea.

August 6: The Atlantic

The USS *Augusta* was on its way back from Europe, and President Truman was having lunch with the crew when an officer brought him a radio message from Washington:

> HIROSHIMA BOMBED VISUALLY WITH ONE TENTH CLOUD COVER AT 052315A (AUGUST 5, 7:15 PM, WASHINGTON TIME). THERE WAS NO FIGHTER OPPOSITION AND NO FLAK. PARSONS REPORTS 15 MINUTES AFTER BOMB AS FOLLOWS: "RESULTS CLEAR-CUT SUCCESSFUL IN ALL RESPECTS. VISIBLE EFFECTS GREATER THAN ANY TEST. CONDITION NORMAL IN AIRPLANE FOLLOWING DELIVERY."

Truman excitedly shook the officer's hand, beamed and said, "This is the greatest thing in history."

A second message arrived from Stimson while Truman was still at lunch:

> BIG BOMB WAS DROPPED ON HIROSHIMA AUGUST 5 AT 7:15 PM WASHINGTON TIME. FIRST REPORTS INDICATE COMPLETE SUCCESS WHICH WAS EVEN MORE CONSPICUOUS THAN EARLIER TEST.

Truman rose and tapped on his glass for silence. He announced that the United States had just dropped a new type of explosive device on Japan, unleashing a force greater than 20,000 tons of TNT. The sailors burst out in applause.

Truman rushed to the officers' wardroom and repeated his announcement, adding, "We won the gamble!"

August 7

Japan's leading nuclear physicist, Dr. Yoshio Nishina, flew over the flattened remains of Hiroshima in an Army plane, then returned to Tokyo and reported to General Seizo Arisue that from his estimation Hiroshima had been destroyed by a uranium type of atomic bomb. In his opinion nothing else could have inflicted such extreme devastation.

He cautioned the General that if the Americans had the capability to do it once, they could most certainly do it again.

The General relayed this grim assessment back to Army Headquarters, who in turn informed the Cabinet.

In Washington, General Marshall, just back from Potsdam, met with Stimson at the War Department. Both men were subdued. Stimson already had photographs of Hiroshima. He explained what had happened to Operation Big Stick.

Marshall was stunned. "What does Groves intend to do?" he asked.

"Not a thing," replied Stimson. "Groves feels it would serve no purpose to drag it into the open. It makes his security apparatus look bad at the very moment when it should have looked its best. And since he can't do anything to bring back the scientists, he's quite content to hush it up. It's bad enough he's got to tell the families that those men were lost in a plane crash."

Stimson leaned back in his chair and looked out the window. "It looks like we're going to have to use the second bomb, George. The Japanese aren't reacting fast enough. And Truman won't have it any other way."

Marshall was silent a moment, then he said, "Haven't we done enough? We've shown everybody what had to be shown."

Stimson swung around and faced him. "It's madness," he said. "And only the beginning."

In Moscow, Josef Stalin shook hands with Russia's five top nuclear physicists, complimented their work, then ordered them to increase their efforts to develop an atomic bomb. Cost was no object, and from now on they would work under the direct supervision of Lavrenti Beria. He ignored the slight shudder this news produced among the five men.

As they left, he signaled Beria to remain. "No further word on that American mission?" he asked.

Beria wiped his glasses with a handkerchief. "Nothing," he said. "We think the plane was lost at sea."

Stalin fixed him with a suspicious glare, then grunted in halfhearted displeasure. "A pity," he said.

August 8: MOSCOW

Molotov had been "unavailable" for weeks, so Ambassador Sato was surprised when he was finally ushered into the Foreign Minister's study.

Molotov rose from his desk and interrupted Sato's attempt to deliver a customary greeting in Russian. "I have here," he said stiffly, "in the name of the Soviet Union, a notification to the Japanese government which I wish to communicate to you."

Molotov read a Russian declaration of war, claiming that Japan's curt refusal of the Potsdam Proclamation had left Russia no other course with respect to her allies.

". . . From tomorrow, that is, from August ninth, the Soviet Union will consider herself in a state of war against Japan."

Sato struggled for control, then asked if he could pass this information on to Tokyo. Molotov agreed, then expressed his personal regret that it had finally come to this.

The two men complimented each other's efforts over the preceding years. Sato was almost convinced that Molotov was truly sorry.

"Let us part with a handshake," said Sato. "It may be the last one."

At the moment their hands touched, Russian police were entering the Japanese embassy. They dismantled and carted away all the radio equipment. Sato was later obliged to send his message via the Russian cable office.

August 9

At 1 A.M. the Soviet armies swept across the Manchurian border and knifed through the weakened elements of Japan's Kwantung Army.

At 11 A.M. Prime Minister Suzuki confronted the Japanese Cabinet and announced that surrender was unavoidable, that Japan must capitulate under the terms of the Potsdam Proclamation of July 26th. He was met with heated objection.

One minute later the B-29 *Bock's Car* delivered the second atomic bomb, destroying the city of Nagasaki.

The hard-liners in the military continued to fight against surrender. The haggling went on until 3 A.M., August 10th, when Emperor Hirohito, breaking with tradition, threw his weight behind Suzuki and ordered an end to the war.

August 7-14: The Pacific

Just before fog started to roll in on the morning of August 7th, Snyder got the first answering flash from seaward. With Nakamura he waded out beyond the surf line. They hooked their arms into the hand straps of the tiny raft and paddled out toward the blinking light.

A black shape loomed out of the darkness and fog, and they followed the low rumble of diesels in for the last leg. They were hit with a narrow spotlight just as they came abeam of a long black hull.

Snyder heard the nasty snick of bolts being cocked and saw armed men silhouetted on the submarine's forward deck, rifle barrels pointing directly at the raft.

"Put up those goddamned weapons!" Snyder yelled. "Somebody throw us a line."

A disembodied voice from somewhere behind the searchlight called out, "Identify yourselves!"

"P.T. Snyder, Major, United States Army, and Shini-chiro Nakamura, Major, Imperial Japanese Army!"

There was silence a moment, a standoff, then the lights flicked off. A voice called out, "Hey, Snyder! What took you so long?"

Footsteps clumped on the deck above and a rope was flung down. Snyder grabbed it, and the life raft was pulled alongside. He held the rope taut while Nakamura scrambled up into waiting arms. Then Snyder was hauled up, turned and gripped by both shoulders.

He stared into a familiar grinning face. "Well, where were you?" Dave Scheff said.

Snyder stared at him in amazement, then snapped, "Stayed for the second show. What are *you* doing here?"

"Waiting for you. These guys were ready to take off yesterday. I had to use Jewish muscle."

"He made a big impression," said an officer approaching from the bridge. "I'm Commander Gronmark. Welcome to the *Pilotfish*. Now if you gentlemen will just get below, I'd like to beat it the hell out of here."

Ten minutes later, the *Pilotfish* was racing out to sea at flank speed. Snyder tried to clarify Nakamura's status with Commander Gronmark.

"That's all well and good," Gronmark said. "You can accept responsibility, but I still want him confined to quarters for *his* safety."

Nakamura was put in the petty officers' cabin. He accepted the situation philosophically, telling Snyder, "Everywhere I go—tiny little rooms."

"Tell you what," said Snyder, "someday you and I will share a suite at the Fairmont in San Francisco. I'll pay."

Snyder left as the pharmacist's mate came in to examine Nakamura.

After changing clothes, Snyder went to the officers' wardroom to have coffee with Dave Scheff, who showed him the dressings on his legs. "Minor burns," he said. "Ain't I lucky?"

"What happened, Scheff? I saw you hit. I thought you were gone."

Scheff lit a cigarette. "I was too low to bail out, so I rode it into the water and just managed to get out before it sank. Had my raft, floated around all night, waiting for this sub to pick me up."

"I must have paddled right past you."

"No, the current took me out. Thought I was going to float all the way to Alaska. I was flashing signals, hollering, singing 'Onward Christian Soldiers' . . ."

Snyder eyed him skeptically.

"Don't knock it—it worked. This tin salami came right up behind me. Damn, I was never so scared in my life. They picked me up and wanted to leave right away, but I made such a *tsimmis*, they had to stay. I haven't done so much fast talking since I thought I'd knocked up Sonya Gabrilowitz in the back room of my dad's deli."

Snyder laughed.

" 'Course, I don't know what made me think you would get out okay. So what happened? Where'd you pick up Nanki-Poo?"

"He's a friend."

"What do you call an enemy?"

"He's been through a lot," Snyder said. "I can't tell you more than that. Do me a favor and don't ask. Okay?"

"If that's what you want. Hey, you hear about the big bomb?"

"Yes."

"Well, what do you think?"

Snyder drained his coffee, rose and said, "I need some sleep."

Scheff watched him go then shook his head in amazement. He leaned back and admired his bandaged legs. Clucking in mock self-pity, he said out loud, "So where's my Purple Heart."

After a few hours' sleep, Snyder prepared a message for General Groves:

> BIG STICK TERMINATED X SECURITY INTACT X NO LOOSE ENDS X ALL PARTICIPANTS BOUGHT FARM EXCEPT POW NAKAMURA NOW WITH ME X ALL SENSITIVE ITEMS DESTROYED X ADVISE X SIGNED SNYDER.

Early the next morning a response came through, relayed from Pearl:

> MESSAGE RECEIVED AND UNDERSTOOD X HAVE ARRANGED YOUR TRANSPORTATION WITH POW FROM PEARL STATESIDE X INSTRUCTIONS WAITING X SUGGEST NO FURTHER CONTACT WITH BIG BOYS X OUT OF SIGHT OUT OF MIND X GOOD WORK X SIGNED GROVES.

Snyder grinned in relief. So he was to stay away from Stimson, and his future was in the hands of General Groves. In that case thank God for the last two words, "Good work."

Snyder pushed his luck and sent another message, asking Groves to contact Beth Martin at Berkeley to let her know he was okay and on his way home. Same message to his parents. And with the General's permission, he would like to stop in San Francisco before debriefing.

A one-word acknowledgment came back: AGREED. SIGNED GROVES.

On the journey to Pearl, all the crew could talk about was the atomic bomb. It was the fourteenth of August and Snyder was staying out of the discussions, except to express the same lack of information as anyone else when the subject couldn't be avoided.

Only Dave Scheff cornered him and said bluntly, "You're full of shit. You know more about it than anyone else aboard. I just want you to know you're not fooling me."

"Wouldn't dream of it. But suppose you keep your mouth shut. I don't want anybody trying to connect the bomb with me and Nakamura. Understand?"

"Sure, sure. I just fly planes. So why should I ask questions?"

He was interrupted as Commander Gronmark's voice came over the intercom, brimming with excitement. "This is the Captain," he said. "I have an announcement to read."

In every compartment the crew fell into a hush of expectancy.

"The Commander-in-Chief advises all fleet units that as of today, fourteen August 1945, we are no longer at war with Japan. The enemy has surrendered—"

He barely got it all out. The entire boat erupted in bedlam. Snyder and Scheff joined the celebration as a ration of brandy was issued to each man. In all the uproar Snyder remembered Nakamura.

He found him alone, sitting on his bunk, neither happy

nor sad. Snyder held out a glass of brandy. Nakamura took it without a word.

"To a better world, Major," Snyder said. They drank, then fell silent, listening to the excitement reverberating outside. Swing music was being piped through the boat.

"What are your plans?" Snyder asked.

"I won't go back to Japan."

"What about your family?"

Nakamura shook his head. "To them I'd still be a disgrace."

"Even with Captain Gohra's letter?"

Nakamura felt it still tucked in his shirt pocket. "It's not enough."

"Look, if you need someone to vouch for you, I'll do anything I can."

"You wouldn't carry any weight with my family."

"You could do a lot of good, you know. As a buffer, explaining about the bomb and what efforts were made to stop it. Smooth over some of the damage—"

Nakamura regarded him sharply, then rose and closed the door. He sat down on the bunk again and faced Snyder.

"Let me explain to *you* about the atomic bomb," he said. "When you described this mission to me back in July, I didn't tell you everything I knew. When I worked with Dr. Nishina at the Riken, we were not merely colleagues in physics. In fact, we were trying to develop exactly what you showed me in New Mexico, our own atomic bomb."

Snyder stared at him.

"I was afraid that Japan might be able to retaliate, and I saw city after city on both sides being destroyed. I could never warn you because I was sworn to secrecy. Surrender has changed all that. Until now I didn't know how far Nishina's efforts had gone. It would seem they've been unsuccessful."

His eyes bored into Snyder's and he said quietly, "But think how close it could have been."